Also by Ed Gaffney

SUFFERING FOOLS

PREMEDITATED MURDER

Available from Dell

And coming soon

ENEMY COMBATANT

PRAISE FOR ED GAFFNEY'S SPELLBINDING LEGAL SUSPENSE

"Full to the brim with thrills, spills and chills . . . electric, tingling fare." —*Los Angeles Times*

Suffering Fools

"Gaffney's second novel is a suspenseful and compelling tale. He keeps the reader guessing right to the bitter end. At every page, you're challenged to turn the next one and figure out exactly what happened." —freshfiction.com

"This is a meticulously plotted, fascinating glimpse at the real justice system. A first-rate, fascinating mystery packed with false leads and a quixotic ending." —*Romantic Times*

"The action is rapid, twisted, and changes in the blink of an eye. *Suffering Fools* is fun to read and powerful."
—*ILoveaMystery.com*

"I guarantee you will not figure out the conclusion of this book. You will feel like a tornado when the results come out. Take it and enjoy this nonstop action."
—*MysteriesGalore.com*

"Here at last is a legal 'thriller' that does not take itself too seriously. The author excels at the various hearing and trial aspects of this book. Gaffney has created a good cast of characters. . . . The plot is entertaining and moves along swiftly with a nice degree of suspense. . . . A great change of pace." —*Deadly Pleasures*

Premeditated Murder

"Great characters in a gripping story, wild twists, and—surprise—big laughs! I love this book!"
—*New York Times* bestselling author Suzanne Brockmann

"Gaffney does a credible job linking these events in this unique thriller filled with intrigue and nonstop action."
—*Romantic Times Bookclub Magazine*

"This is a deep legal thriller that [is] at its best in the court scenes and when the lawyers meet with their client. Ed Gaffney writes a fabulous tale that grips readers from the moment Judge Cottonwood shows his bench bias and never slows down until the confrontation with number seven." —Harriet Klausner, *Midwest Book Review*

"A fast-paced, dramatic ride through the decisions that affect everyone's life since September 11. As a first novel, Ed Gaffney does not disappoint as a storyteller. He paints a picture that is vivid and taut with tension. Readers who enjoy legal thrillers or political suspense will enjoy this novel." —Marie Pyko, freshfiction.com

"A fascinating plot . . . *Premeditated Murder* is recommended reading this summer or at any time that you want to scope out the next thriller that is written 'outside the box.'" —*ILoveaMystery.com*

Diary of a Serial Killer

Ed Gaffney

A Dell Book

DIARY OF A SERIAL KILLER
A Dell Book / April 2007

Published by
Bantam Dell
A Division of Random House, Inc.
New York, New York

Cover art by Alan Ayers
Cover design by Jamie S. Warren Youll

Dell is a registered trademark of Random House, Inc.,
and the colophon is a trademark of Random House, Inc.

ISBN: 978-0-440-24373-1

Printed in the United States of America
Published simultaneously in Canada

www.bantamdell.com

OPM 10 9 8 7 6 5 4 3 2 1

This book is dedicated to my partner forever, Suz.

ACKNOWLEDGMENTS

Thanks again to Kate Miciak and the entire Bantam Dell team for their tireless efforts.

Thanks to my agent, Steve Axelrod, for the kwan.

Thanks to Eric Ruben and Kathy Lague for the research help, and to Suz Brockmann, for all that terrifying reading she did about serial killers.

Thanks to the fearless early readers: Suz Brockmann, Fred and Lee Brockmann, Deede Bergeron, Scott Lutz, Patricia McMahon, and Karen Schlosberg.

As always, thanks to Eric Ruben, whose passion and humor are the inspiration for Terry.

Thanks to the Tribe for their friendship and support.

Deepest thanks to fellow author Lori Foster, whose work for the Animal Adoption Foundation inspired Suz to introduce me to my lifelong friends and companions, Sugar and Spice.

And finally, special thanks to my parents, Bernard and Mary Gaffney, who gave me a near-perfect childhood.

Diary of a Serial Killer

Forty-Five Seconds

THE MOMENT THE MADMAN FIRED HIS FIRST shot, attorney Zack Wilson knew that he had less than forty-five seconds to live.

Which meant that he was going to have to make them a damn good forty-five seconds.

It wasn't that Zack was clairvoyant. It was just that as a criminal trial lawyer, he did a lot of reading about violent life-or-death situations—like, for example, the one he and about a hundred other innocent people were in right now—trapped in a closed and dimly lit courtroom, with a homicidal gunman.

Who just then fired a second shot into the screaming crowd.

Zack knew that the great majority of those caught in such terrible circumstances actually survived, because they did what anyone would expect. They dove to the floor, covered their heads, and waited for the shooting to stop.

But he also knew that there were others who decided, for whatever reason, they needed to confront the shooter. Those were the ones who got killed.

And according to the statistics, they usually got killed in the first forty-five seconds of the attack.

As the echo of the gunshots and the terrified cries of the people in the gallery reverberated around Zack, the world slid into slow motion.

The first bullet had been wild, hitting the main overhead light fixture, showering broken glass down onto dozens below, and shorting out the room's entire electrical system. Now only oddly aimed beams from the emergency flood lamps mounted high on the walls shone through the windowless space. It didn't matter to Zack. He was very familiar with his surroundings. He'd been here dozens, if not hundreds, of times before.

It was a rectangular courtroom, divided in two by a waist-high wooden rail. At the back of the room was a large area where the spectators sat in wooden benches divided in equal thirds by two aisles running from back to front. At the forward end of the room, the judge, the clerk, the stenographer, the jury, the lawyers, and the witnesses all did their work.

Right now, however, the front of the courtroom was empty except for Zack at the far right side of the room, and the shooter, who was all the way on the other side.

But the gallery was close to full, and even though Zack could only catch glimpses of the spectators because of the crazy lighting, what he saw was awful.

A woman with huge eyes was clenching a newspaper in the first row, directly in front of the shooter. She appeared to be paralyzed with terror.

There was an Asian man directly behind her, trying to scramble over the back of his wooden bench.

But the man wearing the short-sleeved shirt two rows behind him was sitting quite still, with a puzzled expression on his face, and a spreading bloodstain on his shirt.

The woman next to him was shouting something into his ear which he didn't seem to understand, as others in their row of seats climbed over them both to get to the aisle.

In the dim light and the chaos, though, Zack couldn't see where his seven-year-old son, Justin, sat. That meant Zack would never be able to reach Justin in time to protect him from any other shots the gunman might fire into the crowd.

And Zack couldn't live with that.

So as the roar of the gun's second discharge pierced the screaming and echoed through the panicked room, Zack didn't dive for the floor and cover his head. Instead, he started moving toward the shooter.

Because that was the only way he was going to be able to keep Justin safe.

And Zack *could* live with that.

At least for another forty-five—now probably more like forty—seconds.

ONE

Five Weeks Earlier
August 15

"ARE YOU TELLING ME SOME SERIAL KILLER took a twenty-year vacation and then all of a sudden started murdering people again last night?"

Police Detective Vera Demopolous put a pair of latex gloves on, and carefully removed the letter from the plastic evidence bag.

She had just walked through the front door of her first murder scene as lead detective—the single-family home at 53 Lakeview Street in the Indian Oaks section of Springfield. She was talking to Sergeant Jimmy Wong, who had almost twenty-five years on the job. Wong had been a rookie on the force back in the early '80s. Right around the time Vera was attending Benjamin Franklin Elementary School in Fairbanks, Alaska.

Jimmy laughed. "I doubt it. Willy Grasso put away the Springfield Shooter back in '84. Alan Lombardo. Real sick guy. I'm just saying, from what I remember, this scene is a little like those—including a note from the killer. At least from what I heard. I was doing mainly traffic control back then. Not too many murder investigations."

Vera turned her attention to the letter. It was on a plain white piece of paper, and looked like it had been run off a computer printer.

To the Detective assigned to this case:

First, please give my regards to Detective Grasso. I hope he is enjoying his well-earned retirement.

As I'm sure you must have surmised, this letter was written before I got here, so I will not, herein, be able to provide you with many details of my activities. But I'm sure the condition in which I leave Mr. Chatham will provide you with more than enough work to keep you busy for some time. Of course I will tape him up, and I will shoot him, but beyond that—well, I will just have to see how things progress.

What I can tell is that I'll be in touch with you soon about the next murder you'll be working on. (Oh yes, I'm one of those kinds of killers!!!)

But I don't want to distract you from Mr. Chatham. You're going to want to pay special attention to him, because he's our first. Go ahead, Detective, look for clues, ask around, see if you can find me before I kill somebody else.

But you won't.

When she finished reading it, she replaced the letter in the evidence bag. Jimmy gestured over his shoulder and said, "Body's over here in the living room."

Vera followed the sergeant as Wong turned left off the entry hall. Forensics and Crime Scene were already well into their work. "Can you fill me in on what you've got so far?"

Vera was lucky that somebody as experienced as Jimmy Wong was at the scene. Murder scenes were always complicated, and for now, Vera was working without any backup.

She had joined the force two years ago, but three of the detectives who had been working when she started were gone. Willy Grasso, the senior member, had retired and moved to Florida. His former partner, Ole Pedersen, was on medical leave recovering from surgery, and John Morrison had died in the line of duty.

Suddenly Vera was one of the most experienced detectives in the shorthanded precinct. When Lieutenant Carasquillo had assigned last night's murder investigation to her, he'd assured her that she'd be getting help soon. And he'd mentioned that he'd left word for Willy Grasso to call her because of the similarities to the Springfield Shooter case twenty years ago.

"Okay. Victim's name is Corey Samuel Chatham. Earlier this morning, around eight-thirty, a software engineer named Muhammed— No, wait"—Wong checked his notes—"Maleek Muhammed, pulled into the driveway to pick up Chatham to go to work. They carpool, and it was Muhammed's turn to drive. Chatham is always on time, ready to go, but today he doesn't come right out, so Muhammed honks the horn. Still no Corey. Muhammed gets out of the car, knocks on the door, rings the bell, no answer. Now he's getting worried, so he starts walking around the house, peeking in windows, and sure enough, he sees somebody sitting in a chair in the living room. He calls 911, the uniforms break in, and it's Chatham, DOA, duct-taped to a recliner. Looks like small-caliber handgun, maybe a .22. Shot twice, in the groin and the eye. There's some red marks on his neck and chest, maybe a burn. And one of his fingers is missing. Looks like it was cut off. The ME hasn't gotten here yet, but the body was cold when the uniforms found it."

Vera felt herself make the mental shift she needed so

she could do her job. Her grandmother called it putting on Vera's grim suit. She had first named it that when she watched normally happy-go-lucky and bubbly ten-year-old Vera sit absolutely still with a frozen expression on her face and say nothing while getting stitches in her leg after falling in the playground on some broken glass.

The modest-sized living room where the corpse was found was furnished with the plush, leather recliner on which Chatham had died, which faced a wooden entertainment console that housed a flat-screen television and a stereo. The shelves of the large console contained an extensive collection of science fiction DVDs, books of art, and hardcover collections of comic strips. There were also framed photos, several featuring Chatham and an orange-striped cat, and a portrait of a young girl in a Catholic school uniform.

There was also one of Chatham, looking both embarrassed and thrilled, at a theme park, dressed in a *Star Trek* uniform.

At right angles with the recliner was a dark red leather sofa, marred only by a very small scratch on one arm. Yesterday's newspaper lay at one end, folded neatly.

In front of the sofa stood a wood-and-glass coffee table, on which sat a remote control for the TV, and two more art books.

The place was almost ludicrously neat.

Chatham, himself, was a very different story.

The victim was a light-skinned African-American, probably in his fifties, with curly black hair that had started to gray. He was average height, and maybe a little overweight. He wore khaki pants and a blue oxford shirt. His feet were bare.

In short, nothing out of the ordinary.

Until you looked at his grotesque wounds.

It would be up to the medical examiner to make the

final call, of course, but from the marks around the eye socket, it sure looked like that shot was taken point-blank.

The one to the groin wasn't as clear, because the pants were so badly bloodstained.

And the missing right index finger looked like it had been severed before he had been moved to the recliner, because the upholstery on the arm of the chair under the missing finger had not been ripped or torn at all.

If the finger had been cut off while Corey sat here, you'd have expected the leather on which it had rested to have been damaged. Unless, of course, the finger had been snipped off with a tool of some kind.

Jeez. People could really suck, sometimes.

Blood had pooled on the seat of the recliner, and on the floor under the chair. It was pretty clear that the victim had been taped here, and then shot. There were no bloodstains anywhere else in the house.

After Crime Scene had taken photos of the victim as they had found him, Vera gently tried to tip the head forward a bit, to see if there was an exit wound, but rigor mortis had already set in, and the head remained rigidly fixed against the seat back. She turned back to Jimmy, and asked, "Where's the coworker—Muhammed—now?"

"We let him go to work after he gave us a statement. I told him you'd want to speak to him later today. I wrote down his contact information." Jimmy handed Vera a small sheet of paper with the witness's phone number and address.

"When was the last time anybody saw Chatham alive?"

"We're still canvassing, but we know that it was Chatham's turn to drive to work yesterday, and he dropped Muhammed home in Linwood last night at six-thirty. That's all we have so far."

Linwood was about fifteen minutes away. So the earliest Chatham could have gotten home was six forty-five.

From the condition of the body, that sounded about right. Under typical room temperature conditions, rigor mortis would be at its peak between twelve and twenty-four hours after death. After that, the body would start to become limp again. It was close to ten A.M. now, and Chatham's body was positively rigid. Time of death was probably between six forty-five and ten o'clock last night.

"Uh huh. Muhammed's story check out?"

"Yeah." Jimmy read from his notes again. "Worked the day before. Wife saw him get out of Chatham's car around six-thirty. Spent the night with her and their five kids eating dinner and watching some Disney video."

Jimmy went over to speak to one of the Crime Scene guys just as Vera's cell phone rang. The display indicated that the call was from Florida.

"Hello?"

"Vera, it's Willy. Was there a note?"

So retirement to Florida hadn't done much for Willy's social skills. Her grandmother would say the guy pretty much always had his grim suit on.

"Hi, Willy. Jimmy Wong just showed it to me a minute ago."

"What does it say?"

Vera read him the note.

"Yeah, that sounds about right," Willy said. "Check me on this, but I think it was after the third shooting, Lombardo started leaving little notes. Always addressed them to me. They were a little simpler than this one, though. More like, 'What do you think of this?' or 'How about them apples?' We couldn't do anything with them until we caught the guy. Lombardo ran them off his computer printer, too."

"He use a .22 in the other shootings?"

"Yep. Every one of the victims was tied up with duct tape and shot repeatedly with a .22 caliber handgun. Most of them lost an index finger just like your DOA. Sounds a lot like Lombardo."

Vera didn't believe in coincidences. It seemed obvious that last night's murder was connected to the ones twenty years ago. "So what do you think? Copycat?"

Willy sighed. "I guess so. Everything you found fits the pattern of the old murders—the weapon, the tape, the note, the finger, even the location. It's not too hard to believe, I guess. I mean all of this stuff was big news in the area when it was happening. Anyone who lived in New England at the time knew about the Springfield Shooter."

Even though a copycat seemed like the most plausible explanation, it still seemed far-fetched. Why wait two decades before deciding to replicate old crimes? "Any chance Lombardo was wrong for the shootings in the first place?"

"No way," Willy replied, gruffly. "It was a good bust. By the book all the way. Found tons of evidence in his home. Must have been thirty witnesses at the trial. He had no chance. The jury was out for all of twenty minutes. Nine indictments, nine convictions. Judge gave him nine life sentences."

But what had happened to Alan Lombardo sure didn't explain why twenty years later someone would start copying his homicidal pattern. She looked again at the killer's note. "And you didn't find any hidden messages in the words of the notes, nothing like that?"

"Nope. We couldn't figure anything out, and since he didn't confess, we never got an explanation from him. We ended up figuring the notes weren't anything more than a twisted creep getting his jollies."

It was worth looking back through the messages left at the nine old crime scenes to see if there was anything Vera could pick up. "Probably right." She idly turned the evidence bag over and noticed that there was something on the envelope that had contained the note. "What do you make of the fact that the words 'Welcome to my world' were on a sticker that was on the back side of the envelope that held the note?"

Willy didn't answer right away. When he did, his voice sounded tight. "Wait a minute. Did you say 'Welcome to my world'?"

Vera looked again at the envelope. "Yeah. It's pretty clear that it came from the same computer printer, I mean—"

But Willy interrupted. "You're telling me that on the *back* side of the envelope at your crime scene, the words 'Welcome to my world' were printed?"

Vera had no idea what was so important about the message being on the back of the envelope, but just to be sure, she read it again. " 'Welcome to my world.' That's what it says."

"Holy hell," muttered Willy. "That's not good."

"What?" Vera was completely confused. "Was that something that Lombardo used to put on his envelopes?"

Willy exhaled loudly. "Yeah, but that's not the problem. You ever work on a serial killer case before?"

"No. Why?"

"I only had two. This one, and another I helped with when I was in the FBI, a million years ago. Anyway, this agent taught me once that in high-profile cases, it's a good idea to try to keep a few specifics of the crime scenes out of the press. He called them hole cards. He'd hang on to them for interrogations, especially when there was a possibility you'd get crackpots turning themselves in. If the guy confessing didn't know about your hole cards, then you'd know he wasn't your guy."

"And—'Welcome to my world'—"

"That's right. Lombardo always wrote that on the envelopes which contained his notes. They were easy to keep out of the press. Those envelopes were my hole cards."

That took a minute to sink in. What it meant was that the person who committed this crime either had—just by chance—happened to commit a murder in the same neighborhood and in the same manner as a serial killer two decades ago, while leaving a clue common to the original crimes that no one knew about, or else . . .

"You know what that leaves you with," Willy said, as if he were reading her mind. "Either the person who did this crime is someone who has access to the original, confidential police files of the Alan Lombardo case—"

Vera finished the thought. "Or the Springfield Shooter is still out there."

TWO

July 3, 1982. It was a hot day, so Bobby was wearing shorts and a T-shirt when I came in. He wasn't expecting me, of course, and surely didn't think I'd come to do anything to him. The shock in his eyes when I pulled out the gun was awesome.

By the time he was all tied up he was crying. Gasping. Sobbing. I couldn't believe it! Snot was pouring out of his nose. He had no idea what I was going to do next. I pointed the gun at his face to see what would happen, and he looked like he was going to piss his pants.

And then, sure enough, he did piss his pants.

It was incredible.

But that wasn't the only thing I was going for, so I waited for a while, until he calmed down a little.

And then I shot him.

But I almost blew it. I wanted to watch his eyes as he realized that he was actually going to die, and I wanted to see what his face looked like as he bled to death, but when I pulled the trigger it looked like I hit him square in the heart and that he was going to die instantly. That would have been awful!

Luckily, the bullet hit him lower, probably in the stomach or the liver, and the blood just started to pour out of him. Was he ever surprised! And scared shitless. He was *actually shaking as he looked down at the blood oozing out of his belly.*

Then I shot him again, lower this time. Intestines, I think.

I wish I hadn't done that, because I bet the first shot would have killed him soon enough, and the second one just messed up the expression on his face. He looked like he was in pain, but then he started to look confused. He didn't look scared enough. And worst of all, he wasn't looking at me anymore. That wasn't right.

So I shot him again to get his attention. By now, he had fallen to the floor, and there was a pretty big puddle of blood on the rug. The third bullet must have hit an artery somewhere, because the puddle really started to grow, and then Bobby began to shudder a lot, and his face got very pale. He wasn't watching me at all now, and it didn't even look like his eyes were focused.

When he stopped shuddering I figured he was probably done, so I shot him in the head to be sure, and left.

It was my first one. It wasn't perfect, but I'd get better. There would be others.

(*Commonwealth v. Alan Lombardo*, Trial Exhibit Number 5A)

Attorney Terry Tallach sat across from his partner, Zack Wilson, in the office they shared in downtown Northampton, Massachusetts. Terry was reading one of several trial exhibits in a case called *Commonwealth v. Lombardo*. Zack said that they were looking into it to see if there was legal support to claim that the defendant—a guy twenty years ago the newspapers had dubbed "The Springfield Shooter"—should be given a new trial. Mr. Shooter was claiming that he was innocent.

Zack had described the case as "somewhat of a challenge."

Which meant that it was going to drive Terry crazier than his father's fascination with twisted Uncle Campbell's set of bagpipes. Every time Terry heard one of those shrieking, plaid noisemakers, he couldn't believe that humankind hadn't already wiped Scotland off the face of the earth just for inventing them.

He focused on the last few lines of the exhibit. *"It was my first one. It wasn't perfect, but I'd get better.*

"There would be others."

Swell. It was always good to have something to look forward to.

Terry closed the folder. He looked over at Zack, who was typing up a hopeless memo in preparation for a hopeless trial they would be handling next week.

Zack didn't look like one of the best criminal lawyers in the state. Although he had decided to forgo his usual jeans in favor of khakis today, the faded red linen shirt still managed to make him look way too informal to be taken seriously. And, like always, his blond hair was just a little too long, a little too unkempt.

But somehow, all of that melted away in the courtroom, when the gavel hit the bench. Because that's when judges, lawyers, witnesses, and juries—especially juries—saw the energy and intelligence in Zack's eyes, and the confidence and, well, the peacefulness in his smile. All he had to do was stand up and say, "Good morning, Your Honor and ladies and gentlemen of the jury, my name is Zack Wilson, and I represent the defendant," and the prosecutor was in serious trouble.

Good thing Terry and Zack were best friends. Otherwise, that kind of thing might be really annoying.

Now Terry got up and walked to the window, looking out at the paralyzingly slow stream of cars passing through the Traffic Cone Capital of the World—the undying roadwork project taking place directly in front of their building. Thirty thousand people in this suburb of Springfield—Northampton was officially called a city, but that was a joke—and Terry would bet that two-thirds of them drove through this goddamned construction site every single day.

And good news for the rest of Northampton—this was a traveling show. The entire city was getting new road surfaces this summer. As soon as the geniuses responsible for this nightmare finished messing up downtown, they were scheduled to start wrecking the residential areas.

Zack stopped typing long enough to ask, "How's it looking out there?"

An immense piece of equipment which was being used to rip the top layer of pavement off of a perfectly good road had recently lost its mind, and had spewed football-sized chunks of stone and tar all over the sidewalk in front of several stores across the street. The monstrosity had apparently chosen to end this morning's effort by coming to a palsied stop in the middle of the busiest and most important intersection in Northampton, half of which was already torn to shreds. The machine stood there shuddering, occasionally croaking out an ominous plume of foul-smelling black smoke, while two part-time cops wearing idiotic-looking orange plastic vests hopelessly flailed their arms, blew whistles, and shouted as traffic worked itself into an impossible knot.

Meanwhile, angry shopkeepers and a crowd of bypassers watched as a group of hardhats scurried around like circus clowns trying to shut the insane contraption down while cleaning up the debris on the sidewalk so nobody got killed on their way to getting an ice cream cone.

And was that blonde down there with the cutoffs the girl who worked at the pizza place around the corner? What was her name again? And why wouldn't that construction guy move so Terry could get a better look at what she was wearing?

What was it that Zack had just asked him?

Terry glanced over his shoulder at his partner, who was still writing. Guess it wasn't that important. "You want to take a break for lunch and get a couple slices of pizza?"

Zack stopped typing, peered at his computer screen, then said, "Um, it's ten-fifteen, Elvis." He took a bite of the corn muffin that he had brought in from the deli earlier this morning and washed it down with some coffee. "Maybe after I finish breakfast." Then he stole a look out the window and turned back to Terry. "Is Heather distracting you again?"

Heather. That was her name. Terry returned to the scene on the street. He still didn't have a full view of Heather, but what he did see was really, really nice. "I have no idea what you're talking about, but if she's wearing a halter top with those shorts, I'm probably going to need to take the rest of the week off." Heather turned the corner, passing out of sight. "And stop calling me Elvis." Lunch today was going to be one of the greatest meals of his life.

Terry spun back to face his partner, who had returned to his keyboard. "So what's up with this case you gave me to read? 'I shot him so he'd look at me?' I'm no shrink, Zack, but I'm betting Mr. Lombardo might have some control issues."

Zack finished typing something, and looked up again from his computer. "You read the whole file already?"

"No. I had to take a break to make sure that Heather made it to work okay. And I never like to rush through my psychopath diary reading." Zack was still looking at him. "I finished the first entry, though. Is there a lot more?"

"He killed a total of nine people."

"Okay. That's more."

Zack picked up his muffin and coffee, and joined his partner at the window. "Yeah. A lot more. And guess who his lawyer was."

By now, a pair of Northampton police cars, lights flashing, were snaking their way up the street, because everyone knows that the presence of multiple police cars with bright blue strobe lights flashing always relieves congestion on the roads. But in an attempt to get out of the cops' way, some dumbshit in an SUV had managed to rear-end a Mini Cooper and blow out one of the little car's back tires. The Mini Cooper driver, who was about six inches and fifty pounds too big for a tiny ride like that, had unfolded himself from his crippled vehicle, and was addressing the situation by repeatedly banging on the roof of his car, screaming at the SUV driver, and pointing at his flat tire. His fellow commuters were fascinated, and many stopped to watch.

In about fifteen minutes, traffic would be backed up to Maine.

"Uh, I don't have any idea who represented the guy," Terry replied. "When did you say he was convicted?"

"1985."

Terry had met Zack in the fall of 1986, in high school, when Zack and his family had moved to Rhode Island. "I don't know," Terry responded. "Your dad?" Zack's father, now Federal District Court Judge Nehemiah Wilson, had been a high-profile criminal defense attorney back in the day.

Zack took another bite of muffin and swallowed. "Bingo," he said.

"Wait a minute," Terry said. "I thought the biggest thing he did was that white-collar case—the George Heinrich gambling thing." On the few occasions that Terry had spent with Zack's father, the old man never failed to bring up his biggest legal victory—the acquittal of "Gentleman George," who went on to become one of New England's quietest but most successful organized crime bosses. For someone who had a great son like Zack, Judge Wilson was a real load.

Zack nodded. "Heinrich was the biggest case Dad ever *won*. Lombardo came later, and it was even bigger. But he lost that one."

"So how come your father wants you to look into it?"

Zack walked back to his desk and sat down. "I doubt he knows I've got anything to do with it." He started to type again. "Harry Baumgartner called me early this morning and asked me to take it as a special favor. You know that shooting in Indian Oaks last night? The facts are just like the ones in the Lombardo case. Judge Baumgartner thinks there might be an argument that Lombardo deserves a new trial, so he wanted us to poke around, see what we could find."

Jesus Elizabeth Christ. Judge Harold Baumgartner was a good guy, and a volunteer on the bar association committee who was in charge of assigning lawyers to court-appointed cases. But the last special favor Terry and Zack had done for the judge had almost ended with some crackpot blowing up the entire Boston Esplanade. And this assignment seemed to have just about the same amount of crazy on it as the last one. "Just because some copycat nut-job shot somebody?"

"Not really," Zack replied cheerfully. "Lombardo had been asking for new counsel for years. The Indian Oaks shooting just pushed it to the top of Harry's pile."

"And were we supposed to ignore the entire Canon of Ethics when we took the case, or just the part about conflicts of interest?"

According to one of the most fundamental ethical guidelines governing—well, supposedly governing—lawyers' conduct, whenever an attorney was involved in a legal matter, he was obligated to put his clients' interests ahead of anyone else's. Including his own. One of Terry's law school professors had explained it like this: "Clients hire lawyers to go to war for them. If a lawyer has to worry about who the bullets might hit when he starts shooting, he's got a conflict of interest."

So, for example, if a lawyer was defending someone accused of a crime, he couldn't take on as a client one of the witnesses against the defendant, even if it was involving a different legal matter—say, a real-estate closing. Because when it came time to cross-examine the real-estate client at the criminal trial, the lawyer would be in a dilemma. It might be in his *criminal client's* best interests to make all of the witnesses at his trial look like liars, but it would be in the *lawyer's* best interests to soft-pedal his cross-examination of the real-estate client, because he wouldn't want that witness to get pissed off and take his business to another law firm.

The conflict of interest facing Zack in the Lombardo matter was just as obvious. It made no sense for Zack to be responsible for checking into a case that his own father handled to see if there were grounds for a new trial. Because if Zack discovered that dear old Dad had somehow screwed up, he would be faced with the dilemma of either keeping the mistake to himself and protecting his obnoxious father's reputation, or doing the right thing for his client, which might end up plastering his father's face on the front page of every newspaper in New England.

Zack finished typing and started printing out the memo. "Yeah, I talked to Harry about that. Turns out that the first two lawyers he assigned to look into Lombardo's case met with the client and then asked to get reassigned. I guess Lombardo's got some personality thing that makes him a little tough to deal with."

"You mean besides the killing-nine-people-in-cold-blood personality thing?"

"Yeah." Zack reached over and took the finished memo

out of the printer. "He's obsessive-compulsive, or has obsessive-compulsive tendencies, or something like that. Anyway, Harry said he would have dumped the whole thing a long time ago, but he thinks there's actually a possibility that this guy is innocent. Who knows? Maybe this latest killing really is by the same creep who murdered all those people twenty years ago. Maybe they got the wrong guy back then. That's what Lombardo claims, anyway."

"Wow," Terry said. "A convicted felon who says he didn't do it. Imagine that."

Zack straightened the pages of the memo. "Anyway, Harry told Lombardo that because he didn't cooperate with the first two lawyers who had been assigned to the case, Lombardo was going to have to represent himself. I guess that really scared Lombardo, because he begged Harry for just one more chance—he'd read about us, and specifically asked Harry for us. Harry agreed, but he told Lombardo that if it doesn't work out with us, he's going to have to go *pro se*."

Technically, any inmate could file a motion for a new trial without the help of a lawyer. The Latin term for this—which lawyers use because everything is so much clearer when it's in Latin—was *pro se*. But realistically, there were so many procedural and other hurdles facing somebody trying to overturn a criminal conviction that the typical defendant stood little or no chance on his own. And somebody like Lombardo, who had been in jail for twenty years, was sure to know that.

"But just because we're Lombardo's last hope doesn't get rid of the conflict problem, Zack. Your dad's not my favorite person in the world, and I know he's done some things that you aren't thrilled with, but he's still your father. There's no way you can pretend that he's just another lawyer when you look at this case."

Zack nodded as he got up to make copies of the memorandum. "That's one of the things I'd like to talk about with Mr. Lombardo when I meet him." He fed the original of the document into the copier, and pressed the start button. "You up for a trip to prison?"

Terry looked back out the window. "As long as it's after lunch," he replied. "I've got plans."

Monster

IT HAD TAKEN MORE THAN A YEAR OF PLAN-ning, and countless hours of painstaking effort, but finally, *finally*, all of the elements were in place. The monster sat down, turned on his computer, and attached his digital camera. His masterpiece was truly under way.

The Corey Chatham experience had been such a plea-sure. Such a *relief*. It all had gone exactly as planned.

When he'd approached the house, he felt a thrill like he hadn't experienced in quite a while. He was smiling by the time that Mr. Chatham finally answered the door, which was terrific, because it very quickly put the rather large man at ease.

Not that he needed much help, thanks to the stun gun. In seconds, Chatham had collapsed to the floor like a demolished building as the waves of shock pulsed through him. In a matter of several seconds, except for some involuntary muscle spasms, he was completely inca-pacitated.

It was like poor Mr. Chatham had been sentenced to die by hand-held electrocution.

But he didn't die, of course. He was just immobilized, until he could be brought to what was obviously his favorite chair—a nice, plush recliner, directly opposite his television.

Dragging him across the living room floor wasn't as bad as it could have been—Corey had good taste, and both his entryway and his living room featured hardwood floors, so he slid rather smoothly from one area of the house to the other.

But getting him into the recliner took some effort, because Mr. Chatham was no lightweight. It was a bit comical, actually. First, he had to pull Corey over so that the unconscious man was sitting on the floor with his back against the chair. Then, while standing on the chair, he had to hoist the limp Mr. Chatham up by his underarms until his rear end finally found its way onto the recliner's seat.

Once that was accomplished, he climbed down from the chair, pushed Corey back into a normal position on the chair, gagged him, and taped him up good.

But Corey was out cold, and it would probably be a while before he came to, so the monster decided to have a look around.

The most interesting things were always in the bedrooms, so he went right up the stairs, and found himself in a narrow hallway, featuring four doors—one right at the top of the stairs, and three at the far end of the house.

He correctly guessed that the nearest door was a guest bedroom. Some dusty books were stacked on a long shelf running along one wall, and some boxes of what looked like old clothes lined the same wall beneath the shelf. The rest of the room seemed to be a holding area for furniture that didn't have a place elsewhere. It looked more like a storage room than anything else. It was totally uninteresting.

He moved down to the other end of the hall, and opened the first door he came to, which was a small linen closet. The second door opened to a surprisingly clean bathroom, and the third, finally, brought him to Chatham's bedroom.

It was furnished with a lot of style. On the far wall, a queen-sized bed sat on a dark cherry frame, on either side of which stood matching end tables.

But it was the framed photos, diplomas, and other memorabilia on the wall to his immediate right when he entered which really caught the monster's eye.

Apparently, Mr. Chatham was something of a do-gooder. Next to a replica of a movie poster for *Casablanca*, there was a framed certificate attesting to the fact that Mr. Chatham had donated more blood to the Red Cross over the past five years than any of his coworkers. Another indicated that he had "adopted" an impoverished family living in some godforsaken place in Africa, and five of the blackest faces the monster had ever seen smiled at him from a photo that was attached.

How noble.

Chatham had attended the University of Rochester, poor bastard, and some high school in Cleveland, Ohio.

Too bad for him he had ended up in Springfield, Massachusetts.

One of the bedside tables was bare, but the other had a prescription pill bottle sitting on it, a bestseller, and a photo of a cat.

Jeez. The guy was sick, *and* he had a cat. God Almighty. The most boring victim ever.

Maybe the first floor would prove more entertaining. He started down the stairs, but before the monster had a chance to see if Corey had a secret den where he kept photos of underage girls, he heard a sound from the living room.

Corey Chatham was awake.

A quick look determined that the hero of the Red Cross was only starting to revive himself, so the monster took a seat on the edge of the coffee table across from his victim, and waited until the man was sufficiently recovered from the effects of the stun gun to enjoy his reaction when he learned that he was about to make his final donation of blood.

And it was worth the wait.

When Corey's eyes finally flickered open, he was quite groggy for a few seconds. He clearly did not understand his situation. He blinked at his attacker a few times, but without real recognition. He tried to stand up, and noticed that he was stuck in place.

And that's when the neurons that had been fried by the Taser started coming back on-line. He looked down at his arms, saw the tape that bound them, looked back at his captor, tried to speak, and then realized he was gagged. Next, he tried to stand, and that's when he realized that his ankles had been taped to the base of the chair.

The look of panic that flashed onto his face at that moment was spectacular. It was like in one moment, he was working hard to free himself, and the next, he was fully cognizant of the fact that he was minutes from death.

It was just what the monster was looking for, and he was ready with his digital camera. The repeated flashes as he took the pictures further surprised Chatham, which was just as well. It was always best to keep victims on their toes.

Figuratively, of course.

Next came the real shooting. The one with the gun and the bullets.

The monster stood up, and moved so that he was directly in front of Chatham. He switched the camera to his left hand, and with his right, he slowly withdrew the handgun that he had been keeping in his jacket pocket. He readied the camera, in case another expression passed over Chatham's face that he wanted to capture.

But by this point, Chatham's expression had become less entertaining. He seemed committed to hyperventilation more than anything else. His eyes merely moved insanely rapidly from the gun to the monster's face and back, repeatedly.

For some reason, this upset the monster, and without even thinking, he jammed the gun into Chatham's crotch, and fired.

Chatham grunted heavily, and, as much as he could with a piece of duct tape across his mouth, began to moan and cry.

This, also, angered the monster. After the fearful looks that had taken over Chatham's face when he'd first realized his predicament, the monster had been hoping for something more unique in Corey's post-shooting reaction than mere blubbering. He screamed "Shut up!", and pointed the gun right at the center of Chatham's forehead. "Shut up, or I will kill you right here, and right now!"

In retrospect, it was a stupid demand. Corey Chatham had just received a bullet to the sexual organs. It was ludicrous to expect that he could just sit there and not make a sound.

But the monster was in no mood for disobedience. Even though Chatham had quieted himself somewhat, he was still making small noises of pain as the waves of agony crashed over him. So the monster stuck the gun in Chatham's left eye, and said, "If you don't shut up, I will shoot you in the eye."

It was actually somewhat pathetic. At that point, Chatham gasped. He was clearly trying to stop making noise, but under the circumstances, that was virtually impossible. The gunshot had probably destroyed his penis— and maybe one of his testicles as well. That entire area of his body must have been on fire with pain.

Chatham groaned, quietly.

The monster responded immediately, and shot him through his eye.

The bullet tore through the man's brain, ripping a path directly through whatever was responsible for telling the lungs to work, because Corey ceased breathing immediately, and death was virtually instantaneous.

The sudden nature of the monster's own assault had taken him somewhat by surprise, but despite the excitement of the moment, he did not forget to take the necessary photos with his camera.

Now, several hours later, he downloaded the images onto his computer, so that he would be able to manipulate them as necessary.

And then, he surfed the internet over to the feed from the webcams that he had installed in the home of the woman who would be his final victim.

Researching her comings and goings had not been particularly difficult, but it had been a critically important part of his preparations. He had needed a considerable amount of time to be able to effectively plant both webcams with their associated audio bugs in her apartment. One was in the kitchen, in the overhead light fixture, pointing at the small table where she ate most of her meals, and the other was in the bedroom, in the housing of the ceiling fan. That one needed to be positioned perfectly, so that when she stood facing her full-length mirror, he would be, in effect, looking at her reflection, from over her shoulder.

In other words, any image he captured from that camera would include both a front and a rear view.

And even though it was wrong to dwell on the fact, it was beyond dispute that she had a very nice front and rear view.

In fact, today he was expecting to capture the image that would serve as the focus of one of his most crucial projects for the coming weeks. This was the first day since he had planted the bedroom camera that she was showering before going to her second job that evening. If she dried herself off in her bedroom . . .

Yes! She was coming out of the bathroom with just a towel wrapped around her, holding a hairbrush in one hand. She came into the middle of the room, turned to face the camera, and then reached up toward it.

Holy shit! Had she discovered the camera? What a disaster that would be. Police would be called, she might put a security system in place, his whole operation could be thrown into chaos.

But it was a false alarm. She was just pulling on the chain to start the ceiling fan. Then she turned away from the camera, checked to be sure that all of the windows were covered with curtains, dropped the towel to the floor, and walked to the front of the mirror, brushing her hair, naked as the day she was born.

Oh my God. This was perfect. But happening so quickly. One minute, his whole plan was on the verge of discovery, and the next minute, jackpot.

Life was really good.

He recorded the images from the camera for the next two minutes, as she ran the brush through her shoulder-length hair repeatedly. When she stepped out of the camera's field of view to dress, he stopped recording, and went to work.

First he reviewed his footage, waiting for the time she took a short break from brushing, and stood, hands by her sides, completely nude, facing the mirror. He froze the video, captured the still image, and saved it to a file he labelled "The Final Moment."

Then, leaving that image on the left side of the screen, he brought up on the right side the image of Corey

Chatham that he had saved from one of the photos he took of his corpse sitting there in his recliner.

Using the photo-editing program, he cut out of the Chatham image the bullet wound that had taken the place of his left eye, and brought it over to the nude photo of the woman. Then, very carefully, he pasted it over her left eye in the picture.

Then, he repeated the procedure with the gunshot he had delivered to Chatham's groin. Carefully taking only that part of the Chatham photo that depicted the lower wound, he excised it, and superimposed it over the pubic area of the naked woman's photo.

"The Final Moment" now was a somewhat macabre composite of the front and back of a naked young woman facing a mirror. The rear view was exquisite—the unblemished flesh of an attractive female. But the front view was quite unsettling, featuring an otherwise perfectly fine-looking person with a hideously disfigured left eye and groin.

He intentionally left the differences in skin coloring, lighting, and other features alone, so that the total effect of the new image was something like that of a ransom note composed of glued-on letters and words cut from a variety of magazines.

Disturbing. Upsetting.

Perfect.

He saved the images on the hard drive of his computer, and then returned to monitoring the woman.

She was dressed now, and had returned to the mirror. She was looking at herself somewhat critically, as if there was something wrong with what she saw.

Hardly. She was ideal, in so many ways.

Because she was the ultimate goal. Corey Chatham, and the others who would follow, were mere appetizers, preparing the palates of all involved for the final, exquisite, main course. These preliminary deaths would all be satisfying in their own small ways. He would take care to make each special, to make each a true contribution to the final moment.

But the deaths of the first victims would not bring to him what he truly craved. For that, he would need to build a pattern of murders, a pathway of evidence, leading to the innocent man who would ultimately bear responsibility for the carnage that had only just begun.

The final victim was the key to this perfect plan. For she and she alone would seal the fate of the innocent man, in so many more ways than one. And so the young woman who was scheduled to die within a matter of weeks must be the focus of his attention. No matter how many others were killed on the way to her death.

He returned his attention to the computer. He saved the file he called "The Final Moment," as well as the images of Corey Chatham, both the terrified expression on his face as he realized that he was being held captive by a man who intended to murder him, and the post-mortem shots of his wounds. He labeled that file "S," and again opened the window that showed the images being broadcast from the kitchen.

She had not yet moved into that part of the house, but she would be coming soon. She didn't have a lot of time before she had to get moving to her night job.

Finally, he heard her say a single word: "Whatever," and then move into the kitchen camera's field of view.

And into the silence of the monster's very solitary sanctuary, he uttered only the words, "I'll be seeing you."

THREE

SPRINGFIELD MEMORIAL HOSPITAL PEDIATRIC nurse Stephanie Hartz glanced in the direction of the full-length mirror standing in her bedroom, pushed a strand of her shoulder-length brown hair back behind her ear, noticed nothing else tragically out of place, then hurried on down the hall to the kitchen, sighing, "Whatever."

Her freshman roommate, an amazingly popular blond firecracker from Tennessee named Michelle Merlan, would have been appalled. "Boobs and butt, Stephanie!" Michelle would cry out in her Dolly Parton accent, if Steph didn't spend the appropriate length of time in front of the mirror before heading off to classes. "Boobs and butt—you better check 'em out, darlin', because everyone else is going to."

Now it was almost twelve full years since Steph had lived in a college dormitory, and significantly more important priorities demanded that all boob and butt checks be indefinitely postponed. In fact, starting about two months ago, when Steph had begun moonlighting at St. Joseph's Hospital in Hartford, there had barely been enough time left to breathe on the days she worked her second job, let alone try to look attractive. Not that there was anything to do about the red-and-white-striped smocks that St. Joseph's made all their nurses wear. Even gorgeous Michelle would have been hard-pressed to look good wearing that catastrophe.

And why in the world was she wasting time day-dreaming about her ugly uniform? Normally, if everything went just right, Steph had exactly nine minutes to eat her gross microwave dinner before she needed to head off to Hartford.

And today everything had gone far from right. Steph was already well behind schedule, in part because her neediest patient, a weepy little boy named Clay, had had a meltdown when he found out that today's Jell-O flavor was lime.

As she hurried into the kitchen, Steph noticed a vaguely familiar image on the little portable television she had set up on the counter next to the stove. The sound on the TV was muted, so she didn't know why the news station was showing some obviously dated footage of a suburban house, and she couldn't remember where she'd seen the house before. If it was important, it would come back to her.

She moved hastily to the microwave, and peeled back the plastic cover from this evening's culinary disaster: Asian vegetable medley. She set it down on the small table in her dining nook. Steam was rising from the dish. It looked—against all odds—almost good.

But as the steam dissipated, the meal slowly began to reveal itself to be just like all of the others she'd been feeding herself these past few months. A bit awful, and quite a bit more pathetic. Fortunately, Steph was too hungry to care. In about twenty seconds it would be cool enough to eat, and she'd wolf it down, no matter what it tasted like. She opened the refrigerator, poured herself a glass of iced tea, took a quick sip, and set it next to her dinner. Then she went over to the window seat where she'd tossed today's mail, looked up briefly to see if the rain had stopped, and oh my God, eighty-seven-year-old Philomena Giordano was in the driver's seat of her ancient Dodge Omni, peering into the rearview mirror, preparing to back out of her driveway.

Steph dropped the mail, bolted to the front hall, threw open her door, and rushed over to her elderly neighbor's car. Thankfully, it was still stationary, idling noisily while Mrs. Giordano struggled to disengage the parking brake. The idea that this tiny, half-blind, and more than half-deaf widow might actually drive on a road traversed by other vehicles was nothing short of terrifying. Mrs. Giordano was lovely and intelligent, but she had no business behind the wheel of a car. It was a virtual certainty that she'd get into an accident, hurting or killing herself and God knows how many others.

Steph tapped on the window, startling the old woman, who had just begun the process of creating a five-minute, two-handed project out of shifting into reverse.

"Mrs. Giordano!" Steph shouted, hoping that her neighbor's very prominent hearing aids would be able to pick up her voice over the rattle of the car's engine. "Where are you going? I thought you stopped using your car!"

Mrs. Giordano's shiny dark eyes looked enormous behind the thick lenses of her gigantic glasses. She labored to roll down her window and said in her high-pitched, halting soprano, "Hello, Stephanie, dear. Don't you think you should have an umbrella? You're getting all wet."

Steph looked at the thin streams of water running down the old car's windshield, and only then noticed the tiny dark spots rapidly appearing on the sleeves of her uniform. Sure enough, it was still raining. She put her hand over her head in a futile gesture to protect herself from the drizzle that seemed to have been falling for the entire summer. Her hair, never a particularly strong point, was going to look truly abysmal in about fifteen seconds.

"I only came over to see why you were driving," she replied. "Aren't you going out this weekend with David?"

David was Mrs. Giordano's son, and way too self-absorbed for any person nearly fifty years old. But he was the family member who lived closest to his mother, and so for the past several years, he had come by every few Saturdays to take her shopping. It was obvious that he didn't like the chore, but at least he recognized that his mother was a peril on the roads.

"David forgot to come last weekend," Mrs. Giordano said, "and now he's in New York on business. I ran out of my heart medication last night, so I called in a refill. I was just going down to the CVS to pick it up."

The CVS drugstore was on Main Street—easily the most heavily trafficked route in town. There was absolutely no way that Mrs. Giordano would make it there and back without crashing into someone or something. And the medication she was taking was very important. She'd already had two heart attacks, and needed to be very strict about taking her pills.

Steph saw no way out. Mrs. Giordano would refuse to take a cab, saying, as she always did, that they were "a waste of perfectly good money," and by the time Steph got home from work that night Mrs. G. would already be asleep, and the pharmacy would be closed. Thanks to David the jerk, Steph would have to be the one to get the medicine, right now. Silently, she bid farewell to her Asian vegetable medley. "The CVS is only a few minutes down the road, and I needed to pick up a few things myself," Steph offered. It was only half a lie. She did need some razors and some hand lotion—she just didn't need them right now. Sort of like the headache that was slowly starting to bloom around her temples. "How about I get your prescription while I'm out? I'll be back in ten, fifteen minutes at the most."

"Are you sure it isn't any trouble?" Mrs. Giordano leaned forward as if searching for something on the side of the steering column. She finally figured out where the ignition was, and then turned off the noisy engine and wrestled her keys free. A surprising silence ensued as the car's motor finally chugged to a reluctant halt. "Normally I wouldn't go out myself, dear, but this medicine—"

"Don't say another word," Steph called over her shoulder, as she headed back through the rain toward her house. "I'll be right back."

Steph raced inside, grabbed her purse off the table near the door, and hurried back outside to her car. If she didn't hit any red lights, and traffic was light . . .

Who was she kidding? She was going to be late. For the second time this week. And her supervisor was not going to be happy about it. Damn David Giordano and his stupid trip to New York. How in the world does anybody forget their own mother? Steph hadn't had anything to eat since lunch, and her headache was getting worse by the second.

But headache or not, there was no way Mrs. Giordano was going to embark on a suicide mission when all it took was for Steph to go a few minutes out of her way to prevent it. And if her boss got so angry that she fired Steph, well, that would be a problem, but not an unsolvable one. Steph still had some money from last year's tax refund tucked away, which she could use in a pinch. If she couldn't get another job fast enough, she'd just dip into her savings account.

She pulled out of the driveway, and headed for Main Street.

Steph's father, Malcolm Ayers, would have been furious if he knew what his daughter had been going through these past couple of months, since she'd taken on her newest responsibility. Malcolm had a short temper to start with, but when it came to financial matters, he didn't have any patience at all. His last pronouncement on the subject—which was no doubt an exaggeration—came immediately after Stephanie had turned down his attempt to give her a ridiculously large amount of money on her birthday last year: "I still have so much money saved up from that damned book I wrote that I couldn't spend it all if I tried." Malcolm had been furious.

And if her father knew that Steph had taken a second job so she could help support a family from Thailand that had lost everything in the tsunami, he would no doubt have had a stroke.

It wasn't that Malcolm—her father insisted that she call him by his first name—was against philanthropy. Far from it. He had always given quite generously to many charities. At the peak of Malcolm's popularity, before—as Malcolm put it, Satan crashed the party—he gave away more than half of what he earned. "What else could I possibly buy?" he bellowed at his accountant, who had suggested that instead of donating hundreds of thousands of dollars to charity, he invest in real estate. "Exactly how many dwellings does one human being need?"

But as generous as he was, Malcolm Ayers firmly believed that people in Stephanie's shoes needed to protect themselves financially, and build up their own wealth, before giving away significant amounts of cash to others in need.

Still, when Steph's best friend from high school told her about an organization run by a few of their classmates to help the surviving residents of the tiny village of Katang, Steph had to help.

Since then, she and her friend had been contributing a few hundred dollars a week, hoping to assist the people of Katang in trying to find a way to put their lives back together without starving to death in the process.

The traffic on Main Street was mercifully light, and

Steph made it in and out of the CVS drive-thru window with a minimum of trouble, then headed back home. She dropped the prescription off at Mrs. Giordano's, and then started right out for Hartford. She decided to grab a snack at Dunkin' Donuts on the way. She wasn't really a fast-food person, but she had to have something to eat, or her headache would turn into a whopping migraine.

Just after Steph reached Route 4, she switched on the radio to catch a bit of the news.

"Last night's shooting bears an uncanny resemblance to a series of brutal murders that terrorized western Massachusetts more than twenty years ago. The infamous 'Springfield Shooter,' Alan Lombardo, was convicted of those crimes in 1985, but authorities have acknowledged that a note left at the scene of this most recent killing appears to indicate that the man responsible for this latest crime was somehow connected to those of twenty years ago."

By now, Steph's heart was racing. Her headache, Dunkin' Donuts, St. Joseph's, Mrs. Giordano, Thailand—everything on her mind was replaced instantly by the memory of that house she'd glimpsed on her television screen. Now she knew exactly why the news station was showing it. She checked in the rearview mirror, then quickly turned off the main road onto a side street to listen to the end of the report.

"A police spokesperson released a statement that the murder took place in the Indian Oaks section of Springfield, between seven and ten P.M. last night. Anyone with any information about the killing should contact—"

By this time, Steph had already pulled out her cell phone, and was frantically dialing her father's number. When Malcolm finally answered, she demanded, almost in tears, "Daddy, where were you last night between seven and ten o'clock?"

Forty Seconds

AS ZACK RACED TOWARD THE GUNMAN ACROSS the front of the courtroom, the completely unbidden realization jumped into Zack's mind that all that separated him from the assailant was sixty feet. The same distance between home plate and first base on a softball field.

And then came the memory of that moment, over seven years ago.

"Hey, Zack. If you're there, man, pick up. Damn. I hope you're on your way. The game's going to start in five minutes. Hurry up, dude."

Zack heard the message come through the answering machine, but there was nothing he could do to respond to the call. And there was no way he was going to the softball game, either. In fact, softball was the least of his worries. At that moment, Zack wasn't sure that he was going to be able to leave his apartment ever again.

Only two days earlier, Zack had returned from the hospital with his adopted infant son. Zack was utterly sleep-deprived, extremely hungry, and doing his best to put a diaper on the little squirming baby he had named Justin, a child who, despite his inexperience at being alive, already seemed to have mastered quite a few neat tricks.

Like screaming incessantly, kicking his legs violently, and defecating repeatedly in brand-new diapers.

And then something strange happened. One minute there was nothing but shrieking and sobbing, flailing limbs and flying urine and mucus, and the next—silence. Zack's left hand was resting gently on the little guy's rising and falling chest, but somehow, Zack's right hand—actually, his right pinky—had become locked in the surprisingly firm grip of a miniature fist. And even though the nurse had told Zack that Justin's eyes weren't really able to focus yet, he would have sworn that the boy was looking directly at him.

For that moment, lasting probably no more than five or ten seconds, as Justin and Zack met for the first time in each other's eyes, there was nothing but a quiet bond, a steady, certain connection.

An understanding that everything was going to be all right.

It turned out to be all that Zack needed. It became the moment he would call upon whenever the uncertainties, the insecurities, and the fear threatened to overwhelm him.

Being a single dad was going to be hard. Harder than he had imagined, and he was only in day two. But that was okay. Fatherhood was an important job. It was supposed to be hard.

Zack would face every challenge, and he would rise above them all.

Whether it be hunger, or lack of sleep, or an infinite number of soiled diapers.

And then the sound of another gunshot ripped through the courtroom.

Or whether the challenge was an armed lunatic, less than sixty feet away, firing wildly into a mob.

FOUR

August 23, 1982. It was raining when I got up, and it just kept raining the whole day, which really sucked. I was planning on doing Stewie today, but the hell with it.

I hung around the house and got drunk instead.

August 24, 1982. Today was much nicer than yesterday. I got some things done, and then, just after sunset, I went over to Stewie's house.

I remember now that he had told me about his family when we met, but I wasn't paying much attention. I was just getting such a powerful image of what he was going to look like when I aced him.

So I really wasn't expecting to find his sister standing next to Stewie when he came to the door.

And then I realized, shit. Now I can't kill him. As soon as the cops start asking questions, his sister would surely ID me as somebody he'd spent time with recently.

But I couldn't very well just show up, knock on the door, and walk away as soon as they answered it. Talk about suspicious. So I made up some bullshit—I told them I was in the neighborhood because I was on my way to get dinner at Fitz's Pub before maybe catching a movie—God, I can't even remember what I said.

Anyway, they invited me in, and I figured I was really screwed. Instead of killing Stewie, I was stuck hanging out with him and his sister.

It was going to drive me nuts.

But then, I caught a break, thank God, and the whole day turned around.

While we were talking, it turned out that Stewie and his sister were also thinking about going to dinner, and they started making noise about how we could go together.

By that time I was starting to feel sick. I absolutely did not want to spend any more time with these two. I needed to find somebody to kill. But before I could even think up an excuse, all of a sudden, his sister said the magic words. "I just need to take a quick shower, and then we can get going."

Talk about a change in plans. One minute, I'm in the shitter, and the next, it's time for a double-header. I said sure, and Betsy left. I think her name was Betsy, but I don't remember. Isn't that wild? About six hours ago I was about as intimate with her as a person can be, and I don't even remember her name.

So anyway, off she goes. A minute later, we can hear the water in the shower start to flow, and two minutes later, I've got Stewie all tied up. I had to wrap him pretty tight, because I left him so I could go get Betsy, or whatever her name was.

I got a little wet pulling her out of the tub after I shot her, but it was worth it. You should have seen the look on Stewie's face when he saw me dragging her body out of the bathroom and over to him. It was almost as good as the look on his face when I shot him.

When I got tired of watching the blood flow out of him, I looked over at Betsy, and noticed something interesting. I had dragged her across the floor by her ankle, so her arms were extended back over her head. And it was weird—her face was all messed up and there was blood everywhere, but her right index finger was extended away from the rest of her hand, which was sort of in a gentle fist. Not bloody, not bruised, nothing. It was just sitting there, perfectly fine, pointing to nothing.

*I don't know why, but I decided right there that I
wanted to keep it, so I went into the kitchen, found one of
those nice steak knives with the wooden handles, and cut
the finger off. Then I cut off one of Stewie's, too, because it
was also in really good shape.*

(*Commonwealth v. Lombardo*, Trial Exhibit Number 8)

Zack looked up from the document he had been reviewing. He was still trying to get a sense of the kind of person
he was being asked to represent, and had decided to look
again at all of the journal entries that a jury had determined were written by him.

He was also looking forward to actually speaking to
Alan Lombardo, but that was going to have to wait.
Because Alan was an extremely slow reader.

Zack was sitting at the table in the attorney's meeting
room at MCI–Bridgewater. Lombardo sat across from
him, currently reading the second page of a three-page,
double-spaced conflict of interest waiver that Zack had
handed to him a very long time ago. The inmate was
probably in his fifties, a little shorter than average, with
thin, graying hair that featured the most severe part Zack
had ever seen in his life.

And his facial tic—an exaggerated and very frequent
blink—was also pretty severe.

Terry was sitting to Zack's left, expending an incredible amount of energy attempting to look like he was the
consummate professional, a man of infinite patience in an
expensive suit, merely waiting for his client to conclude
the review of an important document.

Zack knew it was an expensive suit because Terry
must have mentioned it six times on the way to the prison.

But what Terry was really doing was trying to keep
from becoming the first human being to go super nova. A

bead of sweat ran down the side of his face, and the muscle in his jaw was jumping around like he was grinding his teeth into dust. If Lombardo didn't finish soon, Terry was going to end up leaping onto one of the little plastic chairs surrounding the table, and shrieking uncontrollably.

Zack hoped the chairs were stronger than they looked, because it didn't look like Lombardo was in a hurry.

While the inmate continued to read, Zack glanced at the two-inch thick stack of papers that Lombardo had brought with him to the meeting. It appeared to be a portion of his trial transcript, held together by a large binder clip. Several lines of the top page were highlighted in pink, one in green, and two in orange. There were notes written in the margin, in what looked like a very careful handwriting.

Lombardo sighed heavily, lifted page two with his thumb and index finger, and turned it over, placing it carefully on top of page one. Then he straightened those two sheets, and turned his attention to the final page. But before beginning to read that one, he performed for the third time what was apparently his personal legal document ritual— he tapped the table gently with his right hand, twice, and then laid it on his right thigh.

Unfortunately, as Lombardo began to peruse the top of page three, a puzzled look came over his face, he blinked furiously, and he reached over to page two, carefully turning it over to reread something at the bottom. Then, with the deliberation of a ninety-year-old with advanced arthritis, he replaced page two back on top of page one, straightened them up again, and returned to the final sheet.

A small, strangled sound escaped from Terry, and then, as if watching one more second of Lombardo's craziness were too much to bear, the big lawyer quickly looked down at a legal pad that he had brought to the meeting. He clicked his pen frantically, and then began to scribble something.

It was probably a suicide note.

A moment later, Terry slid the pad in front of Zack. Zack got as far as reading, *Heather is my*—before Alan Lombardo cleared his throat. The convict was looking up through his black-rimmed glasses. In a quiet voice, he said, "I'm sorry it took me so long to read that. The font your printer used gave me a headache."

Terry exhaled deeply, slid his legal pad back in front of him, and closed his eyes. "That's funny," he said, bringing his hands up to rub his temples. "I've got a headache, too."

If Lombardo had picked up on the disgust in Terry's tone, he didn't let on. He merely blinked a few times, and continued speaking to Zack, as if he hadn't heard anything. "So I guess you'd like me to sign this."

"Well, actually, I need to know that you understand it," Zack replied. "And then I need you to sign it—if you agree with it, of course."

Lombardo paused. For a prison inmate, he was extremely well groomed. His face was clean-shaven, his clothes looked freshly laundered, possibly even ironed. His hands were folded and resting on the table. Each one of his fingernails was a perfectly shaped white crescent, exactly the same size.

"I fully understand the document," Lombardo said, looking directly into Zack's eyes. "In order for you to represent me, I have to acknowledge the fact that it might be difficult—and maybe impossible—for you to be objective when you are reviewing the work your father did when he was my trial lawyer."

Zack quickly looked at Terry, who was studying Lombardo carefully. It wasn't often that they represented someone who was both intelligent and articulate. Even if his mannerisms were extremely disconcerting. "That's it in a nutshell," Zack told Lombardo. "Terry and I will do our best to tell you what we think about your chances for getting a new trial. And we'll try to help you get one. But because my relationship with your trial attorney creates a conflict of interests, we have to inform you of the conflict, and advise you that our representation might be compromised because of it. Of course you always have the option of representing yourself—"

"Excuse me," Lombardo interrupted. The blinking accelerated. "I went through all of this with Judge Baumgartner. I know the risks, and I still want you to represent me." He selected one of the several pens and highlighters that rested on the table beside the clipped transcript before him, painstakingly signed the waiver, then passed it to Zack. "I assume that you'll send me a copy of this."

"Of course," Zack said, looking down at the signature. He hadn't seen handwriting so precise since Mrs. Baylor's third-grade penmanship class. He put the waiver in the thin manila folder that he had brought with him to the meeting.

Terry exhaled loudly. "So now that that's out of the way, can we talk a little bit about the case?" He clicked his pen a couple of times and turned to a fresh page on his legal pad. "I was hoping that we could get into how this all started. You know, when you first learned you were a suspect, whether you turned yourself in, or whether you were arrested, that kind of thing."

Normally, inmates jumped at the chance to explain all about how unfairly the police had treated them, or how innocent they were.

But instead of launching into a tirade, Lombardo merely steepled his fingers together, and pursed his lips. Then he moved the pens a few inches away from the transcript that he had marked up, and slid it across the table. "Actually," he said, "I think you'll find that I've already pulled out and highlighted the parts of the transcript that will be most useful in getting me a new trial. And"—*blink blink*—"could you please stop making that noise with your pen?"

Oh, this was going to be interesting. Terry had a nervous habit of clicking his pen whenever he held it in his hand. He probably did it about five thousand times a day. Asking him to stop was like asking him to give up inhaling. It was going to be the battle of the twitches.

Terry looked up from the document. "Me?" he asked in surprise. Then he looked down at the pen in his hand. "Oh. Sure." He put down the pen, flipped through a few pages of the transcript, and then pushed it toward Zack. "Great," he said, picking up the pen again, clicking it a few times, jotting a note on the pad, clicking the pen a few more times and then looking back at Lombardo, who had given up blinking, and was now wincing. "Oops," Terry said, putting the pen back down again.

"Terry and I will read the whole transcript," Zack interjected, "as well as everything else written about your case—but first we'd like to get an idea of how this all unfolded. Like, what were you doing when the police first contacted you? Where were you? What did they say?"

Terry picked up his pen, clicked it a few times, and began to scribble a few things on his pad.

Lombardo reacted to the noise of the pen, but Terry was too busy concentrating on what he was writing to notice. The inmate brought his attention back to Zack. "I really don't see how that will help," he said. "As I mentioned, the transcript is full of errors, which I've already marked for you." He motioned to the stack of paper he'd just passed to them. "In fact, I think you'll see that in the judge's final instructions to the jury on the burden of proof, he made at least three errors that were so serious that there's no question that my case will be flipped. All you have to do is simply prepare the motion for new trial, file it, and we can go from there."

This was getting weird. Did this inmate really expect that *he* was going to call the shots? Terry had finished whatever he was doing, and was now regarding Lombardo with a quizzical look. He clicked his pen twice, stared down at it as if he hadn't remembered what was in his hand, then dropped it hastily.

Zack tried again. "I understand what you're saying, Mr. Lombardo, but I'm still interested in learning everything I can about the circumstances of the arrest, and anything else I can learn about the investigation, at least from your perspective. That's why I'd like you to tell me about how this case first came to your attention. You must have been aware of all the publicity around the case at that time. 'The Springfield Shooter' was on the front pages all the time back then, right?"

Lombardo appeared to consider what Zack said. He blinked his flat, nondescript brown eyes too many times, then took a deep breath. "I guess I'm a little confused," he said. "I've already identified the arguments you can use to support a motion for new trial. I don't really understand why we need to waste a lot of time talking about things like my arrest."

Terry looked positively astonished. But Lombardo smiled, somewhat patronizingly. "Believe me, I've lived with this case longer than either of you will ever have to. Trust me: there's no appealable issue with my arrest, or the indictments, or anything else other than the errors made at my trial." He pointed to the transcripts again. "And they're all in there, marked up and ready to go."

Okay. Now there was a problem. If this guy expected that they were just going to write up a motion for a new trial based on a review of only those parts of the transcript that he figured were important, he was going to be very disappointed. "I'm sorry, Alan," Zack said, "but I'm a little confused myself. Is there any reason that you don't want us to know about how the charges against you were initiated?"

"Of course not. But why spend time looking into issues that have no chance of helping support a motion for new trial?"

Before Terry tried to jump across the table and wring this idiot's neck, Zack stood up. "Tell you what," he said. "Obviously, you have given your case a lot of thought, which is terrific." He picked up the stack of papers Lombardo had prepared for them. Terry stood, and Lombardo followed suit, looking a little surprised. "Terry and I will review the work you've done, but we're also going to read the entire trial transcript, and the appeals briefs, and then we're going to come back and ask you about the arrest, and everything that happened to you starting from that point forward." The two lawyers headed for the door, where Terry signaled the guard that their meeting was over. "By that time, you'll have had a chance to decide whether you are comfortable addressing those aspects of the case. I hope so, because we won't represent you unless you choose to answer the questions that we ask."

Alan clearly wasn't expecting that the meeting would end so abruptly, but he said nothing as he was led away to his cell. Zack and Terry headed in the opposite direction, toward the control area where the guards would process them before leaving the facility.

As they walked down the long, tiled hallway, Terry muttered, "Dude's got issues."

Zack nodded. "If he can't answer the simplest questions, we can't do anything for him."

After a moment, Terry looked back at his partner, but said nothing. It was as if he was waiting for Zack to say something else. "What?" Zack demanded.

The big man blew out some air. "I just want to say that when somebody wears their brand-new, designer, charcoal gray, pin-striped suit for the first time, you're supposed to say something like, 'Nice suit.' "

Now Zack understood why he'd heard so much about the suit. "Oh." They walked another few paces, and then he added, in a ludicrously disingenuous voice, "Hey, Elvis. Nice suit."

Terry shook his head in disgust, and kept walking. "You suck."

FIVE

August 22

STEPHANIE HARTZ LOOKED ACROSS THE TABLE at her father as he cut into the slab of rare prime rib he shouldn't have ordered for dinner. The few strands of white hair still on top of his head did little to soften his thin, weathered face, which carried more lines than the face of a normal seventy-year-old.

"Tonight I renounce poltroonery, my daughter, and henceforth vow to be lionhearted."

Not that there was much normal about Stephanie's father.

"My will is stout, my resolve unshakeable. I have fire in my heart, and brimstone in my liver. That is, whatever is left of my liver."

Tonight's dinner was the latest in a string of surprise gestures that had started several weeks ago. Last month, out of nowhere, he had sent her a card with a reproduction of a Van Gogh painting that he knew she liked, just because he saw it in the store, and "couldn't think of any reason in the world *not* to send it." And two weeks before that, he had called her, without any provocation, to let her know that one of her favorite movies, *Butch Cassidy and the Sundance Kid,* had been released in a special edition DVD.

After more than a dozen years of neglect thanks in large part to his alcoholism, and then a half dozen more thanks to his self-conscious and tenuous sobriety, this recent attention was very unsettling.

"I say now, Stephanie, as I have oft said before, if those self-aggrandizing jackals in the news media so much as whisper the vaguest innuendo, I shall fly on Hermes's winged feet to the halls of justice, and stop at nothing to staunch the flow of their fetid bile."

Malcolm Ayers's aversion to the press was understandable.

Forty years ago, he'd been an English teacher at a high school in upstate New York, and working on his master's degree at night. In his spare time, he had been writing a little novel called *Sally's Gift.*

That's right. *That* Malcolm Ayers.

As if there was anyone who didn't already know, *Sally's Gift* captured the imagination of America like no book in recent memory, and mere months after its publication, middle schools, junior high schools, and high schools across the country began to order the book for use in their English classes. It became widely accepted as an instant American classic.

Everyone read it.

And Malcolm Ayers's life was turned completely and utterly upside down.

"Oh good," Steph replied, exasperated. "Lawyers and Greek gods. Our problems are solved."

Malcolm took another bite of his beef. "Sarcasm does not become you, my dear." He looked over at her plate. "And you've barely touched your dinner."

Steph squeezed her eyes shut. "All I know is that I'd feel a lot better if you had an alibi." She opened her eyes and looked again at her father, as he continued to act as if nothing was wrong. "The idea that this whole thing could be starting up again just makes me so *angry.*"

The tidal wave of fame and fortune that washed over Malcolm after *Sally's Gift* had been published was more intense than even he ever could have anticipated. His mailbox overflowed with letters from readers, his phone rang incessantly, and his small town was overrun with strangers—*tourists*—hoping to meet him, take his picture, chat about his book.

Malcolm had always been a very private person, and the attention he was suddenly attracting was far more than he could bear. He began using alcohol to cope. He quit his job. For years, he went into hiding, assuming that he and his book would soon be forgotten.

He was only half right. By 1973, the public's fascination with him had declined enough for him to move to Indian Oaks, and resume his career as a teacher at nearby Colton College. But the popularity of *Sally's Gift* did not weaken.

Malcolm swallowed a mouthful of mashed potatoes before he answered. "Starting up again? I refuse to allow another family's tragedy to dominate and overwhelm our lives a second time." He took a sip of water, and blotted his lips with his napkin. "And for the record, I do understand that it is not for me to determine how you should feel. However, I would like to remind you that I have always provided the bitterness and resentment in our relationship. If anyone is to be unreasonably angry, kindly allow it to be me, Stephanie. I excel at it."

By 1980, Malcolm was living what he considered an idyllic existence. He had been married to fellow professor Marilyn Inserra for five years, and their daughter, Stephanie, was three years old. He and Marilyn were happy and fulfilled in their careers and as parents.

But then, completely out of the blue, Marilyn was diagnosed with breast cancer. She died within months.

Once again, Malcolm's life had been upended. And as tempted as he was to escape through alcohol, now he had a little girl to care for, alone. And so he resisted.

But as Stephanie grew older and Malcolm's loneliness grew deeper, he began to drink once again, only in the evenings, to help him sleep. By 1982, he was getting drunk almost every night. Yet he still maintained enough control over his life to care for his daughter, however imperfectly, and to hold on to his job.

"May we change the subject to something more pleasant?" Malcolm took another forkful to his lips. "How is your friend Nolan? It's been quite a while since you've spoken of him."

Nolan Fogg was a physical therapist for three local hospitals, including Steph's. During an uncharacteristically glum period about a year ago, Steph had gone out on a handful of dates with Nolan, to cheer herself up. But after a short while, it became clear that although Nolan had graduated from college many years ago, he had not yet emotionally moved out of his fraternity house.

Steph's far-too-early and completely unsuccessful marriage to her college sweetheart had taught her that no matter how big or how old, men who had not left boyhood were not great husband material. She did not hide her feelings from Nolan, and he had seen the handwriting on the wall. So on one of their last outings together, he took Steph to a Red Sox game with Malcolm. It was a shameless attempt to stave off the breakup that he knew was coming, by worming his way into Steph's affections through her father, an insanely devoted Boston baseball fan.

Despite the obvious incompatibility between Nolan and Steph, Malcolm still harbored hopes that Nolan would magically evolve into a fully functional adult, and that Steph would then fall in love with him.

Not so far.

"Nolan is fine, as far as I know. Last I heard, he was dating a kindergarten teacher from Ludlow."

"Ah. Well, if you run into him, please give him my regards."

Steph took a halfhearted stab at her spinach salad. At any moment they could learn that an avalanche of suspicion and intrusive reporters was bearing down on them from this latest murder, and yet here they were, discussing Nolan Fogg, for goodness sakes. "So that's it? The plan is for us to make small talk and just hope that this all goes away?"

"Perhaps the Alcoholics Anonymous philosophy is finally taking hold," Malcolm replied. "I am accepting those things I cannot change."

"Fine. But wouldn't it be easier if you *could* change things? Why not try to establish an alibi? What harm—"

"Stephanie, dear, on the night of this most recent tragedy, I did the same thing that I've done every night for the past eleven years of my life. I stayed at home, reading and working. Alone. It is what I do. I am sorry to disappoint you, but just like those nine murders of twenty years ago, I have no alibi."

"I have no alibi. You're going to have to lock me up, I guess."

Paul Merrone was not amused at the telltale odor of tobacco that wafted into the den as George Heinrich emerged from his private bathroom. "C'mon, Mr. Heinrich. What am I supposed to tell Neil?"

Officially, Paul was Vice President of Heinrich Contracting, a construction firm headquartered in the heart of Springfield's industrial district. But really, Paul was old man Heinrich's bodyguard.

Back in the day—hell, even five years ago—being George Heinrich's bodyguard really meant something. The man ran the entire south side of Springfield from his firm's office. Numbers, loan sharking, protection. Heinrich's influence was everywhere—city and state government, the courts, you name it. George Heinrich had this little area of the world in his pocket.

And his reputation was golden. For a man doing the business he did, George Heinrich was known as absolutely, always honest. Good, bad, or otherwise, if Mr. Heinrich said it, you could take it to the vault. For Paul, that always made his job, even when it got ugly, a little easier.

"Oh, what difference does it make? So I had a cigarette. I'm dying, Paulie. The doctors say if I'm real lucky, I got two more months. You think one more smoke's gonna make any difference?"

Actually, Paul really *didn't* think it was going to make any difference. If it were up to him, he'd let Mr. Heinrich do whatever the heck he wanted for the last few weeks of his life. He'd sure earned it. Smoke, drink, party. Hell, live it up, right?

But Mr. Heinrich's only kid, Neil, was the one calling the shots now, and Neil very much did not want his father to smoke, drink, or party. Watching his father die was killing Neil, and he was fighting it every step of the way.

"I guess it can't hurt," Paul answered. "As long as you don't rat me out to Neil. You ready to go? We're supposed to meet him at The Seaside at noon."

Mr. Heinrich started to answer, but got overcome by a coughing fit instead. So he just waved his hand, and walked past Paul toward the door to the driveway. They got in the car and headed off.

It was strange how it was all playing out. Neil Heinrich hadn't always had his act together. He was plenty smart—he'd even gone to college—but when he was growing up, he was kind of a loose cannon emotionally.

But ever since Neil started with the company, ten, maybe twelve years ago, he had been Mr. Responsibility, showing up every day, working hard with his father, learning how to manage every part of the business.

When his dad had gotten sick, Neil pitched right in to help run things. And when his dad had gotten so ill that he couldn't even come to work anymore, Neil fully took over. Even if he wouldn't admit it to anyone else.

When the coughing stopped, Paul asked, "Do you need your medicine?"

The old man shook his head and made a face. "I hate that stuff. Screw it. I'd rather just cough." He popped a breath mint into his mouth, then said, "Listen, Paulie. I gotta ask you something."

The car turned down First Street toward where most of the downtown restaurants were. "Sure, Mr. Heinrich."

"Neil's gonna need a lot of help with collection, at least at the beginning—you know, after I'm gone. People are gonna see what they can get away with, see how far they can push, you know what I mean?"

They pulled into the parking lot of the restaurant. Paul turned off the engine and nodded. "I do."

Mr. Heinrich cleared his throat. "I talked about a lot of things with Neil, and I'm pretty sure he's going to be fine, but I told him that if he runs into trouble, he's gotta use you, especially down near the river. You know. O'Malley & Sons, Stein's, Best Air, all of those accounts. They know you. They know what you can do. It'll help Neil if they understand that even though I'm not around anymore, nothing's really changed."

Just then, Paul's phone rang. He answered it, and then handed the phone to Mr. Heinrich, saying, "It's Alan Lombardo."

Iris A. Dubinski

IT WAS 8:23 P.M. ON AUGUST 23 WHEN IRIS Dubinski answered the door for the last time in her life.

She was feeling a little stressed, because she'd needed to stay late at the office to rewrite a memo explaining the new overtime policy, and so she was running behind. She had a very early flight the following morning—she was taking a week off at a spa in San Diego, and then going to an important meeting in Los Angeles. She had to pack, close up the house, make sure the cat was taken care of, and do the dozens of other things that she needed to do before she could leave.

When the doorbell rang it didn't really surprise her, because it wasn't unusual for her boss to send her last-minute materials by messenger before a trip. So she didn't hesitate to open the door.

Minutes later, she was lying on her back in the middle of her living room, bound and gagged with duct tape, staring at the terrifying man with the gun, who had entered her house saying only, "Welcome to my world, Iris Dubinski. Two down, four to go."

SIX

August 26

DETECTIVE VERA DEMOPOLOUS GOT A COLD
bottle of water out of the refrigerator, sat down at her
kitchen table, and for what must have been the fifteenth
time since the letter had arrived at the station two days
ago, began again to read.

> *My Dear Vera,*
>
> *I know that we haven't known each other that
> long, but I feel compelled to tell you immediately how
> impressed I was with your decision to keep our little
> communications off the front pages. I expected a very
> unpleasant public debate about the contents of my
> letter, speculation about my next victim, and who
> knows what else?*
> *I so much prefer that our dialogue is private.*
> *And I'm happy to report that this letter is being
> written after my latest work, so I will be able to share
> my diary entry for that exciting day:*
> *August 23. Practice has truly made perfect.
> I don't like to plan too much before I go into*

the house. Sometimes I have a general idea of what I'm going to do after we've gotten started, but most of the time, I just improvise.

Today, I must admit that I was inspired.

Seconds after I knocked on the door, she opened it, I used my friend the Taser, and voilà! I was in the house, and she was wrapped up quite nicely.

You know my preferences—taping my quarry to a chair, or the floor, or whatever is handy, and then shooting for a while to see what happens. But this time, I thought I'd just bind up her hands and feet, but leave her free to wiggle around. And then see what happens.

Vera took another sip of water and skipped ahead to the end of the letter. She didn't need to wallow in this maniac's account of the bloody details of a crime she didn't even know had occurred. If he really did all the things he described in the diary entry, she'd find out soon enough when they discovered the body.

Even though I didn't mean for it to end like that, it was probably for the best, because I had been there for several minutes, and I didn't want to overstay my welcome.

I got the pictures I needed, and then I flipped her back over. I'm happy to report that despite the mess we had made, her right index finger was still in very good shape.

I cut it off, washed up a little, and returned home.

Hello Vera. I am back.

I have to admit, I'm somewhat proud of this one. It was the perfect combination of planning and

*spontaneity. I knew I was going to do her, and when,
and how, but not at the detail level. I waited for the
moment to decide about that, and it turned into
something of a masterpiece.*

*I don't really know you that well yet, but I hope
when you find the body, and verify that everything
you've read is accurate, you're the kind of person who
can appreciate the type of effort that went into that
slaying. It was a work of art.*

*I'm going to leave you now. But don't worry. I will
be in touch soon.*

Vera put the copy of the letter back into the file that
she had brought home with her. No matter how many
times she read it, she didn't feel any closer to finding who
sent it.

The original of the note was still being worked on by
the lab, but Vera didn't expect them to find much more
than they already had. The envelope and paper were ordinary. The labels on the envelope were ordinary. The return address was a fake Springfield post office box.
Anyone who went to the amount of trouble this crackpot
did to write and mail this kind of a letter to the police
about his crime had to be intelligent enough to keep fingerprints and any identifying evidence out of their hands.

The only thing they were relatively sure of was that
the printer was one of the least expensive and most popular out there—a Printex 343.

Vera had also checked into missing persons reports
for an adult female living in the Springfield area, but so
far, no luck.

Normally, Vera was an optimistic person, but even
though she hoped that the description of the murder contained in the letter was a bluff, it sure didn't sound like one.

Thank goodness her new partner would be joining her

any day now. Technically, he wasn't actually a partner—he was a state police detective assigned to assist her in the investigation. But Vera couldn't have cared less. She was going to need all the help she could get, especially if this second murder turned out to be real.

And it was also a good thing that she didn't wear much makeup, because lately she'd been spending so much time in front of those insanely hot television camera lights that if she had, her face would probably have melted off by now. Vera finished her water, got up, and went into her bedroom.

As she changed from her sweaty work clothes into a T-shirt and shorts, Vera said a silent prayer of thanks that her air conditioner worked so quickly.

Not that Vera was complaining about the attention the Chatham murder investigation was getting. Having the lieutenant assign such an important case to her obviously meant that he had a lot of faith in her. Although it was pretty clear that neither of them knew just how important the case really was until they saw the press go crazy about the similarity of the Chatham murder to those of the Springfield Shooter two decades earlier.

Once that story got started, Vera had been spending about as much time dealing with reporters as she had running down leads.

When you've got more than four dogs, put them in the same room at dinnertime and feed them all together. Otherwise you'll spend your whole day opening cans of Alpo.

It was a safe bet that Grandma Burke hadn't thought that her experience raising dog-sled teams in Alaska would help organize daily press conferences in Springfield, Massachusetts.

Funny how Grandma's advice about animals came in so handy when dealing with reporters.

Okay, that was a little mean. Some of these people

really weren't bad. A few of them just wanted to learn the truth and present it to the public.

But most of them seemed interested only in having Vera say something that they could use to generate an inflammatory headline. *Those* reporters were definitely dogs.

Now Vera took a container of chef's salad out of the refrigerator, and brought it over to the little table she had set up in her half living room, half dining room. As she began to eat the leftovers from yesterday's dinner, she opened up the Chatham file and, for the hundredth time in the past ten days, went through the names she had been generating as possible suspects since she first spoke to Willy Grasso.

She started with the police who were involved in the Springfield Shooter investigation twenty years ago. The two lead detectives were Willy and his then-partner, Ole Pedersen. And although Vera personally knew beyond any doubt that neither man was capable of committing murder, she had treated each of them like everyone else on the list. Just another person to clear, or to investigate further.

But eliminating Willy and Ole as suspects took about fifteen seconds. On the night of Cory Chatham's murder, Willy Grasso was in Sarasota, Florida, attending a dinner theatre performance of *Mame* with his wife and a dozen of their friends from their retirement community. And Ole Pedersen had been in the Springfield Memorial Hospital, recuperating from prostate surgery.

So that left her with only about three and a half pages of other names to go through.

Next were the uniformed officers who had discovered the victims. The only one who might have seen the message "Welcome to my world" at more than one Springfield Shooter crime scene was Officer Earl Quincy, who had been the only cop involved in finding more than one victim. He had been the responding officer for victims four and nine, and so he could have seen two of the six notes that the Springfield Shooter had left behind.

As unlikely a candidate as Quincy seemed, Vera checked into his whereabouts on the night of Chatham's murder, and learned that he had left the Springfield force eight years ago, and had then moved to South Carolina. She hadn't yet reached him, so Quincy was still on the list. But not exactly a prime suspect.

And there were dozens of officers, crime-scene specialists, lab techs, and others who had seen the telltale greeting. Running them down was going to take a lot of time.

And there were the assistant district attorneys who had worked on the case, who turned out to be a pretty impressive cast of characters. The lead A.D.A., who later went on to serve as the district attorney for another county, was named Robert MacManus. It was a safe bet that MacManus wasn't involved, though, since he died of a stroke nine years ago. Of the four prosecutors working with him on the case, two had gone on to become judges: Mary Feldman and Charles Gutman. Although she felt a little silly doing it, Vera established alibis for both. Feldman and her husband had been attending a birthday dinner for one of their grandchildren, and Gutman had been vacationing in Denver.

The remaining two prosecutors were Sarah D'Abruzzo, who was now married and had changed her name to Sarah Sandstrom, and Dan Dorrenbock. Both had left the D.A.'s office, and were in private practice. Vera had verified Sandstrom's alibi—she had been working late on the night in question, with four associates, on a brief they were preparing. Dorrenbock and Vera had been playing phone tag for the past three days. So his name was still on her list.

And on and on it went. There were support personnel

in the prosecutor's office to check, and the members of the state police who helped Willy Grasso with his investigation, and the support personnel in that office. All in all, there were probably between one and two hundred names on the list, which itself had taken Vera almost a week just to compile.

But that's what police work was about. Details. Not taking anything for granted.

And staying focused.

Which was why it was time to take a break from the list, and replay that videotape of the crime-scene footage.

If there was one thing that Vera really relied on in her work, it was repetition. She didn't look at the tape of a crime scene once or twice. She looked at it once or twice *a day*. Until she solved the case.

It was just her way of making sure that her memory of the scene was true. It also helped her ask questions. She loved asking questions. It used to drive her older brothers nuts. "Why did you get home from school ten minutes later than usual today?" "Who would you rather have on your baseball team—Sylvester Stallone or Arnold Schwarzenegger?" "If you were walking down the street, and suddenly a gigantic bear started running after you, what would you do?"

Now Vera pressed the play button on the remote, and a picture of the home of Corey Chatham flashed onto the television screen. The officer taking the video had been standing on the street, and started with a wide shot, which included the one-car garage, the short driveway leading to it from the street, with Chatham's sleek sports car parked in it.

Then she zoomed in on the front door.

At least this latest letter had solved one of the puzzles of the Chatham case. If the victim had let the murderer into the house through the front door, he would have seen who he was through its decorative window. And that's probably what had happened. There was no sign of a break-in. No windows were broken, no locks were forced.

So either the killer had a key to Chatham's place, or Chatham had opened the door to someone he didn't believe to be a threat. And then the killer blasted him with a Taser—leaving the burn marks they found on Chatham's neck and chest.

On the one hand, it would make sense for the killer and Chatham to be acquainted. Most murder victims knew their killers. In fact, by far, most murders were crimes of passion. The usual killers were angry husbands and boyfriends. Something went sour in the relationship, they freaked out, and attacked their wife or girlfriend.

By now, the image on Vera's television had changed to the living room, where Corey Chatham's dead body sat taped to the recliner.

Which was one of the many problems with the crime of passion theory. Why duct tape? That didn't make any sense. If you were an enraged lover, you just lashed out and shot. You didn't take the time to tape someone to a chair.

They were still making inquiries into Chatham's life—friends, family, girlfriend, ex-wife, whatever. Maybe they'd find something there, but Vera wasn't counting on it. Sure, the shot to the groin—gross—might have been some kind of sexual payback. But that, combined with the point-blank shot to the eye, the removed finger and the duct tape, just didn't add up to passion. At least not the kind of passion behind most murders.

And how about that note? The lab had confirmed that it had been generated by a computer printer, and not by any printer in Chatham's house. It had to have been written before the killing, and was intended to convince the police that the Springfield Shooter was responsible. The murderer had obviously done a considerable amount of research and planning before killing Corey Chatham.

Vera had asked for the files of the Springfield Shooter investigation to be called up from archives. It would be interesting to compare the weird combination of facts in this case with the facts of those earlier crimes. But that would be tomorrow's work. It was time to take a break.

She stretched, turned off the television, and reached over to sort through the pile of mail she had scooped out of the box on her way in.

It was all junk, bills and catalogs, except for a single, ordinary, white envelope.

Which bore ordinary address labels, and a Springfield post office box for a return address.

But when Vera turned it over to pull open the flap, she saw the sticker on that side of the envelope, which was not ordinary at all. Because it read: *Welcome to my world.*

SEVEN

ASSISTANT DISTRICT ATTORNEY CARTIER: *Detective, what was the first contact you had with the defendant in the context of this case?*

DETECTIVE WILLIAM GRASSO: *On March 13, 1984, we received an anonymous tip that a white car with license plate number XR4 54P was seen driving on Yale Street at about ten P.M. on the night of March 11. The killer's ninth victim had been murdered in her house on Yale Street on that night, at about that time. So we ran the plate.*

Q *I'm sorry. You what?*

A *Sorry. We checked the records of the registry. We learned the license plate was registered to an Alan Lombardo, for a white Ford LTD. His address in the records was listed as 12 Foster Lane.*

Q *At this point, did you consider Mr. Lombardo a suspect?*

ATTORNEY NEHEMIAH WILSON: *Objection.*

THE COURT: *Overruled.*

DETECTIVE GRASSO: *No, he wasn't a suspect. But we sure wanted to talk to him.*

Q *And did you talk to him?*

A Yes. After we got the tip, my partner and I visited Mr. Lombardo at his home in Indian Oaks.

Q Did you call Mr. Lombardo to let him know you were coming?

A No. We wanted to see how he reacted when he was approached by police.

Q And how did he react?

A Well, he was surprised to see us, I think. But he was basically fine. You know. Polite. Although he seemed awfully, well, normally I'd say nervous, but I'm not sure that really covers it.

ATTORNEY NEHEMIAH WILSON: *Objection.*

THE COURT: *Overruled.*

ASSISTANT DISTRICT ATTORNEY CARTIER: *How do you mean?*

A Well, he had this, I guess you'd call it a twitch, or something. Like he was always blinking his eyes. And he had, you know those disposable wet napkins they have now for cleaning babies?

Q Yes.

A Well, he had a container of those and he kept wiping his hands with them while he was talking to us. Over and over again.

Q I see. And did you discuss the reason for your visit?

A Yes. First we got his information, ID, et cetera. Then we asked him about his whereabouts on the night of March 11, and he said that he had spent all night alone at home. And when we told him that a witness had seen his car driving on Yale Street at about ten that night, he said that they must have made a mistake.

Q Was there any further conversation?

A Not really. We left him our card, and told him if he could think of anything that might help corroborate his story that he was home alone that night, that he should call us.

Q Did he call you?

A No.

Q What was the next significant thing that happened in your investigation relative to the defendant?

A Well, I guess the next significant thing was the emergency phone call we got from the housekeeper, Mrs. Perez.

...ASSISTANT DISTRICT ATTORNEY CARTIER: Would you please state your name for the record.

GABRIELLA PEREZ: My name is Gabriella Perez.

Q And Ms. Perez, am I correct in stating that English is not your primary language?

A Sí. But I understand English. I have been taking classes for two year. Two years. Sorry.

Q That's fine. I just want you to know that if you need a translator, we can get one for you. So if you don't understand something, let me know, and we'll try to straighten it out, okay?

A Yes. Okay.

Q Good. Now I'd like to know if you are familiar with the defendant in this case, Alan Lombardo.

A Sí. I know Mr. Lombardo.

Q And can you point him out to the court?

A I'm sorry?

Q Sorry. Do you see Mr. Lombardo in the courtroom today?

A Sí. He's sitting over there.

ASSISTANT DISTRICT ATTORNEY CARTIER: May the record reflect that the witness just pointed at the defendant?

THE COURT: The record will so reflect. Continue.

ASSISTANT DISTRICT ATTORNEY CARTIER: Now Ms. Perez, what is your relationship with Mr. Lombardo?

MS. PEREZ: My relationship?

Q Yes. How is it that you know Mr. Lombardo?

A Oh. Sí. I am his housekeeper. I come to his house every two weeks, and I clean.

Q I see. So were you working at Mr. Lombardo's house on the morning of March 14?

A You mean the morning I found all those fingers inside Mr. Lombardo's freezer?

(*Commonwealth v. Lombardo*, Volume II,
Pages 54–57; Volume III, Pages 14–15)

August 27

Attorney Terry Tallach shifted in his seat. The chair he'd chosen *looked* great, and probably cost close to a thousand dollars, but he was starting to think about an extra trip to the chiropractor after sitting in it for all of five minutes.

Terry was with Zack in the offices of Zack's father, the Honorable Nehemiah H. Wilson, whose official title was Senior Justice of the Federal District Court of Massachusetts. To Terry, however, Zack's father's title was Judge Most Likely to Crush Himself from the Weight of His Own Pompous Bullshit. They were seated in leather chairs around an oval mahogany-and-glass coffee table at one end of the room. At the other was the judge's massive mahogany desk and matching workstation, bookcases, credenza, grandfather clock, file cabinets—Jesus Christ. It was like a freakin' tropical rain forest over there.

They had come to discuss the Alan Lombardo case, which Judge Wilson had handled as a trial lawyer twenty years ago. Zack promised that they would not stay more than a half hour. That was about all Terry figured he could take. Judge Wilson was the worst father and grandfather he had ever known, and Terry had trouble keeping that opinion to himself.

"So, Alan Lombardo has been filing motions, has he?" the judge said, lighting an obnoxious-smelling cigar. Nehemiah had thick white hair which he combed straight back from his tanned, leathery face. He was wearing a midnight-blue Armani suit, a shirt Terry had seen *on sale,* for God's sakes, at Thomas Pink for two hundred dollars, a yellow bow tie, and, of course, braces. He looked like he thought he was the balls, at least in the world of ass-clenchingly reactionary Yankees. And he looked like he wanted everyone to know it. As the judge blew out the match, he called out over his shoulder toward the open office door, "Mary, could we have some coffee in here, please?"

A voice from the waiting room outside the office called back, "Right away, Your Honor."

Judge Wilson turned back to his guests and shook his head. "Alan Lombardo. When I saw that name on the phone message, I have to admit that it came as a bit of a surprise. How did you two end up with this jackpot?"

"Judge Baumgartner gave me a call the other day—" Zack began, but his father cut him off.

"You know, Harry did a good job judging that trial. One of his first murder cases, too. Can't understand what he's thinking, putting you on this, though. Damnedest thing. No question of guilt."

"That's what he said," Zack responded evenly. "But Lombardo has been filing motions claiming he was innocent, and then that new murder in Indian Oaks got Judge Baumgartner thinking. So after a few misfires, he appointed us to look into it. Lombardo waived the conflict of interest, and here we are."

Zack's father studied them as he took another hit off his cigar, settled it in the ashtray on the table, and shook his head again. "Yes. Here we are." He sat back up. "Alan Lombardo. Well. Hell of a thing." He pursed his lips. "Damned frustrating case, but in the end, there wasn't an awful lot I could do. They had him cold for all nine murders. I was friends with the prosecutor, Jim Cartier, but there was no way we could plea-bargain this case. And Lombardo insisted he was innocent, so I didn't even have an insanity defense."

There was a light tap on the door, and then a young, *very* good-looking woman wearing perfect makeup, an expensive outfit, and insanely sexy shoes came into the office with a coffee service. "Thank you, Mary," the judge said, as she placed the tray down on the table before them. "We'll take it from here."

"Very good, Judge." Pretty Mary straightened up, and marched her hot little body out the door. Ol' Nehemiah watched her every step of the way. If Judge Daddy wasn't doing her, it was damn sure he was trying.

Zack cleared his throat, poured himself a cup of coffee, and then asked, "You know, Dad, I always wondered how you ended up with the Shooter case. I mean, especially after the Heinrich trial, I thought you could pretty much pick and choose whatever you wanted to do. This seemed like such a tough set of facts."

Judge Wilson laughed. He picked up his cigar again and took another puff. It was illegal to smoke in a government building, but it was pretty clear that the old man didn't give a crap about that. The room smelled like he spent a lot of time smoking cigars in here. "You're right. I probably should have checked into the case more carefully before I jumped in," he said. "But when Alan first approached me, I really felt for the guy. And then, when he paid the fee that I quoted, in full, in advance, well, I just couldn't turn that kind of money down."

Terry had to know. "How much did you charge?"

The judge looked for a second like he might balk, then a smile came over his face. "Biggest single fee I ever earned," he answered. "Two hundred and fifty thousand dollars." He took another toke from the cigar, and blew a cloud of bluish smoke into the air.

Holy crap. Two hundred fifty grand. No wonder Judge Wilson grabbed the case. For a quarter of a million dollars, Terry would represent a psycho accused of killing nine people.

Wait a minute. He already *was* representing a psycho accused of killing nine people. Accused and convicted. For about fifty bucks an hour.

Zack broke the silence. "Wow. I always thought Heinrich was the biggest fee you got."

"Oh, hell no," the judge replied. "I was on retainer to Heinrich before he got indicted, so I could only charge him my hourly rate. Back then, I was probably billing out at one fifty per. Maybe two hundred. I spent a lot of time on that case, but it couldn't have been more than what? Three hundred hours? What's that? Sixty thousand? At the most."

Terry wasn't sure he heard correctly. "You were on retainer *before* Heinrich got indicted?"

"For years. He ran one of the biggest construction companies in Springfield. Say what you want about the man, his word was his bond, and he was an excellent businessman. He had all kinds of issues—unions, government permits, bonding, insurance, corporate, criminal, you name it. If anyone that was doing work for him needed a lawyer, I was the guy."

Damn. If he was charging two hundred dollars an hour back in '84, no wonder Nehemiah was wearing Armani.

"So, back to Lombardo," Zack said. "He paid the big fee, you took the case, and started getting ready for trial. What was your strategy? Do you remember?"

The judge sat back and ran his hand through his hair. "Funny how that case has stayed with me, even though I handled dozens, if not hundreds, of criminal files before the President appointed me to the bench." He pointed to a picture of Reagan shaking hands with the judge at some black-tie thing. It was one of several photos mounted on the walls, all featuring Zack's father as he socialized with hotshot politicians and other celebrities. In one he looked like he was about to tongue-kiss Newt Gingrich. The display was about as classy as the lobby of a Las Vegas tourist trap. "Ronald Reagan. Greatest president ever."

Terry saw Zack smiling, and then he quickly checked his watch. They'd been in the office less than ten minutes, and Judge Nehe had already mentioned Reagan by name. Shit. He owed Zack twenty bucks.

"Anyway," the judge continued. "My strategy? Alan insisted that he didn't do it, so the first thing I did was try to establish alibis. I thought we might have had a chance to argue that he got framed if we could show that it was impossible for him to have killed these people."

"I read the transcripts," Zack said. "So I can guess how that turned out."

"You've probably met Alan by now," the judge replied. "I don't know what your impressions are of him, but when I knew him, let's just say that he was not your average defendant."

"Yeah. I think it's safe to say that he isn't your average inmate, either," Terry said.

The judge nodded. "Still a pretty strange duck, eh? Well. Anyway. Back in 1984, when the Spam hit the fan and he got indicted, Alan was working as an accountant. Very successful business. You know how those guys are—watching everybody else's money, and making tons of it themselves. He lived alone in a pretty nice house over in Indian Oaks. Had his office in his home. But even with all his money, the guy had no friends, no family. At least none that I ever found. And I put investigators on it, just to make sure. He was an only child. Mother and father both dead. No aunts or uncles living. No cousins. Nothing." The judge twirled the cigar around in his mouth. Talk about disgusting. Terry felt a little queasy. "And here's the topper. Lombardo told me that not only did he have no friends or family, he never left his house after dark."

"Really?" Zack exclaimed. "I had no idea."

"Most of the victims were killed at night, right?" Terry asked. "So if he never went out, he couldn't have killed them."

"Well, he *said* he never went out at night. He lived alone, remember? Like a goddamned monk. There was no way I could prove anything. For all I know, he was out on the town seven nights a week."

"And there were no phone calls, no visitors? Nothing you could document to show he was home when any of these things happened?" Zack asked.

"Zachary, I wish I could have found just one alibi. But

every one of those nine shootings was done at night. And I couldn't find a single thing that would prove that Alan Lombardo was home on *any* of those nights."

"So it was just his word against . . ." Zack let it hang there.

"Exactly. His word against a Tupperware container of fingers that Mexican girl found in his freezer." The judge sighed. "And that awful journal the cops found in his computer."

Thirty-Seven Seconds

IF ZACK HAD THOUGHT TO COMPILE HIS PRE-ferred environments for reaching and subduing a gunman without any weapons of his own, this courtroom would not be on the list.

The shooter was still dozens of feet away, on the other side of the room. One of the beams of the emergency lights was shining directly into Zack's eyes as he approached, so it was impossible to see the shooter's face, but it was clear that he was aiming his gun at the gallery, off to Zack's left, where a room full of terrified people were diving for cover, or scrambling for the aisles, frantically trying to escape the attack.

Zack had to stop the madman before he fired another shot into the crowd, where Justin, Zack's seven-year-old son, was surely scared to death, if not already hit and bleeding.

Or worse.

Zack fought to keep those images out of his head. But his brain was going so fast it was almost impossible to control. He fixed his gaze on the weapon that the shooter was slowly sweeping back and forth across the room. It was only a matter of time before he squeezed off another shot. As Zack ran toward the assassin, he tried to keep his concentration solely on getting to the hand that gripped that gun. If only this room weren't so wide open—

If only Zack knew what the hell he was doing.

He had no training for this kind of situation. He had never been in the military, and had no real interest in military strategy. The only thing he knew about violent confrontations came from a talk given a few years ago at a local bookstore by a former Navy SEAL. The author was promoting his most recent hardcover, called *Fight Smart, Stupid.* The book was all about how SEALs succeeded in almost every one of their operations because they were so careful to prepare. Their overriding strategy was to fight a battle only after manipulating the situation so that every possible aspect of the engagement was to their advantage.

The author said that because SEALs were so committed to putting the odds in their favor, they rarely directly confronted an adversary unless they had already established a detailed plan of how to do so. That was why, he said, when an unexpected confrontation with an enemy force arose, the three most frequently heard words in radio communications between SEALs were "Run away. Over."

Of course, the SEAL at the bookstore had not been talking about being in a room while a nut was shooting bullets into a crowd containing your seven-year-old kid.

Because for Zack, there would be no planning, no manipulation of the odds, and no running away.

Instead, in a few seconds, there would only be a direct, unarmed confrontation with an armed enemy.

The enemy who had just fired a fourth shot into the crowd.

Monster

STEPHANIE EMERGED FROM THE BATHROOM after her morning shower wrapped in a towel, with another on her head.

According to the phone calls she had made last night, she was going to stay home from work this morning so she could go with her father to the doctor.

That was an intriguing change in her normal routine.

She opened the top drawer of her dresser, grabbed a black bra and panties from a jumbled pile of them in there, and threw both onto the bed. Then she walked out of the camera's field of view, only to return a minute later with a pair of jeans and a bright red pullover, which she tossed onto the bed next to her underwear.

Then she stepped over to the mirror, used the towel on her head to dry her hair some more, and then realized that she hadn't remembered to bring her hairbrush out of the bathroom. She went back in to get it.

As she brushed her hair and dressed, he called up on the right side of his computer screen the file he'd labeled "The Final Moment." As the image displayed itself on his monitor, he took the time to call up on the other side of the screen the file he had labeled "A," the pictures he had taken of Iris Dubinski.

As he had done with the Chatham images a week earlier, he used his computer's photo-editing program to isolate and then remove the portions of the Dubinski pictures that specifically displayed the three gunshot wounds she had suffered. Then, he superimposed the images of the three wounds onto the Stephanie Hartz images contained in The Final Moment.

After he was done, he admired his work. Now Stephanie stood before the mirror with a horrendous bloody hole in place of her left eye, a startlingly grotesque gash down the middle of her face in place of her nose and upper lip, a bullet hole in the center of her chest, another in her groin, and in the rear view, bullet holes in each buttock.

He had already predetermined that The Final Moment would be his blueprint for the transformation of Stephanie Hartz from healthy young woman into lifeless corpse, but as he studied the series of injuries that she would suffer, he realized that many of them would take place after she had died. The human body was, of course, a limitation which he was very familiar with, but he found his mind wandering to the final confrontation, and wishing for something more.

As he closed his computer files he returned to watching Stephanie, now fully dressed, as she emerged from the bathroom again. She was wearing makeup! Mascara, maybe a little lip gloss. That was interesting. He'd have to give that some thought as he plotted out the details of her death. Would he like her to be in her normal state, clean, but unpainted, or would he prefer her corpse to display an ironic patina of glamour as it lay there, destroyed by his attack?

As Stephanie left the bedroom, presumably heading to meet her father, he turned off his computer. He pushed his chair back from the table and walked to the closet on the other side of the room where he kept the tools of his chosen trade—a roll of duct tape, a pair of pruning shears, and his collection of pistols and ammunition. He would have to remember to bring an extra clip or two when he put her down. Her body was going to absorb so many bullets he would need to reload.

His glance rested on the pruning shears. Who would have imagined how astonishingly effective they were for the post-mortem removal of fingers?

And then he smiled. Stephanie would be the final movement in this masterpiece. Her death was going to be unique—why shouldn't her dismemberment be unique as well?

He lifted the shears in his right hand, and lightly, *lightly*, ran the tip of his left index finger along one of the blades. Despite all the work he had done with the tool, it was still razor-sharp.

But would it cause the necessary quantum of pain to Stephanie? As she approached the end, his hope was that she would be the source of a spectacular symphony of shrieks and screams, marking with their volume the excellence of his work.

He could, of course, try it on his next victim, and see. But that would mar its use on Stephanie. If she was to be the first to lose her finger while still alive, then he couldn't very well take the technique out for a test-drive on some far less important victim.

And then an idea crossed his mind. An experiment. It would be imperfect, but it would be useful. And, if he were careful, there was no reason it shouldn't work.

Full of excitement, he raced out of his special space into the main part of the house to get the supplies he'd require—a towel, a box of Band-Aids, some gauze, tape, a little plastic bag full of ice, and antibacterial gel. As his hands filled with the items his heart rate increased steadily. This was going to be a fantastic experiment.

He hurried back down to his sanctuary, and set everything onto the table next to his computer. Then he collected the pruning shears and brought them over to the table. He sat down in front of it all, bent down, and untied his left shoe.

If there was an accident, he certainly didn't want any damage to occur to his right foot. That was his dominant side.

He took off his shoe and his sock, and crossed his left ankle over his right knee. And frowned.

The problem was that the target was his pinky toe. He needed to use the pruning shears with his right hand, and there was no way he could do it except in a most awkward manner. He would have to hold the shears to the right of his foot, and have the blades converge on the toe from below. And his only view would be from the left side—over the top of the foot. If he tried to do it this way, the view of his right hand would be blocked almost entirely by his left foot as he leaned forward to see what was happening to his toe.

That would not be satisfactory.

So he uncrossed his leg, pushed back a bit from the computer table, and propped his left foot up onto the edge of the work surface. It was still not ideal, but his pinky toe was now much more accessible to the shears which he wielded in his right hand. It would have to do.

Using his left hand, he carefully took hold of the target digit with his thumb and index finger, and pulled it gently away from the others. It was funny how it always seemed like the little toe was actually clinging to its larger mates, as if for safety. Human instinct was so amusing sometimes.

Once he had made some space between the pinky and

the fourth toe, he slid the open shears into place, setting the base of his toe in the V created by the open shears.

His right hand held the shears carefully. One part of the tool's handle rested at the base of his thumb and across his palm, the other rested across the four opposite fingers. The question to be answered by the experiment had to do with the manner in which Stephanie's digit was to be removed.

When he was cutting fingers off of his previous victims, they were dead, so the method of removal was immaterial. He squeezed the two ends of the handle together, the blades scissored across the flesh and bone, there was a satisfying crunch, and the deed was done.

But when Stephanie was to be mutilated, the effect was not only intended for those who would discover her, but for her. She would be alive to experience it. The question was: How best to create in her the maximum experience of terror?

It was not an idle question. The obvious answer was to cut through her finger slowly, so that she experienced every second of the destruction of that part of her body sequentially, rather than as one rapid event. As the gradually increasing incision grew, there would be time for Stephanie's imagination to create and even dwell on the boundless horrors available to the human mind.

But there were risks. The terror, or the pain, might overwhelm her senses, and cause her to faint. That would be the worst possible outcome. The whole point was for her to be witness to her own fate, her own mortality. Not to fall unconscious as it was happening.

But if the cut was made quick, the pain would be swift, and she would probably be spared some of the physical agony. So it was less likely that she would faint, but would she really suffer?

And suffering was all about psychological pain—

that's where the big money was. What would maximize that?

The monster focused on his relaxed right hand, and then moved his gaze down to the little toe resting between the two blades. There was approximately a half inch of space between each blade and either side of the toe.

Then, slowly, he began to squeeze his right hand.

At first, the tension in the handle resisted him, so that the blades did not move. But then, as he contracted the muscles of his forearm and hand, and put a little more force on the handles of the shears, he could see the blades twitch closed just a fraction of an inch. There was now probably three-eighths of an inch from the edge of the blade and the skin of his toe.

He froze, keeping the blades still at that distance.

This experiment was, of course, flawed in the most critical of ways. He was in control of the blades, and his toe was at stake. That made everything different.

When the time came to cut off Stephanie's finger, she would be well aware of the fact that she was no longer in control of *anything*. And that was surely going to be his most powerful ally in bringing her to the edge of true, raw terror.

He focused again on his toe, squeezing the handle tighter. Now a quarter of an inch separated his toe from the blades.

And now only an eighth of an inch.

It was undeniably exciting to observe, even though he was fully aware that at any moment, he could simply release his grip on the tool, take his foot off the edge of the table, put on his sock and his shoe, and walk out of the room.

When Stephanie reached this moment, of course, she would be in an entirely different situation. She would have no choice about anything. And the emotions she would be feeling would be described as far more than merely "exciting."

Indeed, at the moment that he would squeeze the blades closer to the tender flesh of Stephanie's finger, what the monster would be going for was something closer to terrifying. Or possibly paralyzing. Yeah. Paralyzing would be good.

He realized that, at least at the beginning of their encounter, he would have to tape her to a chair, because if she was going to get the full impact of the experience of having her finger amputated, she was going to have to watch. He'd probably have to force her to watch.

He could live with that.

He squeezed the handle tighter, and now the blades were touching his toe on either side. Just touching. Scarcely even pressing against it.

He was sweating. This was awesome.

Regardless of how he decided to make the final slice through her finger—with a swift, shocking cut, or with deliberate, insistent, and oh-so-relentless pressure—he knew that he would definitely perform this preliminary part of the operation slowly. Make her watch as the separation between the skin of her finger and the cutting edge of the blades of the pruning shears gradually, incrementally, disappeared.

Interestingly, even though the edges of the blades were in contact with his toe, he really didn't feel anything down there. But that made some sense. The nerves at the base of one's pinky toe were probably not the most sensitive.

Ever so gently, he applied more pressure to the handle.

He not only felt the shears' honed metal edge squeezing his toe, but he could see the skin on either side of the digit dented beneath it.

And then he felt something different there. Something hot.

A little bubble of blood formed directly at the contact point between the blade and the toe, and he was transfixed as a tiny but growing bead of glistening crimson liquid pooled on the blade on the outside—the left side—of his toe, where the first incision had been made.

The blade on the right hadn't yet broken skin.

The pain was unpleasant, but bearable, and so, again, he gently squeezed tighter on the handle.

Now the right blade bit in, and the blood on the left blade became a small but steady flow.

The pain was very hot, and now, even though he wasn't applying any more pressure, increasing.

He was breathing hard, and his heart rate was undeniably elevated. The toe, trapped between the blades, was being severed very slowly, just by the pressure of the squeezed flesh against the blades which had cut through the skin on both sides and were pressing ever more insistently.

A droplet of sweat ran from his hairline near the right temple down past his ear to his jawline. The time had come.

Taking a deep breath, and letting it out, he squeezed hard. There was a popping sound, and blinding, searing pain. It was good that he had soundproofed the place, because he was roaring with agony. He felt sick to his stomach, and he was having trouble focusing his eyes. When he finally blinked past the tears and the tunnel vision, blood was pouring out of his foot.

He dropped the shears, grabbed the ice, the towel, and the bandages, and began to stop the bleeding.

He had read once that the nerve endings in the fingers were far more developed and sensitive than those in the toes, especially in the pinky toes.

So that meant that what Stephanie Hartz was going to experience was much worse than what he was going through.

Despite his anguish, he smiled.

The experiment had been a total success.

EIGHT

"YOU CANNOT BE SERIOUS ABOUT GOING PUBLIC on live television."

Stephanie was driving her father to the cardiologist's office. Malcolm went twice a year, because he was at risk for heart attack.

Not exactly a surprise, given the way the man had lived most of his life.

What was a surprise was that he had asked his daughter to come along. Normally, he was pathologically close-mouthed about his health. She feared the worst, and immediately switched shifts with Donna at the hospital so she could go.

"I am gravely serious, my dear. There is a history in all men's lives, and in mine, it is a history of cold fear and cowardly inaction. I have been forewarned that the squalid vultures of the press have again turned their diseased gaze toward my reputation. This time, I have screwed my courage to the sticking place, and I shall not slumber through the attack."

Stephanie sighed as she turned onto the street where the doctor's office was located. Her father had always been in love with Shakespearean prose, but when he got wound up, it could be a little much.

"But Leif Samuelson?" she asked, "Did you have to pick *that* squalid vulture? Have you ever even seen *Public Forum*? What a horrible show!"

"Yes, I have seen it. And of course it's execrable. It's television. But it has the largest viewing audience of any program of its kind."

Public Forum was little more than the opportunity for a blond-haired bully who pretended he was a descendant of the Vikings to kiss up to celebrities who agreed with him, and shout down anyone else. For some reason, people ate it up with a spoon. "But couldn't you have gone on another show that wasn't so . . . I don't know. Unfair? Do you really think you're going to get a chance to say anything?"

By now they had pulled into a parking spot directly across from the doctor's office. They were a good fifteen minutes early.

"I didn't choose Leif Samuelson. He chose me."

"What?"

"The show's producer contacted me yesterday evening, and informed me that the good Mr. Samuelson was planning to do a show on last week's murder in Indian Oaks, and invited me to be his guest. The implication, of course, was that I was going to be a target of the man's evil speculation regardless of whether I was a guest or not. So I took up the gauntlet. Tomorrow evening a camera crew from WFFT will invade my home in the middle of the afternoon, and later that evening, from my own living room, I will make my first live appearance on television. Just Leif Samuelson and I, one on one. No six-way shouting matches, no other distractions. My chance to finally stand up for myself. God help me."

Stephanie switched off the engine, and turned to face her father. Like every day of his life, Malcolm was dressed like the only place in the world to buy clothes was the L.L.

Bean catalog. "Speaking of God help me, you are sure that there is nothing wrong with you, right? This is just a routine visit to the doctor?"

Malcolm cleared his throat and looked straight ahead, through the windshield. The day was overcast, and unseasonably cool. How could it feel like autumn in the middle of the summer? "Do you recall a rather unpleasant exchange between us that took place approximately three years ago?"

Did she recall? It may have been three years ago, but she *recalled* it quite well. And it still got her plenty mad. "You mean the time you contacted me the day *after* you had emergency coronary surgery?"

Malcolm turned in his seat to face his daughter directly, and raised his voice a bit. "While the procedure was, I grant you, *technically* emergency coronary surgery, I can assure you——" But he stopped himself abruptly, looked down for a moment, and then met her eyes again. "Yes," he said, much quieter. "The time I called you after I had the stent put in. After I had the emergency coronary surgery."

Malcolm's abrupt change in tone caught Stephanie off-guard. She couldn't help but back down herself. "Of course I remember."

"Well." Malcolm took a soft breath. "I have given my actions a great deal of thought, and I have come to the conclusion that I owe you an apology for that entire episode. I was, I acted——" He frowned. "What I did was wrong. I should have told you about the diagnosis, and I should have told you about the surgery before I had it."

This was new ground for them both. Stephanie wasn't quite sure what to do. So she just waited.

"Therefore, in order to avoid another such imbroglio," Malcolm continued, with a smile, "I thought that I would give you the opportunity to accompany me on these biannual adventures to Dr. Uppal. He has agreed to speak to us both after my examination, if you are willing."

Stephanie was willing, but increasingly suspicious. "And you are sure that Dr. Uppal hasn't said anything bad about your condition that you have been hiding?"

"I know that your trust in me has been understandably shaken, too often, in our time together. But I assure you, my dear, with all the gravitas I can muster, that I am not hiding anything about my condition from you. That is not why I have asked you to come with me to the doctor today."

"Your condition is serious, but it is definitely better than before the surgery. And there has been no deterioration in the past several visits, so that is also encouraging."

Dr. Uppal was a few inches shorter than Steph, who was only about five foot seven. And although he was somewhere between Stephanie's and her father's age, he had such a peaceful aura that he seemed like he was a two-hundred-year-old holy man in a lab coat. He was almost always smiling, and when he wasn't, it looked like he was just about to. Regardless of what he was saying. For a cardiologist, that was some trick.

"I would like to see your cholesterol level drop a little, and your blood pressure seems stubborn. Very stubborn indeed. You are taking your medicine?"

Malcolm raised his right hand as if swearing an oath. "Every night. Lipitor, Toperol, aspirin. My three best friends."

Dr. Uppal made a note in Malcolm's chart, and nodded. "You could still stand to lose a few pounds. You are trying to get some exercise every day, right? A little walking? Even light jogging, if you are up to it."

"I walk every day," Malcolm replied. "Usually a mile, sometimes a little more."

Well, that was news. Steph considered her father the most sedentary individual she had ever known.

"Okay. Very good." Dr. Uppal looked up at them. "Do you have any questions for me?"

Steph waited for a moment to see if Malcolm had anything to say, but he was just looking at her. So she dove in. "When you say that my father's condition is, um, serious, can you be more specific? I'm a pediatric nurse, so I have a general understanding of why he needed the surgery, but I don't have much experience with treatment plans and prognoses."

"This is an excellent question, Ms. Hartz." Dr. Uppal sat back in his chair, laced his fingers together on his chest, and smiled. "What I am doing when I am treating people with cardiovascular issues is I am helping these people manage their risk. Risk of heart attack, risk of stroke, risk of aneurism, risk of arteriosclerosis."

How could he talk about things like this and look so, well, *jolly*?

"So even though we were able to treat your father's acute condition with the angioplasty, we still know that there are significant risk factors which make him more likely than the normal person to suffer any of these problems. For example, elevated cholesterol, and elevated blood pressure. Age is a factor. Certain arterial walls have already hardened considerably. The management of stress has been a source of difficulty for your father, and that is not a good sign. And of course there are other historical factors which further indicate that we should be cautious."

Malcolm cleared his throat. "What the good doctor is saying, ever so discreetly, is that by abusing my body for decades as an active alcoholic, I have contributed, quite possibly significantly, to my current condition."

Even if Stephanie had wanted to say something, she wouldn't have been able. It was just too much to take in all at once. She knew that her father wasn't in the greatest shape, but to hear it laid out so starkly, even by Dr. Twinkly Eyes, was profoundly upsetting.

And speaking of laying things out starkly, Stephanie had never heard her father speak so bluntly about his drinking. Ever. It was overwhelming. She had to blink away the tears that were suddenly making it hard to see anything.

"I am hoping that I did not mislead you into believing that your father's condition is worse than it is," a blurry Dr. Uppal told her. Still with the smile. "As long as Malcolm continues to take care of himself and live in a healthy lifestyle, there is every reason to believe that he can continue to keep the risks under control so that he can live a full and happy life."

Like almost everything that had happened in the past hour, the doctor's prediction that her father would lead a happy life caught Steph completely by surprise. She didn't know whether it was the absurdity of the notion that the gloomiest person she had ever known would suddenly start filling in the *o* in Malcolm with a smiley face, or whether it was because she was so stressed out, but a spasm of giggles shook her. She knew that it would be rude to laugh, of course, so she wrestled the sound coming out of her mouth into a kind of strangled cough.

Malcolm, however, didn't stop himself from loudly barking out the noise which he used as a laugh. "Doctor," he said, as they stood up and shook hands, "that is a prognosis which I think we can all look forward to proving correct."

And for a few moments, as they returned to her car, Stephanie almost let herself believe that her father *was* happy.

Until they turned on the car radio, and learned that the police had found another murder victim.

NINE

Dear Vera,

I hope that you don't mind me writing to you at your home like this, but I thought that since we are going to be working together very closely for a while, it might be nice to cut through some of the red tape.

Anyway, I trust that you found the crime scene at Iris's place everything I had described it would be.

Of course, I'll let you know when you can expect to see my work again.

(Dubinski Evidence ID Number 40)

Detective Vera Demopolous put the creepy letter down, took a moment to put her feet up on her desk, close her eyes, and rub her neck. She was beat, and it was only two-thirty in the afternoon.

Of course, the fact that a nightmare had awakened her for good at three-thirty that morning might have had something to do with her exhaustion.

And learning that she and Springfield really were facing a new serial killer certainly didn't help the headache.

The second victim's name was Iris Dubinski. She had

been a forty-five-year-old sales rep for Roaring Retail, a local corporation which managed malls on both coasts. She was found early that morning by a taxi driver. Last night, a call had been made to the čab company for a pickup this morning, instructing the driver to ring the doorbell, and then enter through the unlocked front door.

Of course, lying in the entryway was the very cold body of Ms. Dubinski.

Like the letter said, she had been shot three times—twice in the rear end, and once through the face. From the blood smears leading from the floor of the living room to the entry hall, she had obviously been dragged there.

And as promised, her right index finger was cut off.

"Excuse me . . . Detective Demopolous?"

Vera opened her eyes. She saw a forty-something man approaching, carrying two large, overfilled cardboard file boxes. He looked uncomfortable in the rumpled brown suit that he was stuffed into, maybe because he had gained thirty pounds since he bought it. His smile was marred only slightly by the bit of lunch still clinging to the corner of his mouth.

But none of that mattered. Because hanging around his neck was a state police detective's badge. It had been a long time since Vera had seen such a welcome sight. She hastily got up and held out her hand, saying, "Hi, I'm Vera Demopolous."

The detective had friendly eyes and a solid grip. "Sorry to barge in on you like this. I'm Ellis Yates. I was on a special assignment for the past three months, and it took HQ a few days to untangle me from that and switch me over to give you a hand. I guess you guys are a little short-staffed right now?"

Vera couldn't stop smiling. The cavalry. Hallelulah. "A little short-staffed sounds right. Did you meet Lieutenant Carasquillo yet?"

"Yeah. He wanted me to jump in with you on those shootings that look like the old Springfield Shooter case. Like I'm going to say no." He looked down at the boxes he was holding, and then at her desk. "Mind if I put these here for a second?"

"Of course," Vera replied, clearing off a space for the heavy-looking things. "What are they?"

Ellis put the boxes down and pulled the lid off the top one to reveal dozens of file folders, reports, a book or two, some notebooks, some photographs. It was quite a collection, whatever it was. "Lieutenant said you were looking for any stuff we had in storage on the Springfield Shooter, so I went down to archives and dug it up. Hope that's okay."

Vera laughed. "That is way more than okay, Ellis. I've been reading through the official reports that had been entered into the computer, but this backup will really help." She put the latest letter she'd received into the top box, then lifted it off her desk. "Follow me," she told Ellis. "Believe it or not, we've got our own temporary command post."

"Whoa. Sounds pretty impressive," Ellis replied, as he picked up the second box, and they headed down the hallway past the water fountain that no longer worked and the men's room, and turned in to the next doorway.

"Not exactly," Vera explained, as she led Ellis into the nondescript little room dominated by the two-way mirror, the cafeteria-style folding table, and the four metal folding chairs scattered around it. "Lieutenant is letting us use Interview Three because my desk was overflowing." She was wide awake now, completely reenergized by the knowledge that she wasn't alone on this case anymore.

They set the boxes of old file material next to the street map of Springfield that Vera had laid out on the table. She had stuck Post-it notes all over it, indicating where each murder had taken place. On the other side of the map was the stack of legal pads which contained her notes, and a three-ring binder with some of the copies of the exhibits from the Springfield Shooter case. There were also a few manila folders scattered around that Vera had been using to organize some of the information on the Chatham murder.

"The eight yellow stickers are the locations where the original Springfield Shooter murders took place," she explained. "And these two blue ones," she continued, pointing to the Indian Oaks section of the map, where four of the yellow stickers were also clustered, "are the sites of the two murders we're looking into."

Ellis bent over and read the little numbers that Vera had written on each of the indicators. "Funny how murders one through five are scattered all over the place, and then six through nine, plus the two new ones we've got, are all jammed into Indian Oaks."

That fact had been bugging Vera like crazy. It was one of the few patterns she had been able to identify, but she hadn't been able to exploit it in any significant way. It was really getting frustrating.

"Is it possible that we've got two different killers here?" Ellis asked.

Vera was puzzled. There were obviously two different killers. Alan Lombardo was in jail when the two most recent murders had taken place—

Her expression must have betrayed her confusion, because Ellis broke into her thoughts. "No. I mean, uh, what if Alan Lombardo was responsible for the first five murders, and was wrong for six through nine? That would explain this geographic pattern. Lombardo did the first five, a second guy copycats him and does murders six through nine, and then maybe the guy takes a kind of BTK vacation. You know. Kills a bunch of people, then takes a long break, then starts up again."

BTK, standing for "bind, torture, and kill," was a self-styled serial killer responsible for the murders of ten people in Wichita, Kansas, in the late 1970s and '80s. The Midwestern community had been devastated. Then, for no apparent reason, he stopped killing. Until about twelve years later, when, even though it seemed that he would never be caught, the BTK killer reemerged, taunting police with messages. They had been lucky to catch him before he started to murder again.

"That's exactly what I thought," Vera told Ellis. "But I talked to the lead detective on the Springfield Shooter case, and they had this guy Lombardo absolutely nailed for all nine murders." She grabbed the top legal pad off the stack on the table and checked her notes. "His housekeeper found a Tupperware container full of eight fingers in the guy's freezer, next to about a ton and a half of chocolate chip ice cream. They were able to conclusively match every finger in that container to every one of the eight Springfield Shooter victims that was missing a finger."

"Only eight? I thought there were nine."

"He didn't start cutting off fingers until victims number two and three. The brother and sister."

"Oh, that's right," Ellis said, soberly. "I should have remembered that."

"Remembered?" Vera asked. "I just learned about this stuff last week. You haven't worked on this case before, have you?"

Ellis laughed. "Not exactly. I grew up in Indian Oaks. And for about three years, believe me, all I ever heard about was the Springfield Shooter."

Wow. Talk about the perfect partner for the out-of-town girl cop from Alaska. "You mean you're from here?"

"Born and raised in Springfield. Capo High School,

Class of '82. Go Bobcats. Dad ran the family hardware store, the whole nine yards." A smile grew across his soft face. "I still live in the house I grew up in. I'm a total townie." He hesitated for a second. "Anyway, I, well, this is kind of embarrassing, but after I picked up these boxes from archives, I was so hungry, I stopped to get a sandwich at a deli on the way over. While I was eating, I started reading this book that was in one of the boxes. It came out right in the middle of the investigation. *Diary of a Serial Killer*. You ever heard of it?"

"Not before I started reading the file," Vera replied. "But I saw it mentioned in there a few times. I thought that it was mostly fiction."

"Yeah, it is, sort of. Kind of a mixture. Anyway, I just used it to remind myself of some of the details. Like about the fingers. Or that he didn't start leaving notes until the fourth victim, and that's when he started taking credit for the first three killings. Do I have that right?"

"You got it."

"Yeah, well, I'm afraid that's about all I got. I'm usually more of an Internet research guy, anyway. Drives my wife crazy. I spend way too much time on-line."

Vera opened up the box that she had carried in with them, and rummaged around until she pulled out the copy of the book that Ellis had been reading. She turned to the copyright page, and then showed it to Ellis. "This came out in March of 1983, right?"

He nodded. "Looks right."

Vera checked some notes she'd made on another pad. "Like about two months after the fifth murder. And about three months before the sixth."

"Are you thinking that the book had something to do with the delay?"

Vera shook her head. "Not really. I've just been trying to find things that happened between the fifth and sixth murders to make the killer suddenly decide to bunch all of his attacks together like this." She pointed to the Indian Oaks section of the street map laid out on the table. "Do you remember anything in the book about Indian Oaks?"

Ellis laughed. "You mean other than the college professor?"

Vera looked at him blankly.

"You don't remember the professor who was a suspect for about twelve minutes?" Ellis looked incredulous, but then he shook his head. "Sorry. I forgot you weren't living here then."

"No. I grew up in Alaska."

"Yeah. Lieutenant Carasquillo told me. Sorry." Now Ellis was walking around the room. "Anyway, the biggest thing that happened between number five and number six was that this book came out, and then there was a huge scandal about a local college professor being a suspect. He actually got arrested."

"Before they nabbed Lombardo? Really?"

"Yeah. The guy who wrote *Diary of a Serial Killer*, Russell Crane was his name, was pretty much in it just for the money, so he wasn't too careful with the facts. And whenever it made his book better, he just made stuff up. Like his profile for the Springfield Shooter: 'He might be an educated man, quite possibly a high school teacher or a college professor, age such and such, who was an alcoholic,' blah blah blah, whatever."

"So how did the college professor get involved?"

"Believe it or not, some television reporter read the book, put two and six together, and came up with a guy who matched Russell Crane's description. Turns out he wasn't just any local college professor. Turns out he was this real famous author—Malcolm Ayers."

TEN

November 11, 1982. Julie Chang was really hot. That's not why I picked her, of course. I'm not some kind of freak. But damn. The girl was hot.

The whole sex angle didn't occur to me until after I was inside her place. It started just like all of the others— I pulled the gun on her, gagged her, told her to get on the floor, and just as I started to tear off the tape, I realized that instead of taping her hands together behind her back, I could tape one hand to the leg of this huge piece of furniture sitting in her living room, and the other to the radiator, about an arm's length away.

So I told her to lie flat on her back, arms apart, and sure enough. It worked!

Then I taped her feet together, and there she was. Spread out on her back, lying on the floor, looking up at me.

The way her arms were stretched out, it kind of pushed her tits out against her shirt. That's what got me to thinking about sex in the first place. Whew. She was lucky I wasn't a rapist. Because if I was, she would have been a no-brainer.

But the funny thing was that when she saw me looking at her body, she thought I was going to rape her.

That was kind of an interesting twist. So I decided to run with it. I brought my gun over and pointed it at her chest. She was wearing a button-down shirt with the top button unfastened, so I stuck the barrel of the gun between the next two buttons. The shirt was slightly pulled apart at that point, because her hands were taped so far away from each other. I could see the color of her bra. It was blue.

Then I pulled the gun up against the higher of the two buttons until it popped off, leaving her chest just a little more exposed.

She kind of gasped—if you can gasp with your mouth taped shut—and I said, "Don't worry, I'm not going to rape you. I'm just going to look for a while."

I don't know why, but that started her crying. And that pissed me off. I mean goddammit. If I told her I was going to rape her, then fine. Crying would make sense. But I tell her I'm not going to rape her, and she starts bawling.

So I stood up and shot her.

I wish she hadn't made me so angry. I would have liked to have stuck around for a while, but once I got started on her, the crying got louder. And that just pissed me off more, so I shot her again and again.

Before I knew it, I had emptied the clip into her.

That's a lot of bullets for one kill.

Anyway, it gave me an idea for my next one, so it wasn't a total waste.

Then I chopped off her finger, and went home.

(Commonwealth v. Alan Lombardo, Trial Exhibit Number 31E)

August 28

Zack Wilson had read through everything that was in his father's old files on the Lombardo case—the trial transcript and exhibits, the appellate briefs, the printouts of the computer work files Lombardo kept at home, the police reports, the research and the notes. He was now going over one of the most disturbing of the entries found in the sadistic killer's computer journal—the Julie Chang murder.

Zack was especially interested in the description of this crime, because it was the one that was most sexually explicit. Typically, serial killers had a sexual component to their psychopathology. Sometimes there was an actual sexual release at the murders, sometimes the killings substituted in a psychological way for sex, and sometimes the brutality of the acts was a sign of sexual rage.

In any event, it was interesting that in Alan Lombardo's case, with the exception of the Julie Chang murder, there didn't appear to be much of a sexual aspect to any of the crimes. He made a note to talk to his father about psychological testing.

The sound of someone raking leaves caught Zack's attention. He went to the open first-floor window of their oversized old house and looked out into the side yard.

Seven-year-old Justin had set up what looked like a little obstacle course for himself. A line of three lightweight folding lawn chairs, about five feet from each other, extended into the yard. Beyond those three chairs was a picnic bench. And past that, Justin was raking together a huge pile of leaves from last fall's pile which lay about ten feet past the bench. When he saw Zack at the window, Justin dropped the rake, waved, and cried out, "Hey, Daddy! Watch this!" Then he ran toward the house, setting himself up at the near end of the lawn chairs.

A voice from over Zack's left shoulder said, "You sure you don't want to tell him that jumping into a pile of old leaves is the second most dangerous thing a child can do while playing outdoors during the summer months?"

Terry had just finished taking a series of courses on insurance litigation. He was thinking about doing some plaintiff's work for people injured by dangerous products.

Because life as a criminal defense attorney wasn't David versus Goliath enough.

But as a by-product of his recent education, Terry had become a walking encyclopedia of things that you should fear in your daily life.

As if the single father of a seven-year-old boy needed a longer list of things to worry about.

Now Kermit, Justin's tail-wagging companion of indeterminate breeding but unquestionable loyalty, had joined the little boy.

"Being bitten by an animal is first," Terry continued, grimly.

Zack just shook his head, looked over his shoulder at his friend, then turned back to watch his son.

"I'm just saying," Terry persisted.

Justin had reached what had to be the starting line. "Are you watching, Daddy?" he called up over his shoulder, one more time. Clearly, this was a moment that bore witnessing. "Because here I go!" Justin took what was intended to be a sprinter's starting position, but looked rather like he was trying to place both his hands and his feet onto exactly the same blade of grass. Then he shouted, "On your marks, get set, go!" and with that took off toward the nearest chair, with Kermit barking delightedly at his heels.

Stage One was a combination slalom- and twirling-type event which was apparently accomplished by circumnavigating each lawn chair in turn, but in alternating directions, while spinning like a top.

Stage Two involved crawling under the picnic bench. But that task looked far easier than it turned out to be, for Justin had been so intent on circling the chairs at maximum velocity that he was now quite dizzy, and barely able to move in a straight line.

"He looks a little drunk," observed Terry.

Zack ignored the comment.

Apparently, Justin decided that he was less likely to fall off the surface of the earth if he simply gave in to the vertigo. Sinking to his hands and knees, he began to crawl toward the picnic bench. Kermit, now thoroughly confused, approached his friend cautiously, and planted a large, sloppy kiss right on Justin's cheek. Justin giggled and protested, but to his credit, kept moving forward, finally making it under the bench to the other side.

He got to his feet, somewhat steadier now, for the finale. He wiped his hands on his shirt. Then he screeched, "Yahhhhhhh!" and raced toward his personal finish line. Six steps later he was in the air, and then he landed, theatrically, but unharmed, face-first in the middle of the brown and yellow leaf pile.

He scrambled to his feet, splashing dried maple and oak leaves everywhere, and cried out to Zack, "Did you see that, Daddy?"

"I sure did, Justin man. It was awesome, buddy."

"Outstanding," Terry chimed in. "Nothing ever like it in the history of sport."

"I know!" Justin agreed enthusiastically, as he grabbed the rake, and began preparing for his next attempt. "And now I'm going to do it again!"

Zack and Terry turned from the window, and took seats facing each other. To Zack, the room was idyllic—high ceilings, spacious windows looking out toward New England woodlands.

To Terry, it wasn't a serious workplace. At his insistence, they had recently rented the more traditional office space in town. He needed to know the difference between going to work and going over to his friend's house. Zack didn't fully understand, but now that Justin was at school full-time, it was less important that Zack be home almost round the clock.

"Take a look at this," Terry said, passing a newspaper to Zack, pointing to a story on page one. "We might finally be catching a break."

Under the headline "New Springfield Shooter Strikes Again," the article laid out the story of the discovery of the most recent victim. Once again, the killer had immobilized the victim with duct tape, shot her repeatedly with a .22 caliber handgun, and cut off her index finger.

And then Zack finally read the line in the report that Terry had wanted him to see. "*Lead investigator on the case, Springfield Police Detective Vera Demopolous, stated that similar to the circumstances surrounding the shooting of Corey Chatham, this killer has communicated with the police. Demopolous stated, however, that at this stage of the investigation, the content of the killer's message is not being made public.*"

Terry had become romantically interested in Vera Demopolous about a year ago, but she had been involved with an assistant district attorney at the time. The A.D.A. had moved a few months ago to take a new job. Maybe Terry was going to get another chance.

"So? How does this help Alan Lombardo?"

"I don't know," Terry responded, "but I was thinking of calling Vera anyway, asking her to meet with us to talk about her investigation because of our connection to the original Springfield Shooter case."

The only other time they'd worked on a case with Detective Demopolous, they'd shared some information that had worked out to both their advantages. "Good thinking," Zack said.

After a second, Terry looked back at his partner, and asked, "What?"

"I didn't say anything."

"I know you didn't say anything. But you were thinking 'Why doesn't he ask her out,' and I'm telling you that I will. I just want to make sure we aren't on opposite sides of this case first."

Zack just looked his partner up and down, made note of how he always seemed to be dressed up these days, and smiled.

"And don't grin like you think I'm crazy, because that's exactly what you were thinking."

"No I wasn't. I just realized that I'm supposed to say, 'Nice shoes.' "

Terry glanced down at his feet, then shook his head, sighed, and looked back up at Zack. "I've owned these things for five years, you idiot."

Oops.

Paul Merrone watched George Heinrich take another of the morphine pills and swallow it down with a beer. George was at lunch with his son, Neil. Well, Neil was eating lunch, anyway. George Heinrich barely ate anything anymore. Some ice cream, once in a while. And, of course, the morphine.

"Dad, are you sure about this?" Neil had the face of a man way older than his forty-one years. He had been a good-looking kid when he was growing up. But his father's sickness had really taken a toll on him. It looked like Neil was getting less sleep than his old man.

Although that was impossible. Mr. Heinrich hadn't slept more than an hour at a stretch for about the past three weeks.

"The doctor said that the cancer spread into my bones. There's nothing more we can do. Except try to make me more comfortable. Yeah. I'm real comfortable." The old man started to laugh, but that just kicked off a coughing fit. Neil turned to Paul as if to ask what to do, but Paul just shrugged. The coughing fits were coming more and more frequently, and the only thing was to wait them out. This one was real bad.

As the coughing subsided, Neil said, "Dad, I'm not sure what we should do."

When he caught his breath, Mr. Heinrich said, "That's what I'm telling you, Neil. *We* aren't going to be doing anything anymore. It's all yours now. Officially."

The decision wasn't exactly a surprise to Paul, but still, hearing the old man actually say the words out loud was kind of shocking.

"I met with the lawyers the other day, and I signed all the papers. I don't leave the house anymore. I don't listen to the radio, I don't watch TV, I don't read the newspapers. I'm just staying here, enjoying my memories for as long as I can. You can talk to me anytime you want about work. But from now on, the business is yours. Do with it whatever you think is best."

Twenty years ago, if George had said that to Neil, Paul would have bet that the young man would have jumped for joy, and then hired a limo to drive him to the bank so he could get a bunch of money to do something else stupid.

But from the look on Neil's face now, you'd think somebody just told him, well, that his father was dying.

Thirty-Four Seconds

ZACK WILSON HAD LESS THAN THIRTY FEET TO go when the gunman seemed to realize there was something coming at him from his left. He wheeled, facing Zack head-on, and fired.

Although the world was still in slow motion, Zack managed to plant his left foot and push off toward the right just as the sound of the gunshot reached his ears. One of the things that Navy SEAL had said at the bookstore was that the accuracy of handgun fire in movies and television was ridiculously overblown. The typical handgun was accurate only to about twenty feet. After that, it was dumb luck if somebody got hit by a pistol.

So Zack knew that he was outside the pistol's realistic range, and figured that all he had to do was dodge right, and there'd be no way he'd get hit.

Somehow, though, his momentum carried him so violently off to the side that he felt himself actually spinning in the air, and he was extremely surprised and embarrassed to land flat on his ass, with a considerable burning in his left leg.

Damn. He must have pulled a muscle in his thigh. Maybe it was just a cramp. It didn't matter. He had to get moving.

But his leg felt really weird, so he looked down. The first thing he noticed was that his shoe had come off, and was lying a few feet from his right hand. He didn't want to slide all over the place in his socks, so he grabbed it and started to put it back on, and that's when he saw the dark stain spreading on his pant leg. He reached down and touched warm, sticky liquid, which promptly turned his left hand red.

Maybe this handgun was better than the typical one, because Zack had been shot.

And Zack really didn't have time to be shot.

At least not yet.

He rolled over onto his stomach, and looked up, half expecting and half hoping to be facing the barrel of a gun. But the gunman hadn't moved. He'd merely turned away from Zack. That was good news, because it allowed Zack to use one of the clerk's chairs to pull, well, to *try* to pull himself up to his feet. The chair was on wheels, which made it kind of hard to steady. And that left leg really didn't feel good at all.

The bad news was that if the shooter had turned away from Zack, that meant he had turned his attention back toward the crowd of innocent people in the courtroom gallery.

Including Justin.

Screw the leg. Zack let go of the chair and started moving. He didn't care. He'd hop, skip, jump, crawl, whatever. He'd make his way to that gun, and he would stop that madman from doing whatever it was he thought he was doing.

But with the world in slow motion, and Zack crippled by the gunshot wound, the twenty or twenty-five feet still between them was going to take an eternity.

Which, under the circumstances, was now probably less than thirty seconds.

ELEVEN

In many ways, the death of Kevin Spellman was the turning point in the saga of the Springfield Shooter. Before that bloody evening in February of 1983, many residents of western Massachusetts still believed that the murders of Robert Rath, Stewart and Betsy McCabe, and Julie Chang were unrelated. Sadly, the desperate and naïve hope that the Springfield metropolitan area was not being stalked by a vicious and cunning serial killer was to die along with Kevin Spellman, victim number five.

February 10, 1983, was a dreary day. A low-pressure system was sitting over most of New England, and the temperature barely made it into the forties. A light but steady rain began to fall around noon, and it rained on and off for the next three days.

But Kevin Spellman was not the kind of person to let inclement weather put him into a bad mood. According to his friends, Kevin was one of those people who almost always approached his job, and his life, with a positive attitude. He had, of course, a very different perspective than many of us. Because Kevin was legally blind.

On the last morning of his life, Kevin arrived at work at his customary starting time of 6:30 A.M. According to that day's sales receipts, business was good at the newspaper stand at the Amtrak train station in downtown Springfield. It seemed that more people than usual were buying expensive magazines, possibly thinking ahead to the spring.

Amtrak ticket agent Wendy Gold saw Kevin leave that day at 4:45. She remembered calling out something like, "Stay dry!" to Kevin as he left for home.

Of course she could not know that those would be the last words she ever uttered to her friend.

Because well before the morning of February 11, a crazed, homicidal maniac with the soul of a demon would enter Kevin's home, tape him to a coffee table in his living room, and shoot him six times, until he bled to death. If the note left at the scene is to be believed, the killer went out of his way to make sure that Kevin stayed alive during the attack for over an hour.

And as if he was speaking directly to the people that doubted that their world had been invaded by a serial killer, the killer also took pains to claim responsibility for his previous four victims.

The brutal truth was that the Springfield Shooter had struck again.

As this book goes to press, there has been no arrest in the case of the Springfield Shooter. The families of the victims know no closure, and all residents of western Massachusetts know only terror and suspicion.

The obvious question is who? Who could possibly do this? Who would deliberately disable, torture, maim, and ultimately kill normal people like they were animals or laboratory subjects? Robert Rath, Stewart and Elizabeth McCabe, Julie Chang, and Kevin Spellman were good people, people with families and friends, people with lives like the rest of us. People who are now nothing more than cold statistics, the first five entries on a list of victims that threatens to grow larger with each passing morning, with each phone that is left ringing, each doorbell that is left unanswered, every appointment that is not kept.

Law enforcement experts in serial killers, psychologists, and psychiatrists have compiled a set of characteristics common to most of these monsters. Those personality traits, which, with careful study, and placed in the context of what is known about the first five murders of the Springfield Shooter, might lead to a profile which could look something like the following.

The Springfield Shooter might well be an educated man —even a man of letters. Perhaps an educator, maybe a high school writing teacher or even a college English professor. He could be someone who has access to a great deal of wealth. He is by no means poor.

The monster is likely to live alone, or at least without adult companionship. If he was married, he is now divorced, or separated, or his wife has died. Perhaps at his hand.

If he has always been single, it is because he is and was unable or unwilling to make the commitment to enter into matrimony.

The Springfield Shooter is also likely to be an abuser— not just of his victims, but of himself. He is probably an active alcoholic, or a drug addict, or some combination of both. He is undoubtedly gravely mentally ill, but he does not and will not seek help. He is arrogant, selfish, and righteous. When confronted with his crimes, he will be defensive and combative, and he will deny everything.

He could well suffer from a physical impairment of some kind, such as deafness, or perhaps an injury or malady that leaves him with a visible physical abnormality. Perhaps he walks with a limp.

Diary of a Serial Killer, by Russell Crane, Pages 149–151, 334–335

By the time that Stephanie reached her father's home, everything had been set up for that evening's broadcast. He was seated in a chair in his living room, which had been moved from its original position so that it was now in front of a bookcase. A young woman was standing to Malcolm's left, apparently discussing with him some document that was attached to the clipboard she was holding. On Malcolm's right side was a small table, on which a glass of water was resting.

The rest of the room was more crowded and chaotic than Stephanie had ever seen it. A large video camera had been set up on a tripod about six feet away from her father's chair. There were an amazing number of gigantic lights hanging from stands all over the place, and the oriental rug that Stephanie had used twenty years ago for somersault practice was tangled with thick, black electrical cords.

Whatever space wasn't taken up by all of this equipment was jam-packed with people, half of them talking on headsets or cell phones.

The idea that her father was cool with this wholesale invasion of his space was mind-blowing. Especially since it was all because of an interview about the Springfield Shooter. Talk about a loaded subject for her father. Steph wound her way around five people and finally reached him, only to have the lights go on all at once, and someone shout, "Sixty seconds!"

Before she could even say a word, the woman with the clipboard seized Steph by the arm, and moved with her off to the adjacent dining room, where a monitor had been set up, showing what was being aired to the rest of the country on tonight's edition of *Public Forum*. "He'll do fine," Clipboard Lady whispered.

Easy for her to say. *Her* father hadn't spent the better part of the last twenty-five years drinking and flirting with a series of nervous breakdowns. There had been times when just a casual mention of the Springfield Shooter was enough to send Steph's father into a raving fit. The idea that Malcolm had agreed to talk about it on national TV, even in a one-on-one setting, was nerve-wracking.

Just then, someone back in the living room shouted,

"Settle. Thirty seconds to feed!" And at the same moment, the television screen switched from a commercial to the face of Leif Samuelson, sitting in his studio somewhere in New York, or Los Angeles, or wherever. Behind him, a graphic displaying the words "The Springfield Shooter: Act II" in horror-movie lettering, was prominently displayed. Leif smiled into the camera, and began to speak.

"Welcome back. Over twenty years ago, the city of Springfield, Massachusetts was plunged into a nightmare of terror and suspicion. During the twenty-one-month period from July 1982 to March 1984 a serial killer known as the Springfield Shooter, in a coldly calculated homicidal frenzy, selected and then murdered nine people in their homes. He used duct tape to disable and bind his victims, and then he shot them, repeatedly, with a small-caliber handgun, and watched them suffer and die. To add insult to injury, this twisted individual cut off a finger from his victims, as a sick kind of trophy."

A different camera angle was displayed, and Samuelson appeared in profile, close up. Then he dramatically turned to face the screen. The graphic had disappeared, but a banner across the bottom of the screen now displayed the words, *Is the Springfield Shooter still at large?*

Samuelson continued. "Just yesterday, police confirmed that another series of murders has begun in Springfield. First, approximately two weeks ago, a fifty-three-year-old computer programmer named Corey Chatham was shot to death in his home in the Indian Oaks section of Springfield. And two days ago, Iris Dubinski, also a resident of Indian Oaks, was found murdered in her home. Police believe that the murders were committed by the same individual."

"Ten seconds to feed!" cried the voice from the living room.

Samuelson droned on. "But most disturbing is that,

just like the original Springfield Shooter, this new killer bound and gagged his victims with duct tape, shot them to death with a small caliber handgun, and then cut off a finger from each."

"And we are up!" declared the living room voice, just as the television screen changed to show Malcolm, sitting there, looking, well, okay. Steph quickly glanced over her shoulder at her father, and then back at the monitor. It was really happening. Her pathologically shy father was going to be interviewed in public about some of the worst times in his life. Her heart was racing. She had no idea how this was going to turn out. She realized that she was wiping her sweaty palms on her St. Joseph's striped smock. Good thing she wasn't on camera. She was so wound up she wouldn't be able to put two coherent words together.

"We are joined tonight by the bestselling author Malcolm Ayers. Of course, Professor Ayers is with us tonight not because of his writings, but because of his bizarre connection to the Springfield Shooter case, which came about as a result of the publication of a book over twenty years ago called *Diary of a Serial Killer*, by fellow author Russell Crane. Good evening, Professor Ayers."

"Good evening, Leif," Malcolm said. "Although I would take issue with the fact that I'm connected at all to the Springfield Shooter case. And for the record, Russell Crane is less of an author than a fraud."

At this point, the screen split to show Samuelson on the left and Malcolm on the right. "Well, why don't we get right into that off the top?" Samuelson said. "You certainly don't deny that Russell Crane is an author, and that he authored *Diary of a Serial Killer*, do you?"

Stephanie watched as Malcolm stared into the camera. Oh boy. The bait was out there. How was he going to handle this?

"I have no idea who was responsible for that shameless and appallingly vapid collection of poor writing and half-witted guesswork," Malcolm began.

Steph found herself cringing. Her father had never spoken to her about *Diary of a Serial Killer* without completely losing it. What was that going to look like on national television?

But as Malcolm continued, he looked surprisingly under control. "But my charge of fraud is not that Mr. Crane took credit for writing that lurid, parasitic, amoral, and self-serving embarrassment. His crime for that would be conspiring to publish with neither talent nor conscience. No, I say Russell Crane is a fraud because after his book was purchased by tens if not hundreds of thousands of people who were misled by its half-truths and salacious speculation, Mr. Crane, his ego now swollen beyond all understanding, held himself out to the public as an expert in serial killers, and thereby proceeded to do a staggering amount of damage to me personally."

"Harsh charges, indeed," said Leif, looking into the camera, and then glancing down at a sheet of paper he was holding. And just at that moment, Steph saw it. A tiny shift in the blond television personality's manner, or possibly the merest hint of smugness in his expression. But however she knew it, she just *knew* it. Something awful was about to happen.

"As a result of the damage you claim to have suffered to your reputation, Mr. Ayers, did you sue Mr. Crane for libel, or slander, or defamation of character? Did you ever speak to him about your feelings?"

One of teenage Steph's guilty pleasures had been a television cartoon called *The Ren & Stimpy Show*. It was kind of an insane rendering of a ludicrous friendship between a Chihuahua named Ren, and a cat named Stimpy.

In one of the episodes, Stimpy destroyed the universe by pressing a big red button.

Ever since then, Steph identified people's most sensitive personal issues, those that would most likely drive them crazy, as their Big Red Buttons.

The idea of suing Russell Crane, or facing him directly in any way, was Malcolm's Big Red Button. And Leif Samuelson was dancing very close to it.

"No, I chose not to fan Satan's malignant flames. I hoped that Mr. Crane's fundamental stupidity would ultimately bring the curtain down on his moment of glory, and end my personal discomfort without such a confrontation."

And then, the television screen switched to a picture of a tan, handsome man with hair so light colored it looked almost white. He wore an expensive-looking, soft, cottony white shirt with an open collar and a gold chain around his neck, and a wide, plastic-looking smile.

Leif Samuelson's voice continued to come through the television. "Well we'd like to offer you the opportunity for just such a confrontation, Professor Ayers. Joining us from his summer home in Marblehead, Massachusetts, is the screenwriter of the new blockbuster movie *The Suspect's Daughter*, which is opening next month in theatres all over the country. More importantly, of course, this individual has written several books, including his first, and probably most controversial, *Diary of a Serial Killer*. His name is Russell Crane. Good evening, Mr. Crane."

TWELVE

March 30, 1983. I finished Diary of a Serial Killer today. What a joke. Russell Crane couldn't have been more wrong if he tried.

April 5, 1983. It's amazing how a stupid book and a stupid reporter could make themselves look so important. One idiot writes some bullshit about what the Springfield Shooter probably is like, and then the other idiot runs around and decides that sounds a lot like Malcolm Ayers. Unbelievable.

April 11, 1983. Oh my God. How perfect is this? I just was watching the news, and Malcolm Ayers doesn't have an alibi for any of the murders! That is too great. He must be going nuts thinking he's going to get indicted for five murders he didn't do.

April 21, 1983. I was lying in bed last night, and I got the idea of a lifetime. First I've got to find out where Malcolm Ayers lives. I'll start tomorrow. If I can pull this off, I'm going to be one of the greatest ever.

July 30, 1983. It's taken a little while, but I finally found my next winner. It's Candy Obligado, a stenographer I met over at McFarley's last weekend. She checks out, so I'm lined up to do her next week sometime. I cannot wait. It's been a while.

August 12, 1983. This was a new kind of kill, which made it extra special. A little more work, but boy, was it worth it.

First, I waited until about dinnertime, then I went by Malcolm Ayers's place, and made sure he was home. From what I hear, he never goes out, but I didn't want to assume anything. Anyway, no problem there. Malcolm was home, and drunk. As usual.

Then, on to Candy's place. She lived about a half mile from Malcolm, which was fine. I can't make this too obvious.

What was really awesome, though, was that doing Candy was like doing it for the first time. I mean I was really nervous. My hands were shaking as I knocked on the door. No kidding.

Usually when I do these, I rush in, tape them up, and then, once everything's under control, slow it down, see what comes to mind.

But with Candy, I decided to play it smooth, see if I could draw it out a little before I had to tape her up. And thanks to Candy, that worked out great.

She was happy to see me, and was all about getting me something to drink, and hanging out, watching some TV, whatever.

So we watched videos on MTV. Nothing special. I wasn't really paying attention. I was too busy watching Candy to worry about the tube.

Anyway, after a little while, I think probably fifteen or twenty minutes, Candy got up to go to the bathroom, and I decided this would be a good time. So I got out the tape and ambushed her as she was coming out of the bathroom.

She was kind of small, but stronger than I expected, so it took me some time to get her totally restrained. . . .

"Zack, are you going to watch the show, or are you going to keeping reading that crazy shit?"

Terry had brought some Chinese food over to Zack's house to share while they watched *Public Forum*. Despite the fact that the program was pretty lame, Zack was actually relieved to put down the file. The Candy Obligado excerpt from the Alan Lombardo exhibits was especially disturbing.

Public Forum was hosted by a very successful personality who attempted to portray himself as a fair and reasonable regular guy who invited people to speak with him so he could find out the real story in a world designed to deceive people.

He was actually just a loudmouthed bully who had his mind made up about everything long before he ever began his on-air conversations.

Zack had given up on the show some time ago as a source of useful information, but tonight, he had made an exception, because the guest was Malcolm Ayers, a local author who had become, for a short while, a suspect in the Springfield Shooter case back in the '80s.

Zack didn't expect much to come of the interview, but so far, his and Terry's research hadn't turned up much that they could use in support of Alan Lombardo's motion for a new trial. Terry had begun to lose whatever little hope he'd had at the start of the case. As far as he was concerned, Lombardo was guilty, and they were wasting their time.

But Zack was always willing to keep an open mind, until he had explored everything he could reasonably explore.

"Oh, no," said Terry, pointing at the television. "Great. Now Samuelson's sandbagging the guy."

They watched as the show's host, Leif Samuelson,

brought another guest on to the show, apparently as a surprise to Ayers.

The screen was now split three ways, showing pictures of Samuelson and his two guests, Ayers and Crane.

Ayers was speaking. "But you told me this would be a one-on-one interview. I was never informed —"

Samuelson cut him off. "I'm sorry, Mr. Ayers. You were fully advised that there could be additional guests appearing on the program with you. Do you have a problem confronting Mr. Crane with your charges?"

And then, the show delivered another surprise. While Samuelson was talking, a hand reached into the shot of Malcolm Ayers from the left side of the screen, completely startling him. He turned to his right and said something like "Stephanie," but the hand had already unclipped the small microphone that had been fastened to his lapel.

"Better hope that thing's grounded," Terry muttered.

And then the face of a very pretty young woman wearing an incredibly loud red-and-white-striped smock leaned sideways in front of Ayers, and faced the camera. There was something about that woman's face that was really appealing. Her eyes were positively blazing.

Terry reached for the container of General Tao's chicken and said, "You're going to have to tell me what's happening, because whatever that person is wearing has blinded me for life."

The woman's voice may have been a little loud, but then again, that might have been because the mic was so close to her sensuous mouth. Her indignation was palpable, her energy fierce. "Mr. Samuelson. I don't know if you can see or hear me, but my name is Stephanie Hartz. I'm Malcolm Ayers's daughter. And you need to know how incredibly unprofessional it is for you to ambush an interview guest on your program like this. My father specifically agreed to appear on your show because—"

But before she could continue, her father spoke into her ear, and she stopped her address. She turned back to Ayers and said, "Are you sure?" and the professor said something else to her that the microphone didn't pick up. Then she turned back to the camera. "Before I return the microphone to my father, I'd just like to say that cheap tricks might inflate your show's ratings in the short term, Mr. Samuelson, but over the long haul, you might want to look into integrity and a sense of fair play. I understand that at one time they were really popular in this country."

Russell Crane just sat at his desk, smiling his California smile. Samuelson wasn't about to let his program fill up with dead air, though. "Are you staying, or are you going, Professor Ayers? Is there a problem? Is your daughter speaking for you now, sir?"

But while Samuelson blustered, Stephanie Hartz reconnected her father's microphone to his lapel, and stepped back out of the shot. Probably to be wrestled to the ground by security. "There is no problem." Ayers spoke directly to the camera. "I am willing to continue the conversation, despite, as my daughter so aptly put it, your stupefying lack of professionalism."

"Well, I've got to admit, for spending time on a case that we can't possibly win, this is kind of fun," Terry said.

"Tell me about it," Zack murmured. He had never even heard of Stephanie Hartz ninety seconds ago. But he found himself hoping that she would lean back into the shot of her father, so Zack could see the fire in those eyes again.

Russell Crane was speaking. "Mr. Ayers, I never once said that you were the Springfield Shooter. Not in *Diary of a Serial Killer*, and not in any of my public appearances."

"No, you never had the courage to come out and actually say it, did you? You merely exploited the tragedy of five murder victims and their families by further sensationalizing those homicides through the loathsome, so-called diary of what you *thought* the murderer *might* have written, and then you implicated me indirectly."

"No way," California Dude shot back. "The facts are the facts. Just as with these latest two murders. I don't live in Indian Oaks, sir, and I can account for my whereabouts on the nights of the murders. Can *you?*"

And with that question just hanging there, Samuelson went to commercial.

Terry swigged some of the Sam Adams he'd brought over with the food. "Is Blondie serious? Does he really think Malcolm Ayers killed those two people?"

Zack got some rice and shrugged. "Who knows? Crane seems like one of those guys who would say anything, whether he believed it or not, as long as it got him some press."

Just then, Justin came into the living room holding a book. He was wearing his favorite SpongeBob SquarePants pajamas, which were now getting a trifle small. It was tough convincing the little guy that new pjs would probably be a great idea. "Daddy, I'm ready for bed," he announced. "Can I read for a while before lights out?"

"Yes, you may," said Zack. "But I need two things first. Number one . . ." and Zack opened his arms expectantly, raising his eyes heavenward.

"A hug!" Justin shouted, putting his book down, running across the room and launching himself into his father's arms. "I knew that one!"

"You are right!" Zack said, squeezing the boy tight. Then he pulled back and looked at Justin. "And number two, I need to know what you are reading, and how it is going."

Justin got very serious, slid down to the ground, trotted back to pick up his book, and read the cover. "I'm reading *The Reptile Room*," he said. "I'm on page sixty-seven, and it is going great!"

"Whoa," Terry said. "When did you finish the first one?"

"I finished that one, um, I don't remember. Dad? When did I finish the first one?"

"Last week, I think," Zack replied. "Go on up to bed, Justin. I'll be up in a half hour or so, okay?"

"Okay, Daddy." And away he went.

Lemony Snicket was just the latest thing to confirm that Zack was the most ignorant single father in the world.

The lightning fast acceleration of Justin's reading and writing skills had completely blown Zack away. Justin had always loved books, even before he really knew what they were. He'd climb up in Zack's lap while Zack read these gigantic, dry legal treatises. Justin would help turn the pages, and occasionally ask what he knew were silly questions. His favorite, which he would barely be able to utter before collapsing into giggles, was "Daddy, does this book have any pictures of kittens in it?"

Zack had always believed Justin was extremely intelligent, and so he was somewhat taken aback when, in kindergarten, Justin showed average, and occasionally slightly below average, reading skills, despite a ludicrously advanced vocabulary. But then, something happened in first grade, and suddenly, Justin wasn't sitting in Zack's lap listening to his father read books. He was in Zack's lap, reading books to his father.

And then, in second grade, yikes. One day, Justin was asking where the Blue's Clues books were, and the next, he was halfway through *The Unfortunate Beginning*, and asking what the definition of *menacing* was.

The television show had returned, and Malcolm Ayers was speaking.

"I will not be drawn into a bottomless cesspool of

counter accusations," he said. "I would, naturally, be more than willing to speak with any person of authority about any concerns they might have regarding this matter. But please do not expect me to explain myself to this unctuous, sunburned Neanderthal, as if he had any right to interrogate me, or indeed anyone, about these latest tragedies. As far as I am concerned, he is a clay-brained ass, seeking only to profit further from the suffering of others."

Russell Crane was, incredibly, still smiling. It was not clear whether he understood that he had just been insulted. What he did understand, though, was that it was his turn to speak.

"I have reviewed the evidence in the first Springfield Shooter case," he said, "and I have come to the conclusion that there is a possibility—a small one, I grant you, but a possibility—that while Alan Lombardo might have been responsible for the first five murders, the final four killings *could* have been committed by a *second* perpetrator."

"Do you have any idea in the world what this guy is talking about?" Terry asked.

"I'd love to find out how Alan only did five of the nine, but ended up with all of the fingers in his freezer," Zack replied.

Russell Crane was continuing to speak. "I have no definitive proof, of course—"

"That never stopped you before," Ayers chimed in.

"—But anyone can see that there was a dramatic change in the killer's behavior pattern after *Diary of a Serial Killer* was released," Crane continued.

"Do you not realize that the journal entries found on Alan Lombardo's computer speak to that issue specifically? This was widely publicized at the trial. Are you mentally impaired, or do the facts of the matter have no bearing on the offal that spews forth from your hollow skull like some putrid geyser? Thanks to your despicable opus and the rampant, irresponsible speculation about me that followed," Ayers continued, "after the fifth murder, the killer decided to center his killings in Indian Oaks, to further implicate me. And in so doing, he destroyed my reputation, and very nearly destroyed my career. Are you now saying that you don't believe this to be the truth?"

Crane just shook his head and kept smiling. "And even if I am wrong about that," he replied, "I fully believe that the same characteristics I identified in *Diary of a Serial Killer* will apply to the killer of these two new victims."

"If I'm not mistaken," Terry said, staring at the screen, "Surfer Dude just accused Malcolm Ayers of being a serial killer. Again."

And then Ayers responded quietly. "The poisoned ravings of your foul mind, no matter how absurd, can do considerable damage, if broadcast widely," he told Russell Crane. "I implore you to keep your odious and defective opinions to yourself, sir. Let the police do their job. Let them catch this monster who has seen fit to attack us. Stay in Marblehead, or California, or wherever it is that you skulk, and keep to your own tawdry pursuits."

"And that was not exactly a ringing denial," Terry concluded.

THIRTEEN

Dear Vera,

Well. It's been about two weeks, and I'm sure you've been wondering what I've been up to.

The answer is that I've been working on something that I very much hope you like.

But I'll get to that and some other exciting things in a minute.

First, an apology.

The other day, I reread that letter I sent to you about Iris Dubinski, and I have to admit that was not very nice of me. First of all, I spent the entire letter gloating, which is not only undignified—it's downright rude.

And second, I sent the letter to you after I killed the woman. What kind of friend would do something like that? You're a police detective, not a medical examiner. You want to save people, not recover dead bodies. If I had been paying attention to your feelings, I would have sent a letter in advance of the killing, to give you a chance to stop it.

So I apologize. No more gloating. No more letters after the fact.

Here's a diary entry from a couple of days ago that I hope will make up for my insensitivity:

> *September 7. I finally found my next participant.*
>
> *He's a little older than my other participants, which is very good news. I like variety. It keeps the blood flowing. So to speak.*
>
> *I suppose what I like best about someone new is imagining what it's going to be like. For example, what will it sound like when I take the old man's finger? Will the sound be so unusual that I will want to take two? Will his bones be so brittle that the falanges will crackle, like dry sticks, when I use my pruning shears?*
>
> *He must be an independent person, since he's still living alone at his age. But will he fight back? Or will he just succumb to his inevitible demise?*
>
> *And what if, just as we get started, he has a heart attack, and dies before we get anywhere? What am I going to do with a body that I did not kill? I'm not exactly a mortitian.*
>
> *The possibilities are infinite. But one thing is certain.*
>
> *For my participant, it will be a very important and dramatic evening.*

Hello Vera. I'm back.

I know, I know, mispellings. What a crude way to tell you who the next victim will be. I might as well have used onomatopeia. But I thought I would start off with some relatively easy clues, since I feel that I owe you something for being so uncaring in my letter to you about Ms. Dubinski.

Good luck saving the old man's life, but act quickly. It will be all over tonight.

Eternally Yours

September 10

Five minutes ago, when Detective Vera Demopolous first walked through the door of the law office with the latest letter from the serial killer in her hand, she started breaking rules.

Well that was too bad. Because she was running out of time. And like Grandma used to say, in an emergency, rules start to seem more like suggestions.

It was about seven o'clock. Depending on what the killer meant by "It will be all over tonight," Vera might be too late.

The state police lab was frantically running tests on the original of the letter, and Ellis was working with their database, trying to crack whatever code the killer had used, doing anything he could to generate a name or a set of names of people to warn, or possibly to protect.

But Vera couldn't shake the feeling that there was a connection between this serial killer case and the one solved twenty years ago which might reveal the letter's hidden message. She'd called everyone she could think of, even Willy Grasso down in Florida, but so far, she'd come up empty.

As a last-ditch effort, she called attorneys Terry Tallach and Zack Wilson, the two people who now probably knew the most about the original Springfield Shooter case. They agreed to let Vera look through some of the old Alan Lombardo files, in hopes that it might trigger something.

Terry had actually said that he'd been intending to call her for the same reason. Interesting.

Anyway, she and Zack were now standing next to each other at a table, reading the photocopy of the letter that Vera had brought with her.

Terry was pacing the office like he hadn't been fed in about two weeks. Then he stopped. "Are you telling me that this psycho is sending you letters to your *home address?*" His voice was pretty loud.

"I'm having my mail forwarded to the station house," Vera replied, turning back to the killer's message. "Which is why we got this letter as early as we did. If I'd opened it after I got home from work today, we might not have even seen it before the murder."

Zack had pulled a pad in front of him, and was jotting down some letters. "Let's see. The *f* in phalanges is wrong. So is the *i* in inevitable, and the *t* in mortician." He looked at the pad. "*F-i-t.*"

"Yeah," Terry said. "That sounds like what I'm just about to have." He went back to pacing.

Vera turned away from the letter and now began to sift through the documents in the file box that Zack and Terry had made available to her. "We've already run those letters back at the house," she said. "We tried all of the combinations, but if those three letters spell the last name of the victim, we're in trouble. There's no old man living alone in Springfield whose last name is spelled with only the three letters *f-i-t*, in any order. And if they're initials, we don't have a chance to get through all of the possibilities in time." She pulled out the computer journal entries from the Springfield Shooter trial. "Are you sure there wasn't anything like this in the Lombardo case?"

Zack shook his head. "There were lots of diary entries, and six notes at the crime scenes left to Detective Grasso. But the killer never gave hints about who he was going to kill. At least not as far as I've seen." He turned to Terry. "Hey, Elvis. You see anything in the Lombardo file like this letter?"

By now, Terry had joined them at the table, looked at the pad for a second, and then moved off again, for another lap of the office. "No. And can we get back to the part where the serial killer knows where Vera lives? Is it just me, or is that kind of, oh, I don't know, un-fucking-settling?"

The file Vera was looking through contained all of the

diary entries she had seen in the police reports, with a bunch of notes written in the margins, as well as all of the trial transcripts, court filings, other evidence, legal research, and folder after folder of other paperwork that she couldn't even begin to pay any real attention to. "I've got to get back to the station," she said, pushing the file box away. "I can't go through all of this in the time we've got."

But suddenly Zack said, "Hold on just a minute." He went to a bookshelf, grabbed a dictionary, and began flipping through it.

Terry continued, from the other side of the room. "I guess what I'm saying is that if a serial killer started sending letters to me at home, I'd never stop vomiting."

The big man's words did not match up with Vera's experience. A year ago, she had barely survived a kidnapping, and Terry happened to be on hand when she was rescued. He was much braver than he pretended to be.

"The killer misspelled 'misspelling,' " Zack interrupted. "He left out an *s*."

Terry was next to them at the table immediately. "So that means you should add an *s* to the list, right? *F-i-t-s*. Maybe there's somebody with that for a last name."

Something about that didn't add up for Vera. "Weren't we making a list of the letters that the killer used incorrectly?" She took the pad and reread the list. "If he left a letter out of a word, technically, he didn't use *any* letter in that word incorrectly. Maybe the list should be of letters that were left *out* of the words."

Zack grabbed the pad. "Like *ph*, instead of *f*, for phalanges."

Vera consulted the list. "*C* for mortician, and *s* for misspelling."

"And *a*, for inevitable," Terry added. "And by the way, what the hell is 'onomatopeia'?"

Zack started turning the pages of the dictionary. "It's

when the word sounds like—" He paused, reading the dictionary, and then the letter again. "Holy shit."

"All right. I know it doesn't mean *that*."

"No, onomatopoeia is misspelled, too. He left out an *o*."

"So what does that leave us with?" Vera asked.

Zack read the list of letters off the pad. "*P-h-o-a-c-s*. Does that mean anything to you? What about combinations?"

At that, Zack began to write the letters in different order. Saphoc. Pachos. Coshap. Achops.

He kept going, but Vera kept looking at Achops.

Ac Hops.

A. C. Hops.

"Stop right there!" Vera exclaimed, pulling out her cell phone. "The victim's name could be Hops. A. C. Hops. Or C. A. Hops, I guess. Whatever. I've got to call Ellis and get someone started on calling—"

"But there's lots of other possibilities," Terry said. "How do we know—"

Vera interrupted him, waiting for Ellis to pick up. "We don't. But at least we can be doing something . . ." Ellis finally answered the phone.

"Vera, is that you?" he asked. Something was wrong.

"What's up, Ellis? I was just calling because we might have something on the note."

"Never mind," Ellis said. "We just found our victim. Seventy-seven-year-old Laurence Seta. Evening grocery delivery service found the old man taped up, shot repeatedly. There's a note. 'Welcome to my world.' No question. It's our guy."

Paul had picked up a few messages from the office, and was bringing them home to Mr. Heinrich. He had left the twins, Oren and Ira, to watch the old man. But the truth was, there wasn't much to watch. The boss was heading downhill fast.

He had nurses and doctors coming and going all day and night, but there really wasn't much more to do.

It was surprising that Mr. Heinrich even cared about phone messages anymore, but he insisted that Paul check in at work every day. It was probably so that Neil got used to having Paul around.

When he reached the big house on Maplewood, he turned down the side driveway and entered from the back of the house. He headed straight up to the old man's bedroom. Ira, or Oren, he could never keep them straight, was sitting on a chair outside the room, listening to his iPod. He waved as Paul knocked on the door and entered the room.

Mr. Heinrich was lying back in his bed. He was hooked up to an IV, and a nurse was getting ready to leave the room. She smiled sadly at Paul as he went past her, and sat next to the bed.

"Paul, how's business?" the old guy said, in a soft voice. "The nurse just gave me some morphine, so this is a good time."

"Well, things are pretty quiet in the office. Some money came in from Nate and Skelly, and a big check from the Ziggerman job. Neil was spending a lot of time splitting that up." Paul looked down at the messages. "You got a couple of calls from Dr. Choi, one from Bill MacNeal saying he hopes you feel better—"

The old man wheezed a little laugh. Miraculously, it didn't turn into a coughing fit. "Oh yeah. Tell Bill I'm feeling great."

"—And the last one is from a woman named, let's see. Vera Demopolous."

The old man's eyes did not register anything. "Vera who?" he asked.

Paul checked the note again. "Demopolous. She says she's a detective with the Springfield Police. She wants to talk to you about Alan Lombardo."

Laurence L. Seta

IT WAS 5:45 P.M. ON SEPTEMBER 10, WHEN Laurence Seta answered the door for the last time in his life.

He had just finished putting the dinner plates into the dishwasher, and was getting ready to sit down and watch the news. He liked to stay current, not only because it seemed that the world was going to hell in a handbasket, but because it didn't take a rocket scientist to know that the only way to stay young was to keep involved in life, exercise your mind and your body, and spend time with children.

He wasn't expecting anyone, but it was always good to have visitors, so when the doorbell rang, he opened the door cheerfully to the nice-looking man.

The next thing Laurence knew, he had fallen back onto his bad hip. He had no idea how he had collapsed onto the floor, but pain was coursing through his entire body like an electrical current of agony.

And then, through the buzzing in his ears, he heard the door close, and a man's voice say, "Welcome to my world, Mr. Seta."

Twenty-Eight Seconds

GETTING SHOT IN THE LEG WASN'T NEARLY AS bad as Zack would have imagined.

Sure, it had knocked him on his ass, and it burned—a lot—but Zack had pulled himself up to his feet using the clerk's wheeled desk chair, and the shooter was no longer paying attention to him.

Justin's life was at stake. The pain in Zack's leg was going to have to wait. He began to run toward the shooter.

But the moment he put his left foot down, he immediately fell on his face.

Who could ever have imagined that walking could be so hard?

And then a flash of memory raced through his mind like a miniature bolt of lightning. It was six years earlier, and Zack was back in his apartment, speaking to his father on the phone, watching Justin not walking again.

"Zachary, these kinds of opportunities do not present themselves often, and I strongly urge you to take advantage of this one that is practically begging to make you a rich and successful man."

Justin was resting his tiny hand on the coffee table for balance, standing there, smiling a drooly smile at Zack from across the living room. The child had been cruising around the furniture in their tiny apartment for months. The little boy obviously wanted to learn how to walk, but he was afraid to let go of that coffee table. He'd been working on that trick for about two weeks now.

"I really do appreciate that, Dad, but I just don't think it's the right place for me."

Zack's father's idea of a golden opportunity and Zack's were on opposite sides of the solar system. For the past ten days, his father had been trying to recruit Zack to join his buddies at his old firm in Boston. The only criminal law they did was defending their corporate clients against charges of white-collar crime. It was likely that they'd try to turn Zack into a civil trial attorney, defending insurance claims against multinational corporations.

"If you're worried about money, you shouldn't be. Even after hiring a full-time nanny for that child, you'll still be making three to four times what you're making now."

And just then, Justin lifted his right hand off the coffee table and stood there, grinning, completely detached from the furniture. He was going for it.

"I'm sorry, Dad," Zack said. "I'm going to have to pass—"

"For Christ's sakes, Zachary, think of what you're doing. This will be the last time you have a chance to do something important with your life."

At that moment, Justin looked directly at Zack, reached out both hands toward him, and took his first four steps, all alone, wide-eyed and giggling with pride and joy.

"You know what, Dad?" Zack asked, more confident of himself than ever before. "I'm already doing something important with my life."

And then there was the *crack* of a new bullet ripping through the air. And the sound of a new shriek of pain from the gallery.

There had to be another way for Zack to get to this guy.

While the world continued to move around him like a very slow dream full of screaming people, the words of that Navy SEAL from the bookstore came back to Zack again.

"There's always another way. SEAL training is all about learning how to find the other way. You know why SEALs never fail? They just try something else."

Zack may not have been a SEAL, but goddammit, he wasn't about to fail. He had no idea how to stop that shooter, but standing up seemed like as good a place as any to start. He grabbed hold of the seat of the clerk's chair again, and used it to drag himself up onto his right leg. The well-oiled castors on the vinyl floor made the chair dance around, but at least Zack was upright.

Standing on his good leg but leaning on the wheeled chair, Zack turned to face the gunman, who was now about twenty feet away, and pointing his gun out at another victim. Suddenly, as if self-propelled, the chair lurched violently toward the shooter, threatening to roll so far away from Zack that even though he was holding on to it, he'd fall on his face again. So Zack hopped ahead on his right leg to keep up with the chair.

He managed to regain his balance, and looked up again at the shooter.

The distance between them had closed, if only by a few feet. Maybe eighteen more to go.

There's always another way.

Zack pushed the chair forward again, and holding on, hopped after it again. Now maybe sixteen feet separated him and the shooter.

Although the world was still in slo-mo, Zack's mind was blazing along at top speed. How many shots had been spent? Four? Five? How many did a weapon like that hold? If Zack were able to draw more fire, would that exhaust the shooter's ammunition? Or should he try to rush the shooter and hope to catch him by surprise this time? What if the next time he got shot he was hit in a vital spot? He was already assuming that he was going to die, but how could he make sure that his death would guarantee Justin's safety?

Another push, another hop, and now the space between them had shrunk to fourteen feet.

And the shooter, aiming into the crowd, fired again.

Or tried to fire again. Because this time, there was no crack. No bullet. The shooter looked down at his gun, pointed it back out into the crowd, and squeezed the trigger again.

Nothing.

He was out of ammunition. Thank God. Now where was Justin?

Zack spun to his left, trying to spot his son. But the emergency lighting was so poor, and the room so chaotic, with injured and screaming people everywhere, many cowering behind benches or sprawled on the floor, there was no way to find Justin.

Just then, a metallic clatter from the direction of the gunman. Zack spun back toward the noise, and saw a silver rectangular tube of some kind on the floor.

Then he brought his gaze up to the man's hands, and rushed forward.

Because the madman hadn't run out of bullets. The silver thing on the floor was an ammunition clip.

He was merely reloading.

And Zack was still twelve long feet away. With something very important yet to do with his life.

At least what was left of it.

FOURTEEN

September 11

STEPHANIE WATCHED WITH DISBELIEF AS HER father and the crazy-looking little man who was driving them climbed out of the tiny car parked in front of her house and headed toward her.

Stephanie was standing in front of the home of her elderly neighbor, Mrs. Giordano, on a lawn strewn with musty-smelling books, magazines and sheet music, old board games, mismatched sets of glasses, plates, serving bowls and utensils, yellowing photographs, and whatever else she and Mrs. G. had pulled down from the old woman's attic over the past week.

Mrs. Giordano finished talking to the young couple who had just bought an old wooden high chair, and watched as the two men approached. "Do you have to go, dear?" she asked Steph. "It's perfectly all right, you know. David will be by later this afternoon to help out."

For someone she barely knew, Mrs. G.'s son David was turning out to be a real pain in Stephanie's butt. David had basically railroaded his mother into holding the yard sale, in an effort to, as he delicately put it, "get rid of some of the clutter" in Mrs. G.'s life. So Steph felt obliged to help the poor woman with the formidable task of rummaging through her old belongings and making sure, for example, that all of the metal tray tables with the lilac motif were accounted for, and cleaning the three dozen cups that went with the ugliest punch bowl she'd ever seen.

It wouldn't have been so bad if this was something that Mrs. G. had actually wanted. But it was pretty clear that David was the real interested party here, and it sure seemed like it was less about clutter, and more about finding a way for his mom to get her hands on some more money, so David wouldn't have to kick in the lousy fifty bucks or so he spent every month taking her to get groceries.

"No, I'm fine," Steph told Mrs. G. "It's just my father, and, um, a friend. Coming to your yard sale. Amazing."

It wasn't clear which was less likely. That Malcolm had a friend, or that he was coming to a yard sale.

"Well then, I'll be right back with something to drink," Mrs. G. said, heading inside.

Steph became aware that she was holding a copy of the piano and vocal music to *K-K-K-Katy*, and she put it down, hastily, as her father came up to her. He looked nervous.

"Stephanie, I'd like you to meet a friend of mine. This is Mr. Thomas Prieaux. He comes to my regular Alcoholics Anonymous meeting, and several months ago, he agreed, at my request, but against my advice, to become my sponsor." Malcolm turned to the other man. "Thomas, this is my daughter, Stephanie."

Thomas Prieaux looked a little younger than Malcolm— he might have been in his sixties, but he was the kind of person whose smile and attitude made him appear younger than he really was. He seemed to be unaware of the fact that just about everything about his bearing was odd. He walked with his hands clasped together in front of his somewhat rounded belly, his clothes looked clean and pressed, but rather like he was planning to go straight from the yard sale to a '70s fashion show, his haircut was straight out of ancient Rome, and to top it all off, he stood, at most, five feet tall.

Thomas shook hands and exclaimed, "Stephanie, I cannot tell you how pleased I am to finally meet you! Your father is constantly telling me that we mustn't intrude on your life, but after I saw you on *Public Forum* the other night, I told Malcolm, 'Enough, you big chicken. I don't care if I am intruding, I simply must meet this splendid young woman immediately and tell her how much I adore her.' " He looked back over his shoulder at Malcolm, who was fiddling with some salt and pepper shakers that looked like Marilyn Monroe and James Dean, and then back to Stephanie. "And so, here we are. Your earrings are fabulous, by the way."

It was all completely overwhelming. Six months ago, her father had finally acknowledged that he might actually benefit from attending AA meetings. But the idea that Malcolm had actually embraced the program so thoroughly that he had gotten a sponsor—a fellow alcoholic who was far enough along in his sobriety that he could mentor others in recovery—was nothing short of miraculous.

The fact that Thomas looked a bit like a cartoon character was just rainbow-colored icing on the improbability cake.

"It's the hair, isn't it?" Thomas asked, touching his ridiculously short bangs with the tips of his fingers. He turned back to Malcolm, who was now examining an eight-track collection of classical music. "I told you she was going to freak out when she saw the hair, didn't I, Mal?"

Malcolm, or, rather, *Mal*—this was getting weirder by the second—smiled and put down the cartridges. "Thomas is in a play," he said, as if that explained everything.

"They made us cut our hair," Thomas said. "I'm in *A Funny Thing Happened on the Way to the Forum* at the

Longmeadow Players. You should come. It's going to be wonderful."

Stephanie finally found her voice. "Well, it's a pleasure to meet you, Thomas. I, um, I'm so happy you came today."

Thomas squinted, turned back to Malcolm, and launched into another monologue. "She doesn't know anything about this, does she? I knew you weren't going to tell her unless we came here. Too many secrets, Mal, too many secrets. Newsflash, Sweetie. Your daughter already knows you're human and can't do everything all alone. She's a grown woman, and from what I saw on television the other night, quite capable of taking care of herself."

Without missing a beat, he turned back to Stephanie and plunged ahead. "Isn't it incredible how different your father and I are? But what's important is in *here*, isn't it?" Thomas nodded solemnly, and patted the left side of his chest. "And in there, Malcolm and I are like brothers. By the way, your father is doing really well in his recovery. The program is working for him, because he's working the program. I am very proud of him. In fact everyone at the meeting is."

And then Thomas leaned closer, and in a stage whisper, dropped the real bomb.

"But what we really came to tell you is that we just went to the police, because we think that the Springfield Shooter is stalking your father."

At that moment, Mrs. Giordano emerged from her front door carrying a tray of glasses and calling out cheerfully, "Who wants lemonade?"

Zack was supposed to be spending his after-dinner-before putting-Justin-to-bed-time reading a law review article on conflicts of interest, but he couldn't pull himself away from the notes he'd made last week on the letter the serial killer had sent to Vera. It was really hard to believe that the murderer had gone to the trouble to create a random set of false clues. But no matter how many times Zack went through the letter, he couldn't come up with how it led to the name Laurence Seta.

Justin banged on the door, and then came in followed by Kermit the dog. The hems of the little boy's SpongeBob SquarePants pajama pants were now a full inch north of his ankles.

"Hey, you're ready for bed so soon?" Zack couldn't believe it. It seemed like they'd only finished dinner fifteen minutes ago.

"Uh, Mr. Silly Daddy, look what time it is." Justin walked over to Zack to show him the watch he kept at all times on his skinny little wrist. According to Mickey Mouse, it was nearly nine o'clock. Whoa. When had that happened?

"Ooh. Sorry about that, Justin man. I must have spaced out doing this work."

Justin climbed up onto Zack's lap, while Kermit inspected the front left leg of the red leather chair that Terry loved to sit in. Something about that leg really worked for Kermit. The dog spent most of his time in Zack's room sniffing it or lying next to it.

"Daddy, why would anyone want to kill some cornflakes?" Justin asked.

Zack had been through enough of these sessions to know, just from the tone of his son's voice, that the little guy was seriously concerned. Of course Justin was also extremely misinformed. But from personal experience, Zack knew to be careful to find out what was really going on before accidentally reinforcing, ignoring, or ridiculing whatever Justin was worrying about.

As a young child, Zack had spent several years terrified every time he saw someone chewing gum, because he had been told by a kindergarten classmate that if swallowed, ever expanding bubbles would form in the victim's stomach and ultimately kill him. He'd had nightmares well into second grade until his father dispelled him of the myth. Unfortunately, he had replaced Zack's fear with humiliation, by laughing heartily at his little boy's terror.

"I don't know, Justin," Zack answered now. "I never heard of anything like that before. Where did you learn about it?"

"School." Justin was fingering the button on Zack's shirt pocket. A sure sign of anxiety in the sensitive child.

"From your teacher, or from one of the kids in your class?"

Justin stopped fiddling with the button. "Zenita was talking to Trey and K.B., and she said that there was a cereal killer in Springfield."

Zack sighed. Justin was seven years old. From the moment that Zack had first brought his infant son home from the hospital, Zack had been trying to protect him from real world images of violence, like the ones that seemed to be present in every single television news broadcast on every single day. Zack knew firsthand how terrible people could be, and he had hoped to delay for as long as he could their invasion into little Justin's world.

Apparently, the invasion had already taken place, in a second grade classroom, thanks to fellow seven-year-olds named Zenita, Trey, and K.B.

"A serial killer is someone who, well . . ." Zack hesitated. He wanted to lie. He wanted to scream. He wanted to run out of the room. Why did his perfect little boy have to bear this kind of madness?

Zack cleared his throat, and started again. He had to tell Justin, because sooner or later, someone else would. And unless Zenita, Trey, and K.B. all came down with chicken pox tonight, it sounded like it would be sooner.

"A serial killer is a person who is sick, Justin. Mentally

sick. Someone whose brain isn't working right. Because a serial killer is someone who kills a person, and then, later, kills more people. The word *serial* in serial killer sounds just like cereal, like cornflakes, but it's actually spelled differently. And of course it means something very different."

Justin was back to twiddling the button. "So there is somebody in Springfield who has a sick brain who is killing more than one person?"

Zack wasn't going to lie, but he was going to make this as easy as he could. "Well, the police aren't sure if there is a serial killer in Springfield or not. But there have been three killings recently, so the police are telling everyone to be really, really careful about who they let into their homes. And you know our rule about opening doors, right, buddy?"

Justin's dark eyes were solemn. "Right. I don't answer the door unless you are with me."

"You got it." Zack squeezed Justin. "Now I need to tell you three secrets, okay?"

Justin nodded. "Okay."

Zack put his lips up to his son's ear. "First secret. I will never, ever, *ever*, let anything bad happen to you, okay?"

"Okay."

"Good. Second secret. You need new pajamas. The ones you are wearing are so short they are making *my* ankles cold."

Justin giggled. "Daddy," he chided. "C'mon."

"Third secret." Zack pointed to the red leather chair where Justin's best friend was snoring gently. "Kermit is dreaming about the fun day you are going to have with him after you get home from school tomorrow."

And at that very instant, Zack figured out the key to the serial killer's letter.

FIFTEEN

September 12

VERA DEMOPOLOUS SAT AT THE CONFERENCE table and watched as Terry Tallach took the sheets of paper out of his briefcase and spread them in front of her and Ellis. The big lawyer was wearing a dark suit with a nice-looking red patterned tie. Normally, Vera thought that kind of clothing was a little stuffy, but on Terry, it looked just right.

Apparently Terry's partner, Zack, who was stuck in court all day today, had broken the code in the Laurence Seta letter, and he and Terry wanted to get the information into police hands as soon as possible.

"Okay," Terry said. "Here's what we had. The killer misspelled a bunch of words in the letter. *Phalanges, onomatopoeia, inevitable, mortician,* and *misspellings.* And from those five words, we were working with the letters that he had left out—*p, h, o, a, c,* and *s.* And we were rearranging them, hoping that they were going to spell the name of the next victim, until we found out about the latest killing."

Ellis nodded. "That's as far as we got." Poor Ellis was still down on himself for not figuring out the code in time to stop the Seta murder. And he had spilled coffee on the front of his shirt this morning, so he looked as bad as he felt.

Terry handed one of the sheets of notes to Vera. "So yesterday, after dinner, Zack was talking to his son, Justin, about school, and all of a sudden, he remembered one of the combinations of letters." Terry pointed to the one that was circled on the page. *C-a-p-o-h-s*.

"What does *capohs*, whatever that is, have to do with Laurence Seta?" Vera asked.

"The thing was, we were so focused on getting those letters to spell us a name, we overlooked the fact that they might spell something else. Like this." And then Terry took a pen, and wrote *CAPO H.S.*

"Capo High School? Seta didn't live anywhere near the high school." Ellis frowned.

"Right," agreed Terry. "But people who've been in Springfield long enough know that even though everybody calls it Capo High School, its official name is *Stella Capo High School*. Named after some local kid nobody remembers anymore."

Ellis put his hand to his forehead. "Don't tell me. That's how you get Seta's name."

"That's it." Terry pointed again to the page on which he had written the letters *p-h-o-a-c-s*. "To figure out the answer, you have to rearrange the letters he omitted from Stella Capo H.S.: *s-t-e-l-l-a*, the same way you rearranged the omitted letters from the misspelled words: *p-h-o-a-c-s* to spell out *Capo H.S.* You take the fifth letter he omitted, *c*, and move it to the first position. Then you take the fourth letter he omitted, *a*, and move it to the second position. Then the first letter, *p*, goes in the third position. And so on."

Vera picked up a pen. "The omitted letters are '*S-t-e-l-l-a*,' right? So you take the fifth letter in Stella, that's *l*, and it goes in the first position." She wrote down *l*. "Next is the fourth letter. That's also an *l*, which goes in the second position. Next is the first letter, *s*, then the third letter, *e*, the second letter, *t,* and the sixth letter, *a*." By the time she had finished, she had written *l-l-s-e-t-a*.

"The letters spell out L. L. Seta." Ellis opened a folder that was sitting on the table, and pulled out the police report of the Seta homicide. "The victim's name was Laurence Lloyd Seta. L. L. Seta. Jesus Christ. We could have stopped him."

"I don't know about you," Terry said, "but I doubt the killer actually thought you had enough time to solve this and then stop him."

"We had the answer in our hands." Ellis was despondent. "If we'd been fast enough, we could have nailed this bastard."

Terry stood up. "I think he was just yanking your chain. Do you really think he was going to give you the time to solve his little mystery? I think he murdered the guy before you even got the letter."

"He's probably right, Ellis," Vera said. "I just hope that we can use this if he sends us another one."

Ellis rubbed his eyes. "Oh, he'll send another letter. Believe me. Serial killers love to jerk people around. They get off knowing that they're smarter than everybody else. They especially like it when cops run around in circles chasing them. He's probably right under our noses."

Vera hadn't been able to find anything in the Lombardo case that was like these letters. But there had to be something in the connection between the two cases that she could use to help her solve these new murders. And if anyone knew the details of the original Springfield Shooter evidence, it was Terry and Zack. "You haven't seen anything in the Lombardo file that reminds you of these letters, have you?"

Terry gathered up the papers and handed them to Ellis. "Nothing except those computer journal entries. And they weren't clues to anything. They were just gloating. Sometimes I think the guy who's doing these killings has a different psychology than the original Springfield

Shooter, you know? They're both sick, but this new guy, I don't know. He seems more, what? Devious?"

Vera laughed grimly. "More devious than Alan Lombardo? Wow. The man killed nine people before he was caught, and in his spare time, he was a bookkeeper for the mob. I'd say that's pretty devious."

Terry looked stunned. "Did you say bookkeeper for the mob?"

"Are you telling me that you didn't know that back before he was arrested, Alan Lombardo was the personal and business accountant for Gentleman George Heinrich?"

This was one of Mr. Heinrich's good days. They weren't coming that frequently anymore, so the old man was anxious to take advantage of every minute.

He was sitting in his wheelchair at the table in the kitchen alcove, next to the window, soaking up the sun. He was so skinny and frail these days that it was sometimes hard to remember how full of life the old man used to be.

Neil was sitting across from him, having some coffee. Paul was at the counter, in case they needed anything.

"So how are things?" the old man asked. "Paul tells me the Ziggurat job is progressing well, and I understand you landed that contract to redo that strip mall out in New Ludlow. That's really great news."

Neil was trying to be upbeat, but it was obvious that his father's decline was really wearing him down. He looked tired, and not as happy as the company's successes should have made him. He forced a smile, and said, "Yeah, that job's going to keep us busy for months. I always like it when we have a big project going, you know? It keeps the cash flowing, there's lots of places to put the men between the smaller jobs, it just makes sense for a lot of reasons."

Mr. Heinrich nodded, and for a long moment, looked

out the window into the acres of woods that he owned. "I know what you're doing," he said, in a soft voice. "You do realize that, don't you?"

Neil sat forward. "What do you mean, Dad?"

The old man turned back toward his son and smiled. "It's okay," he said. "You don't have to protect me. Even though it's kind of funny, you protecting me from what you're doing . . ." But just at that moment, a coughing attack came on the boss, and Paul hurried over to join Neil. They stood helplessly at Mr. Heinrich's side as the spasms shook his withered body. He waved them away, though. Like usual, there was nothing to do.

When he'd regained his breath, the old man took a sip of water and started again. "I was just saying that I think it's kind of funny that here you are, going legit, and I think you're embarrassed about it. Like you don't want to come right out and tell me."

As usual, Mr. Heinrich was right. Neil probably didn't realize how close his father still managed to stay to the day-to-day workings of the organization. And the boss saw what anyone else would—Heinrich Contracting wasn't pressuring the other companies in the trades for protection money as it normally did, or demanding that those companies hire Heinrich employees and overpay for the privilege of doing so.

After decades of the Heinrich corporate empire ruling the organized criminal world of Springfield and most of western New England, Neil Heinrich was taking the operation legit.

Neil took a sip of his coffee. He was stalling. "I'm not really—"

Mr. Heinrich interrupted him, "Neil. Stop. Don't make excuses. I don't care." He lost his breath again, but at least he didn't go into a coughing fit. "I really don't care if you shut down the whole thing tomorrow, the dirty stuff, whatever. The only reason I brought it up was to tell you that your decision— I'm proud of you. It takes guts. It takes guts in this world to play it like you're gonna play it."

Neil looked like he was going to weep. "Yeah, well, I wasn't trying to protect you, Dad. I just didn't want you to think that I wasn't grateful . . ." But at this point, his voice broke, and he had to stop.

Neither man spoke, and for a little while, all that Paul could hear was the raspy breathing of the father. "You know, you never tell me about Carol anymore. How is she? I miss her, son. She hasn't come to see me for a while. You two are still okay, aren't you?"

Neil had been seeing Carol Pope for about two years. She worked as a sales rep for a marble and granite firm near Worcester. When they first started going out, Neil was obviously trying to keep Carol from getting too involved with his family. But when Mr. Heinrich got sick, all of that went out the window, and the old man and Carol got pretty close. Her mom had died from cancer, and according to Neil, having Carol around really was helping him deal with Mr. Heinrich's condition.

Although there were days, like today, when you really wouldn't know it from how sad Neil looked.

Neil laughed and wiped his eyes. "Yes, Dad, we're still okay. Carol asks about you all the time. She just has felt a little, you know, a little like it would be an imposition—"

"Oh, please, Neil, she's family. I'm surprised at her. C'mon. Tell her to come visit me whenever she wants. I don't have that much time left. I'd like to spend it with good people."

Another heavy silence descended on the two men. It almost seemed like neither wanted to move. Like they could keep things from changing, if they just stayed as they were. Mr. Heinrich, looking out the window into his woods, and Neil, staring down at the table, every once in a while lifting his glance to his ailing father.

Finally, the boss cleared his throat, and turned to face his son. "I'm sorry I have to bring this up, but I need to talk to you about something that might be a surprise to you."

The old man gazed off again into the distance. "It's about Alan Lombardo," he said.

"I still can't believe that the police aren't doing anything."

Stephanie would have enjoyed her father's new commitment to sobriety much more if it hadn't coincided so perfectly with the impact of the second Springfield Shooter on their lives.

Steph and Malcolm were taking a walk together around Malcolm's neighborhood. The houses were big, and the lots were at least a half acre each. Malcolm walked these streets so regularly that he knew exactly where each and every dog in the neighborhood lived. Steph had been bitten as a child by the monstrous German shepherd that lived across her street, and was still terrified of dogs, so they were steering clear of Malcolm's normal route.

"The woman I spoke with, Detective Demopolous, if I remember her name correctly, told me that they would increase patrols in the area." Malcolm walked at a good pace. Maybe this exercise really was doing something for him. Steph hoped so. She knew very well how dangerous Malcolm's condition was. "And she also said that the killer always attacks in his victims' homes. Believe me, my dear, I have no intention of opening my door to any stranger, for any reason, until this madman is caught."

They continued down the sidewalk, passing a large Tudor home with elaborate landscaping. A bus rumbled past, the huge advertisement painted on its side promoting the release of horrible Russell Crane's new movie, *The*

Suspect's Daughter. Steph had read a review of the movie. Apparently, it was about a young, single woman who worked in a hospital and who spent much of the film attempting to shield herself from the mounting evidence that her father was a murderer.

"Daddy, did you get an invitation to that movie?"

In one of Russell Crane's twisted efforts at easing his conscience, he regularly invited Malcolm to the premieres of his movies. "Yes," Malcolm said. "It came in the mail the other day. Not that I have any intention of going."

Steph stopped walking. "I'm probably just being paranoid. But there's a part of me that wants to go, just to see what that jerk is doing. God help me if he's implicating you again."

Malcolm sighed and put his arm around her shoulders. "May I change the subject from an amoral and inept movie writer and his exploitation of some homicidal sociopath's felonies to unutterably beautiful rhododendrons?"

He pointed at the pink and white blooms exploding all along the side of the Tudor house. "Your mother always loved those flowers. I tried once to plant some myself, but my efforts bordered on crimes against nature. I endeavored to redeem myself by cultivating a vegetable garden. Results were again predictably disappointing."

Steph had a hard time imagining her father digging around in the dirt. He always seemed like such a serious person, interested only in books.

And drinking, of course.

Steph's cell phone rang. A number she didn't recognize appeared on the screen. It was from California. Before even trying to guess who it might be, she answered it.

A vaguely familiar and unpleasant voice was on the other end. And as if he had been listening to them as they discussed his movie, the voice said, "Stephanie? We've never met. But my name is Russell Crane."

SIXTEEN

THE CLERK: *Court is now in session. This is the continued matter of* Commonwealth versus Alan Lombardo, *Case number 1984–0616. Court is now in session.*

THE COURT: *Attorney Wilson, we had just sworn in the defendant, I believe. Please continue.*

ATTORNEY NEHEMIAH WILSON: *Thank you, Your Honor. Would you state your name for the record, please?*

ALAN LOMBARDO: *My name is Alan Lombardo.*

Q *What is your occupation?*

A *I am a certified public accountant.*

Q *And who is your employer?*

A *I'm self-employed. I do work for a variety of individuals and businesses out of my home.*

Q *I see. You have an office in your home?*

A *Yes.*

Q *Fine. Now I'd like to talk to you about the night of March 15, 1984. Do you recall where you were on that evening?*

A *Yes. I was home.*

Q   *And did anything unusual happen that evening?*

A   *Yes. The police knocked on my door, and asked me where I was the night of March 13.*

Q   *And what did you tell them?*

A   *I told them that I was home that evening.*

Q   *Was it unusual for you to be home that evening?*

A   *Not at all. I stay home every night. I do not go out after dark.*

Q   *Ever?*

A   *The last time I went out at night was over three years ago. I had to get some medicine.*

Q   *But how about friends, family?*

A   *I am a very solitary person. My parents are dead, and I have no brothers or sisters.*

Q   *Did the police ask any other questions?*

A   *Yes. They asked me if it was possible that someone other than me had been using my car on the evening of the thirteenth.*

Q   *And what did you say?*

A   *I said that it was not possible. I do not lend out my car to anyone to use.*

CROSS-EXAMINATION BY ASSISTANT DISTRICT ATTORNEY CARTIER

Q   *All right, Mr. Lombardo. Let's go back to the evening of March 15, when the police came to your home to question you the first time.*

A   *Okay.*

Q   That must have been quite a surprise, seeing the police at your door, wasn't it?

A   Yes, it was very surprising.

Q   What went through your mind when you first saw them, considering what was in your freezer?

A   I had no idea what was in my freezer.

Q   Oh. You don't know what you keep in your own freezer?

A   Well, yes, I do, but I didn't know anything about that Tupperware container, if that's what you're talking about.

Q   You didn't know there was a container of human fingers sitting next to three half-gallon containers of chocolate chip ice cream in your own freezer at the time that the police first came to your home?

A   I told you. I had no knowledge that that container was in my freezer.

Q   And you live alone.

A   Yes.

Q   No family, no friends.

A   Correct.

Q   And no idea how the fingers of eight murder victims might possibly have found their way into your freezer, in your own home, where you live all by yourself?

(*Commonwealth v. Lombardo*, Volume XIII, Pages 99–101)

Terry Tallach was having a bad day, and it was only nine-thirty in the morning.

He and Zack were meeting with Zack's father again about the Alan Lombardo case, and Judge Wilson was turning out to be even worse than Terry had already believed him to be.

"Just to be sure I understand this—" Zack began, but the old man cut him off.

"I think you understand it quite well, Zachary. Please don't even begin to condescend. Yes, George Heinrich had retained me to provide legal services for him and for anyone who did work for him. And yes, while on retainer, I was hired, for two hundred fifty thousand dollars, by Alan Lombardo, who was working for George Heinrich at the time. Technically, it was an ethical violation, but some of us live in the real world. I had obligations, including obligations to feed and clothe *you*, by the way. When the opportunity arose, I took it."

"*Technically,* it was a lot more than a violation of the rules of ethics. Technically, it was fraud, maybe larceny." Zack was as serious as Terry had ever seen him.

"Oh, what, are you going to turn me in for ripping off George Heinrich? The biggest organized criminal Springfield has seen in the past fifty years? Or Alan Lombardo, the Springfield Shooter? Which one, Zachary? Please. Spare me the lecture. Believe me, it was the lesser of two evils. And Lombardo knew exactly what was going on. Remember, he did Heinrich's books. He knew what George paid, and to whom. It was no secret to him that I was already on retainer to his boss. I assumed he was making sure that I was paid enough to devote all of my time to his case." The old man lit a cigar, inhaled, and blew a noxious cloud of smoke into the air. Lombardo probably hired me with money he had skimmed from Heinrich in the first place."

"Wow." Terry had vowed to stay as quiet as possible in this meeting, out of respect for Zack. But he couldn't stop himself. Last time he heard a bullshit explanation like that, he was defending one of the great rationalizers of all time, Kyle Dracut, King of the Shitty Bank Robbers.

"Excuse me, Attorney Tallach?" For a guy who just admitted to committing some heavy stuff, the judge's tone was pretty snotty. "Do you have something to say?"

Once again, Terry couldn't stop himself. "I guess what I have to say, sir, is—with all due respect—you're a real dick."

The judge pointed at Terry with his cigar. "From what I understand, you're already skating on some pretty thin ice yourself in the eyes of the bar counsel, sir, so I wouldn't be so quick to throw stones."

Screw this guy. He was sounding goddamn righteous for a thief. "Whatever I may or may not have done, which is no business of yours, by the way, doesn't come close to taking a quarter million dollars to do a job I was already being paid to do."

"If I could just interrupt," Zack said. He sounded like he might be addressing a couple of squabbling six-year-olds on the playground. "I was wondering if we could get back to the Lombardo case." How he kept his head from exploding at times like these was a freakin' mystery to Terry.

But the judge was not ready to tone it down. "For the love of Christ, Zachary, will you please stop treating Alan Lombardo like some person worthy of your pity. For God's sakes, you've read the transcript. The man had a computer full of entries detailing every single one of those awful murders, and a freezer full of fingers, in case that wasn't enough. He's a monster who killed nine innocent people. Not some poor waif who needs to be rescued."

"But if he didn't get a fair trial—"

"A fair trial. You're an intelligent lawyer, Zachary. You know as well as I do that that trial was perfectly fine."

"But Massachusetts law on this kind of thing is awfully strict," Zack persisted. "If the ethical violation regarding the fees created a conflict of interest, Lombardo might have real support for a motion for new trial."

Boom. *Conflict of interest.* Cue the mushroom cloud.

For Massachusetts criminal appellate attorneys, it was the atomic bomb of legal theories.

Somewhere in the early 1980s, the judges of the highest court in Massachusetts, the Supreme Judicial Court, made a decision that they probably still regretted. They said that if a criminal defendant was able to show that his trial attorney had a conflict of interest at the time that he represented the defendant, the defendant was entitled to a new trial, regardless of *whether the defendant could prove that the conflict made any difference in what happened at the trial.*

That meant that if Judge Wilson's little two-hundred-and-fifty-thousand-dollar faux pas was somehow able to support an argument that he had a conflict of interest at the time of Alan's trial, Alan would win a motion for new trial.

But Zack's father was dismissive. He put on that smirk Terry had been itching to wipe off his face since he'd first met the man over twenty years ago. "Oh please. I can't even begin to tell you how many reasons that's not going to work. Number one. The very language of the rule governing motions for new trial says that they are to be allowed *only* in the interest of justice. Would you mind telling me who in their right mind would argue that it is in the interest of justice to let Alan Lombardo go through the charade of another trial, dragging the victims' families through that nightmare one more time? And for what? Just to reconvict him?"

Judge Nehe didn't wait for an answer. He was on a roll. "And by the way, do you seriously think that some financial impropriety is going to prove that I was working under a conflict at the time of the trial? And even if it did, how would you prove I did anything wrong in the first place?" He took a hit off the cigar, and blew out another stream of poison.

The judge's last little message stunned Zack. It implied something that Zack spent a good deal of his personal life refusing to face—the fact that his father was not an ethical person.

But no matter how much Zack didn't want to face it, this time, he had to. His father's contention that it would be hard to prove that the judge double-dipped was something that could not be ignored. So Zack took a deep breath, exhaled, and then said what he must have known would seal the deal. "Well, I wouldn't do this unless I was sure that a motion for new trial would succeed, but if I had to, I'd call you as a witness at an evidentiary hearing, and ask you about it in open court."

Zack had always referred to his father as Angry Dad, and it looked like Terry was about to get a firsthand demonstration why. "Oh. *You're* going to call *me* as a witness? Are you serious, Zachary? And just what do you think is going to happen—assuming that I can't quash any subpoena you try to use to get me in there in the first place? Do you think I'm going to sell myself down the river and *admit* I took that money from Alan Lombardo?" He was getting good and worked up, now. "Well think again, sonny. Let me give you a little fatherly advice, okay? Do *not* put me on that stand. Not only will I contradict everything you put in your motion for new trial, but I will tear your buddy here a new asshole, and then we'll see who gets disbarred."

The judge was obviously talking about that time a couple of years ago when Terry threw a well-deserved punch at Kenny Lakey, an assistant district attorney who, at the time, was the biggest douche bag in New England.

"You know what?" Terry couldn't take this shit anymore. "If you're talking about that jerk Lakey, I'll take my chances. He was coaching his witnesses to lie. I heard him in the hallway outside the courtroom, clear as a bell. And for your information, he threatened me first."

By now, Angry Dad's hands were shaking, and his face was baboon's-ass red. "I tell you what, boys," he squeezed out of his clenched teeth as he headed for the door. "You think long and hard about what you want to do. Because I swear to God, if you try to ruin me over this, you are going to find out just how powerful a federal judge really is."

SEVENTEEN

My Dear Vera,

Once again, I find myself seeking your forgiveness.
Not, of course, for Mr. Seta. I realize that it is well
outside of your purview to absolve me of any guilt I
might choose to carry as a result of his death.

Indeed, there may be no absolution available to me
from any source after what I did to that man's face.
What a courageous individual he was. It was a
privilege to take such a life.

But back to my apology to you.

I truly regret the timing of my last letter, in which I
identified Mr. Seta as the next one to die at my hand.

I simply did not give you a fair chance, did I? The
code in that letter certainly wasn't unbreakable, but it
was time-consuming enough to make it impossible to
solve between the time you received it and the time
you learned that my good friend Laurence had met
me, and with me, his fate.

So this diary entry will not only tell you who I am
going to cause to suffer, but when I will do it. You will
see, I trust, that I have learned to be more than

generous not only with my hints, but with the time you will need to act upon them.

September 12.

I have resolved to strike again. And again, I find myself consumed with excitement.

Joy's soul lies in the doing.

But before I begin my work, I must confide in you certain secrets, because as you know, I find myself compelled to share information with Detective Demopolous. I would not wish any companion in the world but her.

She, of course, knows me not. But she is keenly aware that I watch her often, from a respectful distance. I cannot help but believe that there are times she focuses on a face in a crowd, and thinks, "That one may smile, and smile, and yet prove a villain."

Her goal is simple. She must catch me, and thus avoid more killing, more death. So noble a calling, but I fear a futile one. I believe it was Shakespeare who said, "For what is pomp, rule, reign, but earth and dust? And live how we can, yet die we must."

Still, I treasure Detective Vera's efforts, her very presence in my humble life. She makes this little world, this precious stone set in the silver heavens, my playground. And I owe her deeply for that.

My friend, I know that I torture, and that I kill. I know that I am weak. But forbear to judge, for we be sinners all.

Dearest Vera, I am returned to you.

If the good people of the postal service deliver this missive in a manner consistent with their previous

efforts, it should reach you well before my next action.
You should have a minimum of twenty-four hours to
take whatever steps you deem appropriate.

I have a great deal of admiration and respect for
you, Dear Vera, but I do not think you will stop me. I
suspect that when I next write to you, it will be to
bring you tidings of my latest endeavors, and to
assure you that the victim did suffer, before dying.

I remain, Eternally Yours.
P.S. *"All trust, a few love."*

(Seta Homicide Evidence ID Number 13)

September 14

Vera slammed the letter down. Okay. Now she was mad.

That was unusual.

She always felt that one of her strengths as a police-woman was her ability to be somewhat emotionally de-tached from the crimes she sought to prevent, or the criminals she sought to apprehend. Of course she hated murder, and of course she hated murderers, but when she was on duty, she was usually able to let the cooler, more professional part of her take care of the police work.

But this was different.

First of all, she was completely grossed out by the dis-gusting and really creepy way this guy wrote to her and about her, as if he had adopted her as his—whatever.

But worse than that was the way he described what he did to Laurence Seta.

Some of the people closest to Vera were elderly men and women. Her grandmother was now well over eighty, and she was probably the best friend Vera had in the world. And for Grandma's boyfriend, Galen, as he put it, "Seventy disap-peared in the rearview mirror a long time ago."

So the idea that some jerk would deliberately target, torture, and murder an old man was just too much for Vera to take without getting emotionally fired up.

She was getting a headache.

Screw this guy. She was going to break this code, and bust this loser once and for all.

According to the letter, they had until tomorrow sometime.

Ellis walked into the conference room with a folder and a legal pad he had been working on for the past three hours. The cream cheese that had somehow found its way onto his shirtsleeve this morning was mercifully gone.

"You okay?" he said.

Vera exhaled deeply. "I just want this to be over," she said.

"You know if this case is getting to you, you should talk to somebody."

"Yeah," she said. "Easy for you to say. You're married."

Ellis smiled. He had kind eyes. "Listen. I'm just saying if it ever gets to be too much, come on over. We'll have a few beers. *Mi casa es su casa.* Key's always under the mat."

"Thanks." He might be a bit of a slob, but there was no denying that Ellis was a good guy. And then Vera noticed the pad he was carrying. She pointed to it. "You getting anywhere?"

Ellis sat down next to her and showed her the pad. "Okay. We had the time to type this thing into the computer, and there aren't any misspellings. But we do have something, I think."

He showed her a list of sentences he'd written on the pad. "Look at these."

1. *Joy's soul lies in the doing.*
2. *I would not wish any companion in the world but her.*

3. *"That one may smile, and smile, and yet prove a villain."*
4. *"For what is pomp, rule, reign, but earth and dust? And live we how we can, yet die we must."*
5. *This little world, this precious stone set in the silver heavens*
6. *But forbear to judge, for we be sinners all.*

"Do they mean anything to you?"

"Nothing. The language of some of them is pretty strange, but this guy sounds like a pompous loser. Maybe it's just the way he writes."

"Not him," Ellis said. "Shakespeare."

Vera looked again at the list. "These are all from Shakespeare?"

Ellis took another sheet of paper from the folder and showed it to her. "They're pretty much word for word from five different plays. The first is from something called *Troilus and Cressida*, which I've never heard of, and I thought I knew a little about this stuff. The second is from *The Tempest,* the only comedy in the group. The third is from *Hamlet,* the fourth from *Henry the Sixth*, the fifth from *Richard the Second*, and the last one is from *Henry the Sixth* again."

Oh great. Shakespeare. Vera's headache grew. She was a decent student, but her strengths were history and geography. The only time she ever came close to liking Shakespeare was during freshman English in college, when they read one of the comedies. The teacher was so into it that he managed to make it fun for the whole class.

But if it was going to take a knowledge of Shakespeare to figure this out, she was going to be in a world of trouble.

Ellis continued. "We looked again at all the other letters he's written, and there wasn't any Shakespeare in any of them. So we figured whatever he's trying to tell us has to be in these quotes."

Vera looked at them again. "And there's no chance these five plays were all about serial killers, right?"

Ellis smiled. "Well, *Hamlet* is about some pretty nasty characters, from what I remember. But I don't think *The Tempest* is. I don't know much about the other ones, though. I wonder if we should get an expert in here."

But something about the way this murdering creep operated made Vera think that an expert in Shakespeare was not what they needed. The last letter didn't need any kind of expert. Just a dictionary, a little time, and some Crazy Pete Thinking.

Crazy Pete was her grandmother's cat, and he never entered or exited a car except through an open window. He slept on a shelf in the linen closet, and refused to drink anything except water with ice cubes in it.

Grandma always said it was just the way Crazy Pete looked at the world. And when presented with an unusual puzzle or mystery, Grandma always suggested Crazy Pete Thinking. The kind of thinking Zack used when he cracked the code in that first letter with all the unused letters.

"What about this P.S.?" Vera asked. " 'All trust, a few love'? What the heck does that mean?"

"That's one thing we have figured out," Ellis said. "It's Shakespeare again, but it's out of order. It's from *All's Well That Ends Well*. The quote, in order, is 'Love all, trust a few.' "

"So where does that leave us?" Vera asked, stumped.

"Now we have seven passages from Shakespeare that we don't know what the heck to do with."

Vera pulled the list of quotes over in front of her again. The themes of the quotations varied, the lengths varied. Their meanings certainly didn't provide a victim's identity.

Something about that P.S. was bothering her, though. "I wonder if the clue in this message is hidden the same way that the clue in the first letter was hidden."

Ellis looked up from some notes he was making. "I don't think so. Like I said, nothing's misspelled in this letter."

"I don't mean misspellings." Vera took the book of quotations and started flipping through it. "You said these lines are pretty much word for word, right?"

"Pretty much. A few of them have a word wrong, though." He paused. "Holy crap. That's it, isn't it?"

By this time, Vera was already looking up the actual quotes in the book. "Okay. The first one, 'Joy's soul lies in the doing.' That's exactly word for word."

"What about the next one: 'I would not wish any companion in the world but her'?"

Vera flipped through the reference book. "Here it is. 'I would not wish any companion in the world but *you*.' *You*, not *her*."

Ellis scribbled YOU on a fresh sheet on the pad.

"The next one's wrong, too," Vera said. "The actual quote is: 'That one may smile, and smile, and yet *be* a villain.' Not '*prove* a villain.'"

Ellis wrote BE on the sheet in front of him.

Vera went on. And 'For what is pomp, rule,' and all that, should be '*Why*, what is pomp.' 'This precious stone' isn't 'set in the silver heavens,' it's 'set in the silver *sea*.'"

Ellis wrote down WHY, then SEA.

"And the last one, 'But forbear to judge, for we be sinners all,' is also wrong. That should be 'for we *are* sinners all.'"

Ellis wrote the last word down, and smiled at Vera. "We're gonna get this Eternally Yours jackass, aren't we?"

Twenty-Two Seconds

HE WAS TEN FEET AWAY FROM THE SHOOTER when Zack got his chance.

He was finally close enough so that he could just shove the chair at the gunman and hit him with enough force so that if the blow didn't topple him, it would at least knock him off balance. And that would be all Zack needed.

By the time the shooter reoriented himself, Zack would be all over him, and this nightmare would end.

But just as he prepared to push the rolling chair toward the shooter, a powerful wave of vertigo swept over Zack. He clung to the chair for another moment, certain that if he let go, he'd immediately collapse, unconscious.

He inhaled deeply to gather himself, and took aim.

And then, before he could let go of the chair, his vision blurred, the world spun, and the floor came up and hit Zack in the shoulder.

Monster

STEPHANIE WAS GETTING DRESSED, BUT SOME-thing was different this morning. Apparently she had more time, and instead of racing around, in and out of the camera's range, she was standing still, in front of her full-length mirror, trying different things on.

So he was getting something of a fashion show, including long looks at her naked, in her underwear, half clothed, putting clothes on, and more importantly, taking clothes off.

The low-cut tank top without a bra was by far his favorite.

He was getting aroused.

That was wrong. It was unquestionably very wrong for him to be a sexual voyeur like this. Watching *her*, of all people.

But he couldn't stop himself.

The delicious perversion of it made the pleasure all the more intense.

But he didn't want to let this aspect of the project overwhelm him. He had great things to accomplish, and distractions like the ones she was providing this morning were nothing compared to the real excitement he would get when he ultimately made direct contact with her.

She finally settled on the most boring outfit that she had

tried on, and when she moved out of the camera's range, he got back to the work he should have done some time ago.

He called up from his computer the digital images of Laurence Seta, the file he had labeled "L." These would make interesting additions to the portrait of Stephanie that he was generating.

He retrieved the file of the young woman standing naked in front of her mirror with the wounds from the first two victims added to the image. Then he cut and pasted the two shots to Mr. Seta's cheeks and the one directly into his forehead and added them to the appropriate parts of Stephanie.

Now she really looked like something out of a horror movie. Standing naked in front of the mirror with several gunshot wounds to her face, as well as her chest, vagina, and buttocks.

And of course there was the missing finger.

That image turned him on even more than the live girl trying on clothes while he secretly watched.

He shut off the computer before he got hopelessly mired in lust.

It was time to do some training.

He moved into the next room, which he had set up to resemble a shooting gallery of sorts.

It was more of a virtual shooting gallery, because as soundproofed as it was in here, there was always a chance that the report of multiple gunshots would penetrate the barriers he'd set up, and all he needed was for the police to come around asking questions. They'd never find the secret entrance to this most private part of his home, but he liked to be in complete control of all official police contacts.

So instead of firing real bullets, he had a laser pistol, with a variety of targets.

But his training was not to sharpen his aim in the traditional sense. That was unnecessary. His live targets were always immobilized, and it was completely within his power to determine from what range he would shoot them.

This training was for dire circumstances.

Given the way he took care of all of the details surrounding each of his attacks, he didn't believe he'd ever be foiled by the unexpected. He was extremely careful about the victims he selected, and he was always sure that whatever prey he had chosen was securely bound before the execution portion of the encounter began.

What he was training for was the unforeseen. Specifically, an approach from behind.

That's where a lesser individual would fail. Sure, he had reason to be cocky—he'd gotten away with whatever he'd wanted for a long, long time. But just because he hadn't been surprised yet didn't mean it couldn't happen.

And he needed to make sure that if it did, he was ready.

The quiet approach of a relative or neighbor who somehow managed to gain access to the house unbeknownst to him. The unplanned arrival of a delivery when his back was to the door.

Anything.

So his goal was to be able to identify, just from sound, the location of a target, and visualize it so well that he could turn and shoot in one motion, with deadly accuracy.

Because this target would not be taped to a table or a chair. It would not be unconscious, or twitching feebly from countless volts of electricity blasted by a Taser.

This target would be fully mobile, and very motivated to run away.

He would have only one shot, maybe two. He needed to be sure that at least one of those two shots would be lethal.

So he went to the end of the room, and he randomly arranged his eight targets on the far wall. They were all about the size of a human head, and were designed to be used with Velcro, so they could be moved easily. When hit by the beam from his laser pistol, they would register the successful shot by making an electronic-bell sound—*ding*.

He had also purchased a special feature, which was what made this system so perfect for him. The targets were designed so that at a predetermined interval of time, a random one would emit a buzzing sound. That target would be the active one, and the only one that would register a successful hit.

Now he set the time interval for thirty seconds, turned the targets on, and walked about fifteen feet away from the target wall. Then he stood with his back to it, and his hands raised above his head, as if surrendering. The laser pistol was in his right hand.

A buzz sounded over his right shoulder. He said, "I was hoping to get a chance to speak to you—" and between the words *chance* and *to*, he turned and fired.

Ding.

Excellent. When he had first started training like this, it was impossible for him to hit on his first couple of tries. But he was getting steadily better. Now he turned around again, away from the targets. Again, he raised his hands, and waited.

This time, the buzz came from over his left shoulder, a little higher, he thought, than the one before.

"I was hoping to get a chance"—*ding*—"to speak to you . . ."

Yes. Another hit.

He turned again, standing with his back to the targets. *Practice makes perfect.* And for the next fifteen minutes, he took thirty shots.

And hit every one.

EIGHTEEN

WHEN ZACK HAD CONSIDERED THE POSSIBLE conflicts of interest he might encounter in representing Alan Lombardo in a motion for new trial, he never imagined that he might face a choice between—on the one hand—protecting his father from getting disbarred, impeached as a judge, and charged with a felony, and—on the other—doing the right thing for his client.

But here he was, sitting in the office with Terry, researching the Canon of Ethics, the Massachusetts criminal code, and case law defining conflicts of interest. Because Zack had to know the stakes. He had to know that if he did blow the whistle on his father, he was truly representing his client's best interests.

Not that he was anywhere near making his decision.

It was all too miserable.

"Here's a fun one," said Terry. "*Commonwealth v. Baldasian.* In this case, the defendant's attorney not only got his fee from the defendant's brother, but he represented both the defendant and the defendant's girlfriend, who were both charged in a shaken-baby case where the only real question in the case was which one of the two of them did it. What a genius."

The specific question Terry was trying to answer was

whether Zack's father's financial scam actually put him into a conflict of interest when it came to Alan Lombardo's trial.

At first glance, it didn't. George Heinrich was already paying Nehemiah Wilson to represent Alan Lombardo. So Heinrich obviously wanted Zack's father to handle Lombardo's trial. The fact that Alan also paid to have the same lawyer handle the trial certainly didn't seem like it created the kind of conflict of interest that entitled defendants to new trials.

Terry put down the book he was reading. "You are aware, of course, of *our* ethical responsibility to report any ethical violation that we discover."

Zack nodded. "Oh yes. I am fully aware that even if my asshole father didn't put us into a dilemma between turning him in or selling out Lombardo, he's put us into the dilemma between turning him in or violating the Canon of Ethics ourselves. Man, does this suck."

A moment passed, and then the phone rang. Terry answered.

"Oh, hi, Vera. I'm good. How are you?"

The big guy leaned back at his desk, and then sat bolt upright. "No fucking way," Terry exclaimed.

That got Zack's full attention, and he came over to sit at one of the chairs in front of Terry's desk. Terry scribbled *new letter——serial killer* on a pad, and now he shoved it in front of Zack.

"Okay," he said, grabbing the pad back. "Sure. He's here. Fire away."

Terry began to write on the page. Zack read it upside down, as Terry wrote. ARE. YOU. Then Terry said into the phone, "*B-e-e*, like honey bee, or *b-e*, like I am going to *be* really pissed off if this asshole doesn't stop sending you letters?" There was a pause, and then he said, "Okay," and wrote *BE*. Next he wrote down WHY, listened again, and then asked, "*S-e-e*, like 'Who do I see about kicking this guy's ass?' " He waited for a moment, then said, "Oh, okay," and wrote SEA.

Then Terry looked at the pad. "Let me read these back to you. Ready? *Are. You. Be. Why. Sea.* Is that it?" There was a pause, and then he said, "What? Okay." He read again from the pad. "*Are. You. Be. Why. Sea.*" Then there was a much longer pause before he said, "Are you kidding? I didn't do anything." Another pause. "You're sure?" A pause, and then, "Okay. And by the way, is it just me, or is it extremely fucked up that a serial killer is writing you letters? I'd still like to do something about that. I don't exactly know what to do, but whatever it is, I'd still like to do it." Terry nodded. "Okay. Well. Good luck, I guess. Talk to you later." And then he hung up, scratched his head, and turned to Zack. "So, that was weird."

"What?"

"Well, first of all, that was Vera."

Zack closed his eyes. "I got that much."

"Right," Terry said. "Anyway, she called because she got another letter from that Eternally Yours freak, and supposedly tomorrow there's going to be another murder unless they can figure out some clues this guy left in a new letter she got. I can't believe this psycho is actually sending her letters. Jesus Christ."

"Yes, I know."

"Yeah, well, somebody's got to do something about that. Anyway, Vera and her partner were stuck, so they figured since we helped them the last time, maybe lightning would strike twice."

"And?"

Terry pushed the pad back to Zack. "And so she read me these words, and I wrote them down, and just to be sure I got them right, I read them back to her. And then, she asked me to read them again, which I did, and then she started laughing and thanking me and telling me how great I was."

"Damn," Zack said. "Wish I'd picked up that phone."

"Shut up. Anyway, whatever I did—"

The phone rang again. Terry almost jumped on top of it to answer. "Hello?"

This time, there was no grabbing for a legal pad, no scribbling notes, in fact, nothing at all from Terry, except a lot of smiling, a few yeses, a sure, an "I can't help myself," and an absolutely. Then he said, "Yes, yes, yes, yes," and, "Are you kidding me? Of course." And then he said good-bye and hung up.

"Well?"

"Well, it looks like I got a date with Detective Demopolous tonight."

Zack smiled, got up, and moved back to his desk to read some more. "About time, Elvis."

Stephanie knocked on her neighbor's front door, but instead of letting her in, the old woman called out from inside: "Come on in, dear. Use your key. My hands are full."

If the reason Mrs. G.'s hands were full was because that lazy son of hers had found another month-long project for his mother to do, Steph was really going to give him a piece of her mind the next time she saw him. Steph found the emergency key her neighbor had given her, inserted it, and walked into a darkened house. No lights were on, and no curtains were open.

Something was wrong. Mrs. G. never kept her home dark. This was not good. But before Steph could even call out, the lights suddenly flashed on, and a chorus of voices shouted, "*Surprise!*"

Stephanie was so stunned that she just stood there in the entryway with her mouth open, and said nothing.

Mrs. Giordano approached from the kitchen, and her hands were indeed full. With a birthday cake, topped with an embarrassing number of flaming candles.

Her father and his odd little Alcoholics Anonymous sponsor, Thomas Prieaux, appeared with big, bright smiles on their faces.

Thomas launched into a chorus of "Happy Birthday," and the other two joined in.

At least it gave Steph another few moments to pull herself together.

During that part of Steph's childhood after her mother died, birthdays became pretty painful affairs. Although there were times when Malcolm forgot or ignored them completely, those missed occasions seemed like blessings compared to the few times he *did* remember, because that's when things always went really sour. Either he was so distracted and overwhelmed by his wife's death that he would get his little daughter a present she already had, or he'd get so drunk that he would cook her a dinner and bake her a cake that were absolutely inedible.

And then he would make both of them feel even worse by extensively and tearfully apologizing.

Now he stood beside her, holding a shopping bag full of wrapped presents, looking like he was nine years old. They finished the song, Thomas ending it with a dramatic flourish, and Steph went over to blow out the candles.

Everyone applauded, and Steph stepped back from the cake. She was having some trouble bringing her father's face into focus, but it was clear enough that he had opened his arms to her for a hug. As she held him, she realized that she was crying a little bit. It was stupid, but, then again, it had been a long time since somebody had bothered to give her a birthday party, and—well, it felt good.

What didn't feel good was the uncomfortably hard thing that was pressing against Steph's ribs through the breast pocket of her father's jacket, but before she could mention anything about it, Thomas said, "Hey, let's not hog the birthday hugs." Suddenly, Stephanie was hugging the little man, and he leaned up and whispered in her ear, "Your father is so proud of you, I think he might just burst."

By now Mrs. Giordano had brought the cake back into the kitchen and called for them to join her at the table there. "I've got coffee and tea made already," she said. "And now, young lady, I believe it's time for you to cut this cake, and maybe open some of your presents."

It was all simply wonderful. Ridiculous, but wonderful.

Her father had gotten her a writing journal, a book about Shakespeare, a gift certificate to an entire day at an award-winning spa, and two tickets to a Red Sox–Yankees game. Thomas handed her a package and said with a ludicrously obvious wink and total disingenuousness, "This has nothing to do with the fact that I'd love for you to come see our show." It was the soundtrack to the original Broadway performance of *A Funny Thing Happened on the Way to the Forum.*

And Mrs. Giordano presented Steph with the most delicate-looking earrings she'd ever seen, explaining that *her* mother had given them to her more than fifty years ago. "She said they would guarantee that I had good luck in love." Then she smiled, "I'm not giving away any secrets when I tell you that with my Joseph, well, they worked very well." Then her smile broadened. "So I wanted to pass along some of that luck to you. Maybe you'll find some time for a boyfriend."

They all laughed. Clearly Mrs. G. had been talking to Malcolm. It was all just too nice.

And then, as if breaking the spell, Steph's cell phone chirped. She took it out of her purse, and checked the caller ID. "Oh no," she said, pressing the off button and returning it to her purse.

"What's the matter?" Malcolm asked.

It was Russell Crane again. In what had to be one of the most perverse examples of—whatever—in the history of the world, ever since Stephanie had told the detestable Mr. Crane that she had intended to go to the premiere of his movie *The Suspect's Daughter*, he had been calling regularly, asking if he could escort her to the red carpet event the studio was throwing in Boston. Unbelievable. And talk about *gross*.

"Nothing," Steph half-lied. "Wrong number again. I'm going to have to get a new phone."

From the look on his face, Malcolm wasn't buying her explanation, but surprisingly, he did not push.

And despite the intrusion, the good mood of the partygoers overcame the negative energy generated by creepy Russell Crane's intrusive phone call.

Until they had left Mrs. Giordano's house, and were standing on the sidewalk next to Thomas Prieaux's car, saying good-bye.

Because that's when Stephanie again felt the large and very hard object pressing into her through her father's jacket pocket as they embraced. She pulled back from the hug, and gently tugged on her father's lapel. "What *is* that?" she asked, smiling. "I don't ever remember you carrying your wallet in your breast pocket."

But before she could get a good look, her father stepped back abruptly, and shifted his eyes away from her. "It's nothing," he said.

If Malcolm had been holding a sign up that said, *I'm lying about something important and dangerous in my jacket pocket*, he wouldn't have been any more obvious.

"Um, excuse me," she said, stopping her father from getting into the tiny car. "Now I absolutely need to know. What is that in your pocket?"

Still, her father would not meet her gaze.

She looked over the roof of the car at Thomas, who stood, frozen, holding open the driver's door. "Thomas, do you know anything about this?"

The best he could do was say, "Stephanie, dear—" but nothing came to him beyond that.

What could they possibly be hiding from her? It couldn't be a bottle of alcohol. There was no way that Thomas would be a party to her father's descent into that misery again. And then it came to her.

"Do not tell me that you bought a gun."

Thomas and her father looked at each other guiltily, and then back at her. Neither spoke. The pair of them were the worst liars in the world.

"Oh my God," she said, quietly. "What is going on here?" She looked at her father. "How could you?"

And then she turned to Thomas. "And how could you let him? Do you have any idea what would happen if anyone found out about this?"

Thomas swallowed, almost audibly, and Malcolm cleared his throat. "I don't disagree," he began, "but circumstances, er . . ."

Steph couldn't remember the last time her father was at a loss for words.

"Did you buy that thing because you're still being followed?" she demanded. "Because that's exactly what you shouldn't do. First of all, you have no idea how to use one"

"Stephanie, dear, I should explain," Thomas interrupted.

And then Malcolm found his voice. "No, Thomas, it should be me. Earlier today, I received a package in the mail. It looked like it might contain books. But when I opened it, all I saw were those little plastic pellets they use to take up the extra space in boxes."

"You know. Packing peanuts," Thomas offered, with a hopeful smile. Steph did not react.

"And so I dug my hand into the box so the peanuts didn't spill all over the floor, and when I touched what was inside, I just pulled it out."

And in a stage whisper, Thomas leaned over the top of the car, and confided, "You were right, Stephanie. It was a gun."

NINETEEN

JUST AS VERA HAD HOPED, TERRY WAS RIGHT on time, and dressed in a sharp, dark gray suit and red tie. He looked terrific.

She and Ellis had been working very hard for weeks, and they had finally gotten a break, figured out the message the serial killer had sent in his letter, and tomorrow, they were going to catch that monster.

So Vera figured that she owed herself a very nice night off. She had put on her best little black dress, heels and everything, and was going out to a fancy restaurant with a person who really made her feel good.

She got in Terry's slick car, and off they went.

Terry took a folded piece of paper off the console between them, and slid it into the breast pocket of his dress shirt. "I just have to swing by Zack's place and drop this off, if that's okay," he told her. "It's one of those things that's really stupid, but really important, and it has been *such* a pain in the ass to get all the signatures we needed. I wanted to show it to him as soon as I could. His house is right on the way."

"No problem." To tell the truth, there wasn't much that could be a problem for Vera this evening. She just felt so good about so many things.

And tomorrow, when they put that creep away, she was going to feel even better.

"So I thought we'd go to a place called The Harvest," Terry said, "which is not only very chichi, but I know the chef, and he loves making special dishes for people with nontraditional diets. I called to make reservations, and when I told him you were diabetic, he almost burst into tears of joy."

"I have to admit that's a reaction I do not usually get," Vera said, smiling, as they turned into a long driveway toward a big old Victorian. Terry's partner, Zack Wilson, was pushing a seven- or eight-year-old on a tire swing hanging from a tree in the front yard.

As soon as he saw them emerge from the car, the little boy jumped out of the tire. Terry bent down, opened his arms wide, and called out across the yard, "J-man, hit me with a hug."

The dark-haired kid flew across the lawn and into Terry's arms. "Hey, Terry! Want to go on my new swing?"

"Not right now, my man. I'm on my way to dinner."

"To Largeburger?"

Terry laughed. "Justin, say hello to my friend, Vera Demopolous. She's coming with me. *Not* to Largeburger. Vera, this is Zack's son, Justin."

Justin held out his hand to shake. "Wow," the little boy said. "You are so *pretty*."

"Hi, Justin," Vera said, smiling. "That's a very nice thing to say, but you know, I don't usually dress up like this. You know what my job is?"

He shook his head.

"I'm a policewoman. Isn't that cool?"

Justin nodded enthusiastically. "You get to wear a police uniform?"

"I used to," Vera said. "Complete with the badge, the hat, the handcuffs, the works. You should have seen me then."

"Wow!" Justin's eyes were wide. "With fancy shoes and stockings, too?"

"And suddenly, everybody's in therapy," Terry interjected, pulling the piece of paper out of his breast pocket. "Changing the subject to something less NC-17, Justin, do you think you could bring this incredibly important legal document over to your father, and tell him how lucky he is that I am his partner?"

"Yes, sir!" exclaimed the little boy as he enthusiastically grabbed the paper and whirled around to run to his father, who had stopped to pick up a couple of sweatshirts on his way to meet them. Unfortunately, Terry hadn't expected Justin to move so fast, and the big man hadn't let go of the paper in time, and it ripped right down the middle.

Poor Justin looked like he had just committed the worst crime imaginable, and it was only a matter of time before he burst into tears. Terry was fast, though, and before anyone could say a thing, he had scooped Justin up into his arms, whispered something into his ear, and replaced both pieces of the torn document into his breast pocket.

Whatever he said had started Justin giggling, and so the little boy was all smiles as he wiped his eyes, slid back down to earth, darted over to his father, and brought him by the hand to say hello.

"You know what?" Terry told Zack. "I stopped by to give you some work, but let's deal with this tomorrow, if that's okay with you. All this talk about handcuffs and hats has suddenly made me very hungry."

Zack looked quizzically at Terry, and then his eyes registered understanding. He smiled, scooped up Justin into his arms, and said simply, "Enjoy your evening."

* * *

"Okay, I know we said we weren't going to talk about work tonight, but I just have to tell you about the letter. Then we can go back to not talking about work, all right?"

It really didn't matter much to Terry what they were talking about, so of course he agreed with Vera. He was having the best dinner of his life.

The woman was everything he imagined she'd be— well, okay, not everything, because they were in a restaurant and there were other people around, so she had clothes on. But what clothes they were. And she was gorgeous, sexy, fun, smart, and, she really seemed to like him. He could easily see this date leading to another, and another, and then, maybe to something without so many people, or so many clothes . . .

On top of that, the dinner was so good he didn't know what to eat first. The salmon was wild, and fresh, and so delicious—

"So. Remember when I called you for help?"

And then again there was Vera. What was he doing eating when he could be looking at her? God almighty. That dress was the luckiest garment in the universe.

"Yes. Something about a list of words, and how brilliant I was."

"Exactly!" Vera exclaimed. "It wasn't the words, it was that you read them to me."

Terry took another bite of salmon. "Do I stop being brilliant if I don't have any idea what you're talking about?"

"Of course not." Vera cut a little piece of her roast chicken. "You couldn't know how brilliant you were. But here. I brought this to show you."

She took a folded-up piece of paper out of her tiny purse, opened it, and spread it out on the table. It was a copy of the letter from the serial killer. Five of the sentences were highlighted, and in each, a single word had been crossed out and another word written above it.

"The highlighted sentences are all quotations from Shakespeare," she told Terry. "But Ellis and I couldn't get any further than that until we remembered the first message from the serial killer."

"The one with the misspellings."

"Right. We thought maybe he had intentionally made mistakes in the quotes as clues, and we were right. When you look carefully, the quotations are just slightly off. By one word each. We wrote the correct word over the mistake."

Terry looked at the words again. "These are the ones I read to you, right? 'You. Be. Why. Sea.' And 'Are.' "

Vera was smiling. "Exactly. And do you see this quotation here, in the postscript?"

" 'All trust, a few love.' "

"Right," Vera said. "That's a jumbled-up Shakespeare quotation. To put it in the right order, all you have to do is take the last word, and put it at the beginning. See? 'Love all, trust a few.' And it turned out, that was the first key to the puzzle."

"Don't tell me. So what you had to do was reorder the five words that had been wrongly left out of the quotations the same way you reordered the scrambled postscript. So the five words, in the new order, would be, let's see. Put the last one first, right?"

Vera pointed at the words. "Right. So the new order is right here." She pointed at the words written at the bottom of the page. ARE. YOU. BE. WHY. SEA.

Terry looked up at her from the paper. He had no idea what the words meant. "So, when exactly do I understand how brilliant I am?"

Vera grinned. "First you have to do something."

"Okay."

"Close your eyes."

Terry did. "When I open them, am I going to get a surprise?"

"Maybe." The grin was still in Vera's voice. "Now listen while I read these words to you. Are. You. Be. Why. Sea."

Terry worked on the puzzle in his mind. *Are you be? Why sea?* He just couldn't get it. The questions were nonsense. He opened his eyes. "I'm stumped."

"That's because you're not *listening.* You're looking at the words in your mind's eye. Close your eyes again. I'm going to read them a little differently this time. And listen. Don't try to see the words in your mind. Just listen."

He closed his eyes again.

"Ready?" And then, almost as if she were reading quickly through a list of words without any meaning, she said, "Are-you-be-why." Then after a brief pause, she said, "Sea."

"Do it again," Terry said.

"Okay, ready?"

Terry cleared his mind. "Ready."

And then Vera said the words again. But this time, Terry heard, "R-U-B-Y. C."

Terry's eyes shot open. "Oh my God. The words aren't words. They're *letters.*"

Vera nodded. "And I never would have gotten that if you hadn't read them to me over the phone like you did. Do you have any idea how fast you talk sometimes? The words didn't make any sense, but as letters, bingo, we got a name. Ruby Cee, of Indian Oaks, Massachusetts. Now do you understand why you were so brilliant?"

Terry was still talking about dessert as they entered Vera's living room. The man really liked his chocolate. But apparently it was also very dangerous to dogs. Who knew?

Vera had kept the date going not because she was reckless, or impetuous, or inclined to sleep with guys on the first date. Although technically, this was their second date. The first one was last year, on her birthday, the night she'd been kidnapped.

But it wasn't the amount of time Vera had spent with Terry that led her to invite him up to her apartment after dinner. And it wasn't how he protected Justin's feelings when the little boy accidentally tore that important document. It wasn't even that every time she was with Terry, he made her smile, and laugh, and just feel good about things. That was all true, but there was more.

Part of it was instinct. An instinct that Vera always trusted, and that rarely let her down. An instinct that told her that Terry Tallach was a good man, and a man that would be excellent to have as a big part of her life.

The conversation had now turned to the perils of flambé desserts. Apparently, next to choking, being set on fire was the most likely cause of injury to restaurant patrons.

And with that statistic delivered, Terry excused himself to use the bathroom.

Vera lit some candles, got out a bottle of wine she had bought on the way home from work, a corkscrew, and a couple of glasses, put them all on the coffee table, and sat down on the couch, leaving plenty of room for Terry to join her.

The other reason Vera had asked Terry to come in was what Grandma called Vera's *now* attitude. Even as a little girl, Vera was aware that life was extremely fragile, and that tomorrow is not guaranteed for anyone. Her diabetes, her police work, her kidnapping, the loss of so many of her fellow cops on 9-11, all had firmly reinforced her conviction that the only thing that was ensured by waiting before taking a chance was that you might never get the chance again.

And as if that wasn't enough, if tomorrow did come for Vera, it was going to be a very risky tomorrow, featuring a wig, old-lady clothes, and a one-on-one confrontation with a monster in the home of Ruby Cee.

Terry emerged from the bathroom, sat down across from Vera, and launched into a conversation about how champagne corks were much more dangerous than people believed.

He sounded nervous.

Men are foolish creatures, Grandma used to say. *Sometimes you can give them a message clear as Gabriel's trumpet, and they still don't get it. That's why God made high heels and underwear.*

Vera stood up. Terry had moved on to the risks of burning candles indoors. If anything, he was getting more nervous.

Tomorrow is not guaranteed for anyone.

Vera reached behind her, unfastened her dress, and let it fall to the floor.

And finally, Terry stopped talking.

Then he got up off his chair, and came to her.

Thanks, Grandma.

TWENTY

"Excuse me, but before we begin, would you mind switching seats with each other?" Inmate Alan Lombardo blinked rapidly as he stood in the doorway of MCI–Bridgewater attorney-client meeting room #1 and made his bizarre request to Zack. "The last time you visited me, you sat on my right, and Attorney Tallach sat on my left. Now you are the one sitting on my left, and I'm going to have a hard time concentrating."

Zack half-expected to hear Terry come back with something like, "Well I'm going to have a hard time representing you if you don't stop talking like an idiot," but instead there was only silence. Zack looked over to his left, and Terry was just sitting there, looking more relaxed than Zack could ever remember seeing him. "Um, do you care where we sit?" he asked.

Terry let out a small laugh. "Absolutely not." He picked up the legal pad and the pen that were on the table in front of him, and switched seats with Zack, as Alan sat down across from them.

Once they were settled, Zack said, "One of the reasons

we came to see you was to talk about why you didn't tell us that you worked for George Heinrich."

Lombardo did not respond immediately. The rate of blinking surged, and he reached up to make a microscopic adjustment to the angle of his glasses. "I, um, I was afraid that if you knew that, you might not want to represent me."

Under normal circumstances, Zack would have expected to have to restrain Terry from leaping across the table and strangling their client for withholding such important information. But today was far from normal. Terry was in the best mood Zack had ever seen, thanks to an exceptionally successful date with Vera last night. He seemed completely comfortable just sitting there, listening to the irrational thoughts of a convicted mass-murderer.

"Of course I wanted to tell you," Lombardo said, the blinking tic still in overdrive, "but I had no idea how you would handle the news that I was part of an organized crime operation."

Zack stole another look at Terry, but all was well. A half smile was on his face—he did not look like he was thinking about organized crime operations. He picked up his pen, clicked it only twice, made some notes, and put it down silently. Alan was visibly relieved.

"Not to be indelicate," Zack replied, "but whether you were an accountant for a mobster probably wouldn't have had a big effect on Terry and me. We took this case knowing that you'd been convicted of nine murders."

Alan peered at Zack through his black-framed lenses. As always, the severe part in the inmate's hair was laser-beam straight, the clothes creased, the facial tic going at full blink ahead. "Yes, but I didn't commit those murders. I *was* involved in organized crime, though. I'm not proud of it, but if you hold that against me, there's nothing I can do about it."

Alan's attitude shouldn't have been a surprise. To guys in prison, whether you admitted your crime or denied it was sometimes the difference between whether you lived or died. The self-righteous retribution inflicted by inmates on each other was serious, and sometimes fatal.

Still, the idea that Alan thought people believed he was innocent merely because he said so was some pretty serious denial.

"Okay, Alan, let's not get hung up on that. The reason I wanted to speak to you is because once we learned that my father was on retainer to represent George Heinrich and anyone who worked for him, I had to find out why you decided to pay an additional fee for his services."

"An additional fee in the amount of two hundred and fifty thousand dollars," Terry chimed in. "That's a lot of chocolate chip ice cream, my man."

Lombardo sat mute.

"You did know that George Heinrich was already paying my father, didn't you?" Zack asked.

Alan made a little face, and looked back and forth from Zack to Terry and then back again to Zack. "I knew," he said. "I just was afraid that he wouldn't . . ." His voice trailed off. "I just thought that if I paid him enough money, especially since I didn't have to, that he'd put in an extra effort when he defended me. I guess I was trying to use the money as an incentive for him to . . . I don't know. Treat my case differently than the others."

"What do you mean?" Terry asked. "What others?"

Alan adjusted his glasses again. "The other cases he did for Mr. Heinrich's people. You know. Like when one of the truck drivers got arrested for drunk driving, or when there was that big fight at the picket line. That kind of thing."

On one level, Zack understood. Alan Lombardo had severe control issues. The man rarely left his home, he had no friends or family, he needed his lawyers to sit in the same seats every time they visited him—in fact, it was pretty obvious that Alan Lombardo's main mission in life was to have complete command of his environment. That way he would never be upset by repeatedly clicking pens, or headache-inducing printer fonts.

But when you're indicted for murder, how do you manipulate and control your environment then? Alan had decided to try by paying a good lawyer an outrageous sum of money, in hopes of influencing him to represent Alan more zealously than the lawyer's other clients.

And it was precisely because people like Alan Lombardo were vulnerable to this kind of thinking that all lawyers, including Zack's father, were sworn to follow the Canon of Ethics, and not, for example, charge their clients outrageous sums of money, or a fee for work they had already been paid to do.

"Okay," Zack said. "Let's talk a little bit about why this might matter in your case."

Lombardo just sat there, staring at him through the blinks, so Zack continued.

"Right now, Terry and I are looking into a few different strategies, but one of them, which is very powerful under Massachusetts law, is called 'conflict of interest.' I'm not sure whether you're familiar . . ."

"We discussed this when we first met," the inmate interrupted. "I'm quite familiar with it. But I don't see how your relationship with my trial lawyer will do me any good in obtaining a new trial."

"No," Terry said, in a startlingly calm voice. "What Zack is talking about is the possibility that Zack's *father* was under a conflict of interest when he represented you. In other words, we are looking into whether he was completely loyal to you, or whether something was keeping him from doing his best at your trial."

Alan's eyelids fluttered. He looked back and forth between the lawyers. "I don't see how that was possible," he said. "And I also don't see why it would matter."

"Well, we aren't sure there's a conflict ourselves," Zack said, "but when we found out that my father took money from you for a job that he had already been paid by Mr. Heinrich to do, we became somewhat concerned that there was a violation of some important ethical rules."

"Somewhat concerned," Terry echoed, dryly.

"And any time there's an ethical violation by an attorney, there's a possibility of a conflict of interest," Zack continued. "If we were to find one, under Massachusetts law, the state has to give you a new trial, no matter what. It doesn't matter if the case against you was strong, or weak, or in between. If you had a lawyer who had divided loyalties, you are entitled to a new trial."

"But what about the theories that I came up with already?" Alan asked. "What about the mistakes in the jury instructions? I should get a new trial because of those errors, too."

Terry looked like he was running out of serenity, so Zack kept on going.

"Any motion for a new trial is going to contain all the claims that we can make," he told Alan. "So if we find evidence to support an argument that there was a conflict of interest, we'll use it. But we'll also use any other mistakes made at the trial, including the ones you were concerned about in the jury instructions."

"But aren't ethical violations the types of things that get lawyers disbarred?" Alan's blinking was now alarmingly rapid.

Terry looked as puzzled as Zack felt. The big guy shrugged, and answered the strange question. "It really depends on the violation," he replied. "But we won't be focusing on that when we're working on your motion. We're just looking for the best argument to make to get you a new trial."

Lombardo stared at Terry for a few moments, then he started shaking his head. "No," he said. "No. I don't want you to do that. That will not work. That will not work at all."

Zack had no idea what the inmate was trying to tell them. "You don't want us to do what? Work on your motion?"

Alan continued to shake his head. "No. I want you to work on the motion. I just don't want you to look for a conflict of interest. That won't work in my case. It won't work at all. No."

Now that Zack knew what Alan meant, he didn't understand how he could mean it. But Terry had already jumped in.

"Wait a minute. You don't want us to look for support for an issue that would *guarantee* that you'd get a new trial?"

"That's just it," Alan said. "Nobody's going to believe there was a conflict of interest, or any other ethical problem. Attorney Wilson was one of the top lawyers when he represented me. And now he's a judge. A federal judge. There's no way in the world any court is going to decide that something he did, twenty years ago, was bad enough to disbar him, and give me a new trial. There's no way in the world that is going to happen."

He had a point—it was certainly possible that no court would have the guts to throw a popular judge under the bus at the same time they were letting the Springfield Shooter get a new trial. Zack leaned forward. "But even if that's true—and I'm not sure it is—I don't see any reason not to try."

"From everything that I know, I only have one chance at this motion," Alan told them. "If we don't win this, I'm going to die in here, for crimes that I didn't commit. And that means that whatever judge is going to decide this motion has to believe that my claims are serious. If he thinks that I'm trying to disbar a federal judge for something that happened in a case twenty years ago, he's going to think I'm insane. I absolutely don't want you to argue that there was a conflict of interest."

Zack took a deep breath. "So what *do* you want us to do?"

"My life is in danger here in prison," Alan said, "and there's nothing anybody can do about it. I know you think waiting for some miracle problem with your father is the silver bullet, but I don't have time to wait for something that I think won't work anyway. I want you to mark the motion up for a hearing as soon as possible. I want this thing over. If it takes too much longer, it won't matter. I'll be dead."

TWENTY-ONE

A LOT OF POLICE WORK, EVEN WORK WHERE lives were at stake, like tracking down a serial killer, was dreary, and time-consuming. Until yesterday, Vera and Ellis were wading through all of the material in the original Springfield Shooter case to see if there was anything they could use to help them in this investigation, and desperately checking to see if there were any connections—any common threads—that linked the lives of Corey Chatham, Iris Dubinski, and Laurence Seta. Thanks to Lieutenant Carasquillo, they had been able to pass on the seemingly endless job of checking into the people who might have known that "Welcome to my world" was Alan Lombardo's special greeting to a host of other officers.

But there were days, like today, which made all of that drudgery worth it.

Because today was the day Vera was going to take this sick murderer down.

If only she didn't have to do it pretending to be a little old lady.

She was sitting alone in the living room of Ruby Cee, wearing a gray wig, fake glasses, and old lady clothes over a bulletproof vest.

The Eternally Yours killer had told Vera that Ruby Cee

was his next victim, and Vera was going to ambush him as he made his attack.

Ellis was on the second floor, in a bedroom down the hall, ready to tear down the stairs at the first sign of trouble.

Both of them were wired so that Lieutenant Carasquillo and three others from the station who had set up surveillance in the house across the street were able to hear everything, and move in at a moment's notice.

Plainclothes officers were stationed in a wide perimeter around the house, both to spot anyone suspicious approaching Ruby Cee's house, and to close in after the suspect had been identified to assist in the arrest.

Cruisers were strategically positioned, all within sixty to ninety seconds away.

And a state police S.W.A.T. team was on standby.

Whenever Vera went into the field on a dangerous operation, the world got clearer. It was almost as if all of her senses sharpened—colors were brighter, sounds were crisper. She loved it, and lived for it. She would have preferred to go without the fake glasses and the wireless earpiece she was wearing, which interfered with both her heightened vision and hearing, but they had to play this one by the book. They didn't want to take any chances and scare this guy off. They had no idea how long he had been watching Ruby, and no idea how familiar he was with her looks, clothes, and patterns of behavior. So Vera needed to be very careful about her appearance, and how she acted, right until the moment they sprang their trap.

And there was no way she was going into this thing without being able to communicate with her support.

"*Test one two. This is Ellis. Do you read, Vera?*"

"Loud and clear, Ellis. Do you have us both, Lieutenant?"

"*I have you both, Vera and Ellis. Let's go over it again,*" said the lieutenant, as Vera went into the kitchen, pushed the wig back from her forehead a little—talk about itchy—and got herself a glass of water.

And for what must have been the fifteenth time that afternoon and evening, Vera and Ellis repeated the procedure they had set up.

The plainclothes officers would alert them all to anyone approaching the house. When the suspect came up to Ruby's door, a sharpshooter stationed with the lieutenant would take aim. The porch light had been left on so the sniper would have a good view.

Meanwhile, Vera would wait in her living room, pretending to watch television. Apparently, Ruby was a huge fan of M*A*S*H reruns.

When the doorbell rang, Vera would go to answer it, checking through the curtained window at the side of the door. She couldn't pull back the curtains, in case he had a good idea of what Ruby looked like. If she saw any weapons, Vera would begin to turn the doorknob back and forth, explain that the lock was sticky, and that she'd have the door open in a second.

That would be the signal for everyone to move. Ellis would come down the rear stairs, out the kitchen door, and around to the front. The lieutenant and his backup would come in from across the street, the cruisers would block off the street, while plainclothes officers would converge on the scene.

Within seconds, the killer would be surrounded. And if he made a single suspicious move with a weapon, the sharpshooter would drop him on the spot.

If there was no weapon visible, Vera would ask, "Who is it?" to the person at the door. She'd repeat whatever answer she received, so the team would be able to hear how the killer was identifying himself, and then she'd begin to open the door.

Depending on when the killer entered the house, the

lieutenant would make the call for the cruisers and plain-clothes officers to approach, and prepare for an assault. And Ellis would monitor everything from upstairs, just out of sight.

Once the killer was inside, the operation was in Vera's hands. She had a gun in the pocket of the dress she was wearing, but it wasn't as easy to get to as they would have liked, so there were plenty of contingency plans. If she wanted assistance but felt that it would be dangerous to call for it overtly, she'd use the code word "grandmother," and Ellis would make his way downstairs, weapon drawn, while the other officers would come right in the front door.

And naturally, if there was an emergency, Vera would just shout for help.

Of course, she hoped it didn't come to that. In fact, she was kind of hoping that this jerk would figure that a little old lady would be an easy mark, and that he'd be sloppy, pull out a roll of duct tape, giving Vera enough time to draw her weapon, and initiate the arrest.

That was her best-case scenario for today.

And speaking of best-case scenarios, last night really worked for her.

Terry was wonderful, the dinner was wonderful, and the time afterward at her apartment was wonderful. He left that night, very, very late, and in his words, very, very happy.

Just like Vera.

And Lieutenant C. had given Vera and Ellis the morning off, knowing that they'd be working late on this bust this evening. Which made everything that much better. A good day's work, after a good night's play.

"Lieutenant, this is Cordero, on Pinewood. A delivery van just turned down Amelia, heading your way."

"Got it, Cordero. Vera, do you copy?"

"I copy, Lieutenant. Ellis?"

"*I'm ready.*"

Vera went into the bathroom, adjusted her wig, and then sat down in the armchair facing the television, and turned it on.

Hawkeye and BJ were arguing with Major Winchester about something, but Vera couldn't concentrate on the details. She was wearing her grim suit. It was time to stop a murderer.

"*I'm confirming a delivery van heading right for the house, Vera,*" the lieutenant said. "*White van, license number Two-X-ray-Tango, Three-Four-Alpha. We're running the plate now. It's pulling in front of the house. Aw, shit. He parked right in our way. You still have a shot, Isaac?*"

The words of the sharpshooter, Isaac Greene, came through Vera's headpiece with amazing depth. Isaac had the lowest voice Vera had ever heard. "*Clean view of Vera's front door, Lieutenant,*" he confirmed. "*Van's no problem.*"

"*He's getting out now,*" the lieutenant said. "*A white male. Looks young—maybe twenty-five. Empty-handed— No, wait. He's opening up the back of the van.*"

Vera desperately wanted to go to the door, but she needed to play this absolutely straight. She was Ruby, and Ruby loved *M*A*S*H*. Ruby probably wouldn't even have known that there was a van parked in front of her house, so there would be no reason to go to the door and watch as the delivery guy headed up the walk. Especially while Colonel Potter was talking to Major Houlihan.

The fact that the killer was holding himself out as a deliveryman was brilliant. That certainly explained why people who didn't know him opened their doors to a stranger. Who would suspect anything out of the ordinary from your friendly FedEx or UPS guy?

"*He's closing the back of the van now,*" the lieutenant reported. "*Heading for the front door. Looks like he's got one*" *of those overnight envelopes in one hand, and something else in his other. Goddammit, I can't see what's in his other hand. Can you make that out, Isaac?"*

Klinger burst into the office wearing a mink stole and big earrings.

"Negative, Lieutenant," boomed Isaac. *"His back is to me, and he's holding his hands in front of him. He's moving around to the other side of the van now. I've lost visual."*

Ellis did not like what he was hearing. *"I'm standing by, Lieutenant,"* he said, from the top of the stairs. It sounded like he was about one and a half seconds from charging down to the first floor and opening fire.

"I'm okay, Ellis," Vera said.

"Roger, Ellis. Hold your position. Suspect is almost to the door, Vera. Still cannot make out what's in the other hand. Stand by, everyone, he's reaching for the bell. Any questions at all about what's in that hand, Vera, I want to hear about that sticky lock."

"Roger that, Lieu," Vera said, quietly.

The doorbell rang, cutting through the sound of a commercial for dishwashing detergent. It was silly—Vera practically knew what side the killer's hair was parted on, and still, when she heard that bell, she almost jumped out of her skin. Probably the adrenaline. Better keep that under control. No need to add to a tense situation by twitching out every time somebody scratched their nose.

Vera was ready for this. She muted the television, just like she believed that Ruby would have done, and she got up from her chair, slowly, and headed for the door. Ruby was seventy-one years old. These things took time.

The bell rang again.

"Coming!" Vera called out, in what she hoped was an old-lady voice. And then she was at the door.

Vera put her hand on the dead bolt thumb turn as she

peered through the curtained window on the right side of the door, finally face-to-face with her adversary.

As the lieutenant had said, he was a young white man, younger than she expected, judging from the unwrinkled, fair skin of his face, the immature mustache, the hints of acne on his cheekbones. In fact, with the baseball cap, the polo shirt, the matching shorts, dark socks, and sneakers, he looked decidedly nonthreatening.

But that was, of course, all to his advantage. Once he got into the house, everything would change.

He had what looked like an overnight envelope in one hand, but the way he was holding it blocked Vera's view of what was in his other hand.

Vera hesitated, hoping to see something more, and then, the guy moved slightly, and for just a moment, she got a look. It was dark, and shaped like a handgun, although Vera had never seen a gun so big. But it might have been a Taser, and she didn't have any more time. She had to make the call now. If she didn't open the door immediately, he'd get suspicious.

"Just a minute," she called out, in her old-lady voice, as she rattled the doorknob back and forth and pulled on the locked door. "This lock sticks. I'll have it open in a minute."

"*That's a go!*" shouted the lieutenant. "*Go, go, go!*"

Vera heard Ellis thundering down the back stairs and going out the kitchen door. She yanked her wig off, reached into the pocket of her dress, withdrew her weapon, pulled open the door, pointed the gun at the kid, and shouted, "Police! Freeze!"

At that very moment, Ellis came tearing around the front of the house, shouting, "Police! Freeze!" and the lieutenant and three other cops were running up the lawn to the door. The sirens of at least two cruisers wailed as they approached.

"Kneel down, and lie on your face!" Vera shouted at the deliveryman as Ellis came up from behind him. As the suspect complied, Ellis grabbed the letter from one of his hands, and Vera grabbed his weapon from the other.

But it wasn't a weapon. You could hold it like a gun, and there was a trigger, but it wasn't a gun, and it wasn't a Taser. It had a keypad on the back, and a display . . .

It was a *scanner*. This kid really was a delivery guy. "He's not the killer," Vera said.

By now, Ellis had the suspect cuffed, and was reading him his rights. The lieutenant was asking her if she was all right, but she couldn't do anything but repeat, "He's not the killer."

And then, suddenly, she knew.

Taking care to hold it by the edges, Vera picked up the overnight envelope from where Ellis had thrown it to the ground. It was addressed to Detective Vera Demopolous, c/o Ruby Cee, 1235 Amelia. He'd known she would be here.

She looked up and down the block, checking to see if this sick bastard was watching their pathetic little scene. But there was no one in sight except an embarrassing number of police, and a few neighbors.

Then Vera turned the envelope over, and found the little mailing sticker she knew would be there. The mailing sticker that read, "Welcome to my world."

Eighteen Seconds

AS ZACK FOUGHT THE DIZZINESS AND STRUG-gled to his hands and knees to get up again, he felt a change in the room, as if something important had happened. It wasn't the sensation that everything was happening in slow motion—that remained constant. He knew that things were progressing as quickly as ever—it just seemed that they were taking forever to unfold.

But whatever transformation had occurred, he was going to have to work through it, because he had to get to that shooter.

And then, as Zack rose, he realized suddenly what had changed.

The gunman had heard him fall and, instead of facing the gallery full of panicked people, had turned to face him, and was now raising his weapon, preparing to shoot Zack again, this time head-on, from ten feet away.

Zack had not planned for this. If he had been closer to the gunman, he would simply have rushed him, assuming that he would be able to at least tackle him, even if he took a fatal bullet in the process. That was not Zack's first choice, of course, but it just might give the people in the courtroom, including his son, enough time to escape.

But Zack was still ten feet away from the shooter, with

a bullet in his leg. And he had no idea if he could close the distance before a gunshot stopped him.

As the muzzle of the pistol rose slowly toward Zack's chest, he turned to look to see if the rolling chair he'd been using to propel himself across the room was still within reach. Maybe he could shove it at the shooter and distract him. Or maybe he could dive behind it and buy himself a second or two.

But as he looked, Zack saw that the chair had rolled several feet to his right. It was now too far away to grab, or to use as cover.

And as if things weren't bad enough, there was a brief lull in the sounds coming from the room, a slight break in the otherwise incessant screaming and crying. And then, a little boy cried out. As clear as a beam of sunlight through a break in a cloudy sky, the child's voice shouted, "Daddy! *Look out!*"

It was Justin.

And instead of shooting Zack, the gunman swung his weapon toward the crowd, aiming right at the little boy wearing the very bright, ever-so-easy-to-target, white T-shirt.

Andre L. Englewood

IT WAS 11:23 A.M. ON SEPTEMBER 15, WHEN Andre Englewood answered the door for the last time in his life.

Andre was frustrated that someone was disturbing him just now, because he had a lot to do before tonight's rehearsal. He was stage manager for the Longmeadow Players' production of *A Funny Thing Happened on the Way to the Forum*. Right after revising the rehearsal schedule, which he was smack in the middle of, he had to run over to the theatre to check on the sets, then he had to drive an hour out to Kathy's house and figure out what they were going to do about the ridiculous costume Gymnasia needed. Then he had to get back here, write a giant memo with all of the notes from the past three rehearsals, print it out, bring it to Kinko's with the new rehearsal schedule, get enough copies made for everybody in the cast and crew, stop and grab something to eat, and then get back to the theatre, all before six-thirty, because the director said she was getting there a half hour before the seven o'clock rehearsal began in order to go over a few things with him.

Because of the recent news about this scary serial killer who was running around all over the place, Andre had been careful lately to make sure that he looked through the peephole in his front door before letting anyone into his house. But he was so distracted today by everything that had to be done on the play that he just pulled open the door, saying, as he did, "I'm so sorry, but I'm *really* busy right now—"

And the next thing he knew, he was bound and gagged, lying facedown in his entryway.

Eighteen terrifying and excruciatingly painful minutes later, he heard a voice say, "Welcome to my world, Mr. Englewood."

And then he was gone.

TWENTY-TWO

My Dearest Vera,

Welcome again to my world. I'm so happy you are going to be reading this while I take care of my next victim.

I am, of course, flattered that you were so kind as to wait in person for me.

But I must say, with what I hope you understand is the gentle chiding of a close friend, that you did not read my last letter to you carefully.

Oh, you figured out the name that I hid in my missive, but I expected no less. You are a woman of uncommon intelligence.

But you failed to recognize why I identified Ms. Cee to you. I only said in my letter that my diary entry would tell you "who I am going to cause to suffer." I did not say, as you assumed, that I would cause this person to suffer physically.

And that is why, instead, while you waited for me at Ms. Cee's house, I killed Ms. Cee's favorite nephew, Andre Englewood.

(Englewood Homicide Evidence ID Number 1)

September 16

Vera looked up from the letter. Yesterday had been so promising. But in a matter of minutes, everything had turned from triumph to despair. They hadn't caught the killer. Far from it. Instead, another innocent person had been murdered.

All the appropriate steps were being followed. Ellis was looking into the delivery service to find out who had hired them to bring her the overnight letter. The body of the latest victim, Ruby Cee's nephew, Andre Englewood, was being autopsied by the medical examiner.

And Vera was sitting at her desk, with her hands positively shaking with adrenaline. Or rage.

I have high hopes for Mr. Englewood, because as you have probably gleaned by now, I go to a great deal of trouble to arrange these little events in order to bring some drama into my life. Happily for me, Mr. Englewood is himself involved in theatre, so I anticipate he will provide me with an excellent show in his final moments here on earth.

Before I leave you with another diary entry to whet your appetite, I feel compelled to inform you that I will not take another victim until next week at the earliest. Our schedules have been considerably hectic of late, and I would like to be sure that we are both fresh when we next work together.

That will also give you a good amount of time to sort through the puzzle this next entry will present to you. It is somewhat different than the prior ones, so be careful! I have seen how much you care about your work, and so I know that you are going to want to be very certain next time that you have everything figured out before you make your next plan to stop me.

Until then, I remain,
Eternally Yours

Then Vera turned to the copy of the diary entry. The original, along with the original of the letter, were at the lab for analysis, which, so far, was yielding them nothing they could use.

September 14. I have come up with a game to play to lead my friend Vera to where she wants to be.

Here are the clues:

I am not the spawn of Satan.

I am not a crook.

I am not a knight in shining armor.

I am not a bi-sexual, going on a bi-annual trip to bi-shop at the bi-rite bargain store for bi-centennial memorabilia.

I am not asking for help.

Would a hint or two be appropriate? At the risk of breaking the rules, I will share the following: do not forget what you have already learned about playing these little games. And also: keep your focus on the fifth in the first three, and then the twelfth, and finally the fourth.

Then, when you realize what I have left out, put before it the number of squares on the board less ten.

Paul had already seen on the monitors from the security cameras at the gate that the visitor was that young attorney, Zack Wilson, but Paul looked through the glass that had been installed in the front door anyway, just to be sure.

And then he checked Wilson for weapons, before letting him into the house. Because, shit. Just because somebody's a lawyer doesn't mean they can't carry a gun.

But all the guy had with him was a legal pad with a list of questions on it, a pen, his wallet, and his keys, so he was good to go.

"Mr. Heinrich set it up so you two could meet in the kitchen alcove," Paul said. It was where the old man spent most of his time when he wasn't in bed.

The boss wasn't having a very good day, but as he had told Paul this morning, he didn't expect there would be that many days left, good or bad. So even when he wasn't feeling that great, he tried to get downstairs for at least part of the day, just to sit by the window, soak up some sun, and look out toward the woods.

Wilson noticed the medical equipment that had been recently moved out of the bedroom and temporarily placed in the entry hall, and the special lift chair that had been installed on the stairs.

"Is Mr. Heinrich sick?" he asked.

Boy. Was this guy in for a surprise. There was no reason to hide it, though. "Yeah. Mr. Heinrich's got cancer. Started in his lungs, but it's spread everywhere. He doesn't have too much longer."

They made their way back to the kitchen. Mr. Heinrich was sitting in his wheelchair, at the end of the table, and turned to face them as they approached. God, it seemed like he looked worse with every passing hour. His face looked almost skeletal, and the skin on his bony hands was like yellow paper. His breathing was shallow, and his eyes were glassy and sunken.

The boss shook hands with the young lawyer, and Wilson sat down next to him. Paul sat on the other side of the lawyer.

"Thank you so much for seeing me today, Mr. Heinrich," Wilson started. "I had no idea you were sick. I'm sorry for the inconvenience."

The boss smiled, and spoke softly. "I have a great deal of

respect for your father. Please tell him I said hello." He moved to take a sip of water, and Paul got up to help him. The old man's arms were full of liver spots, and badly bruised up from the intravenous needles. Dying really sucked.

Wilson waited until Paul got seated again, and then answered. "I will, sir. He sends his regards, as well."

Mr. Heinrich smiled. "What can I do for you, Attorney Wilson? Unfortunately, we will probably have to keep this short. I don't have as much strength as I used to."

The kid nodded. "Of course. Well, as I mentioned on the phone, I've been assigned to represent Alan Lombardo in a motion for a new trial."

The boss looked somber. "Yes. Terrible thing about Alan. He did good work for me."

The attorney picked up his pen and made a note on his pad, and then looked up. "Before I ask any questions, I do need you to understand that since I'm not your attorney, what we are discussing will not be held in confidence. It's just . . . I represent Alan, and, well, given the fact that you were my father's client, I just didn't want there to be any confusion—"

The old man held up his hand. For the first time in days, there was a spark in his eyes. "Attorney Wilson. I know an honest man when I see one. I appreciate what you just said very much. Ask me whatever you want. I have nothing to hide. Please."

The young lawyer made another note on the pad. "Okay. I guess I need to start by asking you if you paid my father to represent Alan Lombardo."

Mr. Heinrich looked like he was in some distress, but he answered anyway. "Yes. Your father was on retainer to represent me, or anyone that did work for me." He winced, shifted a little in his seat, and continued. "I ran several businesses at that time, and I had dozens, sometimes more than a hundred employees. We were always talking to your father about one thing or another."

The kid made another note or two, and then asked, "So what exactly did Alan Lombardo do for you?"

Clearly, Mr. Heinrich was in pain, and he'd had morphine less than an hour ago. Things were really getting bad. He met Paul's eyes, but turned back to the lawyer. "Alan handled the bookkeeping for our companies," he said simply. "He was our accountant. He did our taxes, all that stuff."

The lawyer went on to the next question on his list. "Sometimes, when one person hires an attorney to represent another, the lawyer is put into an ethical bind, if you know what I mean. The lawyer has to put his client first—"

The attorney was interrupted by a small cry that came from the old man. He was shaking his head back and forth, and trying to shift in his chair to a more comfortable position, but nothing was working. The pain must have been awful. "I'm sorry," he interrupted. He sounded like he was on the verge of tears. "But I'm going to have to go upstairs now."

Paul got up to wheel him to the stairs, but the old man stopped him. "Wait, Paul. Just a minute." Mr. Heinrich took a few breaths, and seemed to calm down a little. Maybe the pain had passed, or maybe the boss's toughness just beat it back. "Attorney Wilson, I'm afraid that I'm so sick that I won't be able to speak with you anymore." The old man gestured to Paul. "This is Paul Merrone. He started with me back before I knew your father. Paul knows everything that was going on back then with Alan and the business." At that point, he squeezed his eyes shut, and tried to move again in the chair. Again, a cry of pain slipped out. Then he seemed to relax, and his eyes opened. "You can get in touch with Paul the same way you reached me. He will tell you anything you need to know about Alan and his work." Then the old man closed his eyes again. "I'm sorry, but I must leave now."

TWENTY-THREE

September 17

What a difference a couple of days could make.

Terry had been really looking forward to seeing Vera the day after their first night together, but she had to work well into the evening, and it hadn't been a good day anyway, so they decided it would be best to meet after work the following day.

So here they were, having dinner together, at Vera's favorite place this time—a little family-owned Greek diner with kick-ass spinach pie—but talk about a different vibe. Tonight, the energy and passion flowing from Vera was as strong as it was two nights ago, but this time, instead of a little black dress with heels, she was wearing a gray sweater, black pants, and boots. Tonight, Vera was much less about sex, and much more about intense concentration.

The serial killer had fooled them all, and Vera was taking it very personally.

"We had a real chance," she told Terry. "We figured out the clues, but we got too cocky. We didn't pay close enough attention to the words in his message." Her beautiful blue eyes were like laser beams as they locked onto his. "I'll tell you one thing for sure. That's not going to happen again."

Oh, she was still sexy as hell. She just wasn't trying tonight.

"I brought a copy of the jerk's latest message. He says nothing's going to happen until next week, but this time we're not taking anything for granted."

Terry looked at the message. "Man. Not exactly the most obvious hidden message I've ever seen."

Vera took a sip of her diet soda. "I've got the feeling this one isn't as hard as it looks. It's got an awful lot already in there. I'm just trying to follow the hints."

Terry had another bite of his spanakopita. It was awesome. Then he checked the note again. "So, okay. What have you learned about this guy's sick games so far?"

Vera ate a forkful of salad and then reached into a shoulder bag she was carrying. She withdrew a pad, and put it on the table beside her. "I started making a list," she said. "Number One. Read everything carefully."

"Right," Terry agreed. "Got that one already."

"Number Two. The puzzles have more than one step. In the first puzzle, the first step was figuring out that we needed the full name of the school, and then the next step was to figure out the name of the victim. In the second puzzle, the first step was to unscramble the quotation in the postscript, then we had to rearrange the words from the other quotations, recognize that they were actually letters, not words, and then, take the step we didn't take—realize that we had spelled out the name of the victim's relative, not the victim himself." She shook her head, and her face got flushed. "Damn it. I can't believe we were that close and we didn't get him."

One thing was for sure. When this monster got caught, Vera was going to be front and center. How in the world had Terry ended up being so attracted to a person who did such an incredibly risky job? "Just remember when you get him that you don't have to do it all by yourself," he told her. "I'm all for nailing this clown, but if you get hurt doing it, there is going to be one oversized Scottish Jew wandering around, looking for somebody's ass to kick."

Vera's expression changed from fierce to frisky in a heartbeat. "I didn't know your dad was in town," she said mischievously.

But Terry was serious. "My dad isn't Jewish. And you know exactly what I mean, Ms. I'll-Just-Dress-Up-Like-an-Old-Lady-and-Hope-the-Bad-Guy-Attacks-Me."

Vera was silent for a second—it was like she was taking a quick trip into the failed past. Then she blinked, glanced at Terry, and returned her attention to her pad. "The last thing I wrote was that the puzzles have all been about what was left out. The correct letters in the misspelled words, the full name of the high school—"

"And those words from the Shakespeare quotes," Terry added. He sure hoped the cheesecake was as good as it looked. "So what's left out of this last letter? It doesn't look like there are any misspelled words. Are any of these clues famous quotations?"

Vera still had a ways to go before her salad was done. She didn't seem too hungry. "It doesn't look like it. At least that's what Ellis said before I left today. He's been all over the Internet and so far, nothing. But I keep coming back to that sentence about the focus. What's the fifth in the first three, the twelfth and the fourth?"

Normally, Steph loved going to the movies. And normally, she really enjoyed a good old-fashioned thriller.

Tonight, however, was going to be an exception.

She stood in the line that had formed down the block from the box office in front of the BigView 8 Cinema. It was the opening night for *The Suspect's Daughter*. And it looked like it was going to be a success. The movie was showing on three of the theatre's eight screens. And from the bits of conversation she was picking up from the crowds of people around her in line, it was the movie everyone was here to see.

Steph wasn't surprised. A gigantic Hollywood marketing machine had gotten behind Russell Crane's latest effort with all the power and money you'd expect for a blockbuster, and advertisements promoting the release of *The Suspect's Daughter* were everywhere. The stars of the movie were on the cover of every magazine, and Steph had even seen the actress playing the lead role appear three nights in a row on three different television talk shows. The story about the insanely cute actress's pet monkey was getting pretty old.

But the more Steph heard about the movie, the more she dreaded it. She knew that she was too close to the situation to be objective about it, but everything she'd seen and heard about the plot of the film made her think that Russell Crane was exploiting her father's horrific experience of being wrongly accused as the Springfield Shooter.

Her cell phone rang, startling her. She answered it without checking the caller ID. "Hello."

"Stephanie, how are you? It's Russell. Russell Crane. Have you seen it yet?"

Unbelievable. "No. As a matter of fact I'm in line to see it right now. I thought I made it pretty clear the last time you called that I had no interest in seeing it with you."

The woman in front of Steph turned around with an interested expression on her face. The woman's husband continued to face forward, but it was clear that he was listening, too.

"Ouch," Crane murmured. "Message re-received, loud and clear. I wasn't calling to ask you to go with me. I just got out of the Boston premiere a few minutes ago, and before I head into the after party, I thought I'd call to get your feedback, since you've been going through a lot of what the heroine of this movie—"

"You know what, Mr. Crane?" Steph was trying to whisper, but she was so angry that she was sure the energy in her voice was broadcasting it at least two blocks away. "I'm not going to this movie because I have any intention of giving you my *feedback*." She leaned on the word, hoping to transmit the scorn that was flowing through her body like hot lava. "I'm going so that I can prepare to protect myself and my father if some irresponsible person suddenly begins to imply that the movie is really about my father and me."

Crane exhaled loudly. "C'mon, Stephanie. You know that would never happen."

"Just like my father getting accused of being the Springfield Shooter *never* happened. Good-bye, Mr. Crane." And with that, she shut off the phone, and paid for her ticket.

Steph left the theatre and began walking to her car feeling better than she thought she would. Not great. But better than terrible. The night was clear, and there was a light breeze. She was happy she'd worn her warm sweater, instead of the one that looked good.

First, the movie was really entertaining. The pacing was relentless and the acting was excellent.

Of course, that didn't excuse what Crane did to create his characters.

He didn't need to make the murder suspect a high school teacher. He didn't need to make the daughter of the suspect a nurse.

And he certainly didn't need to set the movie in a

small town in New England, where, several years ago, a terrible murder had shocked the very same community that was dealing with this new crime.

But thankfully, there were real differences between the movie and reality. In the movie, the original crime had never been solved, and the murderer had used a rope to strangle his only victim.

No serial killers, no diaries of serial killers, no profiles of serial killers, no mention of Springfield or the Springfield Shooter.

And finally, about as far from reality as it could get, toward the end of the movie, the daughter of the suspect hid evidence that she was sure had been planted to falsely implicate her father.

Yeah, like Steph would ever do something as foolish as that. When she had heard about the gun from her father and Thomas, she was so adamant that they report the incident that she almost got in the car and drove with them to the police station that very night.

The sound of rapidly approaching footsteps caught Steph's attention, and she turned around. About a half block away, a young, very skinny woman with fancy hair and wearing a ridiculously improbable outfit—a cocktail dress and sneakers—was running toward Steph with a microphone in her hand. A man labored behind her, carrying a camera of some kind.

The woman waved and called out, "Stephanie! Yolanda Bigelow, Maximum Entertainment Media! I was hoping to get your reaction to *The Suspect's Daughter*. It will just take two seconds."

It took exactly two seconds for Steph to process it all, and then she was turned around, and running to her car. Moments later she reached it, got in, quickly locked the doors, started it up, and pulled away, just as Yolanda Bigelow and her cameraman caught up to her.

Steph wasn't sure, but as she looked in the rearview mirror, it seemed like the cameraman was filming her escape from the interview.

Steph wanted to be furious, but the whole thing was so stupid that she found herself laughing. Paparazzi. Who would have thought that Stephanie Hartz would ever have been chased down the street by the press for her reaction to a silly movie?

Sometimes, the world seemed absolutely stark raving mad.

What was interesting, though, was the fact that the press—at least Yolanda Bigelow—knew that Steph was seeing the movie tonight. How in the heck had that happened? The only people Steph had told about her plans for the evening were her father and Mrs. G.

And Russell Crane. Of course. He wasn't just interested in feedback. He was interested in a little extra publicity from, oh, possibly an interview with a real suspect's daughter. That snake. No doubt after he spoke to Stephanie, he tipped off some network honcho, and they'd sent a camera crew out to catch her as she left the theatre.

As Steph reached the parkway, she realized that her phone was still switched off. It would be interesting to find out if Russell Crane had the courtesy to call and let her know that someone was coming to interview her, or whether he just decided to let them ambush her. Steph dug her phone out of her purse, turned it on, and checked for messages.

There was only one, and, predictably, it was not from Russell Crane. According to the display, it was from Thomas. Uh oh. Why would he be calling?

She pressed the play button, and listened as her world fell apart.

Stephanie, dear? This is Thomas. Thomas Prieaux. Meet me at your father's house as soon as you get this message. I will wait for you, but come soon. Whatever you do, don't call the police. Your father has been arrested, and I need to speak to you before you call anyone else.

Before the message was even over, Stephanie was speeding down the parkway toward her father's house, all thoughts of movies and paparazzi and foolish Russell Crane vanished.

Steph blew by a minivan rolling along at five miles per hour below the speed limit.

Questions were racing through her brain. Malcolm arrested? For what? Was he drinking again? Was that why Thomas was calling her about this? Why did he need to meet her at her father's house? Why couldn't he just leave whatever he wanted to tell her on voice mail?

She exited the parkway at Appleton, and gunned the engine as she approached Old Boston Road. Normally it should have taken her about twenty minutes to get to Indian Oaks from the theatre, but the way she was driving today, she'd be there in less than ten.

Whatever you do, don't call the police. Whenever someone said that in the movies, two things were guaranteed. First, the person who received the message wouldn't call the police, and second, something terrible would happen to them.

She took a sharp right onto Meadowbrook, and immediately found herself behind a school bus. A school bus? What the heck was a school bus doing out at this time of night? Could this get any worse?

Why hadn't her father called her? Had he called Thomas with his one phone call from jail? Or was Thomas with him when he was arrested?

The bus made a right turn, and Stephanie almost sobbed with relief as she raced ahead to make the next traffic light before it turned red. He couldn't have been arrested for anything serious, could he?

There was no question in her mind that Malcolm didn't have anything to do with these murders. She knew him. She knew he wasn't some psychotic who enjoyed torturing people.

It must be that he had started drinking again. That's why he'd called his sponsor instead of her. Oh my God. What could he have done while drinking that would have gotten him arrested? Did he drive drunk and kill somebody? Or somebodies?

The possibilities were endless. And catastrophic.

It was like a nightmare. One minute, Steph was laughing about silly reporters chasing after her for an interview, and the next, she was racing to her father's home, desperate to learn the details of his arrest.

Mug shots. Headlines. Front-page pictures. Leif Samuelson and *Public Forum*. Her father was going to be so humiliated.

And how was his heart going to hold up under the stress of all of this? Would he even survive?

Finally, she made the left turn onto Seminole, and pulled behind Thomas's tiny Volkswagen in the driveway. She jumped out of her car and ran to the front door. Thomas opened it before she even reached it. He had obviously been crying, and as soon as he saw Steph, he hugged her, and sobbed out, "I'm so sorry. It's so terrible. I don't know what to say. It's just too awful. First Andre, and now this . . ."

"Who's Andre? What happened?" Steph pulled free of the hug. "Where did they take Malcolm? Why did they arrest him? What's going on?"

The little man swallowed, and took a shaky breath before he answered. "Andre Englewood was our stage manager. He was the nicest person. And yesterday, he was murdered by this killer, whoever he is. Anyway, the police came here today and said that Malcolm did it. They brought him to the police station. They said they would let him make a phone call when they booked him." He took another rasping breath. "They're going to book him for Andre's murder. Oh God. It's awful."

For a minute, the lights seemed to dim, and Steph felt a dizzying wave of nausea. The last time she felt this was in high school when she fainted on the way to the hospital when she had meningitis.

Damn it, she was too mad to faint. Malcolm was not a murderer, and he needed her to help him prove it. She shook off the feeling of lightheadedness, and then, for the first time, she noticed the house.

The living room looked like a tornado had blown through. Furniture was overturned, books and papers were scattered all over the floor. Even the oriental rug was flipped over.

"What happened in here?" she said, walking through the debris and into the small dining room, where silver-ware and flatware littered the floor.

The kitchen too was in chaos. The cabinets had been flung open, and cookie sheets, frying pans, sauce pots, and lids of every size were lying on the floor.

"I think they had a search warrant," Thomas offered, tentatively.

Steph could barely make her way into the pantry. The shelves were swept almost bare, and the food formerly kept there lay in mounds at her feet.

"What kind of people do this?" Her voice was quivering. "I can't even . . ." She couldn't finish her thought.

Thomas just shook his head. "There must have been a hundred police cars that passed me as I drove here. I was coming to pick Malcolm up to go to a meeting, and I got here just as they were bringing him out of the house in handcuffs. They almost didn't let me talk to him."

Tears flooded Steph's eyes, but she fought them back.

She had to stay focused. She had to take care of this. Unfortunately, she had no idea where to start. It was so overwhelming. Her father, arrested for murder. Again.

Afraid that if she didn't start to do something, she'd just stand there, frozen to one spot, she began to pick up some of the food that had been strewn all over the floor. "Did he . . . Was he drunk when they came?"

"No," Thomas replied. "He was upset, of course, but he hadn't been drinking. Believe me, I'd know. In fact, he made sure to give me the oddest message for you. But he was definitely sober."

Steph paused, a can of split pea soup in her left hand, a bag of onions in her right. "What did he say?"

"Well," Thomas said, and prepared himself to deliver the line.

Steph tried to stay calm. She really didn't need the extra drama that the strange little man seemed determined to add to the moment. "We actually passed on the driveway. I had parked on the street, because there were still a couple of police cars here. And just before they put him into the backseat of one of the cars, Malcolm said, 'Tell Stephanie that everything is all right. I didn't do anything wrong. And tell her not to cheat herself out of a real dinner tonight.' "

As if this day wasn't bizarre enough. Now her father was starting to sound like a madman.

"I hope I'm not speaking out of turn here, but it seemed pretty clear to me that he was giving you some kind of message. That's why I said you shouldn't call the police. Do you know what he means? 'Cheat yourself out of a real dinner tonight'?"

"No." Steph put the onions on a shelf in the pantry, and stepped out into the kitchen again. "I have no idea why he would say that."

And then, suddenly, she remembered. A conversation

Malcolm had told her about that he had had with her mother shortly before they'd found out that her mother was sick.

And Steph realized that she was going to have to check something in the refrigerator, and she needed to do it alone.

"Thomas, I hate to ask this of you, but would it be all right if I just . . . Would you mind if I was alone for a little while? I'm a little overwhelmed, I guess, and I want to clean up this mess before I go to the police station and try to see him."

"Oh my God, of course," Thomas replied. "But are you sure you don't want any help? I feel so awful leaving you with all of this—"

"I'm fine," Steph interrupted. "I think I just need to be by myself right now, if that's okay."

"Girlfriend, I have been there myself. Many, many times." He smiled sadly. "I'm so sorry about all of this. I know Malcolm is a good person, and that he didn't have anything to do with anybody's murder." He hugged Steph again. "If you need anything, you have my number, right?"

Steph nodded. "I do. And I'll give you a call as soon as I get in touch with Malcolm."

"You are a dear," he said, and let himself out.

Steph went to the front of the house and watched through a window to see the little man's car drive off. Just before he got into his car, it looked like he was deciding whether to come back into the house. He hesitated and turned around, but when he saw Steph watching him from the window, he smiled and waved. Then he turned back, got into his car, and drove away.

Steph returned to the kitchen, and opened the refrigerator.

Malcolm's strange message had been intended to remind Steph of a funny conversation he had had with her mother after he had returned home from the grocery store one day. While emptying the bags, he proudly revealed that he had bought an already cooked rotisserie chicken. He was very excited about the fact that his clever purchase had saved his wife the time she'd normally spend actually cooking the bird.

To Malcolm's complete surprise, Steph's mother didn't like the idea of rotisserie chickens. She thought that if a family was going to eat a cooked chicken at home, that they should actually cook the chicken at home. And in the ensuing, very silly exchange, Malcolm and Marilyn debated whether eating a rotisserie chicken was "cheating them all" out of a real dinner.

Malcolm had once told Steph that that conversation was the last time he could remember her mother laughing.

Now she opened the refrigerator, fully expecting to find a rotisserie chicken.

She was not disappointed.

On the second shelf, next to a few bags of precut salad, sat a Big Green Grocery lemon-pepper rotisserie chicken. It was still in its original packaging—a paper bag with a plastic window, and flaps at the end that you could refold. From the date on the bag, it looked like Malcolm had just bought it yesterday.

Steph reached into the fridge, and took the chicken out. Then she picked up a plate from the floor and brought it with the bird over to the kitchen table, which, miraculously, was relatively clear of clutter. Was it possible Malcolm had hidden something in the bag with the chicken while the police were searching the house? How could he have managed that? From the extent of the mess they made, there must have been dozens of cops swarming the place.

Steph put the plate on the table and set the bag down in its center. Then she sat down before it, and carefully, she unfolded the end of the bag, opened it up, and lowered her head slowly, to peer inside.

It was ridiculous. Her heart was thudding. She was peering into a bag containing a rotisserie chicken as if there were a chance that something inside was going to jump out at her. But her hands were actually shaking as she used them to pull back the ends of the bag—

Her phone rang, and she was so startled she almost had a heart attack. She jumped up from the chair, and hurried over to her purse, which she'd left on the counter. The caller ID showed a number she didn't recognize. Maybe it was Malcolm, calling from the police station.

"Hello?" she said. "Daddy? Is that you?"

There was a slight hesitation on the other end of the phone, and then there was a gentle male laugh. "Not exactly," a man said, "but I wouldn't object if that's what you wanted to call me. This is Russell Crane, sweetheart."

"Oh my God, of all the times . . ." Her mind was racing in so many different directions, Steph could barely put two words together. "Would you please stop, you . . ." She couldn't even think of what to call the man who had done so much harm to them. Instead, she clicked the phone shut, turned it off, put it back into her purse, and returned to the table. Russell Crane. If there was one person in the world she did not need to be thinking about, it was Russell Crane.

The chicken sat there in the open bag on the plate. And suddenly, this entire business seemed so incredibly silly. Her father had been arrested for murder, and here she was, expecting something useful from a rotisserie chicken bag. Maybe Malcolm really was crazy. Maybe Thomas had gotten the message wrong.

Still, she reached in and grabbed the chicken, and one of her fingers slid into the body cavity of the bird, striking something solid.

That was strange. Grocery store rotisserie chickens were not supposed to have giblets or anything else in the body cavity. Steph pulled the bird out of the bag, and placed it on the plate. Then using one hand, she pried open the rear end of the bird, and with the other, reached her thumb and index finger inside, and touched what felt like a plastic container of some kind.

It was a very small Tupperware container. A mist had formed on the inside of the transparent plastic, making it impossible to see through. So Steph pulled the top off and looked inside.

The next thing she knew, she was screaming, the Tupperware container, its top, and what was inside were all flying through the air.

But when the three separate items landed on the kitchen floor, Steph could only see one.

The severed human finger.

Eleven Seconds

ZACK WAS OUT OF TIME. HE HAD TO REACH the gunman now, or he was going to shoot Justin.

And Zack was still ten feet away, with a bullet in his leg.

The shooter had completed his turn toward Justin, and was bringing the gun down so that it would point directly forward before he fired.

Zack had no chair to shove at him, no gun to shoot at him, no time to run and dive on top of him.

He had to stop thinking about what he didn't have. What did he have?

His jacket, his tie, his shirt.

The gun rose up. The shooter's arm was almost parallel with the floor. In a moment, he would be ready to fire.

Zack's belt. His pants. His shoes.

The shoe he was still stupidly holding in his right hand.

Jesus Christ. Why hadn't he thought of that before?

And as the gunman sighted along his arm before taking the shot that would kill Justin, Zack let his shoe fly.

He couldn't be sure, but he thought that he saw it make contact with the side of the shooter's head just before he heard the roar of a gunshot.

TWENTY-FOUR

September 18

Paul was surprised by how quiet it was when Mr. Heinrich died.

The old man had had a very rough night, and early on during the day of his death he wasn't any better. He'd managed to have a little water with his morphine, but other than that, he was just lying there in bed, looking tiny, breathing pretty shallow.

So the nurses had called Neil, and he'd arrived around eleven. He took a chair beside his father's bed, and just stayed there, mute and miserable. Paul came into the room a couple of times after lunch, once to see if Neil needed anything to eat, and once to sit by the old man while Neil went to the bathroom.

At around two, Paul went in to check on them, and he found Neil standing beside the bed, holding his father's hand. The old man's eyes were open, and for a minute, Paul thought he was gone. But then the glassy eyes blinked, and the cancer-riddled lungs coughed weakly.

Neil leaned down to say something to his father that Paul couldn't hear, and it looked like the old man nodded.

And then, like he was paying attention to something

else, Mr. Heinrich looked away from Neil, straight up at the ceiling, took a breath, let it out, and that was it.

Paul stood there for a minute, quietly paying his respects to the man who had been his boss for so long.

Then, so as not to disturb his new boss, he silently left the two of them alone.

"I have done nothing wrong, and I see no reason to avoid saying so. I am a recovering alcoholic and I am no longer afraid of the truth. I did not kill anyone, despite what you may think."

Vera watched through the two-way mirror as Malcolm Ayers was questioned by the arresting officers. She had a very good eye for liars, and Malcolm Ayers sure didn't seem like a liar to her.

Of course, that didn't explain how he had come into possession of a .22 caliber handgun that ballistics was testing right now for a possible match to the weapon used in the serial killings.

The officers left the room and turned the questioning over to her.

She already knew how she was going to play this.

Malcolm Ayers was very intelligent. If he was the killer, he might be one of those perps who enjoyed talking to cops. Some serial killers got off on it. As long as they knew something the cops wanted to know, they figured they were in control, so they relished dangling the possibility of a confession in front of authorities. They declined representation, and talked at length with cops, just to see how much they could jerk them around.

Vera walked into the room carrying a file folder. It contained a copy of the written statement that Malcolm Ayers had given the officers when he was arrested, and little else of value—a few old police reports—but they sometimes came in handy as props. You never knew what might put a particular suspect under pressure.

As she sat down, she began to introduce herself, but Ayers cut her off. "I remember who you are, Detective," he said brusquely. "You spoke to me after I reported that I thought this killer was stalking me."

"Okay, Mr. Ayers," she said. "I have a copy of your statement here, and I'd just like to go over it with you, if you don't mind."

"Forgive my lack of tact, but I mind everything about this entire business. I did nothing wrong, and I demand to be released immediately."

Vera looked up from the statement to the face of her suspect. She was going to play this out by the book, but she would be absolutely stunned if he was the killer. She was picking up nothing from this man except honest outrage.

"I'm sure you can understand our position, Mr. Ayers," she said. "We got an anonymous tip that a man matching your description was in the area of Francis Street, acting suspiciously, at about the same time the coroner has determined to be the time of Mr. Englewood's death. We then received another tip, from a different source, telling us that you were seen carrying a weapon."

"That gun was anonymously mailed to me. I merely put it in my pocket until I figured out what to do with it."

Vera looked steadily at the man, trying to pick up any signs that he was not being truthful. "Of course you have no way to prove this."

"I threw out the package it came in, if that's what you mean," the suspect replied. "But my AA sponsor, Thomas Prieaux, was there when I opened the package. He saw me take the gun out of the box."

Whoa. A new version of a lie that Vera must have heard a hundred times before.

I have no idea how those drugs got there. I got nothing to do with them.

It wasn't mine, but I picked it up anyway, 'cause I didn't know what else to do.

I don't know what you're talking about. But whatever it is, it ain't mine.

But somehow, when Malcolm Ayers said it, it rang true. She still had to press him, though. "You understand that a guilty person would probably say exactly the same thing."

"Do you honestly think I would be so stupid as to carry around with me a weapon I used to murder someone?"

"I don't know," Vera replied. "But it's hard to understand why someone who suspected that another person planted a gun in his home wouldn't call the police and report it."

"I did call the police."

"You said you were afraid that you were being stalked. You said nothing about receiving a gun in the mail."

"Maybe it would be easier to understand if the last time you'd dealt with the police, they wrongly accused you of murder, and your entire career was destroyed."

Vera nodded. It was a fair point. "Okay. So a gun is mailed to you, and because of your bad experience in the past with the police, you decide you'll tell them you're afraid you're being stalked, and in the meantime, you just drop the weapon in your pocket until you figure out what to do. How does that explain the fact that the murderer used a stun gun on his victims, and we found one in your bedroom closet?"

The officers had not revealed that to Ayers. Vera had wanted to spring it on him, to see his reaction.

It was dramatic. The man was clearly shaken badly. "What? Where? You found a stun gun in my home? That's outrageous. I'm being set up. You must know that. I've never owned such a thing in my life. I wouldn't even know what one looked like. I guarantee you that my fingerprints are not on it. That was a plant. I am being framed, just like the last time. This whole thing is outrageous."

And again, all of Vera's truth bells were ringing. The lab had not come back with the results of fingerprint testing on the Taser, but she'd be willing to bet that it was clean. Still, there were an awful lot of interesting facts that lined up with Malcolm Ayers.

"You know, we considered that someone might be trying to frame you—"

"Well that's terribly comforting," he shot back, sarcastically.

"But we think that this killer is extremely intelligent, and that leaves us with two very interesting possibilities." Vera sifted through the papers in the file folder for effect. "Either you are the victim of a very sophisticated set up, or, you have decided to take advantage of the fact that the original Springfield Shooter chose to try to deflect blame toward you."

Ayers sat back and smirked. "And how, pray tell, might I have taken advantage of that?"

"By assuming that once you were cleared of the original killings, no one would ever suspect that you might actually be a murderer. In fact, there's even a possibility that you were the original Springfield Shooter in the first place."

At that, Ayers's cynical facade cracked a bit. "Are you serious? Are you telling me that you think that Alan Lombardo was wrongly convicted? That *I* did those crimes?"

Vera flipped through the pages of the file folder again. "Well, I don't know about that. But it's a fascinating theory, don't you agree? After all, if you were the Springfield Shooter, wouldn't it have been terrifying if Russell Crane was right? But not if you spun it the way you did. Not if you took advantage of the Russell Crane accusation to turn yourself into a martyr and deflect suspicion *away* from you."

Ayers was looking at her like she was as crazy as she sounded.

"So Crane says you're the Springfield Shooter, and you decide to start killing people near where you live, making it look like someone is trying to frame you. And in your diary, you write as if you are another person, and tell the world that everyone is so stupid for believing that the real Springfield Shooter is Malcolm Ayers."

By this time, Ayers had recovered, somewhat, from the shock of facing new suspicion that he was the original Springfield Shooter. "So I played along with that empty-headed Crane's accusation by pretending to frame the supposedly innocent Professor Ayers."

"Exactly. And when the computer journal was finally discovered, you, a professional novelist, had done such a good job writing the fictional story of the Springfield Shooter that you managed to convince everyone that it wasn't you."

"I see. And then I waited twenty years before starting to kill again?"

"It's happened before," Vera answered. "But now you're a little older, a lot wiser. So you use a Taser to stun your victims, rather than overpowering them with physical force. And you enjoy intellectual games, so now you leave little clues and word puzzles, all consistent with a man who is familiar with writing, and Shakespeare. To up the ante, you mail yourself one of your own guns and you open it up in front of your AA sponsor. You even call the police and tell them you think the killer might be stalking you. Brilliant touch. Who would ever suspect that the person who seems to be framing you is actually you?"

As Vera's speech came to a close, Ayers just sat there, looking at her carefully, breathing evenly. He was obviously coming to some kind of decision. Vera decided to wait him out.

After about fifteen or twenty seconds, he cleared his throat. "Do you know what I think?" he asked. "I think that you don't really believe that I'm responsible for any of these murders. I think that an anonymous tip led you to my house, where you had to conduct a search, and where you found evidence that is somewhat incriminating."

Vera wasn't sure where this was going, but she was happy to let the suspect speak. It was much easier to learn things when other people were talking.

"And I think you have a great deal of evidence, including some of the old evidence from the Springfield Shooter, that just doesn't add up. By the time the investigation was over, all of the evidence in the Springfield Shooter case pointed to Alan Lombardo, so he got convicted. But now, somebody's started murdering again, and just like the Springfield Shooter. So either Alan Lombardo wasn't the Springfield Shooter in the first place, or somebody new is copying him. And now you're trying out a scenario where I'm the bad guy to see if I get overwhelmed, and just admit to it all."

Vera said nothing. What Ayers was saying was pretty close to the truth, but acknowledging it wasn't going to do her any good in the investigation. Until she was able to put this whole thing together, she was going to have to treat Malcolm Ayers like the suspect he was.

Ayers shifted in his seat. "With due regard for your considerable story-telling abilities, Detective, your scenario with me starring as the villain fails to explain how in the world the journal I supposedly wrote ended up in Alan Lombardo's computer. Nor does it explain how a container full of fingers found its way into his freezer twenty years ago. Believe me, before I saw him on the television during the trial, I had never laid eyes on Alan Lombardo in my life."

Ayers straightened and took a deep breath. "Detective Demopolous, I did not plant evidence in Alan Lombardo's house, and I did not shoot anyone. Not twenty years ago, not twenty days ago, not twenty hours ago. And the sooner you realize that is the truth, the sooner you will catch the real killer."

At that moment, Ellis knocked on the door. He brought a file folder over to Vera, who opened it and turned to the ballistics report inside.

But before she could read it, Ayers said, "Officer Yates, thank God. Would you please tell Detective Demopolous that I am innocent."

Ellis responded coldly. "It's Detective Yates, now."

Vera looked up from the folder at Ellis. "You know Professor Ayers?" she asked.

Ellis ignored the question. Instead, he said, "This time, Professor, I've got different news." He turned to Vera. His expression was grim. "I didn't have much to do with the Springfield Shooter case, but at one point during the investigation a couple of guys who were working on it were out sick at the same time, so I ended up getting assigned to tell this loser that we were releasing him."

That was funny. Ellis never mentioned working on the case before. And it was really unlike him to be so obviously hostile.

Then he spoke again, but this time not to her but to Professor Ayers. "It turns out that ballistics tested the gun you had on you earlier today—the .22 caliber handgun—and it had nothing to do with your latest murder."

"My *latest* murder," the old man sputtered. "I don't know what you think—"

"Enough!" shouted Ellis. "I don't want to hear another word out of your sick mouth."

Vera had never seen Ellis like this before. His normally placid features had been replaced by a mask of fury. He looked downright scary.

"The gun we found on you was used last month to kill your first two victims—Corey Chatham and Iris Dubinski."

TWENTY-FIVE

My Dearest Stephanie,

Please accept these flowers not only as a token of my affection, but as a small apology for whatever I might have done to upset you in the past.

I hope you believe me when I tell you that I never intended to hurt you in any way, whether through my writings or with my other work. I don't pretend to have all the answers, but when I am asked for my opinion, I feel honor-bound to give it, even if it might not be popular with the people I care about.

In any event, I remain hopeful that you can see your way to understanding my position, and recognize that my attentions are nothing more and nothing less than those of a smitten admirer, who wishes to spend time with you so that we can get to know each other better.

As you know, I have a home in New England and another in Los Angeles, so meeting with you would not be difficult.

I merely await your sign.

> *With great affection and even greater hope,*
> *Russell Crane*

Terry looked up from the letter at their new client—her name was Stephanie Hartz. Terry could have sworn when she walked into the office, Zack's eyes started to spin around in his head.

Whatever. She wasn't that hot. Maybe if you went for women with shiny brown hair with slightly exotic-looking but obviously intelligent eyes, a trim, tight body, and a really nice mouth . . .

Okay. Come to think of it, Stephanie Hartz was hot. Maybe not Vera-hot, but hot enough.

Zack had overcome his initial shock, and was asking why she looked familiar. He wasn't kidding—there was something about her that reminded Terry of someone or something, but he couldn't place it. Zack, though, was totally checking her out. Oh, he was being slick about it, but his body language was a lot more nightclub than law office. And every time she smiled or laughed or tucked that strand of hair back behind her ear, she was mercilessly jumping up and down on his Sandra Bullock weak spot.

"No, I don't know why I'd look familiar. I'm pretty sure we've never met. I got your names from one of the court officers at the courthouse."

Zack turned to Terry, who said, "I told you they liked me." Then he faced Stephanie Hartz again. "Did you consider taking this letter to the police?"

The woman hesitated, and then shook her head. "No. We, uh, my father contacted the police about something else before this, and that's, well, it's sort of complicated, but that's why I thought I'd come to see you first."

Zack leaned forward. "So, were you hoping to talk to us about dealing with whoever sent this letter?"

Again, Stephanie hesitated. There was something going on here that was starting to smell a little interesting. Or dangerous.

She took a breath, and said, "Before I tell you why I came, I need to ask a question."

Zack was all smiles. "Of course."

"You know how anything that is between a lawyer and his client is secret, right?"

Uh oh. Terry's experience with clients whose first question is about confidentiality usually involved someone who had done something spectacularly stupid. No matter how good they looked in their blouse with little flowers on it.

Zack nodded. "Right."

"Well," Sandra—Stephanie—continued. "I want to tell you something, but I don't know if, I mean, if I'm not your client yet, how do I know that . . ." She just sort of let the question hang there, unfinished.

"No problem," Zack said. "I know what you're asking, and I'm glad you did. It's something not many people know, but it's a good thing to understand, and it should help you out. Even though Terry and I are not your attorneys, and even though this meeting might end without you hiring us as your attorneys, this conversation is covered by the attorney-client privilege, just as if you were a client. So you don't have to worry about telling us something that you need to be kept in confidence. We guarantee that whatever you tell us will be kept secret."

Stephanie took that in, and seemed to make a decision. "Okay. I need to hire you to represent my father, but I think you are going to need to represent me, too."

Zack nodded, like she'd said exactly what he hoped she would. "Well, why don't you just tell us why you think you need a lawyer, or why you think your father needs a lawyer. We can take it from there."

Again, Stephanie hesitated, but then she finally plunged in. "Well, the reason I think my father needs a lawyer is because he's been arrested for murder."

Good thinking. Zack and Stephanie both turned to face him. Had he said that out loud?

"And the reason I think *I* might need a lawyer, is because I think I might, uh, I might know where some evidence against my father is hidden, even though I know it was planted to frame him, because he absolutely is innocent."

Okay. So that smell was interesting, dangerous, *and* irritating.

"What kind of evidence?" Zack asked.

At that, Stephanie looked first at Zack, and then at Terry, then back to Zack. She was stalling. But clearly she knew she needed help. She wouldn't have come to a lawyer's office if she didn't.

"A frozen human finger," she answered bluntly.

Terry closed his eyes. He imagined what the accompanying sound effect would be if this were a movie. High-pitched violins squealing a menacing chord? A scream?

A gong?

Instead, there was only silence.

A very long silence.

Zack rubbed his forehead as if he had suddenly gotten a headache. "I knew I remembered you from somewhere. You're Malcolm Ayers's daughter, aren't you?"

"That's right." Stephanie clearly didn't see what that had to do with anything.

"I saw you that time you were on TV." Zack looked like he was just about to go crazy. Here was a woman he was very attracted to, who really needed his help, and he wasn't going to be able to do a thing for her.

Stephanie blushed slightly. If Zack weren't already lying on a platter with an apple in his mouth and a spring of parsley on his head, the blush would really have finished him off. "I can't believe you saw that. I am so embarrassed," she said, with a shy smile. "Did you ever do something and then immediately wish that time travel existed?"

"I'm a single dad," Zack replied. "So twice, maybe three times per day." Then he took a deep breath. "Your father has been accused of what? These latest killings in Springfield?"

Steph straightened up in her seat, and all signs of flirting disappeared. That was too bad.

"Yes. I mean, at least one. I mean two. They say that when they searched my father's home they found the gun that was used to kill two people. And they also found a Taser. And then there was that finger—"

"I'm going to stop you right there," Terry said. "Because we need to talk about something that, well, I'm pretty sure is going to make us all very unhappy."

Stephanie looked bewildered. Why not? This was the world of criminal law.

"Right now, Terry and I represent Alan Lombardo. Do you know who he is?"

"Sure. The Springfield Shooter. Why does he need a lawyer?"

"Good question," Terry replied. "We were assigned to represent him by the court. He's trying to get out of jail. He's claiming that he's innocent."

"But the police found all that evidence . . . Oh my God. He's saying exactly what I'm saying. That somebody planted that evidence against him?"

"Well, he's never exactly said that." Zack looked like a kid who just learned he wasn't going to the circus. "But now that another person has been accused of a similar crime, under similar circumstances, it's something we really must look into."

"But why is this going to make us all unhappy? Are cases like this something that you don't like to handle?"

"Oh yeah," Terry said. "I was just telling Zack the other day how boring serial killer cases are."

"No," Zack jumped in. From the look on her face, Steph didn't get the joke. "Terry's kidding. The problem isn't that we don't like these kinds of cases. It's that since we already represent Alan Lombardo, and your father's situation is potentially connected, we can't take them both. Because there might be a conflict of interest."

From the look on Steph's face, she had not reviewed the most recent edition of the Massachusetts Canon of Ethics. "Think of it this way," Terry said. "Suppose that we decided to be your lawyers, and then we found out—now I *know* this didn't happen, this is just a hypothetical—but suppose we found out that your father not only was guilty of these recent murders, but he was also the original Springfield Shooter."

Before he could go on, Zack interrupted. Probably because Stephanie looked like she was going to burst into tears.

"Wait a minute," he said. "We know your father didn't kill anyone. Let's say we learned something else. Like Alan Lombardo, in an effort to convince everyone that he wasn't the Springfield Shooter, hired somebody to commit these new murders just like he used to. And then the killer framed your father. If we found that out, we'd need to report it, right? So we could get your father out of trouble. But we couldn't, because we represent Alan Lombardo, and we're not allowed to do things to get our clients into trouble."

"Generally, we're trying to get them *out* of trouble," Terry offered helpfully. But it seemed like Stephanie had decided by now that Zack was the one she was going to focus on. That was understandable. She probably preferred talking to people who weren't tossing around those suppose-your-father-was-the-worst-serial-killer-in-history hypotheticals.

"Can I ask you a quick question?" Zack asked. "I'm wondering why you showed us that letter. Do you think that has anything to do with all of this?"

"I don't know," Stephanie said. "But you remember the people on that television interview?"

Zack nodded. "Yeah. Your father, Leif Samuelson, and that other author. The one who wrote *Diary of a Serial Killer*. I can't remember his name."

"Russell Crane," Steph supplied. "He's the one who's sending me flowers and trying to take me to premieres of his movie, and sending the press to interview me—"

"Wait a minute," Terry interjected. "Are you saying that the same guy who pretty much told the world that your father was the Springfield Shooter is sending you love notes?"

"I guess you could put it that way. He's a real creep, and it is so disgusting that he thinks I'll ever go out with him, I can't help wondering if he has anything to do with this."

"You think he might have killed these people?" Zack looked like he was on full alert.

"I don't have any proof, of course," Stephanie replied. "But he gives me such an evil feeling, and I can't believe that he keeps calling me." She folded up the letter from Crane and put it in her bag. "It's probably nothing."

"We'll talk to the police," Zack said. He knew that unless someone had a hell of a lot more than an evil feeling, the police would never think of Russell Crane as a serious suspect. Especially when they had someone in custody who was in possession of one of the murder weapons. But he couldn't just let Stephanie sit there like that. "Maybe they'll turn something up."

She nodded, and rose. "Well, I'm sorry that this didn't work out."

Zack and Terry stood, too, and they both shook hands with the woman. She was obviously disappointed, and looked a little lost, as well.

"Would you like us to send you a list of lawyers that we recommend when we can't take a case?" Zack asked. He was dying.

Stephanie smiled, but her heart was obviously not in it. "That would be nice."

And just then, the phone rang. Terry picked it up.

It was the prison superintendent, reporting that two hours ago, their client, Alan Lombardo, had just attempted suicide.

TWENTY-SIX

September 19

Vera got herself another cup of coffee, returned to the mountains of notes that were piled on her desk, and got back to work.

Which, right now, consisted mainly of trying to convince herself that they really had caught the Eternally Yours serial killer.

Because Vera had never felt as unsure of a charge as she did about the multiple-murder rap Malcolm Ayers was facing.

Of course, she was only a cop. Her job was simply to supply whatever evidence she found to the district attorney's office, and let them take it from there. But she deeply believed that her investigation was being manipulated so that she was only getting the evidence that the real killer wanted her to get.

If Malcolm Ayers was a serial killer, she was going to need a long vacation, and a new attitude toward her instincts. Because they had never kicked in stronger than during her interrogation of the man. He was being set up. She just knew it.

But Vera couldn't ignore the facts. Ayers had possession of the murder weapon for the first two killings. His fingerprints were all over it, and he had no corroboration that the weapon was mailed to him by someone else. He also had a Taser, he knew Shakespeare, and he had no alibi for any of the murders.

And any holes in the case against Ayers could be explained. Just because they'd gotten lucky and found him with one of the murder weapons, didn't mean that he didn't have the others hidden somewhere. Many serial killers had secret "lairs" where they stashed weapons, victims, and "trophies" of victims, like the fingers this sicko had taken.

True, the lab had confirmed that Ayers's computer printer was not the one used to generate the notes that the killer left. But that might mean only that he went to an Internet café or some office-supply store to print out his twisted correspondence.

It was a little more disturbing that Ayers's computer showed no sign of any file that remotely resembled the correspondence or diary entries the killer had sent. It was a pretty good bet that this loser took a lot of pride in his manipulative games. Surely he would keep a record of the way he made the cops run around, chasing their tails.

But if Ayers wasn't the Eternally Yours killer, how did that evidence get into Ayers's house? If it was planted, was it possible that the evidence against Alan Lombardo was planted, too? And if Lombardo was innocent, was the Eternally Yours killer the same person as the Springfield Shooter?

Vera had no reason to doubt that Alan Lombardo was guilty, but the case against him had been initiated in exactly the same way as the case against Ayers. An anonymous tip, leading to a search warrant, leading to a house full of evidence, which the owner denied knowing about. Of course, if the Springfield Shooter was the same person as the Eternally Yours killer, it would explain the "Welcome to my world" notes, and the similarities in location, M.O., and weapons used by the murderer. But there was certainly no available explanation for why a serial killer would take a twenty-year break between attacks, and then alter his pattern by starting to use a Taser.

Still, the connections between the Springfield Shooter and the Eternally Yours killer were troubling. For one thing, Vera had never discovered an explanation for how the Eternally Yours killer knew about "Welcome to my world."

One of the first things she did in the Corey Chatham murder investigation was look into the possibility that the new killer was a copycat. But when Vera learned that "Welcome to my world" was not publicly known as the Springfield Shooter's trademark phrase, she compiled a list of people who knew about it.

She was part of the way through the list when the case exploded with the next murder, the letter, the diary entries, and the clues, and so Lieutenant Carasquillo had some of the others in the squad help go through the people connected to the Springfield Shooter investigation.

Vera dug down into the pile of reports and notes stacked at the far right corner of her desk, and found the list.

The other officers had followed Vera's method: contact the potential suspect, establish an alibi, and make note of it to the right of the suspect's name. Then initial and date the entry, and move to the next potential suspect.

Vera scanned the column of alibis. Many of the people on the list had died, or had retired and moved out of the area, or even the state.

She turned to the second page, and continued to check the list. Many had new jobs. One had been arrested, and was now in jail himself.

All had alibis.

She flipped to the last page of the list. Another deceased person, a new resident of Florida, and then, a unique entry in the alibi column.

Because it wasn't an alibi. It was, instead, a note which merely read, *Currently working on this investigation.*

Vera looked to the left side of the page, and then read the name of the only person on the list of people who had worked on the original Springfield Shooter case—the only person who knew that the Springfield Shooter used the phrase "Welcome to my world" in his communications—that had not been checked for an alibi in connection with the murder of Corey Chatham.

The name was Ellis Yates.

As they entered the room where Alan Lombardo was waiting for them, Zack wondered how they were going to play this. In over ten years of criminal defense, he had never had a client attempt suicide.

Zack and Terry took seats across the table from the inmate, and Terry said, "Alan, what the hell were you doing trying to kill yourself? That hearing you wanted us to get is scheduled in less than a week."

Guess they were going to play it blunt.

Lombardo had never looked worse. Their client sat slumped in his chair, eyes bloodshot, expression slack. His facial tic was still there, but it seemed to be far less frequent, and far less severe. In fact, Alan seemed extremely subdued.

Not exactly a surprise, since less than a day ago he'd been depressed enough to try to off himself.

"Did you know that George Heinrich died?" he said. "George Heinrich was a very good man."

The prison staff had informed Zack and Terry that

aside from being watched round-the-clock to ensure that he didn't make another suicide attempt, Alan was on some pretty heavy medication, which might make it hard for him to concentrate.

"We're here to talk about *you*, Alan," Terry said. "Not George Heinrich. I'm not sure you understand, but there have been some pretty significant developments in your case."

Alan's trademark twitching increased slightly. "Developments? What developments?"

Zack slid a copy of a newspaper article across the table to the inmate. "There's been an arrest in the recent Eternally Yours murder investigation."

Alan glanced down at the newspaper, tapped his right leg three times, and then leaned forward to read it. When he was done, he looked up. "I'm sorry. They've been giving me this new drug . . . What does this have to do with my case?"

"Well, we can't go into too many details," Terry said, "but we know at least one person in the police department believes that this guy, Ayers, might be getting set up." Zack wasn't sure that Alan was getting all of this, but he had a right to know. "And we have some other information, which, unfortunately, we have to keep confidential, which makes us believe that you might have been set up, too."

"Why do you have to keep it confidential?"

Sometimes, the rules of ethics were a real pain in the butt. "We can't answer that, either," Zack said. "But I can tell you that it wouldn't surprise me if people on the police force began to believe that you might be in here for crimes you didn't commit."

Lombardo shook his head slowly, back and forth. "If all you came here for was to tell me not to kill myself, you shouldn't have bothered. Psych services is already doing that about three times a day. I know you are both very good lawyers, but I don't believe anything is ever going to change. When inmates bring up legal technicalities, the courts just say the evidence was too strong against them, and that's that."

Alan was right, to a point. "But if we can show that there's evidence that you were set up—"

"I'm sorry," the little man interrupted, with a flurry of blinking. "I can't afford to get my hopes up. I've got to get used to the fact that this is it for me. It's just—well, I think you might not know how hard it is to be the kind of person I am and to be in prison."

Prison was one of the places where you gave up almost all power over everything in your life. For a control freak like Alan Lombardo, one could only imagine what a hell his life had become. "It must be really hard," Zack said.

"Not just hard. Dangerous. It's not like I have any friends in here, you know. How do you think somebody like me managed to survive in here for twenty years with all of my— " He was interrupted by a wave of blinking which washed over him for several seconds. "—Peculiarities?"

Terry said, "You know, I'd wondered about that, but I decided not to ask."

Zack turned to Alan, and said merely, "I don't know."

"From the first minute I was in prison, George Heinrich put out the word that if anyone bothered me, they were bothering him," Alan explained. "It was as simple as that. A week after I was convicted, this guy named Rickets jumped me coming back from the law library. By the time the guards pulled him off of me, he'd cut my arm pretty good." Alan pulled up his sleeve to reveal an ugly, crooked scar on his forearm. "I needed to go to health services for stitches, and before they had released me—it must have been less than two hours—Rickets was brought in. He'd been beaten real bad. Whoever did it broke his nose and his jaw. I never saw him again."

It was easy to forget how violent prison was. Especially when you were dealing with a quiet little mouse like Alan Lombardo.

"I never met a man who was so loyal to the people who worked for him as George Heinrich," the inmate continued. "But now that he's gone, I don't know if my protection is going to hold up. You have no idea what it's like, walking to chow, not knowing if today is the day somebody's going to stab you in the kidneys with a shank. A few mornings ago, I just flipped out."

The medication Alan had taken appeared to be wearing off a bit. The blinking was a little more rapid, and the pace of his conversation had picked up.

"I couldn't stand it anymore," he said. "So I tried to kill myself." There was a pause, and then he said, "I'm really tired, so I think I'm going to go rest now."

And with that, the man known as the Springfield Shooter stood and asked the guard to take him back to the health services unit.

Watching him go, Zack shook his head. No matter how bad things got, he couldn't imagine ever committing suicide.

Eight Seconds

THE TIME HAD COME FOR ZACK TO COMMIT suicide.

From the way the madman had shrieked out the oath that still reverberated in the terrified courtroom, it was clear that Zack had managed to really infuriate him by hitting him in the face with his shoe. That was hard to imagine, since the crazy man was already enraged enough to blindly shoot bullets into a crowd of innocent people. But it didn't matter. The psycho still had enough time to aim and shoot at Justin again before Zack reached him.

So Zack was going to have to make sure that instead, the gunman aimed and shot at him.

In the blink of an eye, Zack instinctively shouted what he knew would be the best way to communicate with the gunman.

Zack's long experience representing criminal defendants had given him invaluable skills in establishing effective working relationships with violent people. He knew that such people were very sensitive to the way others thought of them. Long ago he'd realized that the key to establishing an effective dialogue was to reinforce the notion that despite any class or educational differences that might exist between Zack and the inmate, the bottom line

was that the client and the attorney were both human be-
ings, and both deserved respect. From the way that Zack
treated all of the people he represented, they knew that he
took what they had to say seriously, whether he agreed
with it or not.

But right now, Zack wasn't interested in establishing
an effective dialogue with this madman. He was interested
only in drawing his fire away from Justin. And so, he
shouted the five words that he knew would achieve his
goal: "Hey, you little psycho bitch!"

Because his goal was simple—to get the man's attention.

And he did.

Neil Heinrich

AT 7:55 P.M. ON SEPTEMBER 19, NEIL HEINRICH answered the door for the last time in his life.

It was only the day after his father's death, but Neil was already putting extra hours in at work, burying himself in contract change orders, requisitions, distribution of payments to subcontractors, whatever he could find to occupy his thoughts.

Because thinking about anything was better than dwelling on the dark emptiness that had taken up residence in his soul from the moment his father slipped away. The feelings that raced through Neil's heart were just too much to bear—pain, loneliness, panic.

So when he heard the knock on the front door, his concentration was so deep that it never occurred to him that it was quite unusual for anyone to come to the offices of a construction company at eight o'clock in the evening.

But that all changed when he pulled open the door, and in complete surprise, entirely ignorant of what he was about to suffer, he looked at his visitor and said, "Ellis? Is that really you?"

The struggle was brief, and ended with an extended and considerably vicious blast from a Taser. And if there had been anyone beside the two men in the building, they would have heard the ensuing silence broken only by the words, "Welcome to my world."

Monster

EVEN THOUGH THERE WAS COMFORT AND security in doing things according to an established plan, there was an undeniable thrill in occasionally going off-script.

And this latest kill certainly qualified.

But as the excitement of the murder ebbed, important details pressed in on him for attention.

Most importantly, since the discovery of the body would have to be delayed, he was going to have to move the corpse. And that would require some work.

But hey. This was a construction company office. There were plenty of saws around.

He'd make do.

And if this little change in plans required him to go underground for a short while, well, frankly, it would be worth it.

Vera would understand.

TWENTY-SEVEN

September 20

VERA DIDN'T UNDERSTAND.

She didn't understand why the officer responsible for checking alibis had decided that just because Ellis was working on the case he shouldn't be treated like any other person on the list.

Vera poured herself a cup of coffee from the pot in the station house kitchen area and returned to her desk to wait for Ellis.

Jeez. It wasn't like Ellis was the only cop they were checking for alibis—the list was full of police officers. Most of the people who knew the importance of the phrase "Welcome to my world" were cops.

Another thing Vera didn't understand was why Ellis was late this morning. It was already close to nine-thirty, and he was always in before nine. The state police lab had no idea where he was. They were looking for him, too.

Rather than sit there and try to pretend that there wasn't a tiny seedling of doubt starting to sprout in her gut, Vera called Maurice, up in personnel. And less than five minutes later, he faxed down a summary of Ellis's data sheet to Vera.

And then, against all of her instincts, that seedling began to take root.

Because Vera remembered very well that Ellis had told her that his Internet use drove his wife crazy, but his personnel sheet indicated that he had been divorced five years ago.

And come to think of it, wasn't it a little curious he'd never mentioned that he'd attended Colton College on a part-time basis in the mid 1980s, which just happened to be the same time period Malcolm Ayers was teaching there?

And while none of that proved anything at all, the seedling of doubt was now in full flower.

Vera needed to talk to Ellis, and soon. It was already ten o'clock.

She pulled out her cell phone and called his home number, only to reach the answering machine. She hesitated to go to Lieutenant Carasquillo, but she was starting to get concerned.

And just then, the lieutenant came out of his office holding a piece of paper. "Sorry, Vera," he said, holding up a phone message. "This came in last night from Ellis and I forgot to give it to you. I guess he had some personal thing—said he'd be in late, or he might have to take the whole day off. He said he'd give us a call as soon as he knew."

And then his phone rang, and the lieutenant went back into his office.

Well, that explained why Ellis was suddenly MIA.

But something else about Ellis's personnel sheet had caught Vera's eye, and was nagging at her memory. It was as if there was something important there, but hiding in plain sight. She looked at the page of information again.

Name: Ellis Yates. Date of birth: April 11, 1964. Marital status: Divorced. Address: 43 Laughton Terrace.

Wait a minute.

Vera stood up, taking the information sheet with her into the conference room, where she had laid out all of the information on the Eternally Yours murders and the Springfield Shooter case. She looked down at the big map they had spread out and marked with the sites of all of the attacks, and sure enough. Laughton Terrace.

Ellis lived on the same street as the seventh victim of the Springfield Shooter, Carrie Bernstein, at the time of Bernstein's murder.

Chalk up another thing Vera didn't understand—why in the world Ellis wouldn't mention that he just happened to live so close to one of the original victims.

Still, it was impossible to imagine the big, friendly man intentionally doing harm to anyone.

But instincts never trumped facts. And the facts were that Ellis was familiar with firearms and Tasers. And as a cop, he would have easy access to victims' houses—all he had to do was flash his shield, and he'd be allowed in with no questions. Even locked doors might not pose much of an obstacle for the son of a man who owned a hardware store.

And then there was Ellis's mysterious comment about his non-existent wife.

Vera couldn't wait any more. She grabbed her purse and headed for the door.

Luckily, there was a driveway which led to a parking spot behind Ellis's house at 43 Laughton Terrace, so Vera pulled in off the street, trying to keep out of the view of any neighbors who might be home. Ellis's car was not in the driveway.

She took out her cell phone, and called Ellis again. She heard the phone ringing inside the house, and then the answering machine picked up. She closed her cell phone and returned it to her purse. He wasn't home.

The day was unusually dark—thick, smoky-gray

clouds hung low in the sky. The breeze promised rain soon. Grandma called it "look-out weather."

It was a single-story house—a ranch—with a three-step concrete stoop leading to a back door into what looked like a small kitchen.

A few feet away, there was a bulkhead leading down to the basement.

Although the house must have been at least fifty years old, the hardware on the door and the bulkhead looked new.

And both were securely locked.

There were hedges separating the driveway from the front yard and a little flagstone pathway along that side of the house. Vera walked to the front door, and tried that. No luck.

She approached the two basement windows flanking the bulkhead, to see if she could open either. Both were securely locked.

There were several reasons Vera did not want to break into the house. In her heart she still believed that her partner was completely innocent of anything, and she certainly didn't want to invade the home and privacy of a fellow officer.

But even if she had thought that Ellis was a serial killer, to justify breaking into a home without a warrant, a police officer has to have a reasonable belief that there is an imminent threat, and that such action would address the threat.

And the penalty for an illegal search was for the courts to forbid the prosecution from using any evidence found in the search, as well as any evidence found as a result of the search. Not exactly incentive for cops to willy-nilly bust into houses where they had only a hunch or a fear that something illegal might be going on.

But hadn't Ellis given her an open invitation back

when they first started working together? *Stop by any time.* Mi casa es su casa. *Key's under the mat.*

A gust of wind kicked up a little dust. Vera shut her eyes against the grit which stung her cheeks, and spun around to put her back to the wind. When she opened her eyes, she was facing the little garage.

She could check out what was in there. Why not?

As she approached the tiny structure, it was clear that although it had been built around the same time as the house, it had not been maintained with the same amount of diligence. Paint was peeling over most of it, much of the wood looked rotten, and the roof was missing several shingles.

She peered through a cracked window in the main door, and all she could establish was that Ellis wasn't using the garage for his car. There was too much clutter.

She walked back around the side, and found the door that faced the house.

It was ajar.

Vera put her hand on the old, rusty doorknob, and pushed.

The small, dirty windows in the main door admitted little light into the tiny space, and Vera felt along the wall for a light switch.

She got nothing but a handful of spiderwebs. Gross.

As a kid, Vera had hated spiders, spiderwebs, cobwebs, anything sticky or creepy that was associated with the dark. But as a cop, she had learned that in addition to sending shivers up her spine, cobwebs generally meant that no one had been in the area for a while.

So, while one part of her shuddered, the other part was relieved.

Ellis had not been coming in here regularly with the corpses of his victims and performing God knows what macabre ritual with them.

She peered into the darkness toward the wall on the

other side of the door, but there was no light switch there, either.

Then, as her eyes adjusted to the darkness, she saw a bulb hanging from a beam. A string tied to a short chain dangled from the screw-in fixture, and Vera walked over and pulled it.

Nothing happened. The garage was as dark as ever.

Another creepy but encouraging sign. No one would regularly use a garage if you couldn't see what you were doing.

Still, Vera's instincts led her to return to her car for a flashlight. She didn't expect to find anything nefarious lurking in the corners of the old garage, but part of being a cop was being thorough. Until she could talk to Ellis, she had to assume the worst, even if she didn't believe it.

She got out the oversized flashlight she kept in the trunk of her car, switched it on, and started back toward the garage.

But as she swung around to head away from the house, the flashlight's beam shone briefly onto one of the small basement windows next to the bulkhead. Vera turned back. Maybe she could use it to see into Ellis's house . . .

To have a chance at spotting anything, Vera had to squat down, hold the light right up to the window, and bring her face close to the glass.

At first, the beam hit a bare concrete floor, but then Vera noticed just to the left of the illuminated area a card table with a chair in front of it. She redirected the light onto the table, and gasped.

Open on the table was a high school yearbook, which seemed odd, but innocent enough. But the volume next to it was far more sinister. Vera made herself blink, and look again, just to be sure.

The title of the book, printed in large, bold red letters, was *Famous Quotations from Shakespeare*.

TWENTY-EIGHT

KEY'S UNDER THE MAT.

She was going in.

Vera ran around to the front of the house, lifted the welcome mat, found the key, and put it in the lock. But before she turned it, she rang the doorbell, just to be sure no one was home.

Five seconds passed. Then another five. There was no sound from inside the house.

She turned the key, unlocked the door, and went in.

Almost against her will, little snippets from conversations with Ellis started to march through her brain.

Serial killers love to jerk people around. They get off knowing that they're smarter than everybody else. They especially like it when cops run around in circles chasing them. He's probably right under our noses.

Vera resisted the tug of logic pulling her away from the feeling that Ellis was a trustworthy man. She would just look through his house, assure herself that there was nothing to worry about, and then get back to the station. Ellis was probably there already, waiting for her, working on the latest message from the killer.

She reached for the light switch beside the door.

An overhead fixture came to life—one of its two bulbs shining plenty of light throughout the small room.

It was very cluttered, remarkable only for its almost stereotypical resemblance to any other living room you might expect to find in a single man's home. A remote control, a pizza box, two beer cans, and magazines and newspapers stacked on the coffee table in front of the small, overused couch, which faced the centerpiece of the room—a large television sitting on a metal stand against the far wall.

The walls were bare, except for an old, signed poster of the Boston Celtics, which hung in a cheap frame above the television. Three chairs and a floor lamp were the only other furniture in the room.

There were no bloody fingerprints smeared on the door frames, no hacked-off limbs of murder victims piled in a corner, no biographies of famous serial killers.

Vera began to relax. What she had seen through the basement window was probably perfectly innocent.

She made her way through the living room into the kitchen, which was also small, but tidier than she'd expected. Sure, there were a few dirty dishes in the sink, but the food in the refrigerator was edible.

The freezer held no container of severed fingers.

A dark, narrow hallway led to the other end of the house. Vera flipped on the light, and headed down the hall, and into the first room on the right.

It was a tiny bathroom. A shower/tub, a toilet, a sink, and a medicine cabinet. It could have used a little cleaning, but Vera had four brothers, and was well aware of the minimal hygiene human males seemed to need. In a contest for most disgusting man she'd ever known, Ellis wouldn't even make the semifinals.

The room at the end of the hall was Ellis's bedroom. He slept in a full-size bed, kept his clothes in a closet and a single, modest dresser, except for the pile of laundry heaped in the corner, under a Boston Red Sox poster. On top of the dresser sat three pictures. Ellis's parents and siblings, she decided.

But it was the photo on the bedside table that drew her attention. It was a wedding portrait of a relatively trim Ellis in a tuxedo, holding hands with a very pretty young woman in a veil and satiny wedding gown. It looked like it had been taken in a field somewhere.

I'm usually more of an Internet research guy. Drives my wife crazy. I spend way too much time on-line.

Why would a man who had been divorced for years say something like that? And why would he keep his wedding photo as the only picture by his bed?

Not easy questions to answer, but that didn't mean that Ellis was a sociopath. It was much more likely that he was someone who just couldn't accept the fact that he was no longer married. It wasn't a sign of terrific mental health, but it wasn't a crime, either.

Vera left the room and walked through the last door off the hallway. It was a spare bedroom, furnished only with a daybed and an inexpensive desk and chair. A computer that must have been four or five years old sat amidst messy piles of papers and books. It was connected by a phone line to a jack in the wall.

Vera sat down in the chair and faced the monitor. Here was where Ellis must spend all that time on the Internet.

She wanted to turn the machine on and sift through the files on Ellis's hard drive, but somehow, that seemed more invasive than anything she had done so far. "The key's under the mat" was something much less than "The password to all of my secured computer files is 'psycho.' "

The shelves contained only some software manuals and computer disks. There was no printer at all.

Her relief was short-lived, though, when she realized that there was nothing left to do but to go down to the basement, where she had seen the Shakespeare quotation book sitting next to the yearbook.

Vera was going to feel a whole lot better when she was able to talk to Ellis and assure herself that there was nothing to worry about.

She left the spare bedroom, returned back down the hallway, and went into the kitchen. The first doorway in it led to a broom closet; the second led to the cellar.

There was a light switch at the top of the stairs, and Vera flipped it to the on position, brightly illuminating the way down. Unlike the garage, here there was no sign of spiders or cobwebs. That made it physically more comfortable for Vera, but it meant that Ellis probably spent a good deal of time coming and going from the basement. Yet another in the growing list of things that weren't crimes but still made her unhappy. She would have preferred to find a dark place that no one would ever voluntarily visit.

What she really wanted to find was a nicely bound book with a bow on it, entitled *Ellis's Unshakeable Alibis*.

The basement was unfinished, but dry and cool. The gray floor was spotless, and the exposed cinder block walls were unpainted. There was a dark green, oval area rug on the floor under the chair Vera had glimpsed through the window. And the table she had seen wasn't actually a card table—it was one of those metal folding tables. The high school yearbook and the Shakespeare book were at the end closest to her.

On the part of the table that wasn't visible from the window sat a second computer. This one was not attached to a phone jack. But right next to it was a printer.

A Printex 343.

Vera took a deep breath. It couldn't be him. It really couldn't be him.

The Shakespeare book was extensively dog-eared. To avoid contaminating the evidence with her own fingerprints, Vera took a pen from her jacket pocket and slid it into the book to open it at the marked pages. Several contained the quotations used in the killer's note to her.

They were circled, and above the appropriate word in the quotation, Ellis had written the word that was substituted for it in the note.

The yearbook was from Capo High School, Class of 1982. A piece of paper had been used as a bookmark, and using the pen again, Vera opened to that page. The picture of Carrie Bernstein, victim number seven of the Springfield Shooter, had been circled, and across her face had been written R. I. P.

And on the bookmark itself, she saw a list of names with their middle initials circled:

Corey S. Chatham
Iris A. Dubinski
Laurence L. Seta
Andre L. Englewood

The victims of the Eternally Yours killer.

Then she looked again at the middle initials, and saw that they spelled out S-A-L-L.

And without warning, everything suddenly made sense.

Vera felt ill. For the past several weeks, she had been literally side by side with the most notorious killer Springfield had ever faced. Who was in the process of constructing an elaborate frame-up of Malcolm Ayers by planting evidence, and even by selecting victims whose middle initials would spell out *Sally*, the title character in Ayers's claim to fame.

Vera was willing to bet a lot of money that Ellis's next

victim would have a middle name that started with the letter *y*.

Unless she could stop him.

She pulled out her cell phone to call the lieutenant, but there was no signal. Probably because she was in a basement.

She turned to go back up the stairs, when she heard a *click*, and then an electric hum. She whirled back toward the computer. But the noise seemed to be coming from beneath it.

Vera used her flashlight to illuminate the floor under the far end of the table.

Where there was a small refrigerator.

Oh no. The idea that Ellis could have been keeping trophies from his kills right beside him as he composed and printed out the twisted messages that he sent to Vera was almost too much to bear.

She knelt, and keeping the flashlight in her left hand, she used the pen in her right hand to pry open the door.

Mercifully, the only thing inside was a six pack of Miller Lite beer.

She released her breath in a loud hiss. She hadn't even realized she'd been holding it. She closed the refrigerator, but just before standing up, she noticed a file box sitting on the far side of the refrigerator.

Again, taking care not to leave her own fingerprints on the box or its contents, she dragged it out from under the table, and looked through its contents.

And that's when the nightmare became complete.

Because what was inside were file folders containing information about the victims not only of the Eternally Yours killer, but also of the Springfield Shooter. And the documents weren't just copies from the police files. There was an entire folder of photographs of the Eternally Yours killer's victims, taken during the recent attacks. While they were still alive.

Most of them showing heartbreaking expressions of pain or terror.

Vera started for the stairs so she could call the lieutenant, but then she froze.

Because the sound of the front door opening came down to the basement as clearly as if she were standing right next to it.

And then the door closed.

Ellis was home.

TWENTY-NINE

STEPHANIE WAS SITTING IN HER KITCHEN, talking with Mrs. Giordano on the phone.

While she stared at the paper bag in which she had hidden the Tupperware container with the finger.

"I'm very worried about David," the old woman said. "He just doesn't seem to be himself these days."

There was a considerable amount of irony in the situation, but Stephanie couldn't bring herself to confront her neighbor with it.

If there was anyone who deserved to be worried about in the relationship between Mrs. G. and her son, it was Mrs. Giordano. The woman was living all by herself in the house in which she'd raised David and two other kids. She was more than eighty years old, half blind and mostly deaf, and probably kinder and gentler than anyone Stephanie knew in the world.

And worried didn't even begin to cover what Stephanie was feeling. She opened her freezer, and removed a box of frozen yogurt pops. She emptied it except for a couple of the desserts, then she reached into the paper bag, and removed the plastic container. She put it into the now mostly empty dessert box, and slid it into the very back of the freezer, behind several packages of frozen microwave dinners.

"He seems so distracted lately," Mrs. Giordano was saying. "I was talking to him on the phone the other day about one of his nephews—my grandson Troy. He's applying to college, and is interested in Amherst, but before I could even get two words out, David starts in about this serial killer nonsense. It's almost like he's obsessed with it."

Stephanie hadn't yet told Mrs. G. about her father Malcolm's arrest. She wanted desperately to keep this little part of her life—her friendship with her sweet little old lady neighbor—insulated from all of the ugliness that seemed to be closing in on her these past weeks.

Just then, Steph's call-waiting signal sounded. "Mrs. G., I've got another call. Can we talk later?"

"Of course, dear. I bet it's that lawyer you were talking about. I believe there's a hint of romance in the air."

Although she'd not gone into details, Steph had mentioned Terry Tallach and the very good-looking Zack Wilson to Mrs. G. Now she blushed and mumbled something like "Don't be silly," but the old woman was sharp as a razor. If there was one person in the world Steph wanted to hear from, other than her father, of course, it would be Zack Wilson, saying that the conflict of interest had evaporated, he'd gotten her father out of jail, and he was just calling to see if she was free for dinner. "I'll talk to you soon, Mrs. G.," she said hastily.

And then she clicked over to the other line.

"Stephanie?"

The male voice was obviously disguised—possibly through an electronic device of some kind. It echoed frighteningly, and Steph's throat tightened.

"Who is this?"

"Never mind who this is," the distorted voice snapped back. "Don't try to be cute with the finger. Take it out of the freezer where you hid it, and put it back where you found it."

Steph felt paralyzed with fear. This couldn't be her life. This couldn't be happening to her.

Quickly, she spun around the kitchen, looking toward the windows. But she had pulled the blinds before she had taken the container with the finger out of her purse.

This was impossible.

There was no way that this person knew she had just hidden the finger in her freezer. Whoever he was, he couldn't possibly even know that she had the finger. The only person who knew was her father, and he was in jail. He had to be bluffing.

She did her best to do the same. "I don't know what you're talking about."

"I'm talking about the human finger that you just shoved into the back of your freezer in a frozen yogurt box, Stephanie," the voice said.

Steph spun around again, but seeing nothing different, she opened the freezer, grabbed the Tupperware container, and ran.

Seconds later, she was driving out of town.

Terry was supposed to be reading a new case that had come down from the Supreme Judicial Court on conflicts of interest. But instead, he was gazing out the window, wondering why Vera hadn't called him back. He'd been trying to reach her for hours.

Zack was across the room at his desk. He was supposed to be reading the same case, but even though his eyes were pointed at the computer screen, he was clearly thinking about something else. He glanced up from the monitor at Terry, and said, "How's that reading going?"

Outside, the infinite road construction project had

moved on to the narrow-lanes-bounded-by-concrete-barriers-everywhere phase. Traffic was a horror show. At least the doomsday machine had moved on to destroy other parts of Northampton. "Great." Terry looked over his shoulder at Zack. "How about you?"

Zack sat back and put his feet up on his desk. "I'm having a hard time concentrating, because I'm having a hard time understanding why a man like George Heinrich would go so far out of his way to make sure that a serial killer has an easy time of it in prison."

"Maybe he really thought Alan was the wrong guy."

Zack nodded. "I was thinking that myself. Although that means Heinrich had an awful lot of faith in his accountant. Basically, it was Alan's word against a freezer full of fingers and a computer loaded with incriminating evidence."

"Sounds like Stephanie What's-Her-Name talking about her father. He gets caught with a murder weapon, a Taser, and a severed finger, and she's more convinced than ever that dear old Dad's innocent."

"Man, wouldn't all of that be nice to put into Alan's motion for new trial." Zack had laced his fingers behind his head, and was now staring pensively at the ceiling. "Talk about whether justice was served. He gets convicted of nine murders based on evidence found at his house, which he denies knowing anything about. Twenty years later, a murderer with the same M.O. shows up, and the police grab a suspect based on evidence found at his house which he denies having anything to do with."

"Like the frozen finger little Stephanie Sunshine is probably carrying around right now in her pocketbook." Terry stole a quick look at Zack. "And by the way, she is *so* into you, you hot law-dog."

Zack closed his eyes and sighed. "How do you manage to bring everything down to sex?"

"It is my gift."

Just then, the phone rang.

"That's probably your booty call right now," Terry said. Zack shot him a look, and Terry shrugged. "I gotta be me."

Zack picked up the receiver. "Hello? Zack Wilson."

But it wasn't a booty call, Terry realized. Zack was frowning. Something was wrong.

"Excuse me? I'm sorry, but we don't represent Ms. Hartz. She needs to go to the police. It's way too danger-ous for her to try to do this on her own."

There was a pause. Whatever Zack was hearing, he didn't like it.

"Can you get in touch with her? . . . Well, try to tell her that she needs to tell the police about the phone call."

Okay, this was driving Terry nuts. He scribbled *Who is it???* on a pad and shoved it in front of Zack, who promptly ignored it.

"Doesn't matter if she thinks it's Russell Crane. She needs to go to the police." Zack rubbed his eyes and sighed. "If she tells you where she went, call me, and I'll go to her, okay? Please tell her that if you speak to her."

Oh no. Sandra Bullock was in trouble, and Zack was getting sucked into doing something stupid.

"Okay. Thank you for calling. Good-bye." And Zack hung up the phone.

Terry looked over at Zack and did his best Keanu Reeves. "Don't tell me. There's a bomb on the bus."

"What?"

"Never mind. What's happened?"

Zack was already shrugging on his jacket. Why he even bothered was a mystery. Faded jeans with a jacket were still faded jeans. "Stephanie got a threatening phone call, panicked, and ran."

Terry stood up. If they were going to the police, he

was going, too. He wanted to see Vera, anyway. "Um, I know Stephanie is cute and all, but seeing as how she isn't our client, what does that have to do with us?"

"Because the threatening phone call was from the serial killer."

Vera slowly withdrew her weapon from its holster and approached the bottom of the cellar stairs.

After she had heard the front door open and close, she listened for other sounds, but heard nothing.

She wasn't familiar with the creaks and groans that Ellis's house usually made, but she still would have expected to have heard footsteps above her as Ellis walked around.

Instead, there was only the humming of the refrigerator behind her and the sound of her own breathing. And the thundering of her heart, of course.

She had left the door from the kitchen to the cellar open and the light on. But Ellis had entered through the front. It was possible that he hadn't noticed there was an intruder in his home yet.

Of course there was no way he could have overlooked her car parked in front of the garage behind the house.

But if he had pulled into the driveway, then why did he enter through the front door?

She hesitated. She was still out of sight if Ellis was standing in the kitchen, looking through the open cellar door down the stairs. To mount the staircase, she would have to walk another three feet forward, and then make a sharp right U-turn to begin up the steps.

Her right index finger was already wrapped around the trigger, ready to fire. She put her left hand around the grip and the fingers of her right hand, to steady it. Then she took a deep breath, and spun around the base of the stairs, pointing the gun up at the top.

There was no one there.

Quickly she returned to her previous position and, keeping her right hand on the gun, used her left to untie her boots. She couldn't remember if the stairs creaked when she came down, but she couldn't stay down here forever. It was only a matter of time before Ellis noticed she was here. She had to get up those stairs fast, as soundlessly as she could, and try to take him down.

Now standing in her socks, she whipped around the base of the stairs, gun aimed at the open doorway at the top. But again, there was no Ellis in sight.

Moving as quietly as she could, and as quickly as she dared, she mounted the steps, gun pointed directly up the staircase. And still, Ellis did not show.

When she reached the top of the stairs, Vera hesitated again. Ellis was here somewhere. If by some miracle, he had parked on the street and hadn't spotted her car, she had the advantage. She knew he was in here, and he had no idea she was.

But what was more likely was that he'd seen her car, and was going through the house one room at a time, checking for where she might be hiding. He just hadn't reached the kitchen yet, so he didn't know she'd been in the cellar when he'd entered the house.

When it was time for her to come through the door into the kitchen, she was going to spin around to her left, toward the passageway from the kitchen into the rest of the house. If she was lucky, Ellis was still at the other end of the dwelling, near the bedrooms. If she wasn't so lucky, he'd be waiting for her, and it would simply be a matter of who shot who first.

She took a deep, silent breath through her mouth, let

it out, and moved through the door, turning left into the kitchen.

Still no Ellis.

But now, at last, she heard something. A scratching noise. And then the rasp of paper tearing.

It was coming from her left, through the passageway between the kitchen and the living room.

For whatever reason, it seemed that Vera had gotten lucky. Ellis had obviously parked in front, come in through the front door, was now in his living room, with no idea that she was in the house.

She didn't hesitate. Whatever Ellis was doing, it wasn't standing there with a gun trained on the entrance to the kitchen. This might be her only chance, and she took it.

With a single stride she stepped past the end of the wall dividing the kitchen from the living room, spun around with her gun leading the way, and shouted, "Ellis! Freeze!"

THIRTY

IT WASN'T ELLIS.

It was the same damn delivery boy who had brought the letter to Vera when she was at the Ruby Cee house. He was seated on the couch, filling in a form that was attached to the outside of another overnight letter.

"Police! On the ground, hands behind your head!" Vera shouted, pointing her gun at the kid.

She didn't know where Ellis was, she didn't know why the delivery company hadn't informed them that they'd received another job from Ellis the killer, she didn't know much of anything, except that she was very, very angry.

"How did you get in here?" she demanded, as she knelt and handcuffed the acne-scarred boy facedown on the living room floor.

He offered no resistance, but he was breathing so rapidly it was hard for him to answer. He turned so that his cheek was on Ellis's well-worn carpet, probably in an effort to see her. "The door was open," he gasped. "My boss told me the door would be open, or the key would be under the mat."

Vera had already pulled out her phone, and was calling for backup. In minutes, this place would be swarming with cops.

Next, she pulled out a pair of latex gloves from her pocket, and put them on. Then, she took the envelope the kid had brought to the house off the coffee table, tore it open, and taking care to touch only the edges, she began to read.

Dearest Vera,

I had hoped to reveal myself to you under different circumstances . . .

Goddammit.

She dropped the letter back onto the table. "Didn't Lieutenant Carasquillo tell your boss to inform us the next time you got a job from this guy?"

"I'm sorry," he gulped. "I didn't know. I didn't mean to do anything wrong. Am I going to jail?"

Then, he started to sob.

Under normal circumstances, Vera would have assured the kid that everything was going to be fine, and that he would very likely be released minutes after her backup arrived.

But Vera's faith in what she believed to be good and true had been so badly shaken that she wasn't ready to assume anything.

So instead, she got to her feet, disgusted with herself. And with just about everything else. She had been completely taken in by Ellis, and wasn't ready to risk being taken in by this kid. She hated coincidences, and didn't trust them for a minute.

And for the same kid to show up twice at a potential crime scene, each time with a note from a killer, was one hell of a coincidence.

Thankfully, the sound of sirens came to her from the

distance. Vera really wasn't in the right frame of mind to interview this boy.

What she wanted to do was get her hands on Ellis and stop him before the next tragedy. And she had one more letter to work with. Sooner or later, Ellis was going to make a mistake. When he did, it would be his last as a free man.

She read as the wail of the sirens grew louder.

Dearest Vera,

I had hoped to reveal myself to you under different circumstances, but, as the saying goes, "When life gives you lemons . . ."

Life, as you so well know, is often unfair, so I do not carry undue guilt over my latest crime, even if it was unplanned. I would have enjoyed presenting you with a puzzle before taking action, but certain contingencies arose which required my immediate attention.

At the appropriate time, I will reveal the location of Mr. Heinrich's body to you. Until then, I will be returning to my previous schedule of events.

And that means that we shall be working again together very soon—in fact, as an apology for removing Mr. Heinrich from the scene without so much as the slightest warning to you, I would like to present you with yet another diary entry. As you recall, the last one I gave you identified where I next intend to work. This diary entry is intended to help you identify when.

> *September 16. Some would claim that comparing oneself to great figures in history even with humility—is inherently arrogant.*
> *I disagree.*
> *And so I call out the names of men who, either*

*directly or indirectly, helped bring about death
and suffering on an inspiring scale: Osama bin
Laden, upon his most brilliant and deadly attack;
Kennedy, at his death in Dallas; Roosevelt, at his
famed "day of infamy" speech; Washington, at his
birth; and Columbus, upon his arrival on the
shores of Hispaniola. I ask only that my meager
accomplishments be seen in light of these pivotal
moments in history.*

*I am proud of my work, but not excessively so. I
realize that it pales in comparison to the
stupendous achievements of these legendary
figures.*

*My request is only that it be witnessed as one
man's effort to attain greatness, even if it be only
fleeting.*

Dearest Vera, I am returned to you.

*I understand that our relationship has moved in a
new direction, but I am still anxious to continue
working with you.*

*I hope the feeling is mutual. And as a sign of good
faith, here are a few hints: this puzzle may take you
down at first, and you might be tempted to try to
escape from it, but you'd be better off trying to score
two points.*

*The format you should use is X-XX-XXXX.
And 2011961973142.*

> *Until our next meeting,
> I remain,
> EY*

Oh no. EY. Shorthand for Eternally Yours.
Or Ellis Yates.

It was all so horrible.

Just then, Lieutenant C. and about a dozen other officers and detectives showed up. Vera debriefed the lieutenant, while a pair of officers brought the delivery boy back to the station house and the rest turned Ellis's house upside down for more evidence. And as soon as Lieutenant Carasquillo confirmed what Vera had found, he went public with the news that Detective Ellis Yates was a prime suspect in the recent killings. Within minutes, Ellis's photo and description would be appearing on television screens, fax machines, and computer monitors all over New England.

Vera offered to take the latest message from Ellis back to the station, make a copy, and then bring it to the lab, just in case there was anything else to be learned from it.

Not that they needed to know much more.

Terry was overjoyed that he was getting to spend some more time with Vera.

But Jesus Christ. Who *wasn't* a serial killer?

First it was Malcolm Ayers. Then Russell Crane. And now it was Vera's partner.

Of course the good news was that it was pretty clear that Ellis had set up Malcolm Ayers. The cops weren't going to release Ayers until they were absolutely sure that they weren't going to step on their johnsons by letting him go, but from what they found at Ellis's house, there really wasn't a lot of doubt about it.

So they got Malcolm to call Stephanie on her cell phone, and then Zack got on the line, and then Vera, and they all explained that her father was expected to be released based on new information. They all agreed that Steph would come in with whatever it was that she had, to help them piece the rest of the puzzle together. They assured her that regular patrols would pass in front of her house until any threat was eliminated.

What wasn't such good news was that for too damn long, Vera had been working side by side with one of the most dangerous criminals in America.

After the conference call with Stephanie, Vera sat at a large table with Zack and Terry, and started going over the latest two messages with them. Now that Ellis's true colors had been exposed, Vera was looking for any help she could get solving the puzzles that he had left her. She believed that they were going to identify where and when the next attack was to occur.

Vera's normally shining eyes were pretty dark. She was really upset about her shithead partner. The last time Terry had felt like Vera looked, he'd almost slugged Zack's father, the federal judge. Not the best long-term career move.

"I'm pretty good with history," Zack said. "Want to try to work on this one?" He picked up a copy of the diary entry that referred to Columbus and Washington. "Whoa. What the hell is this number supposed to mean?" He showed Terry the endless string of digits at the end of the message.

"Don't look at me," he replied. "I'm happy to report that I don't think like a sociopath. Vera, remember that list of things you wrote down that you'd learned from all the old puzzles? Any help there?"

Vera nodded. "I'm betting it's about the things he left out again." God, she was pretty even when she was pissed. Probably something to mention at another time. "I wonder if we're supposed to be trying to find the numbers that he left out." She looked away from the paper into the distance. "I cannot believe Ellis was behind all of this." She shook her head. The betrayal she felt was so strong it was like there was a fourth person in the room.

"Maybe we're supposed to pay attention to the years that these things happened. He left those out. Like, 1492 for Columbus."

"And 1941 for Roosevelt's speech, and 1963 for Kennedy's assassination," Zack added.

"Bin Laden's attack was in 2001," Vera added, "but I have no idea when Washington was born."

Terry pulled out his new Web phone, and in less than a minute, read off the screen, "George Washington. Born 1732, died 1799. So now what?"

"If he made this puzzle the way he made the others, we have to figure out what he left out, right?"

Terry watched as Vera wrote the historical dates in a long string of numbers, one after the other: *2 0 0 1 1 9 6 3 1 9 4 1 1 7 3 2 1 4 9 2*. And then, directly underneath, she wrote the other numbers—the ones that were included in the diary entry: *2 0 1 1 9 6 1 9 7 3 1 4 2.*

Then she crossed out the 2 in the lower string of numbers, and the 2 in the upper string. Then she crossed out the 0 in the lower string, and the 0 in the upper string.

Then she did the same for the next two 1s in the lower and upper strings.

"So you're saying that when he wrote actual numbers onto the page, what he left out were *some* of the numbers from the historical dates," Zack said.

"Damn, Vera. That's smart," Terry said. "If you can call thinking like a serial killer smart."

By now, Vera had finished crossing out the numbers that were in each string. The list of historical dates now looked like this: *2̶ 0̶ 0 1̶ 1̶ 9 6 3̶ 1̶ 9̶ 4 1 1 7̶ 3̶ 2̶ 1̶ 4̶ 9̶ 2̶*.

"Maybe I'm not so smart after all," Vera told them "What does 0341129 mean?"

"How about putting it in the format he had in the P. S.? "What does that do?"

Vera wrote: *0-34-1129*. She shook her head. "That

can't be it. The last time we—" She interrupted herself, obviously disgusted. "I thought it was we, but I guess it was really just me, since Ellis wrote the damn thing." She took a breath. "The last time I worked on one of these things, as soon as I got stuck, the hint got me out of the jam." She read from Ellis's message: " 'This puzzle may take you down at first, and you might be tempted to try to escape from it, but you'd be better off trying to score two points.' Whatever that means."

" 'Score two points'?" Zack said. "So suddenly, we're playing basketball."

And then it hit Terry like a slap in the face. "No. We're wrestling. Wrestling with the answer to the puzzle. The hint is full of wrestling terms. 'Take down.' 'Escape.' And he's telling us we need to score two points."

Vera looked at him like he was insane. "You score points in wrestling? I thought you hit people in the head with folding chairs."

"That's professional wrestling, not real wrestling. The only reason I know anything about it is because for about fifteen seconds, I was on our high school team. And to score two points, you need to do a reversal."

"So we do a reversal on the answer . . . Instead of 0341129 . . ."

Zack picked up his pen and wrote the number in reverse. "We've got 9211430."

"And when you put that into the right format," Terry said, "you get what?"

Vera wrote 9-21-1430. Then she put her pen down. "Unless I'm wrong, it sure looks like we just learned that Ellis's next murder is going to take place on September 21, at 14:30. That's tomorrow. At 2:30 in the afternoon. Less than twenty-four hours from now."

THIRTY-ONE

September 21

TERRY PARKED IN THE LINE OF CARS OF PARents who had come to pick their kids up. The students only had a half day because of a teachers' conference. Justin's school looked like the site of a minivan convention. Terry shuddered.

About a minute after he pulled in, the doors to the school burst open, and a flood of children and backpacks and clamor came streaming down the front walk.

Justin broke into a huge smile when he saw Terry's car. He came running over, opened the back door, and threw in his backpack, shouting, "Hi, Terry! Where's my dad?"

But before Terry could answer, Justin slammed the door shut, and then opened the front door and climbed in. He was wearing jeans and a startlingly bright white T-shirt, and looked just like any other kid. But Terry knew better.

The very fact that Justin had become Zack's son was the result of a ridiculous string of coincidences, which Zack believed to be his personal miracle.

It all started because almost eight years ago an old friend of Terry's woke up early one morning with a blinding migraine. On a whim, she called Terry to ask if he'd fill in for her at District Court, where indigent defendants would be making their first appearance in front of a judge after being arrested the night before.

Terry hadn't done that kind of work for years, but he owed his friend a favor, and agreed.

Even so, he never would have met Justin's mother if the sixteen-year-old runaway hadn't been busted the night before. And that never would have happened if the cop that picked her up for shoplifting had taken his normal route home, instead of detouring past the Store 24 to pick up a newspaper, where he spotted a teenager trying to sneak off with a free quart of orange juice and a bag of pretzels.

And Justin's mother never would have mentioned to Terry that she was two months' pregnant with a baby she was going to give up for adoption if he'd had his normal breakfast the day he met her, instead of eating a muffin in front of her which triggered a violent bout of morning sickness.

And none of *that* would have mattered except, the very day before he even laid eyes on the young, pregnant girl, Terry had been speaking to Zack about their future plans, and Zack revealed, totally out of the blue, that he was planning to begin looking into adoption as a single father.

"Hey, J-man. Your dad had to run an errand before the hearing this afternoon, so he and I thought, if it was okay with you, that before we go to Criminal Law City, you and I might grab some lunch at, oh, I don't know . . ." Terry took a dramatic pause. "Maybe, Largeburger?" He pulled out of the parking space, and headed down the street toward Justin's favorite restaurant in the world.

"Largeburger? No way!" Justin said, delighted. "Can I get a milk shake, too?"

In his mock parent voice, Terry replied, "Well, I don't know about that. Were you a very good second grader today?"

"Yes."

"Are you sure? You didn't start any fires? Or do any robberies? Or commit any other serious crimes?"

The little boy was laughing now. The idea that he would do anything like that was so absurd, it tickled him that someone would even mention the possibility. He was probably the sweetest kid Terry had ever known in his life. "Um, I don't think so."

"I see. Well then." Terry turned onto Main Street. Largeburger was only a minute away. "Are you sure you're hungry enough for a largeburger *and* a milk shake?"

"And apple pie!" shouted his companion.

"Well then," Terry responded. "I guess we'll *have* to go to Largeburger."

Zack always flipped through his file one final time before going to court on an important hearing. The Alan Lombardo case was so big, though, that all he could do was review his notes, and some of the highlights. There was just no way to go over it all.

Terry had told him that the judge assigned to today's hearing was Susan "Clear-the-Air" Blair. No matter how trivial, Judge Blair always wanted to have a hearing, just so everyone could get everything out on the table.

Unfortunately, Lombardo really didn't have a chance.

The technicalities Alan wanted them to press were far from significant enough to warrant a new trial. And even though Zack's father had been blatantly and appallingly unethical in his dealings with Alan and George Heinrich, it was going to be hard, if not impossible, to convince the judge that the arrangement had any adverse implications for Lombardo's defense. There was no question that then-attorney Wilson had taken advantage of the situation for his own greedy purposes, but it was also clear that George Heinrich, Alan Lombardo, and Nehemiah Wilson had all been on the same side—they wanted Lombardo to get the best defense possible.

And thanks to the prosecution's overwhelming case, the best defense possible wasn't much.

An anonymous tipster had spotted Lombardo's car at the time and place of the final Springfield Shooter murder. The housekeeper had found a container of victims' fingers in Lombardo's freezer. And the police had discovered the chilling diary entries, describing each one of his nine murders, in graphic and damning detail.

And even though it was now known that Ellis Yates was responsible for the five killings that had taken place over the last month, and some circumstantial evidence might even point to him as the original Springfield Shooter, the case against Alan Lombardo was so strong that it was extremely unlikely that he would be awarded a new trial.

As Zack began to return the various folders and notes into the boxes that held the Lombardo file, something made him stop, and remove the file containing the police reports of the evidence seized in the search of Alan's home.

Zack opened it, and reviewed the contents of the computer and the computer disks the police had taken. There were the diary entries, and an alphabetical list of accounting clients for whom Alan had made files on his hard drive or on disk.

Five minutes later, Zack was on his way to the offices of Heinrich Contracting.

* * *

For lunch, Justin had a burger, a large vanilla shake, and a piece of apple pie. Terry had the same except his shake was chocolate. And they split a mega order of fries.

"Dude," Terry said, as they were walking back to the car, "what's the rule when I drop you off in the courtroom?" This was the third time they were going to have this conversation. But for Terry, there was no way he could be sure enough.

"I stay where you put me, no matter what," Justin answered solemnly.

"And what happens when there's an emergency?" Terry asked.

"I need to talk to one of the court officers. And if it's a super-big emergency, I can go right up to you at the front of the courtroom. But that's only if it's a *super*-big emergency."

They had reached Terry's car. After they fastened their seat belts, Terry looked over at his friend's awesome kid. "Ready, little man?"

"To go to Criminal Law City?"

"Roger that."

Zack had finished his meeting with Paul Merrone, and was headed to the door when he overheard the burly man take a phone call. The Heinrich employee said little, but from what Zack could gather, the police were calling, and they were calling with bad news.

Zack had a few unpleasant calls of his own to make. He got in the car and started off for the courthouse. The first call was to Terry, to let him know that he should alert Judge Blair that she should expect his father as a witness today.

And the second was to Angry Dad himself.

"Hello, Zachary." His father's deep voice boomed

through his cell phone. "I sincerely hope you're calling to tell me what you already know is the case. I will not be attending your little hearing today. It will be a cold day in Barbados when I voluntarily walk into a courtroom and spill my guts to Susan Blair. That woman is the worst judge in the Commonwealth of Massachusetts."

Zack accelerated and merged into the traffic on the interstate. "I'm sorry, Dad, but I just came from a meeting with Paul Merrone. Mr. Heinrich's—"

"I know who Paul Merrone is," the judge interrupted. "What the hell difference does that make?"

"I was going over the Lombardo case this morning," Zack persisted, "and I realized for the first time that in all of the computer records that the cops seized from Alan's home, not one item had anything to do with the Heinrich accounts, despite the fact that Alan was their accountant, and Heinrich was by far his biggest client."

His father made a noise of disgust from the other end of the phone. "I don't know why you continue to pester me with this, Zachary, but I swear to God, whether you are my son or not—"

"The reason Alan had no record of the Heinrich accounts was because he didn't keep any of the records," Zack cut in. "Mr. Heinrich did. On floppy disks, which Mr. Heinrich, or one of his employees, brought over to Alan when Alan was doing work for them. They brought the disks, and stayed, while Alan did the work, then they took the disks away."

"So?" The disdain in the judge's voice was palpable.

"So Paul Merrone told me that Mr. Heinrich, and he, and any number of Heinrich's employees had access to Alan Lombardo's house, his computer, his computer disks. You represented a man for murder who might well have been framed for that very murder by your own clients. It's a classic conflict of interest, and Alan Lombardo deserves a new trial. He might even be innocent."

There was a silence on the other end of the phone. "I had no idea of any of that," the judge said stiffly. "No idea at all."

"From what I learned from Mr. Merrone, that doesn't sound very likely," Zack said. "But as you know, it doesn't matter. The conflict existed, and you're going to testify to it. If you refuse to do so, Judge Blair will find you in contempt, you will be arrested, and you will end up being brought before the court in irons. I suggest you come under your own power. And bring a good lawyer. You're going to need one, Dad."

THIRTY-TWO

Dear Vera,

*By now, you have probably found the latest casualty
in this nightmare, and have figured everything out, so I
suppose the first thing I should do is apologize.*

Vera felt like screaming.

Was Ellis ever going to leave her alone?

The letter had come in today's mail. The original was
being examined by the lab, and a copy had been handed to
her just as she was leaving the station house. Unlike the
others, this one was handwritten. Of course. Why should
Ellis continue to bother trying to hide his identity? Vera
stuffed it into her pocket, climbed into her car, and started
up the siren. She was on the way to this madman's latest
crime scene. She'd read his sick letter after she got there.

She hadn't slept all night, trying to figure out where
and when the next lethal attack was going to happen. And
this morning, when she got in to work, she found out that
she hadn't had any more success than the guys at the lab.

Then, at about noon, she got word that a boy walking
his dog around the Springfield Mall's largest outdoor

parking lot had become suspicious because the dog was barking like crazy at a car's trunk.

And surprise, surprise, when they ran the license plates, they were stolen.

But the model and color of the car matched Ellis's.

So there it was. Ellis had struck again. Hours, if not a full day ahead of when she, Terry, and Zack had calculated to be the time of the next attack.

So either they had made a mistake, or Ellis had been jerking them around again.

And now Vera was on her way out to that parking lot, to find the latest victim. The latest person she hadn't been able to save from this monster.

Vera flew down the highway to the turnoff which would lead her to Ellis's car, and his latest victim. She was going to get this guy. She was going to get him no matter what it took.

This was going to be the last corpse this monster would be responsible for.

She sped down the ramp to the parking lot, and easily spotted the car in question. Two squad cars were there already, as well as a tow truck from a local garage, to help them pop the trunk.

But Vera already knew what was in there. It was just a matter of discovering who.

She reached Ellis's car just as the mechanic had finished unlatching the trunk. The smell hit her immediately. There was no chance that what was in there wasn't a dead body.

The mechanic stepped back, holding a rag over his mouth and nose.

And Vera stepped forward.

The corpse had been thrown into the trunk headfirst, facedown. An adult male, somewhat overweight, wearing an inexpensive suit that looked like it had a stain on one of the sleeves. Vera and the other officers reached in to turn him over.

She grabbed hold of the dead man's shoulder and arm—yes, his index finger was missing—and on the count of three, they rolled the victim onto his back.

And as the corpse revealed itself, his head limply rolled over so that he now faced the police who had arrived too late to save him. His blank, sightless eyes seemed to stare right through Vera, uttering silent accusations, and she felt her stomach tighten and knew she was very close to throwing up.

Because the man in the trunk of the car was Ellis.

And then a radio call came in, and the cruisers both went tearing off to the courthouse, to respond to a report of shots fired.

Leaving Vera alone with her dead partner.

Terry ushered Justin into a seat near the front of the gallery, on the right side, so that he would have a good view of his father during the hearing. Zack had hoped that by allowing Justin to witness the very controlled nature of a courtroom hearing, the little boy's fears over Zack's involvement with a convicted serial killer might be reduced. Terry thought the idea sounded nuts, but what did he know.

They were early—the assistant district attorney, the court reporter, the clerks, the court officers—none of them were in the courtroom yet. Terry decided to hang out with Justin, at least until Zack arrived. Terry showed Justin the door he expected Zack to use, at the front of the courtroom on the right side, so he could keep an eye on it.

There was a decent crowd in attendance—maybe as many as fifty or sixty—and people were still filing in steadily. Somehow the curious ones always knew when something interesting might go down at court. Maybe word that Zack's father was going to be involved had leaked out, or maybe people were here just because it was a chance to get a glimpse of the notorious Springfield Shooter.

Whatever it was, it wouldn't matter to Terry or Zack. They had a job to do, and the job didn't change depending on whether they did it in a crowded room or an empty one.

Just then, Justin tugged on Terry's sleeve, and held up a promotional game piece that he had received with his dessert at Largeburger. "How many of these do I have to get before I get a free milk shake?" the little boy asked.

Terry had no idea. He took the small, brightly colored cardboard rectangle from Justin. It had a picture of a crown on it—

"Justin, man," Terry said hastily, handing the game piece back to him. "I'll tell you in a second." He had just found the missing key to the serial killer's puzzle. "I've got to make a quick phone call. They don't let us take our cell phones in the courthouse, but there's a pay phone in the hallway right outside the doors back there. You want to come, or you want to wait here for your dad?"

"I'll wait here."

"Okay, kiddo. Be right back."

By now, the gallery was quite full, and Terry had a little trouble walking against the flow of foot traffic coming in to attend the hearing. The aisle on the other side of the courtroom was just as busy. Zack's dad and another man were making their way to some seats on that side of the room.

Terry had barely reached the pay phone when he heard the gunshot.

The Final Five Seconds

THIS WAS IT. THE LAST MOMENTS OF ZACK'S life.

He took some comfort in the fact that because of the flood of adrenaline that was surging through his body, time was creeping so slowly he felt like he could see and feel the tiniest increments in movement, and experience the smallest measures of time.

He was four feet from the shooter, who was aiming his gun directly at Zack's heart. His finger was slowly squeezing the trigger.

Zack was sure that the result of this confrontation was that he was going to be shot and killed. But what he also had to be sure of was that he wouldn't die before he had brought the shooter down in a way that gave Justin, assuming he was still alive, a chance to escape.

So he dodged to his right.

Because he couldn't bear any weight with his left leg, and because he didn't want to give up any more ground to the shooter, Zack's feint was only from the waist up. Like a somewhat awkward dance move, or a boxer trying to slip past a jab.

It almost worked.

The bullet struck him high and on the left side of his

chest. Zack felt like he had been punched, hard, and his upper body swiveled back and to the left.

But he did not fall. His brain registered pain, but it was a like a message shouted to him from an enormous distance. He had a single focus, and that was to move forward. And now there were less than three feet between him and his target.

Because the light from the emergency flood lamp was still shining directly into Zack's eyes, the shooter's face was still entirely backlit. For an instant, a flash of hope surged through Zack that all at once, the lights would come on, and the gunman would get startled so that Zack would be able to take advantage of the shooter's hesitation, disarm him, and survive.

But that didn't happen. Instead, the gunman merely re-aimed the gun at Zack. He must have thought that all he needed to do was to plug Zack again with another bullet or two, and Zack would finally give up.

Obviously, the shooter didn't have kids.

Because no weapon was going to stop Zack now.

He had hoped to use both hands to grab the shooter by the throat and wrestle him to the ground, but thanks to that last bullet, Zack's left arm appeared to be in complete rebellion. He couldn't move it at all. So instead, he raised his right fist above his head. Using his arm like a club, he brought it down with all of his force on the shooter's outstretched hand.

Everything seemed to happen at once. The gunshot, the punch in the stomach, the gratifyingly solid contact between Zack's fist and the shooter's gun hand, or wrist, or forearm. Something that made the madman yelp with pain. Excellent.

There was a confused flurry of images—shadows, a flash of light, colors. Zack knew that he had finally achieved full contact with the shooter—he was leaning against him—but he also knew he was falling.

Sounds were registering clearly, though. The incredibly satisfying clatter off to his right must have been the shooter's gun falling to the floor. The sound of the shooter's breath leaving him with a whoosh, just as Zack felt himself crumple into a strangely soft collision with something.

No—he had crashed into the shooter, who had toppled backward with Zack on top of him.

And then there was a curious sensation of being lifted up.

Zack was a very pragmatic person, and a part of him knew very well that he wasn't actually going anywhere, but that knowledge did not erase the feeling that he was actually traveling through time and space, back to that moment two days after Justin had come home from the hospital.

The moment when Zack was changing the little boy's diapers, and each first saw in the eyes of the other what each truly had.

When they both realized that everything really was going to be all right.

Now, Zack decided that all he wanted to do was to pick up his son and hold him.

But strangely, he couldn't move his arms.

And it was getting harder to see Justin.

Zack was fading away.

At least he had done something important with his life.

And then he was gone.

THIRTY-THREE

THE EMTs AND A CRIME-SCENE UNIT ARRIVED only a moment after the cruisers left. That was good, because Vera had been so stunned by the discovery of Ellis's body that she was still fixed to the spot she was in when she first saw him.

As they began their vital but terrible work, Vera remembered the letter from Ellis.

> *Dear Vera,*
>
> *By now, you have probably found the latest casualty in this nightmare, and have figured everything out, so I suppose the first thing I should do is apologize.*

Tears started to well up in Vera's eyes. Not only had Ellis been killed—she had wrongly believed that he was the killer himself.

> *I know I should have followed procedure and taken him in with the whole department, put him in the system, and let the courts take care of it, but I couldn't. I was selfish.*

Because for me, this was personal.

I lived on the same street as Carrie Bernstein, the <u>seventh</u> victim of the Springfield Shooter.

Carrie and I were in high school together. And I had the biggest crush on her.

And the day she was murdered was the day I'd decided I was finally going to ask her out to the movies with me.

I never got over that. When I saw what happened to Carrie, I decided to kill whoever did that to her. It's the reason I became a cop.

But I hardly got a chance to work on the Springfield Shooter case before it was solved.

When I got the opportunity to help you on this case, I jumped at it. I felt like I'd finally have a chance to stop another string of murders that would destroy so many lives. And when it started to look like it was possible that Lombardo wasn't really the Springfield Shooter, I realized that I really was going to get another chance to avenge Carrie's death.

And then I figured it out.

Remember how he was writing all about games in that letter? That was the key to the puzzle. The "game" was chess. The focus was on specific words in the clues. The fifth word in the first clue was spawn— which contained the word "pawn." And the fifth word in the next clue was crook—which contained the word "rook." The other words we had to focus on— "knight," "bi-shop" and "asking"—all contained other chess pieces: the knight, the bishop, and the king.

The one he left out was the queen. Queen Street. And the number of squares on a chessboard—

64—less 10 equals 54. The site of the next attack was going to be at 54 Queen Street. I don't know who lives there, but at least I saved that person's life.

Vera looked at her watch. It was 1:47. She had less than forty-five minutes.

Monster

THIS LAST ONE WAS PROMISING TO BE EVEN more exciting than he had expected.

Technically, he was supposed to wait until 2:30 before killing the old lady, but everything had been accelerated by the Ellis Yates development.

And since it was now going to be a double-header with Stephanie, he was going to need extra time.

Oh well. Vera would just have to adapt.

And realistically, even if she didn't, her disappointment would be short-lived.

Because he was going to kill her, too.

Philomena Y. Giordano

IT WAS 1:49 P.M. ON SEPTEMBER 21 WHEN Philomena Giordano answered the door to her home at 54 Queen Street for the last time in her life.

It was amazing how some days, the doorbell never rang, and others, it seemed like every time she turned around, Philomena was heading to the front hall. It wasn't like she was complaining—she loved visitors. Especially her lovely young neighbor, Stephanie.

But when she opened the door, Philomena was startled to see a young man on her doorstep. Before she could even say hello, he had pulled open the screen door and shoved his way into her home. "Hey!" Philomena cried, stumbling backward, bumping into the little table where she liked to set her outgoing mail. The young man shut the door behind him. "Who are you? What are you doing in here? Get out of my house right now!"

But instead of answering, the man shook his head. With an odd smile on his face, he took a roll of duct tape out of an oversized pocket in his jacket, and said, "Welcome to my world, Philomena."

THIRTY-FOUR

STEPHANIE HAD CALLED IN SICK. THE LAST
few days had been so traumatic that she felt she needed to
sleep for about a week.

But until her father was released, and until they finally put this killer away, Steph was hardly getting any
rest.

She'd spent the morning just taking it slow, but by the
time lunch rolled around, she wasn't feeling any better
than she had for days.

It was funny, but when Steph had imagined finally
hearing from the police that they were wrong, and that
her father had nothing to do with any of these murders,
she had expected to feel joyful relief.

But right now, she was so emotionally exhausted that
all she wanted to do was not think about this nightmare
for a while.

The doorbell rang.

An hour earlier, after unenthusiastically reviewing
her microwave choices for today's lunchtime—Chicken
Teriyaki, Vegetable Noodle Supreme, or Turkey Pot Pie—
she had opted for decadence: an everything pizza from
Maxie's.

She opened the door and paid for the pizza. The

delivery guy started to explain that he was late because of the miserable traffic caused by the stupid roadwork—but Steph's cell phone rang, interrupting his apology.

As she dug her phone out of her purse, she stood at her open door and dreamily watched the delivery person get in his little car and go on his way.

Too bad she couldn't have ordered up somebody to have pizza with. Like that lawyer, Zack Wilson. Now *that* would turn lunch into something exciting. Unless she was reading him wrong, his eyes reflected the same intense interest that she had in him. Intelligent, friendly, charming, *very* good-looking in a kind of relaxed, self-assured way. Donna called guys like that "NFJF"—Not Flashy, Just Fine.

But until her father was out of prison, Steph just didn't have the energy to start trying to hook up with anybody—no matter how fine they were. Even Zack Wilson.

Holding her pizza in her left hand, she opened the phone with her right. "Hello?"

Ten seconds later, she dumped the phone back into her purse, grabbed it, and, still stupidly holding on to the pizza, she ran across to her neighbor's house.

The phone call was from a Lieutenant Carasquillo from the police. Mrs. G. was in some sort of trouble.

Terry pushed open the door to the courtroom and discovered a scene out of a horror movie.

He was met by a small wave of people who pushed past him, out of the room, and into the hallway. Everyone else in the courtroom seemed to be ducking or crawling on the floor. Terrified screams filled the air. It was pandemonium.

The normal overhead lights had been shut off, and only the emergency flood lamps were shining—throwing weird yellow beams in crazy angles across the windowless room.

Terry couldn't see Justin, but he knew where the little boy was sitting, and as he started running down the aisle toward him, trying his best not to step on any of the people who had flattened themselves there, another shot rang out.

Terry looked up, and saw Alan Lombardo, standing at the front of the courtroom on the left side, aiming a gun out into the gallery.

Another shot was fired, and sure enough, Goddamn Alan was going postal in the courtroom.

Well, if he hadn't been a mass murderer before, he was going to be one now.

The screaming intensified, amplified now by the voices of people shouting for help and crying. Terry tripped on someone's outstretched arm, and fell. When he scrambled to his feet, he saw a figure running across the front of the room from the right, toward Alan. It was Zack.

But Alan must have seen him coming, because he aimed his gun at Zack and fired. There was a spray of blood into the air, and suddenly, Terry's best friend of twenty years was flying through the air toward the clerk's table.

Terry kept fighting his way toward Justin. He couldn't remember whether he'd left Zack's son in the second or third row. Justin was on the right side of the courtroom, so as long as he hadn't moved, he was fine. So far, anyway.

Terry could only pray that Zack was fine, too. But from the volume of blood that had exploded out of him, and the way his body acted after getting shot, it sure didn't look like he was fine.

The number of terrified people crawling along the aisle toward the back of the room made it feel like Terry was wading against an impossibly strong human tide. And even if he reached the third row, which was still ten feet away, it was too dark to see down the length of the benches clearly. And with all of the screaming and crying, Terry couldn't imagine locating Justin by voice.

He dove into the fifth row of benches and scrambled up on top of the bench. If Alan looked this way, Terry would be screwed. But fuck it. This was the only way he would have any chance of making progress toward the front of the courtroom with any speed. He stepped up onto the back of the bench in front of him with his left foot, and then stepped over it with his right, bringing it down onto the bench itself.

There was another gunshot. Alan looked like he was swinging around toward this side of the courtroom. Terry didn't have much time.

Again, he put his left foot on the back of the bench in front of him, stepped up, and swung his right foot over the back of the bench, bringing it down onto the bench in the third row. Terry looked down past his feet at the people cowering on the floor. They were all adults. No seven-year-old child.

And then, for no good reason at all, Justin just stood up, facing the front of the room.

He was in the second row—one ahead of Terry—and off about eight feet to his left.

And worse than that, Terry saw Zack, using the clerk's chair as some kind of rolling crutch, still heading toward crazy fucking Alan.

And still worse, when Justin saw Zack, at a tragically coincidental lull in the screaming, the little boy cried out, "Daddy!"

He might as well have painted a target on himself.

Besides Terry, Justin was the only person standing in the entire room. And he was in the second row.

Jesus Christ. Wearing a bright white T-shirt.

Alan didn't miss it. He turned and brought his gun up, preparing to kill the coolest kid in the world.

The next thing Terry knew, he was flying through the air.

Then there was a very loud bang at the exact time as a sharp pain sliced through Terry's head.

And then the emergency lights in the courtroom stopped working, and the screaming seemed to fade.

Terry thought he heard several more gunshots, but he couldn't be sure.

In fact, Terry wasn't sure whether he had fallen, or where Justin was, or just about anything else.

And then it got really quiet.

And then he was gone.

Vera was speeding through the streets of Springfield, siren blaring. She was still at least ten minutes away.

She used the radio to call the station house. Maribel, the administrative assistant, picked up.

"Maribel, this is Vera. I'm heading for 54 Queen Street, Code 6. I'm going to need backup."

"Oh no, Detective." That wasn't exactly the response Vera was hoping for. She started blasting the air horn as she approached the intersection with Main Street. "Every available car is already gone to the courthouse. There's a shooting in progress. Multiple victims."

Vera made a hard left onto Main, tires squealing. She barely missed a stupid cargo van that decided its right turn on red was more important than letting a cop car come through the intersection. "Get somebody here as soon as you can, Maribel," Vera said. "Or I'm going to have multiple victims, too."

Stephanie Hartz

IT WAS 1:51 P.M. WHEN STEPHANIE HARTZ ENtered Mrs. Giordano's house for the last time in her life.

She was still holding the Maxie's pizza box in one hand, so with her other, Steph fished her keys out of her pocket and opened her neighbor's door.

But once Steph got inside the house, she knew that something was terribly wrong. It was too quiet. The police lieutenant said that Mrs. G. had called the police for help and had identified Steph as a neighbor that could stay with her until they arrived. So she expected to see or hear something as she entered.

It was eerie. Mrs. G. was always doing something—baking cookies, cleaning the windows, writing letters. Steph couldn't hear *anything*. "Mrs. Giordano?" she called. "It's Stephanie. Mrs. G.? Are you okay?"

And then she heard it. A noise. Coming from the room to the left of the entryway. Like a soft, high-pitched, what? Moan? The sound someone makes when they're having a bad dream?

Steph set the pizza down on the little table in the front hallway and put her purse on the floor beneath it. Then she hurried into the living room, and saw Mrs. Giordano.

Bound and gagged with duct tape to one of her straight-backed dining room chairs.

Monster

HE HAD JUST LEFT THE UPSTAIRS BEDROOM—
old people's homes were really boring—when he heard the
front door open. And then a woman came inside, closed the
door behind her, and called out for Mrs. Giordano.

He smiled. Of course she'd come. He'd heard her on
the phone with Mrs. Giordano countless times over the
past weeks. The two were obviously quite close. There was
no way Stephanie would stop to think for a second that in
emergencies cops didn't call the neighbors to tell them to
come over.

He waited, silent, until Stephanie moved into the
body of the house. Then he hurried down the stairs, and
stopped. His Taser was out, and he was ready for business.

He had already checked—there was only one other
exit from the tiny house. A side door led to the outside off
the kitchen, the room to the right as you came in the front.
Fortunately, there was a keyed dead bolt which he had secured, and then removed the key.

The kitchen led to the room at the back of the house,
a small formal dining room, which had no exit except to
the living room, where Mrs. Giordano sat, quietly awaiting her fate.

Nobody was leaving this house except through the

front door, where he currently stood, listening, trying to figure out where his second guest was. If she had gone into the house to the right after she entered, she would still be calling out for Mrs. Giordano, because the kitchen was empty.

So she must have gone to the left, and seen the old lady taped to the chair.

That was fine, as long as she hadn't set the old woman free. He enjoyed catching victims, but only one at a time.

No worries. Stephanie had only been in the house a few seconds. Duct tape was tough stuff—it was going to take a while to get it all off.

Still, he didn't want his new participant to be focused on Mrs. Giordano. He wanted her concentrating on her own problems.

So he decided to open communications.

He took his gun out with his free hand, and fired it into the ceiling. The gunshots reverberated throughout the little house, punctuated by the gentle sounds of plaster falling to the floor.

The settling dust drew his eye to a small table and the box on it.

He laughed, and then shouted into the silence, "Wow! Pizza! My favorite!"

THIRTY-FIVE

"WOW! PIZZA! MY FAVORITE!"

The bizarre words of the serial killer rang out even before the echoes of his gunshots had stopped bouncing off the walls.

As she stood there, dead still in the dining room at the back of the house, two competing feelings battled for control inside Stephanie.

On the one hand, she had never been so completely terrified in her life. It was possible that she was literally within seconds of her own horrible death at the hands of an inhuman creature who reveled in the pain and torture of others.

On the other, her senses had never been so alive. She smelled the gunpowder from the shots the killer had taken, the plaster dust in the air, the pizza sitting in the front hall.

She heard the labored breathing of Mrs. G., still taped up in the living room, as if she were still standing next to her.

She hadn't had enough time to free the old woman.

At least she was still alive, thank God.

Plan A was obvious—Steph needed to call for help. But there was no phone in the dining room, and her cell phone was in her purse, which was in the front hall, underneath the little table with the pizza on it.

That left Plan B—get out of the house, and then call for help.

To her right, she could go back through the living room, past Mrs. G.

And to her left, she could go through the kitchen. She thought that's where Mrs. G.'s phone was, and she also thought she remembered there was a door to the side yard off the kitchen. But there was no way the killer was going to let her take the time to dial a phone number, or fiddle with an unfamiliar lock. The house was so small that as soon as he knew where she was, if she didn't keep moving, he'd be on top of her in seconds.

She was going to have to use her newly heightened sense of hearing, and listen for the way he chose to walk around the house. She'd sneak around the other way, reach the front door, and escape.

If she went the wrong way, she was as good as dead. He'd shoot her, and she'd never get away.

Even if her plan worked, it was, of course, a very risky one, leaving Mrs. G. alone in the house with this psychopath. He could kill her in a moment.

But Steph was gambling that if she could make it out the door, the killer would be so intent on self-preservation that he would just bolt, fearing capture if he stayed long enough to murder Mrs. G.

She stood directly in the middle of the dining room, exactly the same distance from the entrance to the kitchen, on her left, as the entrance to the living room, on her right.

The way the room was set up, she couldn't see more than a few feet into either of the rooms to her sides from where she was standing. And it was impossible, no matter how hard she tried to strain her peripheral vision, to see both of the entrances to the adjoining rooms at once. She was going to have to keep moving her eyes back and forth, and try to pick up some hint of the direction the killer had decided to take.

With each passing glance, Steph caught sight of the antique china cabinet standing on the wall directly in front of her. Glass doors revealed shelves of beautiful plates, saucers, and cups.

But beneath the upper cabinets were a set of drawers, which she knew contained potential weapons. Keeping watch for the killer at all times, Steph eased forward, and silently opened the center drawer, revealing a set of flatware.

Including Mrs. G.'s collection of steak knives.

She stood dead still, trying to hear everything. Or anything.

A car drove past the front of the house.

Quietly, *quietly*, using just the tips of her fingers, Steph reached into the drawer, and removed one of the knives.

A lawn mower started up, far off in the distance.

A car horn sounded.

A kitchen floorboard creaked.

As if she had been training all her life for the Olympic house-sprinting finals, she was off like a rocket, knife in hand, flying into the living room, past Mrs. Giordano, heading for the front door, when suddenly, she heard a crash in the entryway. Probably the little table with the pizza.

Then a male voice bellowed, "Shit!"

He was heading toward her through the living room.

She skidded back in the direction she'd come, toward the dining room at the rear of the house. She'd go through that room, into the kitchen, and around to the front that way.

But from the thunderous sound of the killer's footsteps, he had reversed direction, too, and had returned to the kitchen, intending to cut her off again.

Thank God Steph was wearing her cross-trainers today. She planted her left foot, stopped on a dime a few feet into the dining room, and turned around again, once more running past Mrs. Giordano, who sat helplessly in the chair, shaking her head frantically and gargling something in her throat that Steph couldn't understand.

As Steph passed the old woman for the third time, she realized that the killer must have finally committed to coming all the way through the kitchen, chasing her through the dining room and into the living room, because she no longer heard him in front of her.

And then suddenly he was standing there, smack in front of the door, as she tore directly toward him.

The reason she hadn't heard him running was because he wasn't running. He had started back through the kitchen just hard enough and just loud enough to make her think he'd decided to chase her all the way around the house, and then, once she'd committed herself to running through the living room to the front entry, he just stopped, and waited for her to come to him.

As soon as Steph saw him, two things happened.

She slammed to another body-shaking stop.

And he raised what looked like a strange, large gun, and said, "Stephanie, we meet at last. Welcome to my world."

Before the words were out of his mouth, Steph had already turned around and started to run. A crackling sound and an astonishingly painful shock blasted through her, running up and down her spine, into her skull.

It was pain she'd never experienced before. Completely humbling, terrifying, thoroughly disabling agony.

The inside of her head was crackling. She heard nothing but that and a buzzing, ringing sound, and thought she might smell something burning. She lost all control of her limbs, and fell flat onto her face, twitching and convulsing helplessly. Her arms spilled out above her head, the knife—her only hope—skittered away on the hardwood floor.

After an eternity, the electrical current stopped blasting through her body, and the incredible pain ceased pulsing through her, but Steph still could not use her muscles. Paralyzed, she lay there, motionless except for an occasional, involuntary twitch, staring out at the knife, mere inches away.

Desperately trying to put out of her mind the terror, the lingering pain, the buzzing in her ears, the full horror of her situation, she used all of her concentration and willed her right arm to move.

Nothing. So she concentrated on her right hand, and then only on the fingers of her right hand. *Move*. If she could just get control of something, she could get that knife in her hand, and fight this monster off.

But her body refused to respond. She lay there, motionless, staring at her unresponsive arm. Her mouth lay open, and a small puddle of saliva began to form beneath her open lips.

There was nothing now but to wait for a psychotic killer to torture and then murder her.

An image of her father formed in her mind, and a tear ran down her cheek. He didn't deserve this.

She didn't deserve this.

Her hearing was slowly returning, and the sound of his footsteps approached. He was going to pass Mrs. G. on his way to her. But then he stopped.

"You know what, ladies? I'm a little hungry. I think I'm going to get myself some pizza. I'd offer you some, but, well, you know."

And then his footsteps moved away. He was going back into the hallway for the pizza. Moments later, there were sounds from the kitchen. He was opening the refrigerator.

"Mrs. Giordano? Do you have anything to drink?"

The gagged woman didn't answer.

The killer's mocking continued from the kitchen. "That's okay. No—don't get up. I'll get it myself."

Steph focused again on her arm. The electrical shock had so completely messed up her nervous system that the signals from her brain weren't getting to her hand. She kept trying to contract a muscle, to get anything to happen, but her arm just lay there, as if it belonged to someone else.

The refrigerator door closed. Then there was the rasp of a soda can being opened.

How pathetic, Steph thought. Lying here, in a puddle of her own drool, listening to the psychopath in the next room eating her pizza.

And planning to murder her.

Monster

HE DIDN'T USUALLY LIKE PIZZA WITH EVERY-thing on it, but today, he had to admit that it tasted excellent.

He was standing in the dining room, holding the slice of pie he had taken from the box in the hallway and a can of soda. He took a plate out of the china cabinet, put the pizza on it, and set it and the soda can down on the dining room table. Then he walked into the living room, where Mrs. Giordano sat, taped immobile, staring at Stephanie as she lay on the floor.

Poor Steph was not looking her best, lying there in her own saliva.

Well, she was going to be looking a whole lot worse very soon.

He took out his roll of duct tape, tore off a piece, grabbed a handful of her hair, yanked her head back, and slapped the tape across her mouth. Then he dropped her head back down to the floor and dragged a second chair into the living room. He hoisted her limp body up, and dropped her into the chair. She was starting to moan. He wrapped tape around her wrists, binding her to the arms of the chair.

And then he tore off several more strips, and bound her ankles to the legs of the chair.

When he was done, he straightened up, and said, "I don't know about you ladies, but all that did was whet my appetite," and he went back into the dining room to finish his slice of pizza.

THIRTY-SIX

VERA'S GPS SYSTEM IDENTIFIED 54 QUEEN AS the house on the corner of Brookings. According to the display on the screen, she was still over a mile away. At least another minute or two. And the local cops had sent all available units to the courthouse shooting. Vera was on her own.

She knew that the killer had announced that he was not going to act until 2:30, but she couldn't trust him. She needed to be there and *now*.

The speedometer said she was already going fifty miles per hour, and this road was barely safe at twenty.

She urged the car faster. Fifty-five. Sixty.

Sixty-five.

And then, brake lights. Tons of them.

Vera slammed on the brakes, skidding to a halt, and barely avoiding a collision with the stopped car ahead of her. What the hell?

A gigantic piece of construction equipment was entering the intersection ahead, probably lumbering its way up to Northampton and that disaster up there.

Vera waited until the oncoming lane was clear of traffic, and then pulled around to the left of the cars stopped ahead of her.

And then, incredibly, two cars ahead of her, a pickup truck and a minivan both jumped out into the lane in front of her. As if possessed by some mad inclination to completely block the road, a third car—a Chevy—cut into the lane in front of the other two.

The pickup truck slammed right into the Chevy, and the minivan promptly rear-ended the pickup truck.

The road was now totally blocked.

Vera pulled her car onto the nearest lawn, jumped out, and started to run.

"Let me give you a preview of what's about to take place."

Stephanie's heart was racing. She was beginning to feel herself regain some control over her body, but her mind was frantic with panic. What difference did it make if she was no longer limp as a rag doll? The tape made it impossible to move her arms or her legs. The best she could do was to swivel her head and watch as the madman took something out of his pocket.

As he approached he resumed his speech. "Think of these as evidence of my admiration. I hope you don't mind—I took some unauthorized portraits." He held one up in front of her eyes. "I actually think this one's quite good."

Oh my God. It was a picture of her.

A picture of her, *naked*.

"Here's what you look like now. Let's call this the Before photograph."

She was standing, completely undressed, in front of her bedroom mirror. She was holding her hairbrush in one hand. She must have just come out of the shower. The way the picture had been taken, you could see her from behind, and the front of her in the reflection of the mirror.

How in the world did he have a picture of her like that?

He must have been spying on her.

Humiliation, terror, and rage began a battle for control over Stephanie's emotions. But when he showed her the next photograph, terror won.

"And here's what we'll call the After picture."

He was displaying what was obviously a computer composite of the original picture of her standing nude in front of the mirror. Grotesque injuries had been superimposed over the photograph, on her face, her torso, her rear end.

With the amount of adrenaline already pounding through her body, she didn't think it was possible that her heart could beat any faster or harder.

She was wrong.

She looked up at the face of the man who had been stalking her for—how long? Days? Weeks? Had she been a target of this murderer since the beginning of his sick rampage?

He was smiling at her. What kind of twisted person would do this to someone like her?

And to Mrs. Giordano? Oh God. Poor Mrs. Giordano. What was going to happen to her?

As if he could read her mind, he said, "I really wouldn't worry about her right now, Stephanie. Don't you think you've got enough on your plate? I mean, when you consider the very next thing I have in store for you. I'd like you to take a closer look at this one. I realize it might be a little, say, uncomfortable, but try to just pay attention to the detail I'd like to discuss. Your right index finger."

Steph looked at the picture, and this time she saw what he wanted her to see. With all the gore displayed on every other part of her body, she had overlooked the fact that he had also removed from the image her right index finger.

She looked back at him, and in his other hand he now held a pair of pruning shears. She inhaled and snapped her head back in horror. Oh my God. He was about to cut off her finger with that thing. Oh my God.

Right then, he raised his other hand, and a camera appeared, taking a flash picture, which momentarily blinded her. "Stephanie, that was awesome," he crooned. "If you can guarantee that you'll have that kind of reaction as we go through this together, I guarantee that I will make sure that you stay alive for as long as possible before I have to end your pathetic little life. Deal?"

Tears welled up in her eyes and spilled down her cheeks. She couldn't help it. Not only was she crying—she was also now visibly shaking with fear. But it wasn't just fear. There was anger in there, too.

The monster smirked, and took another picture. Clearly, he was eating this up. Which only made her more angry.

A slight change surged through her when she realized that. When she focused on the anger, some of the other stuff, like the paralyzing terror, got pushed further back in her mind.

She knew that it didn't really change anything, but she liked it better, so she tried to stay angry.

"You know what?" The monster was now holding another photo. She refused to look at it. "I didn't think I did a real good job on the finger thing with your photo, so I brought some others to show you."

She kept her gaze steady on him. There was no way she was going to stare at whatever awful thing he was holding. She didn't need to see anything this pervert had to show her.

"Oh, I don't think defiance is your best play here,

Stephanie," he said, in a somewhat menacing voice. He grabbed a handful of her hair and shoved her face toward the image. "I went to a lot of trouble taking these pictures. The least you can do is have the courtesy to look at them. C'mon. I know you've seen one of the fingers I cut off already. What's the big deal? I'll understand if you don't like them. Art is always a matter of taste, don't you agree? But goddammit, you *will* look at these pictures!"

He was getting so enraged that he was yanking her head back and forth by her hair. Even if she'd wanted to look at his horrendous photographs, she couldn't possibly. Her eyes were filled with tears from the pain.

"Fine!" he shouted. "Let's just *do* this."

He flung the pictures to the floor, picked up the pruning shears, stood directly in front of her, and grabbed hold of her right hand with his left.

As he brought the gardening tool closer, she started to writhe. Her wrists and ankles were taped to the chair, but her hands and fingers were unrestrained. They couldn't move away from where they were pinned, but they could move around.

She balled her right hand up into a fist, refusing to give him easy access to her fingers, and began to thrash around frantically in the chair. He wasn't going to do anything to her without a fight. A major fight.

"Okay," he said, somewhat quietly, releasing her and stepping back a few feet. "I see how we're going to have to do this."

The change in his attitude was alarming. Mere seconds ago he was so enraged that he was shoving her face, literally, into a picture of what she assumed was a severed finger.

Now he had gone back to the dining room, and he was returning with the duct tape. He walked around behind her, and then there was the sound of the tape being pulled off the roll.

Then there was a tearing sound.

Stephanie tried to twist her head around to see what he was doing back there, when all of a sudden he was reaching over her with a long length of the tape. He pulled it over her head and brought it down high across the front of her chest. Then he pulled back on it, and wrapped it tightly around the back of the chair.

He was pinning her body to the chair so she couldn't fight him anymore.

Another wave of panic crashed over her. She was in control of almost nothing. She could move her fingers and lean forward and back from the waist, but she had little else as it was.

And he was going to take that away from her.

And then cut off her finger.

The first piece of tape he had used had already reduced her mobility considerably, but he continued to wrap more pieces around her, each one slightly lower than the last, first across her biceps and breasts, then down, near her bent elbows and stomach.

By the time he was finished, she was lashed tightly to the back of the chair. She couldn't bend forward from the waist at all. The best she could manage was to move her head up and down.

Now he moved around to her front. What else could he possibly tape? Her entire upper body was pinned to the back of the chair. Her wrists were taped to the chair's arms, and her ankles to its legs.

He tore off a small strip of the gray tape, and said, "Now I want you to open your right hand."

He wanted to tape her fingers apart.

He was going to make it impossible for her to resist when he chopped off her finger with the pruning shears.

Like hell he was.

She shook her head back and forth, making a strangled noise of anger from behind her gag, and kept her hand tightly fisted.

He sighed, heavily, dramatically, and disingenuously.

"Okay," he said, shrugging.

Then he went back to the dining room, and returned with the stun gun, and shot her.

The pain was fast and brutal, raging through every one of her nerves like an electric current of liquid fire and broken glass. The muscles of her back convulsed, and had she not been so securely bound to the chair, she would have arched her back so severely that she probably would have injured herself.

The muscles in her arms and legs were in uncontrollable spasms. Her teeth chattered, tears ran from her eyes, and then, it was over.

The pain continued to pulse through her long after the electric current had stopped flowing, but more important, she was completely incapacitated. Her muscles were completely out of her control. Her head hung down to her chest, her mouth lolled open.

And her right hand was no longer in a fist.

He was returning with the tape, and there was nothing she could do.

"I really wish I didn't have to do this," he said, as he took the short piece of tape he'd already cut from the roll, and used it to wrap around her right thumb. "I like it much better when you aren't drooling."

Then he taped the thumb down to the arm of the chair.

He tore off another small strip. She looked, helplessly, at her rebel fingers. *Close*, she ordered them. *Resist this monster.*

They lay lifeless, as if disconnected entirely from her nervous system.

He squeezed together her middle finger, ring finger, and pinky, and pulled them slightly away from the thumb he had already taped down. Then he wrapped the new piece of tape around the three digits, and affixed them to the arm of the chair.

He bent down, picked up the pruning shears which he had dropped to the floor earlier, and took hold of her index finger. Then he slid the tool into position, so that the V of the blades surrounded the digit just below the middle knuckle.

He looked up at her face. She wondered what he saw there. She had no idea what expression she wore. Whatever it was, he wasn't satisfied. He squeezed the handle of the tool so that the blades came even closer.

She closed her eyes.

"Don't you fucking close your eyes, bitch," he said.

It was a small victory—more like a tiny one, actually—but moving her eyelids was about the only thing she had control of right now, and she'd be damned if she didn't use it.

"I said open your eyes!" he screamed, his breath warm and disgusting from the onions and garlic of the pizza.

She didn't obey.

"Fine," he said, again using the ominous tone that promised something awful. "I'll just shoot your neighbor here until you open your eyes."

Stephanie immediately opened her eyes, and tried to focus on Mrs. G., but she was out of Steph's field of vision. The killer was still standing in front of Stephanie, but had turned toward Mrs. G., and was pointing a gun in her direction.

"You know what?" he said, his voice laced with false

sympathy. "You can't even move your head yet, can you? You probably couldn't even look scared if you wanted to."

What a despicable jerk. He was getting off on how terrified she looked. This whole nightmare was just getting worse and worse. Steph started to feel control coming back to her body. But she carefully avoided moving. She simply let her head hang there limply, mouth open.

"Tell you what," he said conversationally. "I could use another slice of pizza. So why don't you just sit tight? I'll be right back."

On a good day, in running clothes, Vera could do an eight-minute mile.

But wearing work shoes, long pants, and carrying a weapon was going to slow her down. She was going to have to improvise.

Once she cleared the traffic mess, Vera ran right into the middle of the street. She was heading down Connecticut now, probably still five or six minutes away. She took her shield out, and held it in her hand as she kept running.

The key was to breathe. *In, out, in out.* Never stop, never gasp. *Don't sprint, or you'll burn out, and get there slower than if you just ran at a good, hard, steady pace.*

She was sweating freely now, breathing hard. Probably four minutes to go.

And then, finally, a young woman driving an oldish Toyota began to pull out of her driveway ten feet ahead. Vera bolted to the driver's side window as the woman straightened the car out before driving away, banged on the car door, and flashed her shield. Then she pulled open the door, and shouted, "Get out of the car, ma'am! I'm a police officer, and I'm commandeering your vehicle. *Now.*"

Monster

HE STUCK THE GUN AND THE SHEARS IN HIS pockets, picked up his empty plate and the stun gun from the dining room table, and headed into the kitchen. He needed another drink, which he grabbed from the fridge. He wondered for a second if he should get some ice from the freezer to slow the blood loss after he chopped off Stephanie's finger, then decided against it. She wasn't going to bleed to death from that wound. And he certainly didn't want to dull any of the pain.

He moved into the entry hall, put the soda down next to the pizza box, opened it up, pulled a slice onto the plate, closed the box, and turned back toward his two waiting victims.

Wait a minute. Was that scraping sound one of them trying to move one of their chairs?

He hurried into the room where he'd left them. Mrs. G. hadn't moved, but Stephanie was definitely a little closer to the old lady.

More importantly, her left hand was free, and she was hurriedly trying to untape her right hand from the arm of the chair.

He dropped the pizza and the soda, and held his stun gun out. "You know what, Stephanie?" he said, striding quickly toward her. "You are really pissing me off right now."

But she kept pulling the tape off of her right thumb, as if he hadn't even spoken.

Well, fuck her. As he approached, he really let her have it with the Taser. Her body jerked with the current of electricity he blasted through her.

This bitch was going to learn to obey.

And then suddenly, just as he passed in front of Mrs. G., there was an unbelievably fierce, white hot flame of pain searing through his left thigh, ripping its way down to his knee, and the stun gun was flying through the air, and he was falling forward, almost directly on top of Stephanie.

THIRTY-SEVEN

STEPHANIE HAD BEEN HOPING HE'D COME to her.

She was counting on the fact that he'd be so upset that she'd managed to get a hand free, that he'd walk right by Mrs. Giordano.

And although the devastating effects of the stun gun were tearing through her when it happened, she was still able to take a great deal of satisfaction in the tortured shriek of pain that her attacker uttered as he fell to the floor beside her.

She also thought she might have heard a siren, but that might have been just a ringing in her ears.

Because as she lost consciousness, it, along with all other sounds and sensations, just faded away into the dark silence.

Finally. The corner of Brookings and Queen.

Vera went from sixty to zero in about five, tire-squealing seconds, jumped from the car, withdrew her weapon, and raced toward the front steps.

An anguished shriek sounded from inside the house.

Someone was being attacked.

Vera leapt to the top of the stoop, and without even trying the lock, she fired at it, kicked in the door, and raced inside.

"Police!" she shouted, aiming her weapon into the room. She was still out of breath from the half mile she ran, but she was ready for this.

The scene before her was bizarre. A broken china plate, a slice of pizza, and a spilled can of soda were on the floor directly in front of her. Beyond that, a chair lay on its side in the middle of the room, with an old woman duct-taped to it by her ankles. In her right hand, she held a bloody steak knife. She was moaning through the tape across her mouth. She was in obvious pain.

Beyond her, farther toward the back of the house, a younger woman was much more securely taped to another chair. Her head was slumped over. She looked dead.

To the right of the younger woman, a long, bloody smear ran on the hardwood. It trailed away out of sight, into a room at the back of the house.

Vera approached warily.

The young woman was breathing. From the look of her and the smell of burned flesh, Vera was betting that she'd been Tasered. The older woman was conscious, but she had been gagged with duct tape.

As Vera walked toward her, the woman shook her head, and moved her eyes toward the blood trail staining the floor. She didn't want anyone to bother with her yet. She wanted Vera to get this guy. To finish the job she'd started with the steak knife, God bless her.

"Okay," Vera said, in a strong voice which she hoped would inspire confidence. "Wait here. I'll take care of him."

She hurried past the debris on the floor, through the entry hall, turned left into the kitchen, and then, without a sound, walked into the dining room from that side.

The killer was sitting on the floor with his back to her,

facing the entrance to the living room. His left hand was under his thigh. He was probably trying to stop the flow of blood which continued to pour from him. His right hand held a pistol. It was aimed at the entrance to the living room.

She was about nine or ten feet behind him, and a step or so to the left. It would be an easy shot. But you don't shoot people in the back when you're a police officer.

"Please turn around and try to shoot me," Vera said calmly, "so I can kill you right here."

Monster

DESPITE THE FEROCIOUS PAIN IN HIS LEG, HE smiled. Did this bitch cop really think he hadn't been prepared for her little run-around-behind-him trick? How sad.

He became absolutely still, and then his shoulders and his head sank. He sighed, raised his hands above his head, and said, "Sorry to disappoint you, Detective Demopolous. I give up."

He was concentrating hard, now. The woman's voice was just another buzz to analyze. About eight to ten feet behind him, about five and a half feet off the ground, just slightly to the left.

In his last three practice sessions, he had been thirty-for-thirty.

And that was from fifteen feet away. This was going to be cake.

He began to speak. "I was hoping to get a chance to speak to you—"

And exactly as he had been practicing, between "chance" and "to," he spun around, whipped his arm into shooting position, and fired.

THIRTY-EIGHT

AFTER SHE HAD CALLED OUT HER WARNING, Vera had taken a trembling, silent breath, one large, equally silent step to her left, and then crouched down, held her breath, and waited.

When he turned and fired, the killer missed. High, and to the right.

Vera didn't miss at all.

Squeezing off round after round, she rose and then walked directly toward the killer. His body spasmed with each hit, until he finally flopped backward to the floor.

Only when the house stopped reverberating with the echoes of the gunshots, did Vera hear the comforting sound of approaching sirens.

The serial killer lay on his back, staring blindly up at the ceiling as bloodstains slowly grew on his clothes.

He was a reasonably good-looking man, probably in his early forties.

He wasn't Alan Lombardo, or Ellis. But neither was he Russell Crane. Or Malcolm Ayers.

Vera reached into the man's pocket, pulled out his wallet, and read the name on his driver's license.

Neil Heinrich.

THIRTY-NINE

STEPHANIE WAS WORKING THE LATE SHIFT when Vera came to visit.

It had been three days since the attack. Thanks to Mrs. G. and Vera, Stephanie had escaped with only the Taser burns as injuries.

She hadn't had enough time to fully free her elderly neighbor before Neil Heinrich had come downstairs, but Steph had managed to run into the dining room, grab one of those sharp knives, cut through the tape on Mrs. G.'s hands, and leave her with the weapon before she ran into the dining room to hide.

The only question had been whether the killer would walk close enough to Mrs. G. so the older woman could use it.

And thanks to his arrogant need for pre-murder speech-making, he had.

From the autopsy report, Mrs. G. had done herself proud, inflicting damage not only by severing a small artery and a tendon in Heinrich's leg, but by slicing through his sciatic nerve, too.

The effort at stabbing the serial killer had thrown her balance off, however, and the old woman had tipped her chair over, and broken her left arm in the process.

Her good-for-nothing son had finally stepped up. David was arranging for his mother to live in an assisted care facility near him and several of Mrs. G.'s grandchildren. Mrs G. would be moving into it as soon as she was released from the rehab facility that she'd be transferred to next.

"Vera Demopolous, I need you to come here and kiss me immediately before I die of my grave injuries."

Terry Tallach, Zack Wilson's big, loud partner, was breaking the rules again, and walking around the hallways of the pediatric ward like he owned the entire hospital. He wore a maroon and black bathrobe, and his head was wrapped in a big, bright white gauze bandage. He looked like a gigantic, five-o'clock-shadowed swami. He had been hit in the head by one of the bullets fired in the courtroom melee. Thankfully, the bullet only grazed his skull, so there was no fracture, and no gunshot injury to his brain.

But he'd suffered a serious wound to his scalp and he'd also split his head open when he fell back onto a wooden bench after the bullet had hit him. The gunshot wound had taken eighteen stitches to close, and the gash on the back of his head from the fall had taken another six.

The concussion he'd suffered had been serious, and the doctors wanted him to rest for another few days before going home.

Good luck to them all with that plan.

By now Vera had reached the big lawyer, and they embraced. Terry saw Steph watching them, and called out to her, "I believe it's time for your coffee break, Nurse Hartz. Please come with Vera and me. I think it's about time for my lazy partner to stop faking his injuries and wake up."

Steph looked over at Donna, who was working with her today. She smiled and gave Steph a thumbs-up, and Steph joined Vera and Terry in the elevator up to Zack's private room.

Zack's condition was much more frightening than Terry's. He had suffered three gunshot wounds—one to the left leg, one to the left arm, and one to his abdomen.

The injuries to the limbs were bad enough—the leg had nerve damage, and the arm had a broken bone, but it was the third shot that was the real trouble.

Not only had the bullet perforated Zack's small intestine and peritoneum, initiating a frightening infection, it had made contact with Zack's spine, rather than exiting cleanly.

By the time Zack had gotten help, he had lost a lot of blood, and the emergency surgery, the infection, and the nature of the injuries had put a terrible burden on his immune system, and on his entire body.

He had yet to regain consciousness from the operation. Until he did, no one knew for sure that he was going to make it, or if he did, whether there was any permanent nerve or spinal damage.

When they reached Zack's floor, they turned down the hallway and entered his room.

He looked exactly the same as he had since they wheeled him up here after surgery.

An intravenous tube led into the back of his right hand, feeding him glucose, saline, and an antibiotic. An oxygen tube was looped over his head and attached to his nose. Vitals were being monitored, his left arm was in a cast, and his left leg had a large bandage covering the surgical incision where they'd gone in to remove the bullet.

"Zack, you lazy bastard, wake up," Terry said quietly. "Vera and Stephanie are here. And Stephanie's wearing her nurse's uniform, by the way. I already told her that's your big fantasy, so I don't understand why you're lying there with your eyes closed. She says she thinks guys on a saline drip are hot, so even you might have a chance."

If he survived this, Zack had way more than a chance.

"And Vera said— What?"

Terry was leaning down close to Zack's mouth.

"How's Justin?" Zack asked.

Vera bolted to get the doctor.

"Never better, my friend," Terry said with a grin, and eyes bright with unshed tears. "Completely unscathed. And don't think I've forgotten that you owe me for taking him to Largeburger. Damn check was almost twenty bucks. Kid's a freaking eating machine."

Zack's eyes flickered open for a moment, and his face moved in what had to be the smallest smile in the world, but it lit the room like a sunrise.

"Oh, listen, as long as we're chatting, you mind telling me why you were running *toward* a guy who was shooting you? Seemed a little, I don't know . . . stupid?"

"I . . . had to stop . . . him."

"By bleeding on him?"

Zack was about to reply, but the resident interrupted the visit, and began to examine him. It was clear that the doctor was relieved that his patient had regained consciousness, but there was one more hurdle to jump.

"Zack, I need to know if you can move your foot," he said.

"Do you need me to kick Terry's ass for you?" His voice was really getting stronger now, and his smile was giving Steph's heart quite a bit of exercise.

"Actually," the doctor replied, "we just want to make sure there's no damage to your spinal column."

That got Zack's attention. "Spinal column? He didn't shoot me in the back, did he?"

"The one in your stomach went through to your spine, Zack," Terry explained. "Doc just wants to make sure you can still walk into a hail of bullets if you need to."

"Shut up," Zack said. "I'm fine. Watch."

For a moment, no one moved. Steph realized she was

holding her breath. Then Zack inhaled, and wiggled his right foot just an inch.

Everyone exhaled at once.

Terry pumped his fist and said, "*Yes!*"

And Steph started to sob.

At that point, one of the nursing supervisors came and chased them all out of the room, so Zack could get some rest.

Predictably, Terry grumbled as Vera tugged on him to leave. "Rest? Dude's been sleeping for three days. When do I get to rest like that?"

Then just as they were about to get through the door, Zack said, in the clearest voice they'd heard yet, "Hey! Elvis!"

From the look on Terry's face, if he'd had any doubts that Zack was going to fully recover, they were gone now. The big man in the giant, garish robe, with the huge, bright white bandage wrapped around his head, rolled his eyes, smiled despite himself, took a deep breath, and turned back to his partner, lying there in the bed. "What?"

Zack lay there with a huge smile on his beautiful face, and simply said, "Nice hat."

Epilogue

Two Months Later

TERRY LOOKED OVER THE CHURCH FULL OF people.

Damn straight the church was full.

Malcolm Ayers was celebrating his tenth consecutive year of sobriety at an Alcoholics Anonymous meeting. And Malcolm's sponsor, crazy Thomas Prieaux; Malcolm's daughter, Stephanie; her dates, Zack and Justin; and Terry and Vera wouldn't have missed it for anything.

The outfit Vera was wearing was a celebration all by itself.

If you had asked him four months ago if he'd be here, Terry would have said you were crazy.

But how would he have known that Alan Lombardo's condition would deteriorate so completely that he would lose all control, use his last contact with George Heinrich before the old man died to get hold of a gun, and then shoot up a courtroom full of people in a last-ditch effort to commit suicide-by-cop instead of face life in prison without protection from Gentleman George?

And who could have imagined that Neil Heinrich was the original Springfield Shooter? After Vera finally killed him, the madman's house was searched. His computer, full of rantings and ravings from a very sick mind, told the whole story.

Neil had started his murderous streak back in high school. His old man found out about it, but couldn't bring himself to turn his kid over to the cops. So he shipped the psycho off to Europe with a contingent of bodyguards, and forced him into intensive therapy.

Thomas Pricaux finished his introduction, and now Stephanie was speaking. She had her full Sandra B. going tonight. Once Zack got back to full strength, the guy was going to be toast.

To make sure that suspicion never headed Neil's way, old George planted the Springfield Shooter evidence in Alan's house, knowing his bookkeeper would be the perfect patsy. One of George's henchmen had called in the anonymous tip about Alan's car being at one of the murder scenes. And when the housekeeper found the mutilated fingers in the freezer, that was it for Lombardo.

Except that George always felt secretly indebted to Alan for doing his son's time, so the old mobster made sure that the obsessive-compulsive accountant didn't suffer in prison because of his mental illness.

Meanwhile, the kid managed to control his homicidal impulses and really tried to turn his life around. Neil finished college in Europe, and was very serious about trying to lead a normal life when he returned to the U.S. to help his father with the family business.

And in what must be one of the great ironies of all time, once he got involved in the Heinrich family operations, he started cleaning it up. By the time Old Man Heinrich died, Neil had pretty much turned Heinrich Contracting legit.

Except for the serial killer part.

It seems that when his father's physical health turned

to shit, Neil's mental health slid downhill, too. And soon the Springfield Shooter was back in town.

Of course, he was now twenty years older, and twenty years wiser. He'd seen what kinds of reactions people had to crimes like his, and he'd made special note of the hell that Malcolm Ayers had gone through, thanks to some sloppy speculation and unfortunate coincidences the first time around.

So Neil knew just how to play people for maximum effect. He intentionally threw suspicion on Malcolm, anonymously mailed him one of the murder weapons, and just like his father had with Alan, Neil planted evidence in Malcolm's house.

He couldn't help himself from further muddying the waters when Ellis joined the case, by starting to sign his letters Eternally Yours, waiting for someone to notice the EY clue.

What Neil hadn't counted on was running into a cop like Ellis Yates.

Although no one could confirm it, the best guess was that when Ellis figured out the clue which identified the address of Heinrich's next murder, he was reminded of the chess club that he belonged to briefly in high school. Members got together weekly to play a variety of board games. One of the younger kids in the club, a student who also loved making up puzzles and riddles, was Neil Heinrich.

That was the only connection anyone could ever find between the two men, but once he started looking at Neil, Ellis probably connected the crime lord's son's abrupt relocation to Europe with the discovery of the evidence against Alan Lombardo. Ellis already knew about the connection between Lombardo and the Heinrich crime organization. Any number of other things could have sealed the deal for Ellis—maybe he illegally broke into Neil's house and discovered his sick little annex, complete with shooting range, "trophy" room, and twisted setup for spying on Stephanie.

Whatever led him to his conclusion that Neil was the real serial killer, Ellis probably thought that he'd take his former schoolmate by surprise, but Neil killed him first.

Then, in a brilliantly perverse move, Neil decided to create the illusion that Ellis was the killer. He planted evidence in *Ellis's* house. Figuring he was safe for a while, he took a day off to prepare for the Giordano murder.

Of course, that's where Stephanie and Vera came in.

Now Steph had finished her introductions, and the whole room was on its feet, applauding.

"Hello. My name is Malcolm, and I'm an alcoholic."

Incredibly, Neil's plan was to kill Mrs. Giordano, and then, Stephanie.

The idea was that if you spelled out the first letters of the middle names of all of the victims, you'd get S-A-L-L-Y. As in *Sally's Gift.* Neil's original plan was to frame Malcolm, but when Ellis became an unplanned victim, Neil changed his mind. His gleefully redesigned scheme was to finish off Mrs. Giordano and Stephanie, drive off to some remote place in Ellis's car, and then dismember and hide the cop's body. He figured that the incriminating evidence and Ellis's apparently guilty flight would ensure that Ellis was blamed for the murders, and Neil would escape prosecution yet again.

Until his next life crisis triggered a homicidal spree.

Malcolm was wrapping up his remarks.

"Before I began drinking, I was described as something of a recluse—a rather cautious individual, unwilling to open myself to the society of others.

"And as an active alcoholic, I found myself waking every morning in an increasingly profound quagmire of isolation and self-pity.

"Now that I have committed myself to true sobriety, every day seems to begin with a fresh and growing wave of gratitude for the people in my life, especially my daughter, Stephanie. I expect that I will spend the rest of my life happily attempting to express to her my thanks for her love despite my indiscretions, my anger, and my generally infantile behavior. Thanks in large part to her, I find that my life now is rather insanely joyful.

"As I believe Shakespeare once said, 'Go figure.' "

And the crowd went wild again.

It was another half hour before the meeting broke up, and their group met at one of the side doors of the church.

Malcolm, Thomas, Stephanie, Zack, Justin, Terry, and Vera.

He wasn't sure if it was because he had just come from an AA meeting, or whether it was the company, but it had been a long time since Terry had felt so peaceful.

Just seven good friends, heading out for dinner at Emilio's, one of the nicest restaurants in town, to continue the celebration of everything this past year had given to them all. All seven people on the same page, on the same team, on the same side of the fence.

Not a conflict of interest in sight.

Except for Justin.

He wanted to go to Largeburger.

ABOUT THE AUTHOR

Ed Gaffney took ten years of work as a criminal lawyer, added an overactive imagination, and came up with a new career as a novelist.

Ed lives west of Boston with his wife, *New York Times* bestselling author Suzanne Brockmann. He is shamelessly proud of their two children, Melanie, who is also a writer, and Jason, who is a stage actor. Ed is the author of *Premeditated Murder* and *Suffering Fools,* both featuring Zack Walker and Terry Tallach, and is currently at work on his fourth legal thriller, *Enemy Combatant*, which Dell will publish in fall 2007.

If you enjoyed Ed Gaffney's
DIARY OF A SERIAL KILLER
you'll want to read all of his acclaimed mysteries.
Look for them at your favorite bookseller.

And read on for an electrifying early look
at his next crime novel,

ENEMY COMBATANT
by
Ed Gaffney

coming soon from Dell.

Enemy Combatant

Coming soon

PROLOGUE

My property law professor, J. Keenan Bowles, used to get angry with me whenever I used the phrase "with all due respect," because he thought it was code for "you don't know what you're talking about." Bowles also loved to say that peace was nothing more than a state of mutual cowardice.

And my best friend, Cliff Redhorse, recently told me that according to traditional Navajo teachings, my arrest for murder in the middle of the Gomez terrorism trial was merely the universe trying to put itself back into balance.

With all due respect, Professor Bowles and the Navajos don't know what they're talking about.

The only thing that was out of balance on the first day of the Gomez trial was me. I was exhausted because a cold front had rolled through central Arizona the night before, and Dad can't sleep through thunderstorms.

Right up until his stroke, my father, Henley Carpenter, had been the top assistant district attorney in Maricopa County. He prosecuted all the big criminal cases in Phoenix. He was a quick-thinking, fast-talking, high-energy lawyer in a town where everything seemed to run about two speeds slower than he did.

But by the time that Juan Abdullah Gomez was charged with plotting the infamous Denver Tunnel Bombing, my father had been retired for years, and I was taking care of him in my parents' house up on Payson's Ridge. The injury to Dad's brain had left him unable to speak, unable to move around without a wheelchair, forgetful, and terrified of electrical storms. So I spent most of that night with him in the living room, listening to the greatest hits of Barry White—Dad's favorite CD.

To this day, we still don't know where Dad got his taste in music.

Anyway, from about midnight to a little after dawn, over the background of an alarmingly deep voice musically seducing dozens of devastatingly sexy women, I reassured my father that despite the intermittent flashes of blinding light and air-cracking explosions that rattled our home's windows, we were completely safe, and everything was going to be all right.

Less than a week would pass before I realized just how pathetically wrong I was on both counts.

My naïvete embarrasses me, depresses me, and really pisses me off.

I should probably apologize in advance for my tone. Until recently, I did not consider myself to be an angry person. In fact, before the Gomez trial, I would have told you that I had big plans for an exceedingly bright future. I saw the world as a treasure chest of promise, a complicated but beautiful origami of constantly unfolding opportunities. The perfect day was one filled with discoveries.

My favorite word used to be *threshold*.

I don't have a favorite word anymore.

A perfect day for me now consists of little more than some chores, a bit of writing, and spending time with the few remaining members of my family. I have been told that after a time, my old self will reemerge, and my feelings of betrayal and suspicion will pass, but I'm afraid that I have developed some rather severe trust issues. I wouldn't be surprised to learn that my old self was long gone, and hadn't left a forwarding address.

I guess we'll see.

ONE

It was a fluke that I was in the courtroom at all.

The Juan Gomez trial was sensational by any standard, but for the scandal-starved southwest, it was a thrill-seeker's ambrosia, and the good folks of Arizona were dying for a taste. Phoenix Superior Courtroom Number One was awash with the curious and the vengeful as the trial opened on that fateful June fifth. The defendant was being prosecuted for plotting two attacks: one in Houston, which, thank God, had not yet come to pass, and the one in Denver on that terrible May morning that killed one hundred-ninety-six people, and injured over a thousand. Gomez was the biggest terrorist suspect to be tried in the U.S. since Timothy McVeigh and Zacharias Moussari.

The only reason I got to see the trial in the first place was because Sarge, the chief court officer, had saved a seat for me.

Sarge was a former Marine, and the most physically intimidating sixty-five-year-old man I knew. He started as a court officer at around the same time my dad began his career as an A.D.A. As a child, whenever I accompanied my father to the courthouse, I would always spend a considerable amount of time staring at Sarge's terrifying but mesmerizing flat-top hair. It didn't hurt that he'd sneak me a Tootsie Pop every time he saw me.

My Tootsie Pop connection dried up around the time I became a lawyer myself, but Sarge's affection for my family never did. And he knew that on the fifth day of every June—except for 1995, when my mother's appendix demanded a hasty detour to Phoenix General—my parents, my older brother Dale, and I would attend whatever criminal trial was taking place at the superior courthouse.

It is the one family ritual I continue to honor even after everything that happened. But more about that later.

At the time of the Gomez trial, Sarge was well aware that my mom and Dale were no longer alive, and that it was a real long shot that my father would have the energy to endure the wall-to-wall mob sure to make life in the wheelchair even harder than it already was. But that didn't stop the husky court officer from saving a place for us anyway, just in case.

And so the stage was set for my spectacularly ill-advised pratfall into the unique limelight strictly reserved for mass-murderers.

I was in the third row, shoe-horned between reporters from *U.S.A. Today* on my left and the *New York Daily News* on my right. All the mega-press outlets had swept into town like an Old Testament plague when it was announced that Gomez would be tried here. Fifty of the nearly three hundred seats in the gallery were reserved for them. They complained—hundreds of them were shut out—but they weren't the only ones clamoring for a first-hand view of terrorist justice, Arizona-style. Thousands of ordinary citizens competed for the remaining opportunities to witness what Governor Atlee Franklin, in his ever-annoying drawl, had promised would be a demonstration of "good old-fashioned American West jurisprudence"—whatever that was supposed to mean.

One thing that was definitely not old-fashioned, however, was the trial's television coverage. That entire aspect of the case was being managed by the new, government-run, Judicial Broadcasting System. The idea was to balance the public's right to view criminal trials with the limitations of space by setting up a single camera in the courtroom, operated by a federal employee. That source would then provide a live video and audio feed of the proceedings to any television network or station that requested it.

And according to what I've heard, the system worked very well. Tens of millions watched as Judge Rhonda Klay presided over jury selection on the trial's historic opening day.

I was sorry to see that Judge Klay had been assigned to the case—not because she was one of the meanest judges in Arizona, but because she was one of the worst.

The trouble was not that the small, lizard-like woman lacked the brains for the job. It was, instead, that Rhonda Klay used her considerable intelligence to twist the rules to make it almost impossible for any defendant to get a fair trial.

I realize that last statement sounds like it was written by a defense attorney, and, well, it was. But for several years before the Gomez fiasco, aside from a handful of very mediocre trial performances, I had made my living almost exclusively as a court-appointed criminal appeals attorney. It was my job to review trial transcripts, and to spot judges who didn't follow the rules. I was pretty good at it, too. And usually, when I found a problem, it was because a judge didn't know or understand the relevant legal principle.

What made Judge Klay unique was that she knew and understood *all* the relevant legal principles. She just slithered her way around and through them so that virtually all her criminal trials ended in guilty verdicts. Often in ways that were not ethical.

Or at least they *seemed* not ethical. No one could prove anything, of course.

For example, the pool of potential jurors for the Gomez trial looked almost exclusively Anglo. Considering that the defendant was Hispanic, and that about one-quarter of the population of Arizona is Hispanic, anyone in Gomez's position might well have wondered how twelve individuals culled from an all-white group of individuals could comprise a jury of his peers.

And anyone in Judge Klay's position would surely be concerned, or maybe just puzzled, at the unusual racial composition of the jury pool.

But the woman seated at the head of Courtroom One with the slicked-back hair and the skinny nose looked like everything was just dandy. She knew that potential jurors were supposed to be randomly divided into different groups for different cases behind closed doors, by officials who were sworn to act in accordance with even-handed rules. So she also knew that it was virtually impossible to prove that she'd tampered with the selection process to ensure a racial imbalance favorable to the prosecution.

Why was I so sure that Judge Klay had stacked the deck? Because in every one of the major criminal cases she presided over where the defendant was Hispanic, the jury pool was always disproportionately Anglo. You do the math.

From her perch behind the bench, the judge smiled in the direction of the defense table, and announced, "There being no objections to the jury pool, the defendant may exercise his first round of peremptory challenges."

It was a classic Rhonda Klay move—cheat, then dare anyone to call her on it. What was a lawyer supposed to do? Accuse her of manipulating the composition of the jury without a shred of evidence to prove it?

And then, a surprise. The defendant did just that.

Or at least he tried to. At the judge's words, the brown-skinned man with the curly beard and the wire-rimmed glasses began whispering frantically to his lawyer, stabbing his finger at the potential juror pool, then pointing to himself, then shaking his head. Finally he motioned to his lawyer with both hands, as if urging the man to stand up and say *something*.

But Gomez's lawyer did neither. Which, sadly, was not a surprise. Because Gomez was being represented by Silent Steve Temilow, another disgrace to the criminal bar.

Temilow didn't belong in the courtroom for any number of reasons, high on the list of being that he couldn't lawyer himself out of a bad parking ticket. But Judge Klay had appointed Temilow to the case because Gomez had complained twice during the six months he'd been awaiting trial that his attorneys weren't representing him adequately.

It wasn't particularly unusual for indigent defendants in capital cases to doubt that the same government that was trying so diligently to have them executed was also going to provide them with an attorney who was really going to do battle for them. And Gomez was not exactly your run-of-the-mill indigent defendant in a capital case. Because he was suspected of a terrorist attack, when he was first arrested, he was treated by the government as an "enemy combatant," which is another way of saying that he was held for the better part of eight months without the most basic of civil rights, and regularly tortured in an effort to extract information about future terrorist attacks.

So it was hardly a shock when it was reported that after meeting his first lawyer, Gomez couldn't bring himself to trust the man, and promptly requested another one.

Gomez's complaint about Attorney Number Two—a decent lawyer named Bruno Smithson—was that after months on the case, the attorney refused to do anything except advise Gomez to plead guilty, in the slender hope of avoiding execution. Bruno actually called me a couple of times while he was on the case. The first time, it was because he couldn't figure out a way to convince Gomez they needed a lot of time to prepare for the case. Gomez thought they should go to trial four days after Bruno was appointed.

The second call, several weeks later, was even more serious. Gomez insisted he was innocent, and refused to plead guilty. The problem with that was Bruno had never seen such an air-tight case, one featuring Gomez's connections to the man who actually detonated the Denver bomb, as well as file cabinets crammed with other thoroughly damning evidence that the government had found when searching Gomez's home. Bruno couldn't accept that it was in Gomez's best interest to force a trial, and their inability to get over that disagreement led to his dismissal.

Enter Silent Steve Temilow, the human doormat.

Now Gomez's gesticulations were getting more exaggerated, so Steve appeared to take yet another tack—pretend that the heated whispers and the flailing arms to his left were nothing more than the products of a curious phantasm, which were best ignored. Rather stiffly, the lawyer shuffled through some papers on the table before him, clearly stalling.

Judge Klay preferred a more direct approach to the situation. "Mr. Gomez, kindly control yourself—this is a court of law. And Mr. Temilow? Is there a problem? May we have the defendant's first set of peremptory challenges, please?"

There would, however, be no denying Juan Gomez. As Temilow rose to address the judge, the defendant rose, too, unwilling to let his attorney off the hook, his increasingly insistent body language demanding eye contact. But Silent Steve soldiered on, bravely disregarding his client's sleeve-tugging and table-banging by adopting a some-what robotic posture—his neck, shoulders and upper back so rigidly braced that he seemed almost physically incapable of turning and acknowledging the desperate pantomime taking place at his elbow. Staring straight ahead at Judge Klay, he finally spoke.

"Um, Your Honor, I'd first like to personally apolo-gize—and to apologize on behalf of the defendant as well—both to you and to the ladies and gentlemen of the jury pool for, well, for any impropriety that may have taken place over the last few minutes at the defense table."

Gomez looked dumbfounded. Could this get any worse? The answer, incredibly, was *yes*.

"And with further apologies for any delay—and for any inconvenience caused by such delay—I would like now to address the court's inquiry regarding the compo-sition of the jury."

As he realized that his attorney was finally, *finally* go-ing to confront the extremely non-Hispanic-looking ele-phant in the room, Gomez seemed to relax a bit, and the expression on his face became somewhat expectant. That expression would soon disappear.

Temilow droned on. "First, Your Honor, the defense specifically waives any objection to the composition of the jury pool, it being well-understood that the process by which these candidates were selected as potential ju-rors for this case was a random one."

When Gomez processed this capitulation, he began shaking his head back and forth, glaring at the judge, and pointing at Temilow, in silent, negative commentary.

The lawyer awkwardly twisted his entire upper body so that although he was still facing the judge, his back was now fully to this client. Temilow seemed to hope that by maneuvering Gomez out of his field of view he might make the distracting little man disappear from the court-room entirely. "And further, Your Honor, the defendant will also waive any peremptory challenges, as he is confident that any member of the community will render a fair and just verdict in this case."

It was at that point that Gomez could no longer restrain himself. "Oh no!" he said, continuing to shake his head, but now raising both hands above it as if Temilow had just scored a touchdown for the wrong team. "No, no, no. I am not waiving anything. And I am not apologizing for anything, either. I am firing this man. Right now. I want a new lawyer, judge. This one is not working for me. He is waiving everything, and apologizing, and he is not listening to me at all. I do not want to waive anything. I just want a new lawyer."

With the exception of the frenetic scratching of reporters' pens and pencils against paper, the courtroom became deathly silent. Gomez lowered his hands, and just stood there, as if not quite certain what to do next. Then, suddenly, he sat down, and simply said, "That's it. I'm done, Your Honor. I need a new lawyer."

Apparently, it was time for someone else to talk.

Yet it was not clear that poor Steve Temilow was up to the task. He had managed to keep his back to his client for the entire tirade, but Gomez had failed to dematerialize. Worse, the unpleasant fellow had added a sound track to his heretofore silent performance.

So Temilow did what he did best—he waved a white flag.

"Um, Your Honor, if I might attempt to address the court—with deepest personal apologies, of course—for the unusual nature of this situation."

Judge Klay, however, was not so easily assuaged. "Your apology is *not accepted*, Mr. Temilow," she snapped, glaring at the defendant all the while. "I rather think that it is Mr. Gomez that needs to address this court. Mr. Gomez?"

The defendant rose from his seat before speaking. "Yes, Judge?"

"Am I to understand that despite the fact that you stand trial for multiple counts of murder and for conspiracy to commit murder as well as a number of other extremely serious crimes, you wish for me to discharge Mr. Temilow from the case?"

"Well, Your Honor, I don't know about any discharge. All I want is a new lawyer. This one isn't doing anything for me. He sounds like all he wants to do is give up, but I didn't do anything wrong, so I don't want him representing me."

The judge took a deep breath. She glanced over the defendant's head at the jammed courtroom, the reporters, the television camera, even those members of the victims' families who had made the trip down to see this fiend get exactly what was coming to him. Of course I don't know exactly what was going on in Rhonda Klay's mind at that moment, but I would have bet you a stack of pancakes that she was thinking there was no way in the world she was going to be shown up in her courtroom, in front of millions of Americans, on the first day of the slam-dunk trial of a mass-murdering terrorist.

She looked down at some papers that were laid out in front of her on the bench, and then she looked back up at the defendant with her black eyes, a clever smile pinching her narrow face. I knew, right then, that whatever the judge was going to say, it was going to be bad news for Mr. Gomez.

"Very well, sir. Here is my ruling: You are entitled to have an attorney appointed to represent you, and according to the case file, you have had not just one, but *three* lawyers assigned to your case. And you have chosen to find fault with each one of the three."

She closed the file, rather melodramatically, I thought, and then decreed: "I find that this is nothing more than a pattern of behavior deliberately designed to delay the trial. You have had ample time to prepare, sir, and ample representation. I will not indulge your behavior any further. Here are your choices, Mr. Gomez. You will either withdraw your request to have Attorney Temilow removed from this case and accept him as your lawyer, or you will proceed without any representation at all, and serve as your own attorney for the remainder of these proceedings."

It didn't take a legal expert to analyze that pair of options. There was no way in the world that Juan Gomez, warehouse shipping manager for Pottery World, could possibly defend himself in a multiple-murder trial before Judge Klay. And using Steve Temilow on a case like this was like trying to stop a runaway train with a butterfly net.

But to Gomez's credit, the man did not back down. "Your Honor, you talk about a choice, but that is no choice at all. I do not want Mr. Temilow as my lawyer, and I do not want to represent myself. All I am asking for is an attorney that will stand up for me here. They are saying I did this terrible thing, but I did not do it. I need someone who will say that to the jury."

While this exchange took place, Steve Temilow was standing off to the side of the defense table, looking less like the attorney of record, and more like a spectator at a sporting event that had mistakenly walked out onto the field of play.

And the ball was in Judge Klay's court, so to speak, which she did not like one bit. It came whizzing back at the defendant with quite a bit of attitude. "Sir, you have heard my ruling." Pulling back the sleeve on her robe, the judge took a look at the watch she was wearing. "If you do not withdraw your request that I discharge Mr. Temilow from the case in the next fifteen seconds, I will discharge him. Consider your decision carefully. You now have . . . eleven more seconds."

THE SUSPENSE WILL KILL YOU....

VICTOR GISCHLER

GUN MONKEYS	$6.99/$10.99
THE PISTOL POETS	$6.99/$10.99
SUICIDE SQUEEZE	$6.99/$9.99
SHOTGUN OPERA	$6.99/$9.99

MORAG JOSS

FUNERAL MUSIC	$6.99/NCR
FEARFUL SYMMETRY	$6.99/NCR
FRUITFUL BODIES	$6.99/NCR
HALF BROKEN THINGS	$13.00/NCR
PUCCINI'S GHOSTS	$22.00/NCR

ASA LARSSON

SUN STORM
$12.00/$15.00

STEPHEN BOOTH

BLIND TO THE BONES
$7.50/NCR

ONE LAST BREATH
$7.50/NCR

CODY MCFADYEN

SHADOW MAN
$24.00/$32.00

LISA GARDNER

THE PERFECT HUSBAND	$7.99/$11.99
THE OTHER DAUGHTER	$7.99/$11.99
THE THIRD VICTIM	$7.99/$11.99
THE NEXT ACCIDENT	$7.99/$11.99
THE SURVIVORS CLUB	$7.99/$11.99
THE KILLING HOUR	$7.99/$11.99
ALONE	$7.99/$10.99
GONE	$7.99/$10.99

Ask for these titles wherever books are sold, or visit us online at <u>www.bantamdell.com</u> for ordering information.

BD SUS 2/07